# Books by Jaz Primo

## The Sunset Series

SUNRISE AT SUNSET

A BLOODY LONDON SUNSET   (* forthcoming)

Published by Rutherford Literary Group LLC

You can find Jaz Primo online on Facebook
and at the following locations:
**Website:** http://www.jazprimo.com
**Blog:** http://primovampires.blogspot.com

# SUNRISE AT SUNSET

## Jaz Primo

RUTHERFORD LITERARY GROUP
www.rutherfordliterary.com

Published by:
RUTHERFORD LITERARY GROUP L.L.C.
1205 S. Air Depot, PMB #135
Midwest City, Oklahoma 73110-4807
http://www.rutherfordliterary.com

This is an original publication of Rutherford Literary Group.

ISBN: 978-0-9828613-0-1

1. FICTION_FANTASY_PARANORMAL
   2. FICTION_FANTASY_URBAN LIFE
      3. FICTION_OCCULT & SUPERNATURAL

Library of Congress Control Number: 2010911428

First Printing: September 2010.
10  9  8  7  6  5  4  3  2  1

Set in Century Schoolbook.
Cover art by Albert Slark.

Printed in the United States of America.

# ACKNOWLEDGMENTS

This novel is dedicated to my grandfather, Henry, who taught me that all things are possible with determination, hard work, and perseverance.

Heartfelt thanks to Lori for all the love, support, patience, and encouragement that a human being could possibly offer. Without her, this accomplishment would not be possible. She is truly my sunrise at sunset...

My sincere thanks and appreciation to Al Slark for amazing work using his mastery of the graphic arts, his confident professionalism and patience, and for accepting a challenge to do something fresh and unique in his realm of artistry. Special thanks to Brandon for all his mad technical web skills, artistic eye, and keen creative sense for all things "fonty".

Many thanks to Jimmy, Jessica, Shannon, and Derek whose invaluable friendship, support, advice, and proofreading helped this novel to come to fruition. Countless thanks to my friends Jessica, Teresa, Crystal, Lisa, Nancy, Amie, David, and others for their beta reading, feedback, encouragement, and kindness. Thanks to my editor, Julia, for positive, essential feedback, and for passing along valuable insight that helped me to further hone and improve my writing skills. Thanks to Selina for your impromptu feedback, and being the sounding board that only you can be. Thanks to all those mentioned and unmentioned for their words of encouragement to persevere against insurmountable odds in the conquest of a singular goal: climbing the writer's Mount Everest, known best as the nefarious world of publishing.

# Prologue

# A Reason to Live

*T*he beginning of an end is sometimes just the start of something new. And once in a while, it's the genesis of something wonderful.

The clear skies of predawn held the promise of another sunny day for the small community outside of Columbus, Ohio. A beautiful, fair-skinned woman appearing to be in her late twenties stood among the tall grasses of an empty field. Amber Simmons smiled as her green eyes looked with anticipation beyond the line of trees towards the approaching sunrise. It would be her first sunrise in many human lifetimes, and she stood statue-still, gazing hopefully at the sky.

She absently ran her fingertips through her short brown hair while contemplating the simplicity of the moment. With her keen hearing, she heard the birds chirping around her and a rooster crowing in the distance. As someone who typically planned things out with meticulous precision, Amber was momentarily amused that she'd merely pulled her car to the side of the road and randomly walked through the woods until arriving there.

*This will do nicely*, she affirmed.

In silent homage to her lifelong commitment to structure and order, she recounted what had brought her to that moment. She was a strong-willed person and not prone to depression or morose fixations, but she was at what could be described as a vampire's mid-life crisis. Having led a rich life, she'd enjoyed wealth, means, and free reign of the globe for the most part, as long as one excluded daytime. Daytime reigned as the most lethal environment for her kind, to be avoided at all cost.

However, Amber had grown dissatisfied in recent years. It wasn't so much the series of failed relationships. Granted, those typically ended viciously...for them. It wasn't that she was necessarily tired of living; she simply no longer saw the point in it. She'd been shocked by the realization that she was ready to see her last sunrise. The epiphany came upon her rather suddenly, without brooding or melancholy.

Amber confided in a few close vampire relations. However, most of them also struggled with their own need for diversions and were merely helpful in sympathizing with her situation. There were two vampires in particular who sought to intercede directly on her behalf before she watched that final sunrise, but both were half the world away, and time wasn't on their side.

As she patiently waited, her only regret was the inability to appreciate the sun for very long before meeting her end. She missed the sunshine, really. As a human she had loved the mornings and the hopeful sense of optimism that morning brought to each day. For hundreds of years, she'd only caught fleeting glimpses of the burgeoning dawn before being forced into darker surroundings to await the reappearance of evening. Even at such a maudlin moment, she felt strangely at peace for what would be her last day.

As the sun began to rise, Amber marveled at the beautiful, yellow-orange glow forming above the tree line. It was terrifying in its majesty, and the innate urge to avoid it began to grow despite her resolve to meet her end. *Reflex only*, she mused reassuringly.

Moments later, the repercussion of the sun's ultraviolet radiation began to take effect on her skin. At first it was merely an itching, but quickly it became painful. Her exposed skin blistered, and seconds later the core of her body erupted with fire. Amber tightly shut her eyes against the sun's rays as they crept to the top of the trees and immediately heard a sizzling sound, quickly realizing it was coming from her own body.

With the sunlight nearly full upon her, a peculiar thing happened to the resolute Amber Simmons: she changed her mind.

Harnessing speed that humans couldn't readily comprehend, she propelled her body westward into the tree line, holding the pain inside so she wouldn't scream. Although her lungs were burning with agony, she yearned to release anguished, primal feelings to the world. Instead, she ran while containing the painful wail building within her.

Amber's only hope was to seek refuge from the blazing sunlight using the nearest opportunity for shelter. In a matter of seconds, she raced towards a small, wood-framed garage that quickly appeared before her. The old garage stood alone, some thirty feet to the side of a paint-peeled house located on the small acreage across which she was running. She barely registered the side doorway before she was speeding through it in a blur of movement. Amber slammed the door shut behind her, seeking refuge beneath a tarp-draped and partially refurbished Chevrolet Camaro.

Within seconds, she lay on her back appreciating the cool, though grimy concrete floor. Her skin still sizzled as the burns covering her body felt catastrophic. Pain coursed through her system, and she breathed air in short, gasping breaths. *Great,* she thought, *now what?*

Amber needed fresh blood for her body to begin the healing process properly. But she had deliberately fasted for many days in hopes of accelerating the process of death by morning sunshine. After facing her imminent demise firsthand, she considered it had been a really stupid notion. *Naturally, I left my blood supply at home,* she thought. Sighing with exasperation, she immediately felt her body racked with intense pain for her indulgence and drew air into her lungs through clenched teeth.

She heard the small, creaky door to the garage open and promptly smelled a human. By the sounds of the small, awkward footsteps, it was a small human, likely a child. Her presumption was confirmed in the simple word the visitor uttered next.

"Hello?" inquired a short, sandy-haired young boy. As he bent down to tie his shoe, Amber noted his faded blue jeans and a T-shirt emblazoned with cartoon characters from Walt Disney's The Lion King.

Amber held her breath so there was as much silence as possible. One glance to his left, and the child could probably see her. She needed blood badly, but one of the few resolutions she had made since becoming a vampire was not to hurt children. She hoped that the boy would lose interest and quickly leave.

"I heard the door slam," he said. "Where are you?"

Amber clenched her jaw tightly and snapped her burnt eyelids shut while striving to keep the burning pain coursing through her body in check. *Great, a kid saw me*, she thought wildly. Then she heard the edge of the tarp lift near her and the little boy's gasp.

"Gross! What happened?" the child demanded. "Are you hurt?"

She barely opened one of her eyes to gaze back at him. She must have looked, and smelled, like a burned corpse at that moment. "You need to leave, little boy," she urged as clearly as possible through the pain. "It's not safe for you here."

"I can help, really," the boy persisted.

*Help?* Amber's mind raced for a solution of some kind, but the only thing that occurred to her had little hope for success. For years, she had been a good customer of the blood bank set up by a very old vampire some years ago that catered to a unique clientele. The idea was that a domestic supply of blood might improve the chances of vampires seeking to blend into society without having to hunt humans. The corporate venture capitalized on local blood banks to broker blood supplies to its customers. And best of all, they ensured prompt delivery in most major cities around the world.

"What's your name, little boy?" Amber asked as levelly as possible.

"Caleb," he stammered excitedly. "Caleb Taylor."

"Hello, Caleb," she said while trying to control the tremors of pain in her voice.

"Hi," he replied in a friendly tone that only an innocent child could evoke successfully.

*Well, at least he's polite*, she thought. In fact, he seemed like a child with a pleasant, gentle disposition. Amber tried to clear her mind of her agony and asked, "Okay, Caleb. How old are you?"

"I'm eight," he proudly replied.

Her mind raced as she gauged the aptitude of the average eight-year-old. "Caleb, I'm an angel, and I need for you to call heaven for me," she explained. "Can you do that?"

Caleb frowned. "Call heaven?"

Amber stifled a moan as the burning began to subside only marginally. Her body must be trying to heal itself. But she needed fresh blood to do the job correctly.

"Can you use a telephone for me and not tell anybody?" she asked.

"Not even my mom?" he countered.

Amber considered the merits of a fleeting thought, but quickly discarded the idea of draining his mother dry. *Some angel I am, the angel of death!*

"No, Caleb, not even your mom," she urged.

"Is it a secret?" he inquired.

"Yes, it's a secret," she answered with all the patience she could muster.

The boy was silent for a moment and replied doubtfully, "Well, okay."

She nearly screamed as a wave of renewed pain shot through her body and bit her bottom lip so hard that she drew blood.

"Who should I call?" Caleb asked.

"Get a pencil and paper, Caleb," she insisted.

"Okay," he said before running out of the garage, slamming the side access door behind him.

Amber lay there wondering if she would ever see him again, or if the child's mother or father would come through the door next. She passed the time frantically determining if the sunshine outside threatened the interior of the garage. There was a small pane glass window opposite from her on the side of the car where the boy had been, but the canvas tarp seemed to offer enough protection to keep the sun's rays from reaching her.

After a time, she heard the door open and shut again, followed by the sound of little footsteps. Seconds later, the boy's excited face reappeared beneath the tarp.

"I got a pencil and paper," he said.

"Okay, Caleb. This is very important," she began. "I'm going to give you a phone number to call, and then you just give the person that answers a long number and your address. Do you know your address, Caleb?"

The boy nodded and recited his address with a practiced tone.

*Smart kid*, Amber admired. She gave him a phone number and a special access code and told him to give the person his home address. Caleb repeated the information and promised to go make the call without telling his parents. All the while, it took all her willpower not to reach out and grab the child for the immediate source of the blood that she desperately needed. Instead, Amber waited as she heard his departing footsteps and the sound of the door closing.

Caleb returned some undetermined time later while Amber lay beneath the car gritting her teeth and enduring the searing pain that reignited through her body.

"I made the call to heaven," Caleb said. "Angel Bruce said he'll come soon."

*Unbelievable*, she thought. "Can you bring me the box when it arrives, Caleb?" she asked as gently as possible.

"Okay, but I have to eat breakfast first," he said.

She panicked slightly. "Caleb, are your parents home now?"

"My mom is," he said. "Should I get her?"

"No!" she urgently snapped. The boy jumped slightly.

"Sorry, Caleb. I'm hurt," she earnestly explained. "I need you to get the box from the angel in the truck before your mom sees it. Your mommy may not want me to get the box, Caleb."

The boy considered what she said and replied, "Okay."

Then a woman's voice called, "Caleb, breakfast!"

"Okay, Mom!" he yelled before getting up and running out of the garage.

"Please hurry, Angel Bruce," Amber muttered through clenched teeth.

After what seemed like hours, Amber heard a truck pull onto the gravel shoulder of the street outside and stop. The engine idled, and she vaguely heard a man's voice, followed by Caleb's. Her hearing was normally many times better than a human's, but at that moment the pain in her body blocked a great deal of her acuity and concentration.

A few minutes later, the boy entered the garage carrying a small plastic insulated cooler. He sat it down onto the floor next to the car with a heavy thump.

"The box is here," Caleb said. His pale blue eyes came into view while he peeked beneath the tarp, adding excitedly, "The angel drove a truck!"

"You're an angel now, Caleb," she whispered.

"I am?" he asked with wide eyes.

"Yes, Caleb. You're an angel from now on," she promised as she began crawling towards the edge of the car. "But you need to go now. You can come back later, okay?"

"Okay," he suspiciously replied before leaving the garage, shutting the small door behind him.

Despite the pain, Amber's shaking hands managed to tip the cooler onto its side while avoiding the sunlight streaming in through the garage window. The container was filled with small plastic bags of human blood. She grabbed two, pulling them underneath the car. She snapped the cap off the first one and squeezed the cold blood into her mouth, drinking hungrily. Quickly draining them both, she reached out for more, repeating the process until the cooler was empty.

She stored the drained blood bags inside the cooler with the lid shut, not wanting to scare her new angel, Caleb. While lying beneath the car on the cool, grimy floor, she could feel her body rapidly healing. She closed her eyes to rest.

By late afternoon, Amber heard a car pull into the driveway, followed by the sound of heavy footsteps and a door to the house opening and closing. Eventually, Caleb returned to check on her, at which time she was feeling much better. Fortunately, her pale skin had already healed, with the exception of some remaining welts here and there. Caleb said that he needed to eat supper but would check on her again before bedtime. She silently marveled at the child's interest in her.

As the evening sun prepared to set, Amber heard a commotion coming from the house. She clearly heard shouting between a man and a woman. Then she heard the sound of an altercation and a person being slapped, followed by a woman's cries, as well as Caleb's voice screaming for his dad to stop hitting his mom. Finally, she heard Caleb cry after more shouting and another slapping sound. Anger rose in Amber's chest and spread throughout her body.

A few minutes later, the side garage door opened and Caleb entered, crying. But instead of coming to the side of the car as he had the previous times, he sat in the corner next to some old tires, rubbing his eyes with his knuckles. His sobbing eventually stopped, and he was reduced to sporadic post-crying convulsions.

"Angel Caleb?" Amber quietly ventured.

He looked towards her from where he sat. She could see that one side of his face was noticeably inflamed. "Angel Caleb, are you all right?" she asked.

He slowly nodded his head. "Yeah."

"Does your father do that to you and your mom very often?" she asked gently, trying to keep her voice in check.

He shook his head and offered between sniffles, "Some-times."

Amber grit her teeth and tightly shut her eyes. *There's too much of this crap in the world*, she thought grimly.

The side door to the garage abruptly opened, and she heard a large person enter.

"Caleb Taylor! What're you doin' in here?" demanded a gruff male voice. "Didn't I tell you not to play in the garage?"

The poor child was too scared to move. His eyes were wide as saucers, and his mouth was agape as he stared up at the man with terror. Amber detected the pronounced smell of alcohol.

"Damn you, boy! I'll blister your ass good this time!" the man threatened as he slipped the leather belt off from his jeans and viciously snapped it at Caleb. The belt impacted the boy on his left arm, breaking the skin and leaving a small line of blood.

A feral growl emitted from deep in Amber's throat, and in a flash she was out from under the car, protectively standing before Caleb.

"Who the hell are you?" the man demanded while stagger-ing backwards with surprise.

Amber's eyes blazed bright green, and she scowled while taking in the medium height and build of a middle-aged man with receding hairline and dark eyes.

"I'm Angel Amber," she growled. "And I'm your worst nightmare!"

She punched the man in the jaw with a lightning-fast right hook, causing him to spin to the right and fall back against some old metal shelves stacked with car parts. Amber imme-diately turned to Caleb, who was sitting on the floor in shock. She picked him up and hugged him to her body while carrying him to the side garage door. She hastily ushered the young boy outside away from the altercation.

The man recovered and swung a tire iron at her back as she spun around and caught his wrist. She effortlessly stripped the iron from his hand and tossed it onto the floor.

"What the hell --" the man spat with alcohol-laced breath.

Amber grabbed him by the throat with one hand and snapped his neck with a single, loud *crack*. She let his lifeless body drop to the floor with a heavy, meaty, thumping sound.

Hearing a gasp from behind her, she spun around to see little Caleb blankly staring up at her with wide eyes from the doorway. She determined that he must have been in a state of semi-shock based upon the empty expression dominating his face.

Her breath caught in her throat, and her eyes continued to glow bright green as she stared down at the young boy. She immediately cocked her head to listen, expecting the boy's mother to investigate. Silence reigned. Squatting down, she held her arms open for him in a welcoming fashion. "It's okay. Nobody will hurt you now. Come here, Caleb," she beckoned soothingly.

He stared at her for a moment and bravely, but slowly, walked into her embrace. She hugged him to her and patted him on the back. After a moment, she picked him up and took him back outside into the cool, night air.

"Show me your arm, Caleb," she said while lowering him to the ground and squatting next to him. He held up his arm, which was still bleeding slightly.

"I can do some angel magic to make it feel better. Is that okay?" she asked.

His eyes were huge, and he quietly nodded while holding his arm out to her.

"Okay, but don't move, Caleb. It takes an angel's kiss to heal it," she said gently. She placed her tongue against the wound and held it there for just a couple of moments. The small taste of his blood was unlike any she had consumed in recent memory and was extremely powerful to her. But she mastered her temptation and removed her tongue from his skin. His hand immediately went to probe at the wound area.

"Don't touch it for a few minutes, Caleb," she gently instructed him.

"It feels funny," he ventured curiously.

"That's the angel magic," she explained. Vampire saliva had healing properties, which were helpful for removing a prey's bite marks. "Did it stop hurting?"

He nodded. "Yeah." Then his eyes began to stray back towards the direction of the garage, and a blank stare formed again.

"Good," Amber cooed soothingly. "Now, I need for you to look into my eyes, Caleb."

His pale blue eyes gazed intently into her glowing green ones. She had only tried mild hypnosis with dogs before, and she wasn't certain how effective it would be on a human child.

"Okay, Caleb," she offered in a calm, neutral voice. "Look into my eyes. Forget the bad things today. Just remember playing with your toys..."

Her mantra continued for a few minutes longer, but soon afterwards, the oblivious young boy was in his backyard playing with his toys as nighttime fell. Nobody was around to notice a tall, brown-haired woman carrying a body and a plastic cooler across a dark open field. That day, Amber Simmons found a renewed interest in life: Caleb Taylor.

Amber's life was rejuvenated somewhat by an unexpected intervention from her little angel, and it was her turn to return the favor. She carefully disposed of the body of Caleb's abusive father, although the title of "father" to describe the man carried little weight with her. Later, she made her way to her home in an upscale neighborhood of Columbus, Ohio.

Her current identity as Amber Simmons needed to come to an end before long. But first, she wanted to use her resources to aid Caleb and his mother to the best of her ability. She wasn't about to let her little aid-angel down.

Over the next couple of weeks, she discreetly researched the Taylor family. Her trappings of wealth and contacts in human society meant that she could acquire information rather easily when she needed it. She discovered that the Taylors were a struggling middle-class family suffering from exceptionally high financial debt. They maintained a high balance on multiple credit cards, a mortgage on their small acreage, and a higher-than-reasonable car payment on a very used car.

Caleb's mother, Wanda, graduated high school with a rather good transcript. She was only nineteen when she had Caleb, and was married to Caleb's father, Ted, a few months before the child's birth. He was an automobile mechanic by trade and brought in just enough money to keep the household running. Now Caleb and Wanda were faced with additional financial problems.

Amber owned Columbus Mortgage, a small mortgage processing company that she didn't run directly, though she maintained the power of strategic decision making. She found that the more humans she involved herself with, the more questions were asked about her over time. Keeping a low profile with humanity was a necessary part of a vampire's continued survival. It was part of the reason being a vampire could be a lonely existence. The implied glamour from the numerous Hollywood films involving vampires was altogether wrong.

Amber needed a discreet way to engage Caleb's mother with a job opportunity. So, she waited a couple of weeks following Ted's abrupt disappearance before making an uncustomary, after-hours visit to the gentleman serving as the company's manager. Given that she was the owner of the company, it took very little effort to convince Bob Fletcher of her intentions under the premise that she was reaching out to a family in need. Ever the corporate manager, he conceded the positive public relations potential from the gesture.

Within days, an invitation letter was mailed from Columbus Mortgage's human resources department specifically soliciting Wanda's application for employment. They made sure to include the company information sheet on benefits, such as medical coverage, retirement, daycare, and vacation options. Amber prided herself on making sure that her employees were well compensated. She never forgot that the company's staff was doing her a favor without even realizing it. For Amber,

who had sheltered her accumulated wealth in multiple locations throughout the world, the issue was now about social
camouflage rather than capitalism.

In the end, Wanda was eager to take the bait. Amber had
to hand it to Wanda: the woman cared enough about Caleb
to step out of her comfort zone once the abuser had left the
house. Amber made unannounced, unnoticed visits during the
evenings to check up on Caleb, as well. She was pleased to find
that Wanda wasn't an abuser herself.

Amber remained in her identity longer than she'd expected
just to make sure Wanda and Caleb settled well into their new
life. Via progress reports from Bob Fletcher, Amber was very
pleased to discover that Wanda had a real talent for independence when given the opportunity. In just a couple of years,
Wanda worked her way from the mailroom up to a clerical support position. She also learned that Caleb had settled into his
single-parent life and was doing well in school.

Amber's final direct impact on the Taylors' lives occurred
when the company sponsored a raffle to provide a college fund
for up to three employees' children. Of course, Wanda Taylor
was one of those winners. The night of the award dinner, which
Amber uncharacteristically attended, was the sole time that
Amber recalled having her picture taken as part of a company
function. She posed with each of the three employees, minus
their children. Caleb's presence might have proven disastrous.

Finally, Amber had to disappear, and a new identity needed to be forged. She sold her company to Bob Fletcher, whom
she had been carefully grooming for the role.

Her new identity included a welcome return to her natural
red hair color, and her name changed from Amber Simmons to
Katrina Rawlings. For the time being, she chose to travel the
globe, and would settle down somewhere later. *The rest will
fall into place eventually*, she mused.

As Katrina journeyed the world over the years, she did
something else that was a first for her. Instead of letting her
old identity completely fall away, she periodically checked in

on the status of the Taylor family via calls to Bob Fletcher. Wanda had progressed well in the company, as expected, and Caleb continued to prosper.

Time passed as Katrina renewed regular contact with some fellow vampires around the world who she had neglected over the years. Time was rather relative for vampires.

On a final call to Bob some years later, Katrina learned a shocking bit of news. Wanda had died of cancer suddenly a couple of months prior. Caleb was in his final year of graduate school pursuing his master's degree at Georgia State University in Atlanta, but had taken time away to settle his mother's estate. Then he returned to complete his work at college. Discreet inquiries revealed that he remained in Atlanta with hopes of securing a teaching position. In history, no less.

The shock of the developments rang through Katrina with surprising strength. Her thoughts were immediately of Caleb and the loss he must be enduring. It was then, from her basement apartment in France, that she resolved to seek a permanent residence. And against her better judgment, the area around Atlanta suddenly called to her.

# Chapter 1

◦◦◦

# Reacquainted

*K*atrina took a number of months to establish herself in the area around Atlanta, Georgia. She settled into an upscale, secluded neighborhood in nearby Mableton. As customizations were made to her large estate, she began to familiarize herself with the area. Georgia was a state in which she had never spent much time, though she loved the variety of forest environments that blended into the suburbs and city areas. It was a perfect environment for a vampire, and she wondered why she hadn't visited there before.

She selected an appropriate mode of transportation. Though Atlanta was a large metropolis, it held the opportunity for enjoyable driving experiences. She typically preferred a traditional luxury sedan, but she bought a new jet black Audi sports coupe. It implied fun and speed, without seeming pretentious. The car was sleekly contoured for speed, a style of vehicle that was something entirely new and different for her. Maybe it was that, for the first time in recent memory, she actually felt as young at heart as her nearly thirty-year-old appearance suggested. After only one test drive across the I-20 highway at high speed, she knew that she made the perfect choice. It made her feel playful.

Unlike previous identities, Katrina decided to forgo the diversions of a career. This time she intended to utilize her accumulated wealth to its fullest, allowing her more time to focus on independent projects. She had a couple of diversions in mind, but only one of them had sandy hair and pale blue eyes.

Her careful searching revealed that Caleb was living lo-
cally, and she easily located him on the Website for Robert Fulton Community College in downtown Atlanta. Professor Caleb
Taylor was teaching sections in history for the college as one of
their recently-hired faculty members.

Katrina hadn't seen Caleb since he was a pre-teen, when
she had secretly attended an evening baseball game at his junior high school. He'd been a sandy-haired, lanky youth with
an awkward manner about him, which she found both endearing and amusing at the time. Years later, she had seen a photo
of him standing in the back row of a group of high school baseball team members as part of a newspaper article about their
winning the state championship.

She decided to enroll with the college and take the only
evening section of U.S. History that Caleb taught in the upcoming fall semester. *It'll be fun*, she mused. Her last college
course was in the 1960s at Pennsylvania State University. *Suffice to say, I won't be transferring my transcript*, she added with
a smirk as she completed the online enrollment application.

It was Monday night and the end of the first day of fall
classes at Robert Fulton Community College. Caleb shuffled
his lecture notes for about the fifth time as he sat in his closet-
sized office that was barely wider than the doorway that led
into it. His desk faced a wall-sized window, which at least gave
him a view of the campus grounds, though he hated having his
back turned to the door. There was barely room for a bookshelf
on the right and a narrow computer hutch on the left next to
his guest chair. Nevertheless, he was grateful for the opportunity to teach full-time, being twenty-six and fresh out of graduate school. The marketplace had been competitive due to the
state's recent poor economic conditions. It was a small community college, serving only about four thousand students each
spring and fall semester. But Caleb loved academia, unlike
many of his friends who had primarily valued the socialization
of their collegiate experiences. Knowledge was a passion, and

now a labor of love for him.

He glanced at his watch, realizing his evening class was about to start at eight-thirty: the last section of the day, as luck would have it. He picked up his notes and textbook and made his way upstairs down the simple-tiled hallway lined with classrooms. His was Room 203 on the left about midway down the hall.

When he walked into the classroom on that first evening, he glanced around at the faces before him. There were four rows of tables and chairs split on two sides by an aisle up the middle, to accommodate up to thirty-two students. Only twenty-one were enrolled, and he had been warned by the associate dean to expect two or three students to drop.

There were a variety of stories represented in the faces he saw. Some were younger high school graduates trying to start their college career with poor ACT/SAT scores who couldn't yet qualify for university admission. Others were working adults striving to get an educational edge or promotion in their careers. A few others were interested in avoiding the large general education class sizes of Georgia State for a more intimate setting. There appeared to be a half-male, half-female distribution, and he noted that it was his first class that semester that didn't have anybody sitting in the back row.

After welcoming everyone to his Early American History class, he began calling roll, glancing up at each face in turn to try and associate names with faces: Bibbons, Cosby, Darby, Franks...

Katrina was running late. She had nearly forgotten to get a textbook and was making her way from the college bookstore with her notepad and text in hand. She wasn't sure whether she would actually attend the entire course, her main interest being the opportunity to see Caleb after so many years and listen to him lecture. Her curiosity intensified as she mulled her prolonged absence in his life.

*Absence*, Katrina chastised herself. *As if I've had any real part in his growth or development.* Any tie that she felt to him was solely based upon the memory of his youthful aid on that fateful summer day. Aside from killing his abusive father, she had merely played the role of an anonymous financial benefactor for him and his mother. After that, she'd restricted herself to only watch from a distance. Nothing more. *But then, wasn't that the plan, to stay out of his life and allow him the opportunity to grow up in a "normal world?"* Her previous attempts to develop close relationships with humans always ended badly and, more often than not, fatally for the humans in question.

Katrina broke from her reverie, darted into the classroom as roll was being called, and slipped into a chair at the back of the room. Then her green eyes darted towards the front, following the sound of what had to be Caleb's very mature-sounding voice.

When her eyes settled on the fit young man standing at the podium, she arched one eyebrow in surprise. The Website photo didn't do him justice. His features were accented by a masculine, yet gentle face framed by neatly-maintained sandy brown hair. She was happy to see that his eyes were still the beautiful, pale blue that she remembered from when he was a child, though she readily admitted the term "child" hardly applied to the strapping man that stood at the front of the classroom.

His conservative navy blue slacks and tie looked professorial, while his white Oxford shirt fit snugly to his muscled chest, further accentuating his athletic build. Caleb's pleasing appearance was completely unexpected, and she felt an immediate dual desire rise within her. Part of her appreciated him sexually, while another part was sizing up her prey. She still considered humans as prey, even though her hunting activities were curbed many years ago by the easy access to blood bank supplies. Somehow blending into society was easier if she weren't being hunted by humans for draining people of their blood.

*Oh Caleb, how you've changed since I last saw you,* she contemplated as another wave of desire washed through her.

Caleb continued to call roll. "Jill Parker, Melvin Peterson...
"Katrina Rawlings?" he queried in a friendly tone.

"Here," a firm, but silky voice answered as he looked up to
meet the face hosting such an enchanting tone.

When his eyes fell upon Katrina, he nearly lost his breath.
He guessed that she was in her mid-to-late twenties. Her pale
features were punctuated by deep green eyes and shoulder-
length red hair pulled back in a tight ponytail. She wore a pair
of stylish black denim jeans and an emerald cami. A gold Greek
key necklace adorned the pale skin of her neck. She could easily have been a fashion model. But, much to his surprise, the
most notable aspect about her was her eyes. He could see her
beautiful emerald eyes from the front of the classroom staring
back at him in a penetrating manner.

His pause was somewhat noticeable, and he swallowed
once to moisten his throat before forcing himself to glance
down with a raised eyebrow and continue calling roll. A few
students turned around to glance back at Katrina, the men's
eyes lingering before turning back to the front.

Following roll call, Caleb passed out a copy of the course
syllabus to each student. When he arrived at the back of the
room to hand a copy to Katrina, his hand was starting to shake
slightly, so he simply placed the paper onto the table before
her.

Her hand reached out deliberately to retrieve the syllabus
without taking her eyes from his. The left corner of her mouth
started to curl into an amused smile. He forced himself to look
away and return to the front of the room, noticing that his
pulse was elevated slightly. After pausing to regain his focus,
he discussed the syllabus information, textbook, and the course
objectives. Caleb dismissed the class early and watched as Katrina rose quickly, departing before anyone else.

He exchanged pleasantries with some students following
class, but would later be unable to recall anything he said. He

was still somewhat mesmerized by the beautiful woman who had sat in the back of the class. *Wow*, he thought wildly while walking down the hall. *That was unexpected.*

Yet, even considering her beautiful appearance and penetrating eyes, there was something nagging at the back of his mind. She somehow seemed familiar to him, but he couldn't quite place why. It was as if some tidbit of recognition was on the tip of his memory, yet masked behind a dark curtain.

A couple of younger male students walked behind him, and one asked the other, "Hey man, did you get a look at the redhead in back? I'd tap that in a second!"

*With my luck she'll probably drop the class,*Caleb thought silently as he made his way down the stairs. Still, he already couldn't wait until Wednesday evening.

He arrived at his office and found his girlfriend, Melanie Baxter, waiting for him. They had been dating regularly for about six months. She was a records specialist at the state's Department of Public Safety office downtown, where he'd met her while paying a traffic ticket. Melanie was a year younger and few inches shorter than Caleb. Her straight, dishwater-blond hair draped to her shoulders, and her face was accented by bright hazel eyes. Her fashionably faded blue jeans and white lace trim tank both presented a form-fitted appearance that Caleb found very appealing. She was holding a red apple in one hand and looked bored.

"Hey, Mel," Caleb greeted her.

She grinned, gave him a quick kiss on the lips, and handed him the apple. "There you go, teacher," she said.

"Thanks," he replied smoothly. "You been here long?"

Melanie's grin faded to a more sedate expression, and she replied, "Not too long. I remember you said the first day of class is always short because you just give them an assignment list."

"Yep, pretty much," he absently supplied as he took a bite of the apple.

"Ew, aren't you even going to wash that?" she asked with a pained expression.

"I'm a firm believer in the power of stomach acids," he quipped between bites while dropping his handful of notes and textbook onto his desk.

She just shook her head at him with disdain before adopting a speculative expression.

"So, Candace dropped me off here on her way home," Melanie began tentatively. "I thought you might want to get something to eat with me after class."

Caleb perked up, as he was feeling somewhat hungry. His last meal was around midday at the student center cafeteria. "Yeah, that sounds good," he agreed with a smile.

"Then maybe on the way back to my place you could drop me by this new department store at the mall. They're staying open extra late hours as part of the grand opening," she ventured with anticipation.

"Yeah, sure," he replied with a tired sigh as he flipped off his office light and closed the door behind them. *Shopping...*

Melanie chatted about her day and the upcoming sale at the mall department store, but Caleb only processed a few bits and pieces at dinner. His mind kept wandering back to the strange effect Katrina Rawlings had on him.

Wednesday rolled around again in no time, and he was looking forward to his evening history class. *Or perhaps I'm looking forward to one student in particular.* He almost made it to the classroom before realizing he had forgotten to grab the handouts for the essay that he planned to assign.

Caleb whirled around abruptly, nearly losing his balance, and almost ran directly into Katrina Rawlings. She immediately grabbed his arm and held him in place with a surprisingly strong grip as he righted himself.

"My bad!" he exclaimed with embarrassment.

"Is everything okay, Ca –" she began with concern before abruptly correcting herself. "Professor Taylor?"

"Yeah, sorry," he apologized sheepishly while feeling the heat rise in his face. "I forgot the essay handouts." He took a quick moment to discreetly appreciate the tall woman before him. That night she wore white knit slacks, a royal blue ruffle trim blouse, and a pair of strappy white stilettos. She definitely looked amazing, again.

He glanced down at her hand, which was still firmly gripping his arm. Her eyes darted to his arm briefly before quickly releasing her hold.

"Um, you go on in, and I'll be right back," he stammered before heading back down the hallway. He took only seconds to retrieve the handouts from his office and made his way back to the classroom. *Fast reflexes*, he mused as he contemplated the brief hallway incident. *Strong grip, too.* He rounded the doorway and entered the classroom in a hurry, noting everyone already patiently waiting for him.

"I apologize, everybody," he began. "I forgot the essay handouts on my way up here. And I know how much you'd hate to miss out on them."

An assortment of groans emitted from the students, except from Ms. Rawlings and a couple of others. Caleb took roll, only this time he recognized a few of the faces, most notably Katrina's. She smiled at him in an amused fashion from the back row of the room, but still projected a penetrating, appraising expression in her green eyes that distracted him.

"So, in the next few days, feel free to move around the room until you find a seat you feel most comfortable with, okay?" Caleb neutrally offered, although he quickly glanced at Katrina and fleetingly at two empty seats on the front row off to his left.

Having been studying him so intently, she noted the implied meaning in both his actions and words. Her slightly amused smile added to the twinkle in her eyes. *Baiting me?*

He handed out an essay assignment sheet to everyone and set into his lecture on a brief review of European explorers who had visited the New World as a precursor to the westward expansion of larger scale European settlements.

"Well, can anyone tell me what primarily influenced Portugal to decline Christopher Columbus when he begged funding for an exploratory expedition to seek a western route to Asia?"

Caleb asked curiously.

The room was silent as he scanned the faces. His eyes fell on Katrina's gaze, which seemed to bore directly into his.

"Since Vasco de Gama helped initiate the profitable Portuguese control of trade routes to Asia around the Cape of Africa, Portugal believed there was little need to seek additional passageways," Katrina's voice broke the silence.

Caleb's right eyebrow shot up with some surprise. "Correct, Ms. Rawlings. Very good."

Most heads in the class turned to silently stare at Katrina. She maintained her gaze directly at Caleb with a slight smirk, and everyone's attention returned to him. The lecture proceeded from there, and Katrina offered little more in the way of responses throughout the remainder of the class. As soon as Caleb dismissed the class, she was once again the first student to depart.

Weeks passed with Katrina sitting in the back row of the classroom, much to Caleb's disappointment. She displayed varying degrees of interest and often smiled to herself, which Caleb found slightly unnerving. He also noted that a couple of women in the class chose to move to the forward seats in the classroom, paying more than a normal degree of attention to him, which he found flattering. Meanwhile, most of the males in the classroom seemed to gravitate further to the back rows of the room where Katrina sat. Still, she focused exclusively on Caleb, as if studying him even more than the material being discussed.

After two exams, which Katrina passed without error, Caleb wanted to interact with her outside of class. He still struggled to determine what seemed so familiar about her. But after each class, she always departed before he could approach her.

It wasn't as if he were going to ask her out or anything. He was well aware that would be inappropriate and a violation of college policy. It could get him fired, and he'd worked hard to get on the final interview list for the job. Caleb had to be resigned to the fact that Katrina was simply the elusive type.

At the very least, he looked forward to their brief interactions within the classroom.

On a particularly drizzly evening two weeks before the end of the eight-week semester, the parking lot lights fluctuated as Caleb walked from his car to the building. In passing, a maintenance worker said they were troubleshooting a systemic electrical short. With the budget cutbacks due to the poor economy, it seemed that even parking lot lighting was being piecemealed together just to remain operational. It never ceased to amaze him that during poor economic times, when the influx of students was greatest, community college funding was at its lowest levels.

Caleb went to class as usual, and once again, Katrina departed just as class was dismissed. Not being in a hurry to get home since Melanie was shopping with her friends, he chose to stay a little later to catch up on grading some essays. After an hour, he decided to leave and noticed that the parking lot lights were completely out in a large section where his car was located, giving the area an ominous feel.

As he reached the door to his blue older model Honda coupe, he thought he saw something move out of the corner of his eye. He was immediately confronted by a large-framed individual wearing jeans and a dark hooded sweatshirt. He couldn't make out the man's face in the darkness, but he did see the glint of a long steel blade being wielded in the person's right hand.

"Give me your wallet, asshole!" the man demanded.

"Whoa, just take it easy," Caleb urged, wide-eyed with his hands held up slightly. "Listen, I'm just a teacher. You've probably got more money in your pocket than anybody around here."

"Shut up!" the man ordered. "Just make this easy and give me the wallet!"

Caleb couldn't believe what was happening. He glanced around nervously, but saw no other people around, and the security car that normally patrolled the parking lots was nowhere to be seen.

"Okay, okay," he said anxiously with his eyes focused on the guy's knife. While reaching into his back pocket and slowly withdrawing his wallet, he considered trying to wrestle with the guy, but he had never confronted an armed person before. Despite his athletic build, Caleb abhorred violence and strove to avoid physical conflicts. He struggled with too many bad memories of abuse at his father's hands as a child. *It's just a wallet.*

The man reached out to grab the wallet from him, when suddenly Katrina appeared at Caleb's side. Her right leg shot out, and the heel of her knee-high boot caught the guy in the ribs with a small crunching sound. The fellow heaved a groan while bending over, and then abruptly turned to run away across the empty parking lot. He disappeared between some nearby old buildings overlooking that side of campus, still holding the knife in his hand and clutching at his midsection with his left arm.

Katrina watched the man flee and felt the strong, immediate desire to pursue the assailant. No, not pursue, but rather hunt him down and drain his blood. Instead, she turned to look at Caleb with concern.

He was speechless as he still clutched his wallet in a shaking hand. "Th-thank you" he stammered. "That's never happened before," he anxiously added as he glanced around the area.

Katrina reached out to gently grasp his arm with a look of concern. "Caleb, are you okay?" she asked.

He nodded and nervously ran his right hand through his hair as he gazed up into her eyes. "Yeah...fine...thanks," he muttered.

He didn't seem to notice that she had called him by his first name as his heart pounded away in his chest. She studied his body language and proceeded to lean him back against his car as she protectively wrapped her left arm around his shoulders.

"Listen, I don't know how to thank you," he said in his most grateful-sounding voice possible.

She smiled at him in a supportive, reassuring manner. "Maybe some bonus points in lieu of an out-of-class project?"

He nervously chuckled and scanned the area around them. "Yeah, as if you needed bonus points. I'd wager you'd teach the section better than I do," he ventured as he began to feel a little better.

She smirked. "Knowledge isn't everything. I find that a good presenter always enhances the material."

Caleb wanly smiled while considering the dubious merits of standing in a dark parking lot immediately following an attempted robbery. *What if that guy decides to return for a second attempt?*

Katrina regarded him with an intense expression as she listened to his pounding heartbeat, and an urge rose within her. At that moment, she felt the strong call of his blood. Her predatory instincts were screaming for action, and she wrestled to curtail them.

Caleb could have sworn at that moment that her green eyes seemed to emanate a slight glow, and he stared back incredulously. Then the parking lot lights abruptly snapped on, slightly startling him.

"Well, you better go now while it's safe. I'll see you in class," Katrina calmly urged as she turned to head across the nearly empty parking lot.

As if snapping out of a trance, he shook his head and called after her. "Hey, wait! At least let me drive you to your car."

But she just shook her head slightly and kept walking. "No need. Drive carefully on your way home."

He glanced down to unlock his car door. "Maybe we should go by the security office to report this!" He looked back in Katrina's direction to see if she had heard him, but she'd already disappeared from view. He scanned the well-lit parking lot, but could find no trace of her. There weren't even any cars within view that she could have gotten into, and he didn't recall hearing an engine start. *Strange*, he wondered.

He drove to the other side of campus where the security office was located so he could file a report. It occurred to him that the campus could use some of those emergency call boxes in the parking lots, and some battery-backed up security cameras. Somehow he doubted with their state's poor economic conditions and declining budgets that either of those ideas would be coming to fruition anytime soon.

The would-be robber pulled his black hoody closer around his face against the evening's renewed drizzle as he hurried down the neighborhood street, still clutching his left arm to his ribs. They ached furiously, and he anticipated that at least one was probably cracked.

He paid no attention to a lone sports car driven by a red-haired woman glaring out the window at him as it passed. Instead, he stared at the sidewalk and angrily kicked an empty beer can out of his way. He was furious about the failed encounter back at the parking lot. *That should've been fast and easy. That college guy was an easy mark for quick cash. But who the hell was that crazy woman with the boots?* he fumed. It was as if she came from nowhere. He felt embarrassed and pissed off, and his ribs badly ached where her boot heel had caught him. He cursed to himself as he abruptly turned down a trash-strewn alley between two older brick buildings.

It was a shortcut he had taken many times before. Experience had taught him that survival depended on knowing where to go and how to get there with a minimum of visibility. He tramped across papers and debris and was halfway down the alley when he heard boot heels clicking not far behind him. He stopped and palmed his knife from the sheath concealed underneath his hoody as he turned to see who it was. The lady from the college parking lot had stopped approximately thirty feet inside the alley and just stared at him with a flat expression.

He sneered back at her. "Well, if it ain't boot lady!" he growled. *Maybe the night just got a little better. She has to be one crazy bitch to be following me.*

"Miss me?" Katrina asked with a sadistic grin while patiently standing her ground. Her hunting instincts sang with life as she felt her fangs extend inside her mouth.

"Come here and let me show you how much," he snarled as he stalked towards her.

She stood patiently with her hands out to her sides. He was almost to her when he lunged over the last couple of feet while bringing his knife to bear with a swipe. She deftly caught his wrist and twisted. Pain shot through his wrist as the knife harmlessly clattered to the grimy concrete.

"Bitch!" he yelled, and punched her in the face with a solid blow from his left fist.

Katrina took the blow fully on the jaw, causing her face to momentarily twist in the other direction. Her head swiveled back to stare at him, and he could have sworn that her eyes were glowing!

"What the fu --" he started before he cried out in agony as she snapped his right wrist bones with a quick twist of her hand.

She slammed him against one of the old brick buildings bracketing the alley while using her left hand to pin his face against the wall. Before he could react, she sank her fangs into his jugular vein and sealed her lips against his sweaty skin. He tried to yell, but all he heard was strangled gurgling.

He attempted to struggle, but she pinned his body to the wall like a fixture, and within moments he felt the strength leaving his body. His legs soon buckled, but she held him upright. A strange sense of calm washed over him, even as he felt sluggish and a growing sense of weakness. A euphoric feeling overcame him just before he blacked out to the sounds of slurping and swallowing. Then nothing.

Katrina withdrew her fangs and wiped her mouth against the material of his cotton hoody. In one swift jerk, she snapped his neck between her hands and let the body drop to the concrete. She felt a wave of satisfaction wash over her as she relished the warmth of his blood beginning to metabolize in her system.

"Creep," she muttered under her breath while picking him up by the worn belt around his waist and hauling him down the length of the alley.

There was an old paint-peeled trash dumpster at the rear of the buildings beyond the alleyway. She casually threw the body through the dumpster's open metal window, landing atop the refuse and empty cardboard boxes inside. Sensing no onlookers, but still visually scanning the area, she removed a small can of Zippo cigarette lighter fluid from her jacket pocket and sprayed the contents onto the boxes and body. Immolation was her time-tested, favorite method for eliminating evidence.

She lit a single match and tossed it and the empty canister onto the body. It quickly ignited, the contents protected from the drizzle by the closed dumpster lid. Katrina walked to the front of the alley, the only sound the clicking of her boots on the damp pavement. As she traversed the wet sidewalk along the street to where she had parked her car, she scanned the area around her again to ensure that she hadn't missed any public cameras.

Her thoughts soon gravitated to Caleb and the grim satisfaction she felt for tying up the loose ends with the cretin who had tried to rob him. She couldn't risk the creep making an attempt on someone else. Honesty set in as she confessed it wasn't through any innate concern for the general public. *It's really all about protecting Caleb, isn't it?*

Katrina slyly smirked as she got back into her car and drove away. Caleb was definitely getting under her skin, and her Audi seemed to automatically navigate its way in the general direction of his apartment building.

Caleb was still in a degree of shock as he drove to his apartment across town. Fortunately, his building paid for all-hours gate security services for the small guard shack at the entrance to the underground parking garage. It meant he paid quite a bit more for rent on an already Spartan income, but that night it seemed perfectly worth it. He pulled into a spot not far from the elevator and made his way up to his apartment on the third floor. He entered and immediately set the deadbolt after shutting the door behind him.

He glanced around his small, somewhat cluttered apartment. Aside from the medium-sized bedroom and attached bathroom, there was a living room that opened into the combined small dining room and kitchen.

After dropping his keys onto the small counter that separated the kitchen from the living room, he draped his leather jacket over one of the two barstools. Frowning, his mind kept repeating the flurry of events that comprised the attempted robbery. He marveled at how Katrina seemed to appear out of nowhere to help him. Actually, it was more like she came to his rescue. He smirked at that.

He plopped onto the worn leather sofa and reached over to the television remote sitting on one of the glass end tables. A small entertainment center sat in the corner next to the twin, medium-sized windows that looked out onto the fire escape. He pointed the remote at the TV and then changed his mind. Gazing towards the sheer curtains, he couldn't help feeling watched. He got up and looked out one of the windows, but only saw the aged red brick wall of a nondescript warehouse across the alleyway. Immediately outside was the rather unattractive, black metal fire escape platform that ran across each floor of the building. He sighed, chuckled, and silently berated himself for his paranoia.

Then his phone rang, which startled him. *Damn it.* He stormed to the kitchen counter.

"Hello," he answered in a terse voice.

"Caleb?" Melanie asked.

"Yeah," he replied with a heavy sigh.

"What's wrong?" she pressed as her TV played in the background.

He absently ran one hand through his hair and explained, "Well, I got mugged in the college parking lot tonight."

Melanie gasped slightly. "That's terrible! Did they take

your wallet?"

His eyes widened with surprise, and he demanded incredulously, "My wallet?"

"Well, yeah," she insisted. "If so, it's a real pain! My friend at work, Terri, had her purse stolen, and it took like forever to cancel her credit cards and get her IDs remade."

"Huh?" he muttered in confusion as he took the phone away from his ear and stared at it with disgust. *You're kidding, right?* he thought wildly before putting the phone back to his ear. *What about me?* "Well, he didn't get my wallet," he said. "Thanks to Katrina, of course."

"Katrina? Who's Katrina?" she demanded in an annoyed voice.

Caleb took perverse pleasure in her response. "Katrina Rawlings. She's one of my history students," he proudly replied. "She's leading the class average by a mile, in fact."

Melanie paused, and the TV clicked off at her end of the line. "When did all this happen?" she asked with sudden interest.

"About an hour ago," he said as he glanced at his watch. "It's a good thing she was there because the guy was carrying a huge knife, Melanie. I tell you, I was-"

"An hour ago? Didn't class end way before that?" she abruptly interrupted.

His mind reeled, and he frowned. "Well, yeah, I guess. I was working late in my office grading some essays, and-"

"And was Katrina in your office, too?" she interjected.

"What?" Caleb asked incredulously. "Melanie, what are you trying to say? I get mugged, and maybe stabbed if it weren't for Katrina, and you don't seem too damned concerned about that," he snapped.

She sighed in a huffy manner and retorted, "Of course, I'm glad you're okay, Caleb."

He didn't think she sounded too convincing. "Well, I was alone in my office, thank you," he replied matter-of-factly.

"Okay, fine," Melanie replied. "I'm glad that you're okay

and that you didn't lose your wallet."

"Thanks," he said, unconvinced.

"Do you want me to come over or anything?" she asked.

He thought about it for a moment and was surprised to find he really didn't feel like her company. He felt exhausted, wanting only to take a shower, have a beer to calm his nerves, and maybe go to bed. "No, that's okay, Mel," he said tiredly. "I'm beat. I just want a shower and some sleep."

"Well, call me tomorrow, okay?" she insisted.

"Sure," he replied. "G'night, Mel."

"'Night," she said before hanging up.

He laid the phone on the kitchen counter and headed to the refrigerator for a beer.

Katrina quietly leaned against the black metal railing of the fire escape outside Caleb's apartment window, well to the side in the shadows so that nobody could see her standing there. She was easily able to hear his voice as she watched him through the sheer curtains of his living room. While concerned for his well being, she felt a little like a stalker.

She sighed. It wasn't like she could just call him or stop by his apartment to check on him. Katrina readily detected his interest in her, and the feeling was certainly mutual. But she didn't want to jeopardize his job. It was all she could do not to seek him out after each class ended. Still, there were only two weeks left before the semester ended, and she would end her brief stint at college. She was going to miss listening to him lecture; he had a real talent for teaching. But more than that, she longed to just sit and chat with him, or sit and kiss those soft-looking lips of his.

From the warmth growing inside her, she felt a longing to do other things with him, as well. She longed to share his body, to partake in his blood. She let those thoughts playfully linger for a moment as she observed him.

One thing she knew for certain, based upon Caleb's conversation with his girlfriend, she definitely didn't like Melanie at all.

*He deserves someone much better. Someone like me,* she mused with a sly smile.

As she watched him drink his beer and head into the bedroom, she decided it was time to go. While it was fairly dark where she stood, she didn't want to press her luck on being noticed. Instead, she quickly but quietly negotiated her way to the ground level and headed down the alley to where she had parked her car.

Much later that night as Caleb lay in bed, he kept thinking back to the robbery attempt and how quickly Katrina had reacted. She seemed unusually calm and collected about everything, while he had felt scared to death. Maybe she was just cool under pressure, but he somehow felt there had to be more to it than that.

Those same feelings of familiarity began to stir in him again. *What is it about Katrina that keeps nagging at me?* However, no answers were forthcoming by the time he fell asleep well past midnight.

Katrina sat at her home computer, partaking in the variety of diversions that marked her time in seclusion during daylight. Though engaged in a variety of online financial evaluations and investment activities, her mind kept wandering back to Caleb. She adored listening to him and watching him lecture in her evening history class, and once again she considered how he seemed to have a knack for instruction. Katrina was an avid history fan herself, having appreciated the considerable culmination of personal experiences and observations as a vampire.

Her brief time around Caleb brought an appreciable, fresh dimension to her existence, making it feel more like a life and less of a drudgery. She had enjoyed their brief interactions and longed for more. *The semester will be over before I know it. Then we'll see what happens.*

She sighed and diverted her attentions to email. Since her

reintegration into the world nearly two decades ago, she had reacquired a sense of enjoyment in the interactions with others of her kind. There were a number of fellow vampires from her past that she reached out to again and was pleased to find that most of them returned her interest.

Unfortunately, she was having trouble lately getting a response from a vampire named Garett who'd been living in Paris. He was usually very good about keeping in touch, so she was surprised. However, vampires were often reclusive, so Katrina anticipated that she would hear from him again soon.

She marveled at how much easier technology made everything for her kind. Blood supplies were delivered to nearly anywhere in the world via a specialized courier service. Email and text messaging made quick communication as personal or impersonal as she liked. Transportation around the world was effortless, though often at a considerable cost. Cable television provided hours, or even days, of alternate reality immersion. Every film ever made was available either on demand, online, or on DVD. And the wonderful virtual conduit known as the Internet provided hours of information and online distractions.

Her reverie was interrupted by a text message on her cell phone from a vampire named Alton, who was as close a friend as she'd ever known: *Lost contact with Octavia in Trondheim. Just arrived in Paris.*

Katrina frowned. *Strange*, she mused. *Maybe Alton will at least be able to contact Garett for me.*

The last two weeks of the semester passed very quickly. And while Caleb felt a sense of accomplishment at having successfully taught his first semester for the college, he was somewhat remorseful that one particular evening history section was coming to an end. On the last class meeting, he passed out the final exams. He lingered at Katrina's location for a moment longer than the others, smiling down at her with a hopeful, yet melancholy pause as he sat the exam before her.

Katrina felt an emotional stab of pain reach to her heart

as she took in his expression, and she returned a reassuring smile. "Don't worry, I studied," she offered with a wink. He smiled genuinely, and it warmed her heart for a moment. She couldn't read his thoughts, but she had accurately assessed his mood.

As was customary, Katrina finished before anyone else. She brought the exam to the front of the room as more than one set of eyes in the classroom followed her. She placed it onto the podium in front of Caleb while her eyes never left his, and she offered him a generous smile. With her back to the class, it was discreet enough that nobody was the wiser.

*I'll miss you,* he silently declared as he stared into her beautiful green eyes, wishing that propriety didn't prevent him from whispering his thoughts out loud to her.

Her hand faltered as it hovered over the exam that she placed before him. Her smile faded as she read every emotion in his pale blue eyes, which seemed to call to her in an almost helpless manner. As she withdrew her hand with a quick, smooth motion, she managed to caress the tips of her fingers gracefully across the top of his hand as he gripped the side of the podium. She audibly heard his heartbeat skip in that instant, and she smiled slyly at him and nodded her head ever so slightly before turning to walk away.

He watched her go with his eyes, even as his face was tilted towards the top of the podium, and his mind raced with the desire to call her name. However, he remained silent and turned his gaze to the remaining students with a sigh.

Caleb spent the next week grading exams, meeting with students regarding their grades, and trying to bring order to the chaos often accompanying the end of a semester. It was the first time he had experienced the process completely from the opposite side of the podium, and he gained immediate sympathy for his previous college professors.

He sighed. On top of the hectic pace at work, Melanie was annoyed with him. His responsibilities had ruined her plans for them to join some of her friends on a weekend getaway trip to Florida. He tried to explain that his evenings and upcoming weekend would be swamped with a litany of semester-ending activities, but she brokered no sympathy for him. *Never mind that in October it's too late to fully appreciate the beaches.*

On Thursday evening, he sat alone at his office desk wearing a pair of blue jeans and dark blue T-shirt with the college's name emblazoned across the front of it in large white letters. He had just finished posting the grades for his evening history class, in which Katrina made a perfect "A." Her accomplishment, while uncanny, somehow failed to surprise him. He found her to be quite a remarkable woman at many levels. *Melanie would kill me just for thinking that,* he realized.

His cell phone rang, and he noticed it was Melanie's number. *Speak of the devil,* he mused.

"Hey, what's up?" he absently asked as he filed away some graded essays in a small filing cabinet drawer for safekeeping.

"Hi," she replied in a surprisingly perky manner.

*Everything must be forgiven,* he resolved.

"So, I was wondering," she tentatively ventured, "How would you feel if I went ahead and joined my friends on the Jacksonville trip this weekend? I mean, you're just going to be distracted most of the time with school stuff anyway, right?"

He considered her logic with a raised eyebrow. "Well, sure, Mel. I don't mind if you go without me." He wasn't sure exactly how much time he'd have to devote to her on the upcoming weekend anyway. *And if it makes her less angry with me, so much the better.*

"Great!" she replied with renewed excitement. "I knew you wouldn't mind."

*She must know me pretty well after six months of dating,* he considered.

"Jodi said that a friend of hers, Greg Betwich, was going by himself. So it evens up the couples count again."

"Greg Betwich?" he asked with uncertainty.

"Yeah, you remember Greg? He was the guy at the Valentine's costume party we went to who was dressed as the peanut

M&M," she explained. "The accountant with the odd sense of humor."

*Oh, that Greg.* He recalled Greg Betwich, all right. Greg was the guy dressed as the M&M who kept asking women if they wanted to prove he melted in their mouth and not in their hand. *What a creep!*

"So, this Greg thing," Caleb began carefully. "Are you planning to be with Greg while you're there?"

"Huh?" she asked. "Me and Greg? No silly, he's just going to even out the numbers for our group."

*Much better*, he corrected. At least she seemed to appreciate his concern. "Oh, well, that's okay," he replied more smoothly.

"I mean, we'll probably sit together and may do some dancing," she casually added. "But it's not like we'll be staying in the same hotel room together. He already booked the room across from me."

*They already booked the rooms, and she's just now calling me? Okay, so maybe she doesn't appreciate me as fully as I thought*, he considered as an afterthought.

He grit his teeth. "When are you guys leaving?" he asked with an edge to his voice.

"Well, probably early tomorrow morning so we beat the Friday afternoon rush," she answered. "We're all piling into Candace's minivan."

"Well, call me when you get there, so I'll know you're okay," he insisted in a resigned tone.

"Will do," she replied matter-of-factly. "And don't stay too late up at the college. There might be more muggers out there or something."

"Sure," he replied. "Talk to you tomorrow then."

"'Night!" she said before the line went dead.

Caleb shook his head and stared out the window at the campus, although it was so dark outside and so much lighter in his office that he really couldn't see anything. Reaching up, he turned the blinds down so he wouldn't feel like a fish in a bowl. He noted how eerily quiet the building was. It was only around eight o'clock, but most of the faculty had left for the day, and finals were over so there weren't any students around anymore. It felt lonely to him, actually, and sort of matched his mood at that moment.

"You're quite the night owl."

Caleb nearly bolted out of his chair, and his heart felt like it stopped in its tracks. "Holy –" he exclaimed with a start.

Katrina smiled down at him with a mischievous grin while folding her arms across her chest.

His breath was having a hard time returning to him, but it wasn't because of surprise. Caleb took note of her snug black denim jeans and brilliant blue, long-sleeved turtleneck sweater. Her red hair was pulled back into a ponytail, giving her a sexy, yet edgy, appearance. She was simply beautiful.

"Sorry to startle you," she playfully offered.

He grinned and shook his head despite himself. "You got me there," he conceded.

She raised an eyebrow at him and muttered, "Lucky me."

He stared at her for another moment in silent admiration. "So, Katrina, what brings you up here at this time of night?"

"I thought I might find you here," she answered simply.

"Oh, really?" he asked with raised eyebrows. "Were you wanting to know your final grade? It should be no surprise that you made a perfect score on everything, including the bonus questions." The completely unusual nature of that registered on him with remarkable impact. Suffice to say, while not impossible, it was a highly unusual level of performance.

"Thank you. That's nice to know," she absently replied. "Actually, I came by for you."

*Came for me?*

She noted the momentary look of confusion on his face with silent appreciation. *Slow down, Katrina,* she silently chided in a split second's time. She warmly smiled at him as she listened to his pulse, noting he had a strong heart. From where she stood, she could almost hear the blood rushing through his body. His blood momentarily called to her, and she steadied the innate desire for it that rose in her system.

"I was hoping that we could talk, actually," she amended with a gentle tone.

"Sure," he replied while gesturing to a small guest chair next to his desk. "What's up?"

She tentatively smiled with a sparkle in her green eyes. "Actually, I was thinking that maybe you'd like to talk over coffee somewhere."

He was disappointed as a small warning bell went off in his head. His smile faded, and he responded, "I'm sorry, Katrina. I shouldn't; what with you being one of my students and everything."

But her smile was confident as she raised an eyebrow and countered, "Have you posted our final grades?"

"Well, yes, as a matter of fact," he carefully answered. "But you're still a student."

"Really?" she asked. "I don't believe I'm enrolled here anymore."

A momentary look of surprise played across his face. "I don't understand," he ventured with confusion. "Aren't you enrolling in other courses?"

She shook her head in an almost self-satisfied manner.

"But –" he paused. "Your potential is amazing. Surely, you want to finish a degree or something."

Katrina smirked, regarding his confusion with a sly expression. "No, my college experience has come to an end," she replied. "It provided me with all that I needed."

Caleb blinked once and asked, "Well, what other courses have you completed?"

Her expression turned serious, and she paused before answering in a quiet voice, "History."

His mind momentarily reeled at the odd implications of her simple statement, and his thoughts seemed to seize as he got lost in the pair of beautiful green eyes staring back at him.

"Coffee?" she ventured while never losing eye contact. "I'll drive."

In the parking lot, Caleb stood before the sleek, jet black Audi sports car in awe. Even by the dim lighting it was a spectacle of automotive engineering. He couldn't even dream of something like that given his salary. "*This* is your car?" he incredulously asked.

Katrina smirked at him as she unlocked the doors with her remote. *Ah, he likes it,* she complimented herself. "Hop in," she offered while sliding behind the driver's seat.

He gingerly sat in the passenger seat and reveled in the luxurious leather interior. The vehicle fit him like a glove, and he glanced sidelong at Katrina with a wide-eyed expression. "This is new," he noted while breathing in the scent of the new car smell mixed with fresh leather. "Cool."

Katrina smiled during their drive through the Atlanta city streets as the radio played alternative rock tunes. She basked in the sense of anticipation emanating in small waves from him and took pleasure in having piqued his curiosity.

She studied Caleb with interest as they sat across from each other at the Starbucks on Northeast Moreland Avenue. The place was bustling with people at that hour, but the atmosphere still felt cozy as they secured a small table in the corner of the room near the magazine rack. Pleasant acoustic guitar music serenaded them over the speakers, and they viewed the busy street outside through the front window. Despite the invitation to coffee, Caleb carefully sipped at a mug of Darjeeling. Realizing it was still too hot, he sat the cup down and smiled at Katrina as he noticed her intently observing him.

She enjoyed just watching him sip his tea. It was satisfying simply to sit across the table from him with no impediments to her interest in him. Gone were the premises of the college environment in which she initially sought him. He was hers to focus on entirely. She momentarily paused to consider the possessive nature of her thoughts and found that they suited her.

"Do you like it?" she asked. "Granted, it's not coffee, as I originally suggested."

"It's tasty, actually," he conceded with a hint of surprise. "I don't drink a lot of coffee anyway."

In truth, he didn't tend to stray too far outside of his comfort zone, even when it came to tea. But that night had a different feel to it; somehow daring, yet surprisingly comforting to him. "Yes," he added, his mind back on the tea. "It's light, but there's a sweet hint of nuts and something buttery."

She nodded with a smile while sipping appreciatively from a cup of the same flavor. She relished that vampires could appreciate many beverages and even some foods, though they derived no nutrition from them. In fact, large quantities of human food usually caused her unpleasant digestive effects.

"What did you want to talk about?" he asked.

She regarded him for a moment, once again reveling in the intimacy of their conversation. "Anything," she said simply. "Tell me about yourself."

He smiled, not having expected such an open-ended invitation. And yet he frowned ever so slightly as he considered whether it were appropriate to be sitting across the table from her.

"Am I complicating anything?" she asked in an intentionally vague fashion. While Katrina didn't want to cause him undue guilt over being here with her, she also didn't really care what Melanie might think. The more that she learned about Melanie, the less she liked her.

"Um, not complicated, really," Caleb offered awkwardly before pausing to collect his thoughts. The truth was that after the conversation with Melanie earlier that evening, he wasn't at all certain just how much more complicated anything could be between the two of them. Even after six months or more he still wasn't entirely sure where he and Melanie stood as a couple. Just when he thought he had it figured out, another unexpected event sprang up. Overall, he sometimes felt that he was just "Mister Right Now" when it came to his girlfriend.

Katrina noted his struggle and patiently waited for him to continue.

"What I mean is, I want to be here with you," he said finally with a sheepish smile.

*He's cute,* she mused. *Much like when he was a child.*

"I'm glad to hear it," she answered with an encouraging smile. "Because I want to be here with you, too."

They sipped their tea for a moment, silently appreciating each other's company. Then something that had been on Caleb's mind since he first saw Katrina in class came to the forefront of his thoughts.

"Forgive me if this sounds strange," he tentatively began. "But do we know each other from somewhere? And not from class, of course. What I mean is, have we met somewhere before?"

Katrina curiously arched one eyebrow at him, and fell silent for a moment. *He still doesn't remember,* she confirmed. She was surprised that the little hypnosis trick during his childhood had worked so well. *However, he obviously has some orphaned sense of awareness in the back of his mind,* she assessed as an afterthought.

"You're looking at me like I'm the subject of a study," he noted with a hint of amusement.

"Sorry," she apologized before carefully answering his original question. "I've only been in Atlanta for a few months now. I relocated here earlier in the summer."

He frowned and nodded. "Oh, I see."

Katrina hoped that would be the end of that line of thought for the moment.

"Well then, what about pastimes? Shopping? Reading?" he politely inquired, but with an immediate sense that it was a horribly generic place to start.

"Oh no," she gently chided. "I asked you to tell me about yourself."

He grinned at her and remarked, "Busted."

"Indeed," she observed with mock-imperiousness.

Caleb thoughtfully sipped his tea before continuing, "I grew up in Ohio near Columbus. My mother raised me from a fairly young age as a single parent."

"Divorced?" Katrina casually asked.

He frowned. "Abandoned, I think."

She raised an eyebrow at that and gently ventured, "You sound as if you're not certain."

His frown deepened as he stared into his tea. "My father wasn't necessarily a kind man, you see," he explained in a vague manner. "And he drank. But one day he simply disappeared. My mother said he just left, and then we never heard from him again."

Katrina was fascinated by his recollection. *Your father was a sadistic, despicable man, Caleb,* she thought to herself. *I'm glad I killed him,* she added. Still, she maintained a neutral expression for Caleb's benefit.

"Mom raised me from that time. But something changed in her after my father left," he recalled. "She ensured the household was stable again. She had a great job in Columbus working for a mortgage processing company, and she worked her way up to senior mortgage processing supervisor before she passed away. She never remarried though; never dated much, either. Although she didn't like to talk about that much."

"Your mother sounds like a remarkable woman, Caleb," Katrina said.

"For the most part," he agreed with a frown. "But she was kind of a paradox to me sometimes."

"Oh?" she tentatively asked.

He smiled as if remembering something and explained, "After my father left, Mom became pretty obsessed with security around the house. She took a self-defense class, bought a shotgun, and made sure we had a great home security system. But she never wanted me involved with any of that. When I asked if she would take me to the self-defense class so we could do more together, she wouldn't let me. And when I asked her to take me shooting, she nixed that pretty quickly, too. It was as if she wanted to shelter me or something."

Katrina silently nodded as she absorbed and analyzed every word. *She wanted to keep you away from violence. She feared it would take its hold on you, as it did your father.*

"I asked her once what she was afraid of," he added almost as an afterthought. "And she would never really answer me. But I kept thinking..."

Katrina's eyes darted to meet his. "Yes?"

The corner of one side of his mouth rose slightly. "I know it's crazy, but I kept thinking...it's like she was waiting...waiting for something to come after us."

*Your father,* she mused. *Don't worry, Caleb. He's gone forever,* she willed with her piercing green eyes as she bored into his with a sudden intensity.

He stared into Katrina's eyes, which fleetingly appeared so cold to him, and felt a shiver go up his spine before abruptly looking away from her.

"Are you okay?" she softly asked after practically seeing the shiver run through his body.

"Sorry," he replied. "It's nothing."

*I scared him,* she silently chastised herself. Katrina reached out and caressed her fingers lightly across the hand holding his tea, and he looked up with a shy smile. "Thank you for sharing that with me," she offered sincerely.

"It's strange, but I feel like I could tell you anything," he earnestly observed. "And we barely know each other."

"Nonsense, we practically traveled through history together for a whole eight weeks," she countered with a grin.

They both laughed and quickly sipped their tea for a few moments. Then Katrina broke the silence. "So, you had some questions for me, as I recall," she ventured in an uplifting tone.

Caleb nodded, but felt suddenly unprepared for where to start with his questions. Unfortunately, she recalled his initial lame series of questions.

"Reading? Absolutely. Shopping? On occasion," she answered. "Although mostly I'm a people watcher, you could say."

"Really?" he inquired with interest, eager to engage her with anything remotely relevant that he'd failed to ask at the beginning of their conversation. But something in her response struck a chord in him; perhaps it was in the way she said it. "Do tell," he urged. "About people watching, that is."

She pursed her lips while considering him from across the table. "People hold a special interest for me," she said. "I guess you could say I'm a hopeless student of humanity."

"Ah, hence the history class," he confidently replied. "Was there something about the class that caught your interest in particular?"

The left side of her mouth upturned in a clever half-smile. "You could say that."

"Well, I hope I was helpful to you," he offered as he took a sip of his cooled tea. He was surprised how much he enjoyed the flavor and made a mental note to order it again.

"Oh, you were," she assured him. "I'm feeling much more confident moving forward with my informal research now."

"Good," he replied appreciatively. "I'm glad to hear it. What's the topic?"

*You, of course*, she thought. "Initial history-related teaching techniques of new faculty at community colleges," she replied matter-of-factly.

"Ah, so you were auditing me then," he teased with a knowing smile.

"Exactly," she stated, all too aware of how close he was to the truth. *And you passed with flying colors.*

"But tell me more about you," he insisted. "Where are you from? What brought you to Atlanta? Do you have family nearby?"

She genuinely appreciated his refreshing sense of curiosity instead of focusing entirely on himself, like so many other men she had met over the years. But she knew a little more about him than the seeming strangers that came and went in her life. *Her life*, she sardonically mused. *A life of what?*

He seemed to note her momentary distraction and misunderstood the nature of it. "But I'm being too nosy tonight," he muttered with reservation as he finished off his cup of tea.

She considered him with an amused smile. *So shy*, she

mused. *How very charming and uncommon today.* "Not at all, Caleb," she proceeded before backtracking. "May I call you Caleb?"

He seemed taken aback that she would ask and replied, "Please do. It's not like you're my student anymore. Now we're just two people getting to know one another."

*Sure,* she thought. *But only one of us is a person. The other is a vampire.*

"I felt a strong pull to be here, though I've never lived in this state before, much less the city of Atlanta," she began. "As to where I come from, I'm a resident of the world. And I don't have family here, or anywhere. Any family I had are already dead."

His face fell with a sudden realization. "Really? Me, too."

He relayed to her that his mother had been his only family to speak of. Her parents were older when they had her, and she had no siblings. His father, Ted, had an estranged relationship with his parents, so Caleb never got to know them. He wasn't even sure if they were living or how to get in touch with them. Ted had a brother named Brian, but Caleb had only met him once as a child, and he wasn't sure where his uncle even lived. He explained to the beautiful, red-haired woman before him that he was alone in the world, just as she was.

Katrina closely listened to the story of Caleb's family, but frowned with concern when he suddenly seemed ashamed for a moment, and then quickly fell silent.

"I'm sorry," he apologized as his face turned a shade of crimson. "I've monopolized the conversation again."

She warmly smiled at him from across the table and reached out to grasp his right hand he'd placed before him. His fingers smoothly wound around hers in return, and he smiled.

"Caleb, I want to know everything about you," she insisted. "We'll learn more about each other with every topic that comes up."

He was simply awestruck by Katrina. He had chatted more about his past with her in the coffee shop in an hour than he had the whole six months with Melanie, perhaps more than with any other woman he had dated. And it wasn't as though he didn't get along well with women, it was just that the women he had dated weren't as interested in him as much as in what he could do for them.

Katrina noticed his distracted expression and offered, "A penny for your thoughts?"

He smiled across the table at her. "That's quaint. Nobody says that anymore."

She adopted a smirk and countered, "Well, I'm a bit of an old-fashioned girl."

He absently nodded at her and marveled that he was actually sitting at a table with such a beautiful, articulate, and gentle woman.

"And being an old-fashioned girl," she continued, "I better get you back at a decent hour to get your car, or your girlfriend will be scandalized."

Caleb immediately frowned and asked, "How did you know I had a girlfriend?"

Her expression remained pleasant, but her mind raced for an answer. *That's what happens when you let your guard down so easily*, she scolded herself. Then it hit her.

"Well, the first night after class," she innocently explained. "Wasn't there a woman holding an apple outside your office?"

He slowly nodded, and his frown dissipated somewhat.

"I mean, I'm old-fashioned, but absolutely no students actually do that anymore," she offered with a smirk.

He smiled back at her with a nod, while she inwardly smiled at her good fortune and quick thinking.

# Chapter 2

## A Myth-Understanding

Caleb was elated upon waking the morning after his chat with Katrina at Starbucks. While shaving, he fondly reflected on their visit. After brushing his teeth, he contemplated his Friday; the last weekend before the second eight weeks of the fall semester started. He was grateful for being scheduled to teach only day classes this time. Instead of dwelling on Monday, he focused on spending the day pursuing his own interests, which included working out at the indoor gym on the top floor of his apartment building. It was another perk that, in addition to the parking garage, helped rationalize the increased rent that he paid for his otherwise small apartment.

As he worked out on the elliptical and upper body equipment, his thoughts shamefully wandered to Katrina. Despite the guilt over thinking about her instead of Melanie, his thoughts took on a journey of their own. He realized that his subconscious was trying to tell him something, but he stubbornly insisted that Melanie was the individual who was supposed to be the center of his attention. Following his workout and a shower, Caleb dressed and called Melanie, just to see how the Florida trip was going.

"Hey, Mel," he pleasantly offered.

"Oh, hi, Caleb," she tentatively replied.

"Did I call at a bad time?"

"Oh, no," she offered matter-of-factly. "Greg and I were just talking about stuff as we followed behind Candace's car."

"What happened to the original plan of carpooling in the

minivan?"

"Well, the van was idling funny, so Candace loaded four people into her car, and Greg offered to drive the two of us behind them," Melanie explained. "Wasn't that nice of him?"

*Oh yeah, Greg's a real hero,* Caleb thought with annoyance. "Yeah, real nice," he muttered darkly.

The connection's signal strength seemed to falter, and Melanie said, "Listen, I think we're losing the cell tower signal out here, so I'll call you tonight from the hotel."

"Sure," he replied. "Be careful, okay?"

"You got it," she absently replied before the line went dead.

*Call it paranoia, but I've got a bad feeling about this trip,* Caleb irritably considered.

Katrina lounged before an elaborate oak computer hutch in an oversized basement serving as bedroom, entertainment room, and study at her estate. Daytime was often a boring period for her as she awaited dusk. She had already checked her various foreign and domestic investment accounts and shifted some funds to her bank account in Atlanta. She was passing the time Web surfing, following up on some emails with fellow vampire acquaintances around the world, and longing for sunset.

Her mind was preoccupied with contacting Alton and reviewing the information he had provided to her regarding the lost contact with two vampire associates in Europe. It appeared that Garett from Paris had disappeared entirely, and Alton had found no trace of where he might have disappeared to. Equally curious was the question of why Garett had gone underground so hastily. There was also the odd matter of Octavia from Trondheim, who was normally rather social for a vampire, but who had stopped interacting with her peers as abruptly as Garett.

Vampires didn't require a lot of sleep, so Katrina had a lot of time to mull over both situations, which were beginning to appear connected. Unfortunately, there were still too many unanswered questions, and she hoped Alton's continued investigations would prove more fruitful.

Despite her attempts, her normally unshakeable concentration was distracted with thoughts of Caleb. Katrina had enjoyed their brief visit the prior evening, and longed to spend more time with him. Needless to say, he definitely held her interest. The only problem was that his social life was complicated by Melanie, which meant that Katrina's own interests in him were also handicapped by the woman.

*Oh, how I dislike Melanie*, Katrina mulled with a clenched jaw. She realized that she needed a viable, innocent reason to try to interact with Caleb again. *Something that won't put me on Melanie's radar too much.*

*Maybe I should just kill Melanie*, she brooded.

Katrina felt that she was supposed to feel a pang of guilt for thinking so shallowly about humans. But for some reason, guilt failed her at that moment. Instead, there was a prospective sense of feral satisfaction.

She banished the idea from her thoughts entirely, though not because it might cause Caleb some degree of sadness, but because she needed to keep the body count to a minimum in order to avoid raising suspicion among the authorities and starting unnecessary manhunts. As a matter of practice, thanks to the blood bank, she usually lived in an area for rather long periods with virtually no need to kill anybody. Already, she'd dispatched one human in the short time since arriving in Atlanta. But that was to protect Caleb. Katrina resolved with complete clarity that no body count concerns would deter her from protecting him. It seemed that her concerns for him were still as strong as when he was a child.

"Angel Caleb," she sighed out loud with a contented smirk as she considered the formerly innocent little boy who'd grown into such an attractive, intriguing young man. *He's unlike the other men in my past*, she mused, *but in a good way. So kind, endearing, and sincere. Yet, there's a definite vulnerability in him, a weakness, perhaps. He's damaged from his past.*

*Strength lurks dormant inside him, but he doesn't seem to realize it yet. I can help him harness that over time, I think.*

She froze in place, wondering why he meant so much to her when so few humans had during her time as a vampire. *Because he's special to me,* she determined. Such a connection springing from a solitary day surrounding a singular event nearly twenty years ago might seem unlikely to most. Yet it had been pivotal to her continued existence. If not for him, she would likely be dead. *I'll be grateful to him forever for his simple, guileless effort; an act of selfless assistance.*

But could someone rationally expect to base a relationship on such a flimsy premise? She scoffed, breaking the silence around her. Many in her past had presumed to claim more from her and under much less pretense. *And they all died for their selfish efforts. But not Caleb. He's altogether different,* she confirmed with a smile.

Whimsy struck her, and she picked up her cell phone from the tabletop.

After time spent doing laundry that afternoon, Caleb was once again at the office that evening, preparing some minor changes to his lesson plans, when his cell phone rang. He'd expected it to be Melanie, but noted that it was Katrina.

"Hello?" he asked with a distinctly pleased tone.

"Hi, Caleb, It's Katrina," she greeted him cheerfully.

*As if I wouldn't recognize her beautiful voice in the middle of a hurricane,* he considered, stifling a chuckle as he realized his unintended pun. "Hi, Katrina," he replied with a smile. "What's up?"

"Just a quick history-related question," she began mysteriously. "If I wanted to read up on Andrew Jackson, what authors would you recommend?"

He smiled, pleased that she was calling to ask him for advice. "Well," he began as he playfully swiveled around in his desk chair, "the bio by H.W. Brands is a gold standard, but I actually enjoyed the Jon Meacham bio even more."

"Excellent, thanks for the suggestion," she replied.

His eyes glanced at the small bookshelf in his office, and he spied the very book he had just mentioned. "In fact," he began hopefully, "I happen to have the Meacham book right here in my office. I'd happily loan it to you."

"I have some errands to run, so I maybe I'll drop by and pick it up," she ventured. "That is, unless you were leaving soon."

"Oh, it's no problem," he confirmed a bit more energetically than he'd intended.

He had no way of knowing that she was pausing to grin on the other end. "Great, I'll be there in…shall we say, half-hour?" she asked.

"Perfect," he confirmed with a smile before snapping his cell phone shut.

Approximately fifteen minutes after Katrina's call, Caleb's cell phone rang as he thumbed through Meacham's biography of Jackson. As he reached for his phone, he hoped it wasn't Katrina calling to say something came up. Instead, it was Melanie. *She must've reached the hotel okay.* "Hey, Mel," he answered contentedly. "How's Florida?"

There was a pause at the other end before Melanie spoke. "Hi, Caleb. Wow, you sound pretty happy-go-lucky. Where's the party?"

Even Melanie's sardonic wit didn't impair his good mood at the prospect of seeing Katrina again. "No party, just here at the office finishing things for Monday," he said, but with a more subdued tone than before.

"Now that's the Caleb I know," she said. "We made it to the hotel this afternoon and just got back from dinner. I'm changing clothes, and we're gonna head out for some club-hopping."

"Sounds good," he politely offered. "Having fun?"

"Actually, yeah," she replied with a surprised tone. "It's been better than I expected. And Greg's really been good company, too."

"So, do you miss me?" Caleb smoothly asked.

There was another pause. "Well, do you miss me?" she countered somewhat evenly.

"I think I asked you first," he fenced. *Boy, as if that wasn't a junior high response*, he chided himself.

"Well, sure," she offered a little weakly in his opinion. "But sometimes it's good for two people to do their own thing, don't you think?"

"Yeah, I agree," he diplomatically agreed. He heard a male voice in the background and frowned. "Who's that?" he pointedly asked.

"Oh, it's just Greg," she explained with hesitation.

"I thought you said you were changing clothes," he recalled with some annoyance.

"Well, I just finished," she defensively countered.

He heard another faint noise in the background. *Was that the sound of a zipper being zipped, or unzipped?*

"Listen, I better get going," she insisted with sudden urgency. "The others are waiting for us."

*Waiting for us*, he levelly repeated in his mind. "Sure," he conceded. "Have a good time, Mel."

"Bye then, Caleb," she offered a little too politely.

He was still contemplating the conversation with Melanie when Katrina arrived. She was dressed in a pair of dark denim jeans and an emerald blouse underneath a stylish black leather jacket. Her red hair cascaded casually around her head and down below her shoulders. *She looks amazing.*

She glanced down at him with a smile as she practically posed in the doorway. Her green eyes took in the faded blue jeans he wore, as well as the way in which his trendy, dark blue T-shirt fit snugly over his muscular chest. As her eyes met his, she noticed that his eyes appeared to be slightly strained, or perhaps agitated. Her smiled faded somewhat, and she adopted a concerned expression.

"Caleb, is everything okay?" she asked.

He considered her for a moment before realizing he was feeling happier once she arrived. There was no need to mention the conversation with Melanie. "Me? I'm great," he replied. "Thanks for asking. You?"

"Great," she answered with a friendly smile that didn't quite meet her eyes. *He's being evasive*, she mused as she noted the slight change in his pupils, the sound of his voice, and the almost negligible change to the muscle tension in his face. As vampires went, she was a very observant predator.

"I'm really glad you called earlier," he genuinely offered.

*That's honest*, she noted by reading his body language and voice inflections. She returned his smile in earnest.

He handed the paperback book to her and offered, "Please, keep it as long as you like."

She took it, making sure to flip through to the table of contents before casually scanning the description on the back cover. "Thanks," she offered before carefully probing, "You're up here late again, and on a Friday night no less. Shouldn't you be out entertaining...what's her name?"

"Melanie," he offered with a wry expression.

*Ah, so that's what's bothering him*, Katrina considered, feeling far happier about that than she thought she should have. "Sorry, bad topic?" she casually ventured.

He frowned. "I'm beginning to think so."

She arched an eyebrow at him, but her smile widened wickedly. His heart rate increased slightly as he noted her expression and misinterpreted it as potentially negative. *He's nervous about that*, she noted.

"You know, Caleb," she began innocently, "Nobody's perfect. Relationships aren't easy for any of us." *A major understatement in my experience, and perhaps his*, she thought. The latter postulation was based upon her own intuition more than anything substantive.

He wanly smiled and admitted, "Guilty as charged."

She supportively smiled at him and subsequently heard his stomach growl. An amusing thought crossed her mind, and she struggled to avoid grinning. "Well, I'm ready to render judgment," she smoothly announced with a sober expression.

His eyes playfully glinted up at her from where he sat.

"I sentence you to dinner with me tonight," she declared with a note of finality.

He grinned and held his wrists out to her in mock submission. "Haul me away," he quipped with the flash of a cute grin. "I'm yours."

*Oh Caleb, you really shouldn't have said that*, Katrina thought slyly as a sudden surge of desire ran through her body.

As they walked out to the parking lot, he felt embarrassed about the prospect of driving Katrina around in his older Honda. Fortunately for him, she offered to take them to the restaurant in her Audi. He again marveled at the impressive driving experience the sleek automobile offered, and that was just from the passenger seat. But while he was grateful for Katrina shuttling them around town, he insisted on paying for dinner.

They selected one of his favorite restaurants, the popular and swanky Café Circa downtown off of Edgewood Avenue and Boulevard. Caleb assured her that the food and service were fantastic every time he went there. It was bustling with people that evening, adding a lively energy to its atmosphere. Katrina scanned the room, noting one of the interior walls was lined by a lengthy, finished oak bar with wooden barstools. Behind the bar was a series of backlit shelves lined with every variety of alcohol known to mankind. The dining area held an array of varnished oak bistro tables surrounded by oak barstools, and the lighting was moody and rather romantic.

She smiled at Caleb as he arranged for seating. They sat across from one another initially, but after a moment of taking in the atmosphere, she moved to one of the stools next to him.

"Do you mind?" she asked with a playful sparkle to her eyes.

"I'm flattered," he replied with a proud grin.

They both ordered a beer on tap, and he requested chips and salsa. Caleb ordered Chicken Panini, while Katrina settled for a plain house salad made with the restaurant's signature pumpkin seeds and empanada strips. They chatted as the crowds bustled around them amidst the sound of trendy music.

"So, what do you think of this place?" Caleb asked with a grin.

Katrina looked around, absorbing the atmosphere. Her heightened senses registered the overload of human scents, voices, and emotions. She liked it immensely and felt the hunger for fresh blood rise in her, requiring additional effort to keep her senses in check.

"I love it," she replied with a warm smile. "It suits you."

He nodded appreciatively.

"Is this your hangout of sorts? A favorite spot to take all the prospective women in your life?" she playfully asked.

He chuckled. "Actually, it's one of my favorite spots, but Melanie hates it for some reason. She said it's just not her style or something."

"Well, it's a place I can really sink my teeth into," Katrina countered.

After laughing for a moment at her strange remark, he lost himself in her beautiful green eyes.

"Tell me more about your life, Caleb," she gently urged. "I want to know everything."

He was flattered by her interest and described his experiences growing up with his mother and how he seemed to do much better in school after they moved away from their old acreage home for the Columbus city limits. He and his mother created fresh memories in the new house and tried to leave many of the past, painful ones behind.

His grades improved in junior high and high school to the point where he received a scholarship to Georgia State. He was grateful for the wonderful college fund made available to him after Wanda won a raffle from her workplace. It helped pay for his tuition all the way through graduate school.

Katrina warmly smiled at him, fully pleased to hear her efforts to help him and Wanda had worked out so well. Though it wasn't as if she was trying to make amends, or strike some karma-balance for what she was. Being a vampire was a merely a fact that she had long since reconciled in her mind. She was proud to be who she was and harbored no illusions of what living meant for her. It meant blood for sustenance and clandestine living among the human population to protect her secret and longevity. She broke out of her reverie to realize that he had fallen silent and was intently watching her.

"I guess my life's been pretty boring for the most part," he conceded.

Her face fell as if she'd been scolded, though she had heard every word he had said to her. "Oh no, Caleb," she insisted. "I was just envisioning what you were telling me. It's inspiring how well your life has turned out given so many challenges." She reached out to touch his arm, and he smiled while placing his hand over hers.

"Thanks," he offered. "You're one of the few people who seem to care to listen to me drone on like this." Caleb sighed as the realization hit him that, aside from Melanie and a few of her friends, he still hadn't yet formed any close friendships in the Atlanta area. Many of his college friends had moved away to new locations or returned to their home towns where they grew up. And he was still so new in his position at the college that he was still getting to know everybody there. The majority of people in his life at the moment were friendly acquaintances.

"I'm not like other people that you know," Katrina earnestly clarified.

"No," he agreed after a moment's pause. "You're not. And I've never been happier."

She bent her free arm up on the table and propped her chin on her hand as she smiled at him. He swallowed once and moved his face closer to hers. It felt like an imaginary string was pulling him to her as he gazed into her penetrating stare. She slyly smiled like a predator that had snared its prey and was relishing the catch. As their lips almost touched, their meal abruptly arrived with the appearance of their server.

To Katrina's amusement, Caleb turned his head to look up at their waiter with a forced, false grin, offering, "Wow, that was amazing timing."

Once they began to eat, Katrina mostly picked at her salad as they talked about topics ranging from favorite historical periods, to favorite aspects of the Atlanta area, to how the
Braves were already looking to next season for their race to the
pennant. They enjoyed each other's company immensely and
shared a rich chocolate dessert between them.

Caleb regretted that the time had passed so quickly. He
was rather quiet on their return drive to campus, but felt very
happy. He sensed strong chemistry with Katrina and realized
for perhaps the first time just how poorly matched he and Melanie were.

Katrina was flush with emotions as she drove the two of
them back to the college. She remembered how close they'd
been to a first kiss at the restaurant and was startled by how
much she had craved it. She felt a palpable attraction to him,
both physical and emotional, and his personality seemed both
genuine and endearing. She also relished the diversity in con-
versational topics and how well-informed he was. It surprised
her how strongly, and how quickly, her feelings for him were
growing in more directions than she could have anticipated.

As she pulled up next to his car in the campus parking
lot, she put the Audi in park but left the engine running. She
looked over to him and effortlessly smiled.

"Thanks again, Katrina," he offered as he released his seatbelt. "I really had a great time tonight."

"Me too," she softly replied.

He seemed confused as to what to do and chose to open
the passenger door. He wanted to reach across the seat and
kiss her, and yet his mind screamed that he was technically
still dating Melanie. And while he felt a sense of betrayal over
seeing Katrina behind Melanie's back, he was still happy he'd
done so. Not that he approved of that sort of thing, it was a first
for him, but rather being with Katrina just felt right. He de-
spised the situation he was facing, but knew the only clear way
to any form of redemption was being honest with both Melanie

and Katrina.

She watched him silently, seeing the conflict wash across his features, and waited patiently. She realized somehow she had helped propel them both down this path, but she left free will in Caleb's corner. That is, if trying to deny the temptations directed by one of nature's most powerful, deadly predators was free will at all. *No*, she realized, *human free will is altogether something just as powerful as I am regarding affairs of the heart.* The word "affairs" stuck in her mind.

"Have I created complications for you, Caleb?" she asked with a hint of sympathy.

He looked across the seat at her hesitantly and conceded with a sigh, "I think I've done that all by myself."

She smiled briefly and reassured him, "I'm not going anywhere."

Caleb frowned slightly, realizing his next question might ruin everything, and asked, "What is it about me that compels you to say that? Because I don't know that I would if it were I in your place."

Katrina regarded him for a moment, and she heard his heartbeat increase rapidly. *He's terrified that honesty is going to doom him*, she mused, *along with what I'll say.* But she had a small surprise of sorts in store for him in her response. "Well, you're just going to have to un-complicate things a little and find out," she offered with a smirk.

At first he seemed stunned, and then surprise gave way to hopefulness. He dared to smile. "I'll call you," he promised.

"Good enough," she responded resolutely. "Good night, Caleb."

"Good night, Katrina," he replied with a hint of appreciation.

He watched her drive halfway across the parking lot before stopping the little black sports car, the taillights shining brightly as the brake was applied. He frowned at her delay and unlocked his car door.

*Get into your car, Caleb*, Katrina thought as she watched

him in the rear view mirror. *Parking lots aren't very safe for you, it would seem*, she added with a twinkle in her eyes.

As Caleb closed his car door he saw her pull away into the night. *Was she waiting on me, or did she change her mind about me?* he wondered. Then another, somewhat odd notion made its way to the forefront of his mind. *Watching over me, maybe?* The idea filled him with a strong sense of satisfaction. Once his father had left, Caleb's mother changed into a very protective figure in his life, and somehow Katrina's behavior reminded him of those same feelings of safety. Certainly, it wasn't as if Caleb viewed Katrina as some sort of maternal figure. Far from it, in fact. Merely that the perceived sense of protectiveness Katrina showed to him felt similar.

He chuckled at the outlandishness of the idea and began his journey home. *I'm imagining the whole thing*, he resolved.

As he drove home, a sense of dread and foreboding began to grow, and his mind went immediately to what he would say to Melanie about his conflicted feelings. He was never one for confrontation, but firsthand experience already taught him Melanie was.

The weekend turned into a last-minute dash to update his lecture notes along with changes that had occurred to him during the previous semester. Melanie didn't call at all on Saturday, and he dreaded the upcoming conversation that he needed to have with her. It was obviously better that he waited until she returned from Jacksonville so they could speak in person.

*Great, then Melanie can have the added benefit of yelling and cursing at me in person*, he considered darkly. *It should be very cathartic for her.*

Caleb had learned that Melanie never lacked animation when it came to her temper. Fortunately, he was the peaceful type who only argued back verbally. On one occasion, Melanie actually threw something at him in the middle of an argument, but he managed to dodge a paperweight effectively. The experiences of dodging errant pitches in baseball came in handy at such times. Caleb's mother had preached to him since he was a child that violence was no solution to interpersonal conflict. Additionally, he still had bad childhood memories of when his father was physically abusive with him and his mother, and those experiences added to his personal abhorrence of physical violence.

Saturday evening, he tried calling to check on Melanie, but his calls went to voicemail on all three occasions. Finally, he fell asleep on his apartment couch watching movies on cable and skimming through the pages of the latest biography on Harry Truman. He fell asleep sometime after 1 am, completely unaware of a lone figure peering in at him through the sheer curtains of his living room from the fire escape.

Katrina couldn't help herself on Saturday night. She was restless, and her mind kept wandering through a series of thoughts, all of which ended up on Caleb. She soon found herself observing him from his fire escape in the darkness. Fully realizing she was obsessing over him, the truth was undeniable: She enjoyed his company and couldn't wait to see him again.

*Actually, the truth is I'm smitten with him, and I hate the thought of being apart from him for very long,* she silently conceded.

There was so much more Katrina wanted to ask him about his life, his dreams, his favorite things, and a host of other topics ranging from the magnificent to the benign.

Vampires were like that. They obsessed when they were focused on something intently. Perhaps it was due to the predator or hunter instinct geared towards tenacity when seeking prey. Either way, it merely added to the focus she had for Caleb.

But there was an added element to her interest in him. Ever since the episode with the mugger in the college parking lot, she was concerned for his safety. Caleb was not in a particularly hazardous job or environment, and obviously he was less vulnerable in adulthood than as a child, but she still felt very protective of him. It was an aspect of herself she could freely offer to him, and it made her feel useful in his life.

After watching him at length through the curtains, Katrina determined it was probably time for her to depart, as she wanted to ensure her presence went unnoticed. She'd have to resign herself to other diversions until she could see Caleb again. She realized he needed time to resolve his conflicting feelings for both her and Melanie, who frankly didn't deserve his attentions in Katrina's opinion. Katrina conceded that her own efforts at attracting him weren't helping his dilemma. Still, she was feeling both confident and patient regarding what she considered an inevitability.

*We vampires are focused and tend to shape our own realities.*

When Caleb awoke on the couch Sunday morning, it was to the sound of his cell phone ringing. He sleepily reached over to retrieve it from the end table as the sunlight created a halo of light through his sheer curtains. It was Melanie, and she apologized for not having returned his calls on Saturday night, but they'd been out on the town until after midnight, and she hadn't wanted to wake him. She said she would drop by to see him at his apartment that evening after they got back to Atlanta. He noted that her voice had been pleasant, but distant.

He spent the remainder of the day cleaning house and using his home computer to organize the notes and PowerPoint presentations he had brought home from his office on a portable drive. He tuned the TV in the living room to one of the all-hours alternative rock music channels. The day passed quickly, as weekends and holidays always seemed to, and evening arrived before he knew it.

Sometime around 8 pm, as dusk changed to night, Caleb's doorbell buzzed. He went to the door, peeked through the peephole, and welcomed Melanie in. She held a firmly resigned expression on her face to accompany her otherwise pleasant smile. She wore jeans and a Jacksonville Jaguars sweatshirt, which must have been one of her weekend acquisitions. She absently clutched a small stack of music CDs.

"Hi, Mel," he greeted her with a hug and a platonic kiss. "Welcome back." *So far, so good,* he thought with encouragement. "How was the trip? When did you guys get back?"

"Oh, we all had a great time," Melanie replied congenially as she perched on the edge of one of his kitchen stools. "We just got back a couple of hours ago."

He glanced at the clock on his kitchen stove while moving towards the refrigerator for a cola. He was surprised she hadn't called sooner. He noted the CDs in her hand and asked, "Buy some new CDs?"

"No, these are yours," she answered with a glance down to them. "I'm just returning them."

"Want a Coke?" he asked absently as he reached inside the refrigerator.

"No thanks," she replied. "So Caleb, there's a little topic that we...that is, that I wanted to bring up."

His eyes darted up from his can of cola to Melanie's face with momentary suspicion as he heard the word "we" slip out.

Katrina anxiously waited for the Georgian sunset to give way to nighttime. She hadn't visited with Caleb since Friday and was going a little stir crazy. She absently wondered if he had met with Melanie yet. More than anything, she wanted to just sit and visit with him more. She realized she should probably just wait for him to call, but for some reason her patience was wearing thin.

She yearned for an excuse to drop by to see him. However, first she would carefully observe him from the fire escape before committing to the visit, just in case he seemed busy. *Or the blonde might be there*, she considered darkly. Then inspiration struck in the form of Darjeeling tea.

Katrina changed into a pair of gray Capris, a turquoise long-sleeved cotton shirt, and a pair of flats and stopped by Starbucks. She made her way to Caleb's apartment as darkness was in full bloom and climbed carefully up the fire escape with the tea secured safely in a Starbucks sack. But she soon frowned as she viewed Melanie sitting at the kitchen counter talking to him. Her acute hearing took over as she slid into the shadows near the window.

"Is everything okay?" Caleb asked Melanie with a hint of suspicion.

"Oh sure," she hedged.

He took the high road and waited patiently for her to continue.

"So, there's something we probably need to talk about," she continued. "I had a really nice trip spending the weekend with Greg, and it got me thinking. How would you feel about us seeing other people for a while?"

He let her question sink in and realized that she and Greg must have made a connection over the weekend. "So," he ventured carefully. "You and Greg had a good time this weekend?"

"Well, we kinda hit it off and had a fun weekend," she replied somewhat sheepishly.

Instead of disappointment, he felt a welcome release of tension. It was as if the sense of dread he had been feeling had lifted from him and departed. He suddenly didn't feel so bad about conveying similar feelings to her and adopted a hopeful expression.

Melanie frowned.

"Actually, Mel, I've been thinking recently about us as well," he began agreeably. "I just feel like things haven't gelled with us the past couple of months. So maybe your suggestion would be good for both of us."

"Just what do you mean by that, Caleb Taylor?" she demanded irritably as she flipped her hair away from her face with a flick of her left hand. "Have you already been seeing someone else?"

That caught him off guard to say the least. *Hadn't she just tried to convey her own feelings for Greg a moment ago?* "Well, the past couple of days I've kind of been getting to know some-one," he conceded.

"You mean that Carlita woman from class?" she demanded. "I thought you said she was just a student of yours?"

"You mean Katrina?"

"Whatever!" she chortled.

"She's not my student anymore, actually," he hastily ex-plained. "In fact, she stopped taking classes altogether."

"So, you're leaving me for some college tramp?!"

"You're kidding, right?" he replied dumbly. *Didn't she just tell me that she and Greg made a connection over the weekend?*

"You cheating bastard!" Melanie yelled as she reached down to the CDs in her hand and began throwing them like Chinese throwing stars.

One zinged past his right ear to break against the wall be-hind him, but the second caught him squarely in the middle of the forehead. "Ow!" he shouted in pain as he bent forward and away from her while shielding his face with his hands.

Katrina heard the argument between Caleb and Melanie and tensed as she viewed their exchange. *That woman is crazy,* she silently fumed.

She watched with fury as the CD case hit Caleb in the fore-head and nearly charged in through the living room window. Instead, she turned to leap over the railing and off the fire es-cape balcony to the street level below with a cat-like pounce and landing. Her feet no sooner hit the pavement than she was speeding around the deserted corner of the building to the side entrance, bag of tea still in hand.

Katrina wasn't merely angry, she was enraged.

Four remaining CD cases landed against or around Caleb until the barrage stopped from lack of ammunition. For the most part, he managed to avoid further damage, but the cut on his head began bleeding profusely. He recalled from some first aid training that even minor scalp cuts would bleed more than other places on the body. It stung like hell, too.

"Melanie!" he shouted as he maneuvered around to the living room to stand with the couch between the two of them. "Damn it, just chill out!"

The abrupt sound of the doorbell startled them both.

Katrina exited the stairwell door on the third floor of Caleb's apartment building. She immediately sensed the presence of a person at the end of the hallway standing next to the elevator and briefly glanced at a man dressed in jeans and a Jacksonville Jaguars T-shirt. He was young and muscular and watched her with interest but otherwise seemed non-threatening. A few seconds later Katrina stood outside Caleb's apartment door with slightly glowing green eyes and pressed on the doorbell firmly.

*Three seconds more and this door is coming off its hinges,* she vowed in a rage. Then she heard the sound of a deadbolt unlocking.

Caleb opened the front door to his apartment while holding his bleeding forehead with his left hand. His eyes widened as Katrina stood in the doorway looking less than happy. Was that a glint in her eyes he saw?

"Katrina?" he asked vaguely while squinting against the pain in his forehead.

"Are you okay? What happened?" she demanded with concern as she bodily pressed her way into the apartment, putting herself between Melanie and Caleb.

Katrina's eyes immediately swept the room to fall upon Melanie in a piercing manner. Melanie's eyes widened momentarily with surprise at their intensity, but returned to an outraged expression. Katrina's expression remained steely, at best.

"Who are you?" Katrina demanded with authority as she drew out each word. She loved the appalled expression on Melanie's face in response.

"Well, just who the hell are you?" Melanie demanded back.

Caleb had enough of his wits about him at that moment to remain silent.

"I'm the person who's very angry her friend's forehead is bleeding," Katrina replied with a lethal edge to her voice as she carefully selected her words.

"Melanie, this is Katrina," Caleb offered weakly as he removed his left palm from his forehead and glanced at it to gauge the severity of bleeding. "Katrina, this is Melanie, my ex-girlfriend."

Melanie's eyes darted to him at that last qualification, and Katrina's expression changed to one of grim satisfaction. In fact, she scowled slightly at Melanie.

"You can have him," Melanie fumed as she moved to slip past Katrina. "Jerk!"

Katrina nearly reached out to choke Melanie as she passed by, but restrained herself for Caleb's benefit, not to mention the desire to stay off the Atlanta police department's most wanted list.

A man's voice was quickly heard in the hallway outside, followed by Melanie demanding, "Just never mind. Let's get the hell out of here, Greg."

Caleb's eyes shot up and to the hallway outside his apartment with a mix of surprise and incredulity. Katrina's eyes darted to Caleb's for a split second before her hand swiftly darted out to slam the front door shut behind Melanie. His heart jumped at the swift, loud sound of the door slamming so abruptly. Katrina's eyes looked to Caleb with concern, having sensed the growing darkness in his mood.

"She brought Greg," he fumed.

"Just nevermind that. Let's get you cleaned up," she interrupted gently as she steered him to the bathroom.

He found Katrina's sudden attention to him unusually forceful, but somehow welcome. He partially grasped the idea of her seeming very protective towards him, but his mind was also still racing from the emotional exchange with Melanie.

The scent of Caleb's blood acted fully upon Katrina's sense of smell, and she felt her mouth water slightly in anticipation. She repressed the strong desire to kiss -- no, lick his head wound, and instead grabbed a washcloth hanging on the towel rack in his bathroom. The blood was starting to run again from the small gash in his forehead, and her jaw tightened with the resolve not to do anything foolish that would either disturb or terrify him.

"Really, I can take care of this," he insisted. "Don't trouble yourself."

She regarded him with an arched eyebrow for a moment that seemed to register in his mind as a mild challenge. He got the idea that she was asserting herself with him, although not in a particularly threatening way. Instead, it made him feel safe. He swallowed hard as he gazed into her beautiful green eyes and decided he was perfectly content to let her look after him for the moment.

"Or I could just be very grateful you're here," he conceded softly as he released the washcloth to her grasp.

Katrina smiled. She rinsed the washcloth in cold water and asked, "Antiseptic?"

He pointed to the split mirror in front of him that was also a dual-sided medicine cabinet. She removed a still-sealed bottle of first aid antiseptic and held the washcloth to his head wound. It was superficial, but would likely leave a nasty bruise, unless...

"Press this over the cut for a moment," she instructed him as he held the washcloth over his forehead, partially blocking his vision.

She darted into his kitchen, retrieved a couple of paper towels, and gathered saliva in her mouth. She walked back to the bathroom, opened the antiseptic, and held the bottle up near the paper towel as she quickly applied her saliva instead. Taking the washcloth from him, she held the moistened area of the paper towel to his wound.

He noticed immediately that the small gash in his head

began to feel numb, and was quite happy with the effect. She smiled happily at him as he regarded her with appreciation. Something jogged in his memory for just a split second. It was as if he had felt the sensation sometime in the past, but he couldn't recall when or where exactly.

"It wasn't as bad as it looked initially," she offered as she quickly removed the paper towel, leaving only the appearance of a nearly sealed line of scar.

"Yeah, I guess not," he muttered as the numbing sensation continued.

"It shouldn't even bruise too badly," she ventured as she put the lid back on the antiseptic. "And there shouldn't be any permanent scarring, either."

"Wow, that's some powerful stuff," he commented as he glanced down at the bottle before she replaced it in his medicine cabinet.

"Yep, good thing you had some handy," she replied with a satisfied smile.

"Hey, how did you know where I live?" Caleb asked as the subject suddenly occurred to him. He was surprised to see Katrina at his apartment door that evening, though not at all disappointed. Yet he didn't recall exchanging addresses with her.

Katrina returned her best casual expression and replied, "You'd be amazed what you can find on the Internet today. And besides, I wanted to surprise you with some Darjeeling tea that you liked from the other night."

He followed the direction of her pointed finger to see the Starbucks bag sitting on his end table and smiled appreciatively in return. She was suddenly very happy for the distraction the tea provided. Since he didn't pay property taxes against the apartment, it had been harder than she had expected to track down his home address when she' ha first settled in Atlanta.

"That's very kind. Thank you," he replied sincerely.

She was feeling very pleased with herself at that moment.

But the subject of Melanie quickly returned to the forefront of Caleb's thoughts. "I guess I should explain the little event that was going on when you arrived," he ventured anxiously as he gestured for Katrina to take a seat and then sat next to her on the couch.

"Was she the complication you spoke of the other night?" she asked.

"Yeah, and it's not what it looked like," he supplied earnestly. "I never raised a hand at her. We were just arguing, and –"

"It never once entered my mind," she interrupted him with sincerity. "I could tell when I arrived that you were calmer than she was, and she was quite animated after my arrival, whereas you seemed to be seeking to diffuse the emotion in the room."

Caleb nearly gaped at her frank and rather accurate assessment of the situation. "That's pretty much it," he muttered absently. "She thought I was cheating on her."

"And were you?" Katrina asked plainly, despite recalling the presence of Greg in the hallway. She was curious how he would respond. Melanie had obviously already decided that Caleb was no longer of interest to her, and her own assessment of Melanie was already rather negative after all she had overheard, observed, and discerned. *All the better for me*, Katrina thought.

"Yes, it could be viewed that way from a certain perspective. At least in my opinion," he replied, suddenly critical of himself.

"Oh, really?" she asked. It was important to know that Caleb could take responsibility for his own actions with a degree of honesty. *Score one for Caleb*, she noted.

"Well, I did go out with you while I was technically still supposed to be exclusively dating her," he mused. "But it's felt so wrong between Melanie and me these past few weeks. I don't know. I'm still feeling a little confused about everything right now."

"So, would you say you have devotion issues?" she pressed with a mild injection of teasing.

He considered her question and searched deep within himself for a moment. Nobody had ever asked him questions like this before. He swallowed as he gazed into her eyes. "I really don't think I have devotion issues with the right partner," he assessed as openly as possible.

She smiled slightly and considered him. *Yes, I suspect he's correct*, she determined.

"I wouldn't blame you if you thought poorly of me," he added self-consciously. "Or even if you got up right now and walked right out the door."

"Would you like for me to go?" she asked softly as her green eyes bored into his. She read the answer from the reaction in his pale blue eyes before he uttered a response.

"No, not at all," he insisted gently with a vulnerable expression. He wanted more than anything for her to stay. He realized things had happened so quickly that evening with Melanie, but he'd already been thinking about Katrina very soberly the past few days. He was fully aware how special her introduction into his life already felt to him.

She smiled back at him, adopted a more quizzical expression, and asked, "You seem innocent enough, but why do I get the impression that you get into trouble a lot?"

He briefly recollected the campus parking lot incident, as well as that evening's event with Melanie. "Just my luck, I guess," he quipped with a grin. "I'm just walking, talking trouble, I suppose."

Her smile turned predatory as she countered slyly, "Well, I think I know just how to take care of troublemakers."

Maybe it was the way she looked at him, or perhaps it was the sound of her voice at that moment, but no matter the reason, Caleb felt an immediate urge to kiss her. And unlike the night at the restaurant, he leaned his body towards her without hesitation until his face was nearly touching hers. She didn't move an inch as his mouth neared hers. He ever-so-gently brushed his lips once against hers. There was warmth as their lips touched, and his eyes softened as his face hovered before her.

Katrina listened to Caleb's accelerated heartbeat and felt his warm breath against her lips. She was feeling extremely satisfied with how he had conducted himself. Now she understood his intentions even better than he probably did, and it pleased her.

Her right hand went immediately and gently to the back of his neck, where she cupped the base of his head, and her lips pressed with firm, deliberate pressure against his. She drew deeply against his breath for a single passionate moment, and he responded with a shudder that went through his body as he returned her kiss in kind.

She drew back from him, gazed into his eyes, and whispered, "I don't have devotion problems either, with the right person."

A surge of adrenaline shot through his body, and his heart raced. At that moment, he wanted so much to be the right person in her life. It was stronger than most anything he'd felt before. But he was suddenly lost in a sea of uncertainty as to what he should do next. "And now?" he asked quietly and with a sincere desire for guidance from her.

Katrina smiled, having read the question in his eyes as he asked it. "Now?" she replied as she pulled away from him slightly. "Now we call it a night, and I let you get some rest. Tomorrow will be busy for you, as I'm sure the first day of the semester usually is."

His eyebrows rose with some surprise at her response. He certainly hadn't expected that. "And?" he queried with a grin.

She playfully smiled back at him, but replied with a sober tone, "And we take it one day at a time."

He was amazed by the seemingly uncanny sense of experience emanating from her. She appeared to be no older than he, but she spoke so sagely and with such confident reassurance. She was an anomaly to him in so many ways. And yet he trusted her implicitly.

"Count me in, coach," he agreed as he sat up and reached to

examine the bag of tea still perched on the table.

He was prepared at that moment to do the right thing, no matter what that was. He felt convinced that there was something very special about Katrina, mysterious and enchanting. And he meant both to discover and experience all of it.

For approximately two weeks, they exchanged emails and text messages during weekdays, while conversing over the phone any evenings they didn't see each other. There were dinner dates, a movie, and taking in an evening at one of the local art museums. No matter the activity, they both thoroughly enjoyed each other's company.

However, even as Caleb openly shared his own background, he found Katrina's to be continually vague. She rarely provided straightforward answers to questions about her youth, her family history, or even what kept her so busy during the daytime that she was never available for lunches or entire days together.

Caleb didn't really feel that Katrina was deliberately trying to mislead him, but rather that she felt uncomfortable confiding in him with details. That prospect bothered him quite a bit.

What he didn't realize was that Katrina was all too aware of his concerns. She expertly gauged his body language and voice inclinations, as well as the context of his statements. Furthermore, she realized the time was very near when she would either have to reveal herself and her true nature to him or risk losing all they had worked towards.

Of course, she realized from the beginning of her journey with him that the day would come when she would have to make a delicate and serious decision on how to proceed with him. If she left him now, he would perhaps never be the wiser and might live his life out within the traditional parameters of human existence. However, if she pursued him further, he would face an important decision of his own, one with potentially grave consequences for both of them.

Katrina came to a swift decision regarding Caleb. She

needed to reveal her true nature to him if there were any hope their relationship could continue to grow. *Will he accept who I am? Will he still desire me, or will he be repulsed?*

It was a beautiful mid-November Friday evening at the sprawling and secluded private neighborhood where Katrina lived. The exclusive Pine Valley edition was located just west of Atlanta within the suburb of Mableton in Cobb County, Georgia. Caleb met her at her home for the first time since they met, though she didn't actually invite him to enter the interior of the beautiful estate itself. He parked his car in her driveway in front of her four-car garage, where she met him and proceeded to guide him to the park-like area skirting her five-acre property. She explained that all of the surrounding properties were at least five acres in size and sported their own individual gate access to the sprawling park area.

They accessed the area via a black wrought iron gate leading from her property, which was itself surrounded by tall wrought iron fencing interspersed with tall red brick support columns. Caleb was thoroughly impressed as he walked next to her along the beautiful and romantic pathway. They strolled along the park's small sidewalk that wound its way through carefully manicured trees. The sidewalk was furnished with short black metal lampposts and wrought iron park benches positioned sporadically along its length. It was a scenic oasis for the residents of the Pine Valley edition.

The moon appeared as a small glowing orb high in the sky casting a dim pallor over the outdoors. A vast host of stars filled the clear dark sky like a sea of tiny white pinpricks. The varieties of trees of the surrounding forest were awash with the colors of fall, except for the tall pine trees, which still remained green. Caleb considered it the perfect setting for a romantic walk with Katrina.

"What are you thinking?" she asked while peering sidelong at him.

"Honestly, I was just thinking how grand all this is," he replied sheepishly. He thought it must cost the residents a fortune to have it developed and maintained in such fine order.

She read between the lines of his statement by gauging his shy facial expression. "It's a shared expense between my property and the other estates in the area," she explained. "The area extends forty yards or so on either side of the path. Then it reverts to native forest and undergrowth, as well as the original rough topology of the land. Still, it's peaceful and more secluded than most parks in the area."

She added that the topography was very hilly and some areas were still dangerous until the contractors skirted them with proper fencing or barriers. She remarked that many of the perimeter areas were particularly hazardous at night despite the lampposts sprinkled through the park.

"Still, it's safer than most college parking lots," he quipped with a grin.

She laughed lightly. "For you, that's true."

They walked in silence a little further as she anticipated how to proceed with the serious topic on her mind. Even at that late moment she wrestled with the question of whether to tell him the truth about herself and her true nature.

He zipped his slightly worn leather jacket halfway up to keep out the chill of a gentle breeze and noted with a quick glance that her black leather jacket was wide open. "Aren't you cold?" he asked.

"Me?" she replied with surprise. "No, not at all. I like the cool evening breeze."

"Warm natured?" he asked with upraised brows.

She smiled pleasantly back at him as they walked. "Something like that." Then she amended, "More like cold-tolerant, really."

He found it to be an unusual quality in a woman. Most of the women he had known or dated would have complained they were chilled to the bone after walking outside for just a few minutes on such a late fall evening. But he already realized that Katrina was no ordinary woman. That appealed to him in so many ways, actually. For years, he pursued dating in a traditional manner, but always somehow managed to select the wrong type of person in his endeavors. Meeting Katrina was the first time that a woman took the initiative to pursue him, and it was an appealing quality for him.

Both of them remained relatively quiet for a time as they each pondered their own thoughts and feelings, albeit on entire different lines of thought.

"Would you like to sit down?" she finally broke the silence in a resolute voice, having made her decision on how to proceed.

"Sure," he replied suspiciously as he broke from his own silent reverie. He noticed the more serious tone in her voice, which momentarily concerned him.

She guided him to the next park bench, where they both perched tentatively on the edge of the seat so they faced each other. She reached out to take his right hand between both of her own, appreciating how his hand felt soft and warm. He had the hands of an artist, a gentle soul. It made her smile warmly at him. However, Katrina noted some concern in his eyes. Or was it suspicion? *Are his childhood memories beginning to return?* She pushed the thought from her mind as she considered the topic at hand.

"Caleb, I think honesty is so important between two people, and there's something I want to tell you," she began with a resolute expression, her green eyes catching his pale blue ones intently.

"Yes?" he asked after locking eyes with her gaze.

Her hands felt soft around his, but they had grasped his hand tighter after her last statement. *Is she bored with me?* he wondered. *Or worse, maybe she doesn't feel the same connection to me that I'm feeling for her.*

"I've had a number of relationships in my time," she began awkwardly. *In my time*, she thought ironically. *If he only knew. But then, perhaps in a few minutes he will.*

*Oh no*, Caleb thought, *maybe she senses something in me that reminded her of a previously failed relationship.* His hand flinched between hers.

She quickly detected his flinch and asked with concern, "Is something the matter?"

"Me? Not at all," he replied a little too quickly.

She narrowed her eyes at him slightly before reverting to a more relaxed expression. "Relationships are hard for me. It's hard for people to accept me as I am," she continued carefully.

"Okay," he nodded. *Oh great*, he thought, *she's going to tell me she's a lesbian.*

"You see, I'm not like most people you know," Katrina continued.

He raised his eyebrows.

She immediately realized that things weren't proceeding like she'd hoped. She was stalling, and it was apparent he was becoming confused. The palm of his hand had already started to perspire a little between hers.

"For example, I'm not a day person at all," she stated matter-of-factly. "In fact, I can't be in sunlight. You might say my sunrise begins at sunset."

His eyes widened slightly. *Okay*, he thought, *she has a disease that keeps people from being in sunshine?* "Oh, I saw something about that on a Discovery Channel program about a year ago," he offered encouragingly. "It's not as uncommon as you might think, really." *It might help explain why we're were never able to get together during the daytime*, he thought with some relief.

Katrina arched one eyebrow and shook her head. "No, you don't understand," she tried to correct him. "Those people have a disease. I don't have a disease. It just hurts me to be around strong ultraviolet radiation."

"Um, okay," he replied with a single nod and a deepening frown. *UV radiation sensitivity*, he contemplated wildly.

"It's the result of a genetic mutation," she explained.

"Like a medical treatment gone wrong?" he inquired with an expression of disbelief.

"No, it wasn't a medical treatment. It's..." she tried to continue.

"Government experiment?" he interrupted.

She frowned at him and corrected, "This has nothing to do with the government." *Thank goodness*, she thought to herself as an afterthought. Her kind definitely tried to keep governments from being involved, which would probably be disastrous, at best.

Her clarification seemed to stump him for a moment, but she could tell that his thoughts were already racing. She had no way of knowing that he doubted her sanity at that moment.

"Okay," he conceded politely. "Anything else?"

"I don't like to eat most normal human foods," Katrina added carefully.

Caleb winced. *What the hell?* he wondered wildly. *Normal human foods?* It was turning into a conversation from hell for him. *Well, she does normally order salads when we go to restaurants,* he recalled. "So, you're a vegetarian?" he asked hopefully as he started to pull his hand from between hers.

*Uh-oh,* Katrina thought as she allowed him to withdraw his hand. She hadn't realized that she had been holding her breath, and she exhaled a heavy sigh. "I'm what society would best describe as a vampire," she said finally.

Caleb actually laughed out loud once, then seemed suddenly ashamed, and quickly clasped one hand quickly over his mouth. *And I thought Melanie was half-crazed,* he mused darkly.

"I'm so sorry," he apologized. "You just sounded so..."

"Serious?" she offered helpfully.

"Um, no," he corrected without actually using the word "crazy."

"I'm quite serious," she insisted evenly.

"It's just that vampires aren't real, Katrina," he added with a growing sardonic grin. "I mean, I love vampire horror films as much as the next guy."

His tone sounded somewhat condescending, and she resented his speaking to her like some superstitious child. "Oh, but we are real, Caleb," Katrina retorted heatedly as her eyes glowed green in the dim light of the lamp.

Caleb jolted slightly in surprise and demanded, "How did you just do that?"

Something dark stirred in his memory for just a split second, and it sent a chill up his spine. Then it was gone, like some fleeting flash from the past.

Katrina took a deep breath to relax and regained her composure as her eyes returned to their normal green hue. She didn't want to upset him further and risk continued misunderstanding. *Have I just made a terrible mistake?* she wondered.

"Caleb, it's what I've been trying to tell you," she continued gently.

Had the light from the nearby lamp merely caused an optical illusion? he wondered. *And yet, why did the sudden change in her eyes seem somehow strangely familiar to me?*

He suddenly felt edgy and irritated that the evening had taken such a negative turn. Mostly he was disappointed by it all. He' had hoped their connection was the beginning of something special. Now it just seemed that Katrina was just another of society's misguided souls suffering from some sort of mental illness. He sighed, and she looked into his eyes curiously.

"Caleb?" she asked tentatively and reached out to grasp his hand in hers again.

But he pulled back from her outreached hand with a jerk and rose to stand from where he sat next to her. "I'm very sorry, Katrina, but I think I better go," he said nervously.

She sat where she was but pleaded gently, "Caleb, please sit back down so we can discuss this."

He shook his head and turned to depart in the direction from which they came. "I'll call you, Katrina," he added almost as an afterthought, but it was an empty comment that he immediately knew he didn't mean.

He felt about as disappointed as he could recall in his adult life. Katrina was supposed to have been someone special to him. He'd been falling in love with her, after all. Now everything felt like it was melting away in a matter of minutes. The help she needed was far beyond his ability to cope with, and at that moment he felt he just needed to leave so he could sort out what just transpired between them.

"Caleb," she called as she watched him walk away, his pace quickening after he briefly glanced back over his shoulder at her. "No," she whispered angrily. "Not like this."

She was determined not to let him depart on such bad terms. At the same time, she silently berated herself for not having taken a better tack with him on the subject. It had been so many years since she'd confided her secret with someone she thought she could trust. She'd obviously lost her touch completely. In a split second, Katrina rose from the bench more quickly than any human could and raced ahead of him in a blur of motion.

Caleb was staring down at the sidewalk as he walked, but he thought he heard something swish by him in a dark blur to his right. He glanced up and saw Katrina standing in front of him with her arms folded across her chest. He frowned, glanced back to the empty park bench down the path, and looked back at her. His eyes narrowed slightly.

"How did --" he started to ask.

"Please, Caleb," she began.

He shook his head and turned to walk in the opposite direction. "Goodnight, Katrina," he said as he walked away. This time, he kept his face upwards but realized he was going in the wrong direction. He rolled his eyes upwards and muttered, "Crap."

Suddenly she appeared before him seemingly out of nowhere. "You're going the wrong direction, Caleb," she offered gently.

His eyes widened with complete surprise, and he jumped slightly as he realized that he hadn't even heard her footsteps before she appeared before him. He backed away from her quickly, and this time he kept his eyes on her as he withdrew.

Katrina seemed to stay where she was, and he turned

to walk quickly away from her. Only this time his pulse was quickening and his nerves felt deeply unsettled. *What the hell?*

She heard his heart racing even from the distance between them and called after him, "Caleb, please stop."

He began running down the path and glanced over his shoulder to see if she were still there, but she was already gone. He quickly jerked his head forward and saw her waiting with her arms crossed in front of her again. Only this time, her eyes were burning with a bright green illumination.

Abruptly, something sharp triggered from deep in his memory. His eyes widened as he stared back into her eyes. An intense shock went through his body, hammering at his chest and burning in his stomach. He didn't understand where it came from or why, but he knew immediately what it was: sheer terror. His heart felt as if it was going to burst from his chest. Something visceral from his distant memories yelled, *Run!*

Katrina saw the nearly simultaneous transformation in his eyes and heard his heart suddenly erupt in thundering beats. Confusion ran through her as she tried to gauge what just happened to him.

Caleb spun to his right and sprinted perpendicular to the sidewalk path and into the nearby trees. Terror gripped him like a claw tearing simultaneously into his mind and heart. All that he knew was that he needed to escape. He picked up speed and dashed through the trees, thinking he could elude her somehow.

She watched him divert from the path in a blaze of sudden speed as her mind raced for an answer to what was happening to him. She hastily recalled something about the topography of the area that forced a sense of dread through her stomach and swiftly began to pursue him while shouting, "Caleb, stop! There's a ravine!"

Caleb was unknowingly heading towards the deep drop-off located beyond the trees just past the manicured portion of the park. It fell off for about forty feet from the ground with a number of large rocks interspersed among the low brush all the way to the bottom.

He thought he heard Katrina calling to him again, but he kept running and maintained an impressive speed as he sprinted across the grass and between the tree trunks. Suddenly, the grass was taller and small bushes appeared, but he kept sprinting blindly into the darkness. He was winded, but still making good time and glanced over his shoulder to see if she were pursuing him. Suddenly, there was emptiness under his right foot, and he felt himself tilting into open air.

Then his left leg was caught in what felt like a steel vice, and his body's momentum shifted back to the direction he had been running from. His body spun around in a counterclockwise direction before landing directly onto the ground. He flopped onto his stomach with a heavy thud that momentarily knocked the air from his lungs.

"Caleb!" Katrina exclaimed with relief at having caught him in time. She deftly rolled onto the ground beside him. "You're fast, I'll give you that," she muttered with a relieved sigh as she lay next to him.

He turned his head to stare at her in complete disbelief. Rolling onto his back, he began using his elbows as leverage behind him to elevate himself off the ground. While kicking his legs into the ground, he managed to back rapidly away from her in a crablike fashion.

Her relieved expression disappeared, turning into a heavy frown in the dim moonlight. "Caleb," she cautioned him gently. She didn't like the desperate look in his eyes, like a cornered animal. *Doesn't he realize that I just helped him?*

His hand absently touched a small fallen tree branch that felt solid in his hand. Though it was nearly twice the length he was used to, he leapt up and brandished it like a baseball bat. "Get away from me," he warned desperately.

Her features turned to stone as she took stock of the wild, panicked look in his pale blue eyes. It was the look of someone not completely in their right mind. "Caleb, please, just stop. I'm not going to hurt you," she insisted gently.

He seemed uncertain as to what to do next and started backing away from her while brandishing the limb as if ready to strike. His mind kept seeing those blazing green eyes from somewhere deeply imbedded in his memory as the terror in him pulsed like a warning clarion.

She moved forward slightly and cooed soothingly, "No harm, Caleb. Just calm down."

Katrina gradually advanced towards him, and he desperately swung the limb. It *whooshed* through the air towards her at a furious speed. Her left arm went up to counter his right-handed swing, and the branch broke effortlessly in half. His eyes were full with surprise at seeing that, and his hands vibrated from the shock of the branch's impact. Before he could move, she twisted her arm to grasp the remainder of the limb and pulled him to her with a single, swift jerk.

Her eyes were ablaze with a green glow as she stripped the branch from his hand and warned in a harsh voice, "I swear, slugger, if you try to hit me with another branch..."

Caleb's jaw dropped in amazement at her speed as he realized she was standing directly in front of him again. "Oh, God," he began, but was interrupted by her swinging him around and pinning his right arm behind him. She easily forced him to his knees before her.

"You're going to calm down now," she ordered as she let go of his arm and spun him around to push him backwards onto the ground. The truth was that she was scared, scared for him and for what suddenly happened to his mind to cause him to act that way.

Caleb immediately fell on his butt before her. Katrina was working very hard not to hurt him because she easily recalled the abuse that he had suffered at the hands of his father as a child. He had come so far as an adult, and she was striving not to rekindle violence in his life. She felt an abrupt pang of guilt over the earlier threat that she issued to him. Still, he hadn't been entirely peaceable towards the end, either.

He was shaking like a leaf in a storm and appeared to be

going into shock right before her eyes. He sat silently, pulling his knees up to his chest while wrapping his arms around them. That worried her greatly.

Katrina stopped seeing the young man before her and instead recalled the frightened young boy from so many years ago in the small garage cowering at the malice of his abusive father. Suddenly, she realized with revulsion that she had unwittingly become the next abuser in his life. It touched something deep inside of her that she had last felt in the small, dreary garage so long ago. Mixed with the taint of disgust from that memory were the feelings of sympathy and caring for him which had touched her so viscerally when she had first met him as a child.

"I'm not going to hurt you," she promised as she kept her hands close to her body and slowly squatted down onto her knees in front of him. Her eyes were only dimly glowing green by that time as she strove to calm herself.

Minutes passed where neither of them said anything as Katrina quietly continued observing him. The only noise was from the cool wind rustling through the trees, and she noted that he was still shaking uncontrollably.

"I may have handled tonight rather poorly," she whispered with resignation. *How I wish I could start the whole evening over again.* But there was something more to his earlier reaction, something deeply disturbing in his eyes that she noted.

He merely stared at her with a dumbfounded, wide-eyed expression. His mind and body felt completely numb, as though none of what was happening were real.

"I'm moving to your side, but I'm not going to harm you," she assured him soothingly.

His eyes were wide as he watched her scoot across the short distance between them to sit beside him. He was still shaking as she placed her left arm gently around his shoulders and pulled him to her. He gratefully felt the welcome warmth from her body begin to penetrate through his jacket.

They sat together in the cool silence for what felt like an

eternity. After some time, he had stopped shaking and was merely still as he sat beside her. She sensed his heart rate had slowed a considerable amount, which was a welcome improvement.

"You're a vampire," Caleb said matter-of-factly.

Katrina was so happy when he finally spoke again. She hugged him to her and whispered, "Yes, Caleb. I'm a vampire."

However, she inwardly always hated the word "vampire" despite its reasonable use for her kind. It wasn't as if her kind had any other official title or name. Years ago, the term "night denizen" had been issued to her upon her turning to describe her condition. But Hollywood took such errant liberty in describing the being she was now. Stereotypes were difficult, even among eternal creatures.

Caleb breathed in deeply and exhaled. "I'm not dead," he said carefully, as if in sudden realization.

She frowned warily, somewhat relieved that he couldn't see her expression. "You're quite alive, Caleb," she replied carefully. "And you should try to stay that way."

"I'm sorry I hit you with a branch," he muttered sincerely but with an almost dull voice.

She chuckled lightly as the corners of her mouth upturned slightly. "Apology accepted. But no more branches, Caleb."

He shook his head slightly and promised, "No more branches."

The silence drew out between them again for a time. The sound of the wind through the trees was almost soothing to him. Finally, he asked in a quiet voice, "Can I please go home now?"

She considered his request and heard his heartbeat increase slightly. "Yes, but you have to promise me something," she stipulated quietly.

"O-okay," he agreed.

His voice sounded so quiet and small to her.

"You have to promise to keep my secret about being a vampire," Katrina began. "It's very important that you don't tell anyone. Do you understand?" Despite the evening's drama and tension, this was something she had to insist upon before she could let him depart.

Caleb was silent for only a moment. "I promise, I won't tell anyone."

His voice sounded sincere to her, and she was too concerned for his emotional state to press the matter further. It would have to do. "Okay then, let's get you home," she said softly.

She grasped both of his shoulders in her hands and helped stabilize him as they stood. He was silently amazed, as he had barely engaged his legs before he was standing upright. He swayed for only a moment, and her hands were still firmly grasping him to keep him steady.

"Okay?" she asked gently.

"Okay," he replied as they slowly walked back to the dimly-lit park path.

Within a short time they were standing before his car in the driveway in front of her multi-bay garage. She noted his hand was shaking as he withdrew his keys from his pocket, and they jiggled slightly as he handled them. She anticipated that he must still be in some mild degree of shock laced with fear, because his movements were jerky, and she could hear his elevated heart rate.

"You shouldn't try to drive, Caleb," she gently offered.

He used his other hand to steady the hand holding the car key and slipped it into the lock. He felt somewhat embarrassed by his body's reaction but was determined to keep moving. "I'm okay, thanks," he replied. "I'll be okay."

He was trying to reassure himself as much as reply to her. As he withdrew the key from the lock, he abruptly dropped the entire ring of keys. They landed in Katrina's hand before falling more than six inches, and he gasped in response as her pale hand suddenly appeared before him.

"I'm driving you home, Caleb," she insisted resolutely as she palmed the keys.

He merely nodded and opened the door for her. She smirked

at his chivalrous gesture and slipped past him into the driver's seat. He closed the door and walked around to the passenger side. "A vampire's taking me home," he muttered incredulously before opening his door.

After he dropped into the passenger seat and shut the door, she smiled at him and answered, "Yes, one is."

He glanced over to her slowly with a surprised look in his eyes.

She turned to look at him and read his expression. "Good hearing," she said with a grin as she pointed her index finger to her head.

He nodded mechanically and tried to file the tidbit away for future reference. He started to look away but noted she continued to stare at him, and he frowned back at her.

"Seatbelt," she recommended.

Caleb nodded absently again and belted himself in place as she started his car.

They were both silent on the short journey across town to Caleb's apartment building. There was very little traffic to watch at that time of night, so he just stared blankly out the passenger window trying to collect his thoughts. *I have to be crazy*, he thought to himself. *The whole thing is insane, right?* He realized that he hadn't needed to promise to keep Katrina's secret. Nobody would believe him anyway.

Before long, they pulled into the parking garage beneath his apartment building. The part-time gate guard noted the decal on Caleb's windshield and waved them through the gate without a second glance. It was at that moment Caleb realized how easily a vampire could pass for a human. *Vampires*, he thought silently, *who would have guessed they'd be real after all?*

Minutes later, Katrina neatly parked the car in a well-lit spot near the elevator.

"You're home," she stated simply and was out of the car before Caleb even finished opening his door.

She stood next to him as he exited and handed him his

keys. "Good night, Caleb," she stated with a reassuring smile.

"Good night," he responded with a vague nod as he shut his car door. He started to walk away, but she just stood there watching him intently.

He made it barely six feet before she cleared her throat audibly to get his attention. He slowly turned to gaze back at her and frowned slightly. "Huh?"

Katrina nodded in the direction of his car. "The remote. Lock the doors."

He nodded, and the sound of two beeps emitted from his car. She smiled at him warmly before turning to walk towards the stairwell leading to the street level.

"Wait," he called hesitantly. She turned back towards him with a curious expression, and he offered, "I can call you a cab. It's safer."

But she only grinned. "Oh, I'm safe enough. And it's a nice night for a walk."

"Oh," he muttered somewhat numbly as Katrina turned and disappeared through the door to the stairwell.

Caleb turned, pushed the elevator call button, and waited for the doors to open. He felt both mentally and physically exhausted, but was suddenly so happy to be home and alive. He still felt like the evening was an experience outside of reality. Perhaps he would wake up and it would all have been just a crazy, bad dream. However, if it were real, he had a lot to think about. But he was just too tired to think clearly. He hardly remembered the journey from the parking garage to his apartment as he closed his front door and engaged the deadbolt. He swayed slightly as he made his way through the dimly illuminated room over to his couch and collapsed in exhaustion.

Outside Caleb's apartment on the recently repainted fire escape, Katrina watched silently through the sheer curtains covering the windows to his living room. She felt relief when she finally saw him enter the apartment and lock the deadbolt on his front door. She observed him sway and nearly leapt up to the window to his aid. But she quickly stopped and thought, *Oh yeah, crash through his living room window now. That should send him completely over the edge.*

She sighed, not certain what the future would bring between them. She liked him -- no, she was already convinced she loved him. To her, he was the adult embodiment of the young boy, her saving angel, who had fought against a stacked deck imposed by his past and managed to maintain his innocence. *Time will tell,* she mused hopefully.

Following a quick recollection of their evening, she still wished that she had handled things differently with him. She turned silently to retrace her steps to street level for the journey back to her home. *It's a nice night for a walk,* she conceded. Besides, vampires could move very fast when they wanted to, just as Caleb discovered.

"Nights like this are precisely why I've stayed single for so long," she muttered to herself as she made her way down a side alley.

She was very angry with herself for the night's events, and she berated herself for somehow causing his emotional reaction. *Reaction,* she reconsidered wildly, *it was more like an explosion!*

# Chapter 3

## A Fresh Start

**C**aleb saw green eyes blazing out of the darkness in his dream and abruptly awoke on his couch Saturday morning. His heart was pounding, and he struggled to catch his breath as his eyes wildly scanned the room around him. A halo of sunshine emanating through the living room curtains was suddenly quite comforting. The fleeting, peaceful moment passed before a flood of thoughts and emotions once again screamed through his mind with lightning speed.

*Katrina's a vampire!*

He had trouble processing the reality associated with that thought. Images from every vampire horror film or novel he'd seen or heard of ran though his mind at once. All the popular attributes of vampires began registering in his mind: pasty skin, fast movements, incredible strength, sharp fangs, vicious bites to a victim's neck, fear of wooden stakes, aversion to garlic, no reflections in mirrors, transforming into a leathery flying bat, and being the embodiment of the eternal living dead!

It was nearly brain overload. He realized that he needed to sort things out individually.

*Okay, she never met with me during the daytime. Oh God, does she sleep in a coffin during the day? No, wait, she chatted on the phone and text messaged me during the daytime before.* A vision of her texting on her cell phone while the screen illuminated her face as she lay in a velvet-lined coffin ran through his mind. He would have laughed if not for the very palpable fear he had felt the previous night.

His mind raced through a host of brief recollections about her. *The pale skin -- but then, lots of people have pale skin. She's a redhead, and I've seen numerous redheads with pale skin before. Heck, I'm hardly a sun worshipper myself.*

*Okay, there was the college parking lot incident where that guy tried to rob me. Katrina seemed to come from nowhere. But then, I wasn't really looking for her, either. The guy's nasty-looking knife captured my focus elsewhere at the time. And lots of people know martial arts, right? Okay, dead end there for now.*

He shivered slightly.

*Was she intending to kill me last night? No, wait. She tried to explain everything, but I thought she was crazy.* A pang of guilt touched him only momentarily before his thoughts flew onward. *She saved me from falling over that ravine last night, right? People who want to kill you don't save you.* She had only ever showed him kindness. *Vampires don't do that, right?*

The speed of her movements filtered through the noise of his raging thoughts. It was like she had been everywhere at once. *Nobody moves that fast!* He ran like a rocket, and yet, it had been as if he were running in one of those nightmares where whatever is chasing you can move fast while you feel like you're running in quicksand.

He shivered once again at the memory of the previous night. Rising from the couch, he stretched his sore body, noticing that his right shoulder still ached from where she had briefly twisted his arm behind his back. A singular thought struck him with shock. *I tried to hit her with a tree limb last night!*

A sickening queasiness ran though him to the pit of his stomach. He had never raised his hand against anybody in anger before. He had never even been in fights with kids as he was growing up. *Hell, my own father used to beat on me, and I swore I would never do that to anyone. So, what got into me last night?*

He sighed. Then a vision hit him like a hammer to an anvil. *Katrina's eyes, those green eyes of hers. Sure, her eyes are beautiful, but they took on a whole new quality last night.* The piercing, illuminating green had been like tiny orbs cutting into him. Just the recollection made his heart race. *But why does that also seem so familiar to me?*

That's where the terror had started: her eyes beaming into him with a penetrating green quality. It struck at something hidden and terrible deep in his memory, and his heart began beating rapidly again. *What the hell does it all mean?*

*Better yet, what am I going to do now?* he wondered.

His thoughts were interrupted by his cell phone vibrating on the end table. He picked it up and noticed a new text message from Katrina.

*R U OK? I'm worried for U.*

His breath caught in his throat, and his mouth felt dry.

He thought of her gentle face, cute laugh, kind nature, and beautiful smile all at once, and the memory stirred a warm feeling in his heart. He thought he had really been falling for her. *So, what changed?*

*She's a vampire. But she's still the woman that I'm smitten with, right?*

"Crap," he muttered wearily as he decided that she at least deserved a reply of some kind. *Better to text her than try to talk to her right now*, he decided.

He typed out his reply carefully, slowly, and as honestly as possible. *Not sure. Confused.*

The reply from her came only a few seconds after his. *Take time to think. Call me. I care about U.*

*Wow, fast typist*, he mused. *Fast moving, for that matter.*

*OK*, he texted back to her.

He started to set his cell phone down, but another message arrived.

*No need to fear. Worried about you.*

*That's easy for you to say*, he thought while laying the cell phone on the end table. And for some reason, as he read her last message, Ivy's "Worry about You" played through his mind.

*How odd.*

He realized that he was still wearing yesterday's clothes and went into the bedroom to take a shower and change.

Katrina wore a pair of green cotton lounge pants and a matching cami with her hair falling around her shoulders as she sprawled across her large, four-poster bed with her cell phone in her hands. Caleb's replies to her text messages were brief, but she had anticipated he might still be in shock somewhat after last night's events. Just her recollections from the night before sent a surge of sadness through her, followed closely by a feeling of intense curiosity. *What happened to him last night?* she wondered furiously.

His face had changed in an instant as she'd glared at him. Katrina readily conceded she had been annoyed with him at that point, but she certainly hadn't felt angry towards him for trying to walk out on her. *I just wanted him to talk things out, that's all.*

But the vision of the horror in his eyes before he turned to flee from her had been striking. She easily recognized a look of terror, and his was textbook. It was as if his mind had suddenly snapped or something.

*But why,* she considered furiously. *What did I do?*

A feeling of worry mixed with dread ran through her.

*What if he won't see me again,* she thought. *What if he's too scared?*

An even darker thought crossed Katrina's mind. *What if I ruined one of the only things sparking my renewed interest in life for the past eighteen years?*

And for the first time in a long, long time, a tear began to form in the corner of her eye.

Caleb spent most of Saturday at home staring at the walls, the TV, and out of the living room windows. He was thinking about Katrina and wondering what to do. Eventually, his mind was too tired to consider aspects any further. He needed more than anything to have some sense of normalcy back in his life. So he tried to stop thinking and focused instead on simpler diversions.

He cleaned the bathroom, changed his bed linens, and went to the apartment building's central laundry area. He listened to his iPod and replied to a few text messages from some old college friends. Doug from Texas was still helping his father run the family sporting goods store following his dad's heart attack. Nancy from Massachusetts was just offered a position at a law firm in Boston. And Martin from South Carolina just proposed to his girlfriend, Brenda. But then Caleb's eyes glanced at the earlier messages from Katrina, and he found himself reading them over and over while the washer and dryer continued their monotonous cycles.

He spent the evening at home watching TV and eating pizza he had ordered from a delivery service. For some reason, he noticed that the cooks used a lot more garlic than normal.

*Garlic. Vampires don't like garlic, right?* He shook his head and tried not to think about that. *Of course, it's not as if Katrina's going to be breaking into my apartment and sucking the blood from me until I'm dry, right?* He considered the idea for a moment, once again recalling the text messages she had sent him. Somehow he felt he was safe and that Katrina's intentions weren't hostile at all.

He sighed and tried to concentrate on the television before him as he munched on his pizza. That was his Saturday in a nutshell.

Caleb spent Sunday continuing to distract himself with anything "normal." He organized quizzes for two of his history classes, prepared some notes for his upcoming lectures that week, and cleaned out his refrigerator.

He went to a local bookstore to browse and found himself gravitating to the horror and science fiction sections. He glanced at the covers of nearly a dozen novels all relating to vampires. He browsed the cinema section and noticed a pictorial on the life of Bela Lugosi, one of the world's most famous horror film actors, best known for his classic rendition of Dracula. Admittedly, his appearance was nothing like Katrina's, although, the vision of her wearing a dark cape and baring her fangs seemed to work. *She does have fangs, right?*

In the end, he purchased a discounted book on the historic maps of the American Civil War and proceeded to the grocery store for a few items he needed at the apartment. On the way back home, he drove past a Starbucks and sighed as he recalled the first time that he and Katrina met for tea and their first lengthy conversation. It seemed like a long time ago.

In the end, Sunday had been as equally unsatisfying for him as Saturday.

Katrina tried to be patient and wait for Caleb to gather his thoughts, but it was very difficult. She emailed a couple of close friends, including her former mentor, Alton, about Caleb. As fellow vampires, they sympathized with her, but in the end they seemed hesitant to offer any specific advice.

*Some friends*, she thought bitterly.

By Sunday evening, Katrina had enough of waiting and decided to check in on Caleb. She waited until after dark and drove around the city to contemplate her feelings while listening to some CDs she'd created for just the occasion. Fiona Apple was perfect for her mood, as well as some lilting classic jazz from the 1960s. She added a couple of melancholy French tunes from the 1940s. One thing you could say about long-lived vampires, their music selections were usually eclectic. Around 11 pm, when "Malibu," by Hole, began playing, she was ready to head towards Caleb's apartment.

Dressed in some black denim jeans and black leather jacket, she crept quietly to his fire escape and peeked in from the shadows into his living room. He was leaning back on his couch with his head bobbed backwards against the cushion. A novel he had been reading had fallen into his lap and been forgotten. He looked endearing as he slept with his mouth partially open, and she almost laughed, which helped soften her melancholy mood. She lingered for a short time watching him sleep and decided it was time to go. At least he appeared to be okay, which was more than she could say for herself.

"Goodnight, my Caleb," she whispered as she blew him a kiss across the distance between them. *At least I hope he will become my Caleb*, she thought darkly.

Seconds later, she walked out of the alleyway and back towards where she had parked her car.

Caleb began the work week teaching at the college, but he was frequently distracted. His lectures were passable, but lacked the usual energy and enthusiasm. It was obvious to himself that he was merely going through the motions. And though he had only been a member of the Social Sciences division for a short time, a number of his fellow professors and division office staff noticed his subdued behavior. One of the secretaries named Betty, a kind woman in her mid-forties, even asked him if he was feeling under the weather.

*Well, at least it's nice that people are taking an interest in me around the office after a semester*, he considered.

On Tuesday, he only taught two sections of history in the morning, so he had most of the afternoon free after his office hours. By the time he walked out to his car on that sunny, cool November afternoon, he'd already decided that he needed to return to the scene of his recent mental collapse with Katrina. He needed to understand what had happened to him. He was floating in a state of limbo and wanted to be on solid ground again.

Instead of bothering to change clothes, he remained in his khaki slacks and long-sleeved blue shirt. He grabbed a sandwich and bottled water from a sub shop and drove out to the exclusive Pine Valley edition. She had given him the access code to the edition gate entrance and the code for the wrought iron gate to her driveway on Friday, though he had no intention of trying to go up the driveway or even approach the house itself.

Everything looked quite different by daylight. Things

didn't seem quite as ominous, though it was still distinctly remote and secluded with the edition's sparsely populated residents and heavily forested surroundings.

He was pleasantly surprised to find that the edition entrance code still operated correctly for him as he drove between the large rock columns. The asphalt road winding through the neighborhood presented a series of leisurely curves to negotiate the somewhat hilly terrain. There were large areas of densely forested sections between the various five-acre or larger plots of land. All the homes remaining visible from the street were large estates, each with their own architectural style. One aspect they had in common was how stately everything was maintained. The trees, shrubs, and lawns were manicured meticulously, though each reflected unique landscape artistry.

Katrina's property was further into the edition near the still-developing section of a particularly hilly area. He drove to her property's gate entrance and glanced up the winding driveway as he passed. He saw the house through the dense trees and shrubbery looming in the sunshine like a castle. Caleb rarely had the opportunity to appreciate such properties from a distance, much less actually know someone with the capability of owning any. *Dream homes like this are more like pure fantasy on my salary*, he considered silently. *You don't choose a career as a teacher or professor with hopes of getting rich.*

He stopped at the side of the road next to a more gently sloping area that he thought he would be able to negotiate on foot. He wanted to revisit the park area next to Katrina's property, while not going too close to her house. Caleb felt that daytime was best because he didn't want to risk an uncomfortable meeting in person just yet, and he recalled her comment about staying out of sunshine. *Classic vampire issue*, he mused. What with the day being so sunny and bright, he considered conditions were about as safe as they could get for him. *Just great*, he chided, *too scared to skulk around at night. Instead I'm sneaking around in the daylight!*

He scowled at the thought that he was actually taking all of these things seriously and even felt a little foolish. But his memories of her physical feats from Friday night engendered a more sober expression on his face. In fact, his pulse increased noticeably as he focused on his current intentions.

He strode up the hilly incline to the scrub and trees scattered at the top. If not for the serious nature of his visit, he might actually have taken the time to appreciate his surroundings. Instead, he sighed and tried to focus his thoughts on the events of Friday night.

After a short time, he made it to the top of the incline and looked back downhill to where his car was parked. He felt a cool breeze in the air and noticed that considerably more leaves had fallen since Friday.

He made his way back to the central park area, soon reaching the winding concrete pathway they had walked together. Pausing to glance towards her estate, he began slowly walking in that general direction. He was pleased that conditions seemed much less ominous on such a sunny day.

Before long, he stood outside the black iron gate separating the park area from Katrina's property. He studied the large house looming across a relatively wide expanse of partially green lawn dotted with pine and oak trees. After a sigh, he stared up at one of the windows of the house, though he saw no activity present. The blinds were turned down completely.

He turned and focused on the events of last Friday evening.

Katrina sat at her computer and glanced up at a flat panel display off to her left that hosted approximately two dozen miniature viewing screens, each hooked up to a camera viewing both internal and external parts of the estate. Her eye caught movement from one particular camera located on the side of the house facing the gate to the public park area.

She breathed in sharply and immediately enlarged the window to full screen.

Caleb stood beyond the trees at the gate. *Has he come to*

*visit me?* she wondered.

A hopeful feeling washed through her. She zoomed in on his face as he stared towards the house, the sunlight bathing his gentle features in light. Yet he had a focused expression. She frowned as he turned to gaze back in the other direction and slowly walked away.

*What's he doing? Maybe he came to discuss the revelations I sprang on him last Friday evening. Maybe I should call his cell phone or text him,* she ventured with uncertainty.

Something occurred to her which sent a small chill through her. *He probably came during the daytime because he knew I couldn't go to him. He must be here for some other reason.*

She watched him walk away until the camera could no longer focus on him and sighed deeply with resignation. Despite the strong desire to see him, to talk to him, she would have to remain patient.

Caleb's memory began replaying the events in his mind as he perched on the edge of the bench he and Katrina had sat on that night. He recalled how disappointed he'd felt when she tried to be honest with him about her secret identity. He stood, took a moment to recall his actions that evening, and walked the path leading towards her house. He paused and then proceeded in the opposite direction. He halted suddenly, unsure if he were in the exact spot as before. Frowning, he concentrated intently to recall the sight of her glowing green eyes. A momentary flash appeared in his mind's eye, and his heartbeat fluttered. He turned slowly and began walking off in the approximate direction in which he had run into the trees that night.

He recalled the feeling of flight, running for his life. But now, his pace was deliberate and measured. He marveled at how far he must have run as he trudged slowly among the trees and bushes. A short time later, he stood at the edge of the drop-off where he had nearly fallen before Katrina caught him.

*She caught me, spun me around, and threw me to the*

*ground.*

Looking down, he noticed a broken branch on the partially sandy ground, realizing must be the branch he had grabbed that night. He picked up one piece and inspected it more closely. It was a rather solid-looking length of wood, and he had swung it at her with what he believed had been an impressive velocity. But he recalled how it broke against her arm as if nothing more than a flimsy yardstick. Illustrating that point, he lifted the piece of branch and popped it into the palm of his other hand. *Solid chunk of wood,* he ventured with a frown before absently tossing the branch back to the ground.

*My God,* he realized suddenly, *it should've broken her arm, or at least knocked her over.*

His eyes widened while marveling once more at how Katrina was indeed no ordinary woman. *If she'd been able so easily to withstand such an attack, then she could've effortlessly killed me,* he suspected. But she didn't, for which he was extremely thankful.

"That should count for something," he muttered hopefully.

But there was an underlying feeling after going through his brief mental exercise: wariness. Despite how kind and helpful she had been to him, he felt a degree of unease. *Is it a simple aversion to the unknown or something else?* He supposed that only time would tell.

He considered a very important question while returning to his vehicle. *What am I going to do next?*

Wednesday passed quickly for Caleb. By the time he went home from work, he had finally determined how to proceed with Katrina. He still had feelings for her after everything they had experienced together and felt he owed her the benefit of at least talking things out to see how they both wanted to progress.

He was deeply intrigued by her, but couldn't deny the thought of her being a vampire still unnerved him quite a bit. The whole situation was still a little unbelievable to him. All his life he thought the concept of vampires made for great films, but never once had considered there could be an ounce of truth to any of it. But what was the truth to separate from the fiction? That was a question only Katrina could answer.

He picked up his cell phone while leaning against his kitchen counter and dialed her number. It rang only once.

"Caleb?" ventured Katrina in a soft voice.

He still loved the sound of her voice, among a host of other appreciable qualities. "Hi, Katrina," he said. "Is this a good time to call?" His eyes gazed out the living room window to note the sun just beginning to set.

"Sure," she offered curiously. "You've called me during the afternoons before, you know."

He nodded, wondering why this was so difficult for him. It wasn't as if he hadn't been interacting with her for months. He felt he was starting everything from scratch.

"Sorry, you're right of course," he apologized. "Katrina, I've been doing a lot of thinking the past few days, and I..."

"Yes?"

"I'd like to know if you'd mind meeting with me to chat," he asked.

She paused, and he thought he heard a small sigh from her end, as if she'd been holding her breath.

"Of course, Caleb," she replied with a hint of relief evident in her voice. "I've been hoping you'd call."

The edges of his mouth upturned marginally, and he proceeded with a more confident tone, "Great. That's just great. What's your schedule look like this week?"

"You mean like tonight, for example?" she asked.

"Uh, no. How about tomorrow instead?" he clarified.

She paused. "Day or night?"

He hadn't expected that. "You can do daytime?"

"Daytime is harder, Caleb," she answered with amusement. "But I can prepare the house to accommodate your preference, especially if it makes you more comfortable."

He considered her offer for a moment, but felt it might seem an affront to select an uncomfortable setting deliberately. He respected her too much to do that, though it was at least nice that she was willing to accommodate him. *That's good, right?*

"Evening's fine, actually," he said.

"Good," she accepted gently. "Come by around sunset then."

As he said goodbye and disconnected, he smirked at the way she'd said that and realized if he didn't know she was a vampire, he probably wouldn't have given it a second thought.

Thankfully, Thursday went by quickly for Caleb, because he was anxious for the arrival of evening. He changed into a pair of dark casual slacks and a red oxford shirt and sat on his couch watching the sun begin its descent. A list of questions mingled in his mind, and he hoped none of them were particularly insulting to her. It wasn't every day someone told you they were a vampire and actually meant it.

Caleb grabbed his leather jacket and drove across town on the I-20. He proceeded north on the I-285 towards the Mableton area. As he neared his destination, his anticipation grew to a fever pitch.

Once again, the onset of night gave the secluded edition an ominous feel. Despite the various driveway lampposts, lawn lighting, and house lights surrounding the visible homes, large patches of darkness permeated the uneven landscape and clusters of thick trees within the edition. The scene seemed out of character for the normally well-developed regions throughout Atlanta. He momentarily considered how perfect it was for a horror film, but felt a pang of guilt for associating such thoughts with Katrina.

When he arrived at the gates blocking the entrance to Katrina's winding driveway, he entered his code on the small, metal kiosk and proceeded up the drive. Perhaps for his benefit and comfort, all of the exterior lights around the estate were turned on, creating a subtle glow in the night. He parked his car in front of the garage and emitted a heavy sigh before exiting his car.

Caleb walked up the steps leading to the grand front entrance of the house, once again marveling at its considerable size. He noticed many of the windows emanated an inviting luminance from inside, suggesting that many lights had been turned on throughout the house. He reached the front entrance and barely had time to ring the doorbell before the door opened to reveal Katrina standing before him with a bright, encouraging smile.

She was a vision of beauty, and his mind seemed to forget she was anything but the attractive, intelligent woman who had begun to win his heart. She wore a pair of form-fitting gray pocket pants, a silver and white patterned silk blouse, and a pair of strappy, silver, high-heeled shoes. Her neck was adorned with a simple silver necklace, and her hair was pulled back tightly into a ponytail with a sterling hair clasp. *One thing for certain, Katrina's a fashionable vampire*, he mused.

Caleb mirrored her bright smile and offered, "Good evening, Katrina."

"Please come in, Caleb," she invited by standing aside as she held the door open. "I'm really glad you agreed to see me again."

He entered with a polite nod and took a moment to appreciate the grand interior. A large banister led up to the second floor to the right and wound upwards in a semi-circle to reveal a large open area, allowing someone to look up into the part of the second floor walkway that accessed the other rooms. The lighting was subdued enough that he didn't feel like it was blaring at him, instead providing a warm, welcoming atmosphere. The floors were richly tiled in the main areas, but he could see into a nearby room, which contained an elegant blend of carpeting.

His attention returned to Katrina, and she gestured towards the sitting room to his left, directly across from the grand staircase. The room sported a high ceiling and a series of large windows looking out onto the front yard and circle driveway in front of the house. The furniture was contemporary and mostly earth tones, tastefully accenting the lighter carpeting in the room. Mediterranean artwork decorated the walls.

He considered the large couch, smaller sofa, and two reading chairs expertly placed to allow a grand view of the room and chose to perch on one end of the couch. He glanced at the oak end tables and coffee table, which added a classic touch. A small fireplace stood against the far end of the room on an exterior wall, though likely it didn't receive a lot of use considering Georgia's generally mild winters. *Nice place*, he thought.

She sat next to him, though with enough distance between them that he didn't feel uncomfortable. He admitted to feeling somewhat anxious and noticed his pulse increase slightly. Though not necessarily scared of her, he still felt a little wary. His eyes studied her at length as if seeing her for the first time, and very much liking who he saw. He wasn't really sure why he should have expected something different in her appearance from earlier last week, but still found himself doing so.

"Can I offer you something to drink?" she asked with a smile, well aware of his closer inspection of her. She assessed his body language for the second time that evening, having heard his increased heart rate the moment she opened the front door. It was habit with her normally, but her skills took on special meaning that evening because she wanted to make sure there were no unpleasant misunderstandings. She was glad to see him, grateful he'd seen fit to allow her another chance for them to visit openly before making any decisions regarding their possible future together.

"Thanks, not just now," he replied with a more supportive expression than he felt. *I'm a little too old to have butterflies in my stomach*, he chastised himself irritably. He felt like a timid school boy on his first date. "I want to start by thanking you for saving my life the other night," he began and then added sheepishly. "I suppose the park isn't necessarily 'Caleb-safe' just yet."

She found his awkward manner somewhat amusing. "Yes, I emailed the neighborhood association suggesting that a guard fence should be installed soon. Children could easily get hurt by falling over the incline."

"Adults too," he amended in a respectful tone.

"Well, fleeing blindly into dark, foreign areas could be dangerous for anyone," she replied with a slight edge. He winced at the mild admonishment.

*Easy Katrina*, she warned herself. She was annoyed because she cared for his safety, and he'd acted somewhat recklessly that night.

"Nevertheless, thanks for helping me from a possibly bad fall," he offered sincerely.

"You're welcome," she accepted in a more conciliatory tone. "And I'm sorry if you were handled a little roughly during the event." She had tried not to hurt him. She hoped he understood that she merely endeavored to calm him that night, never mind being nearly breathless with shock as he went over the edge of the ravine. *Glad that I was able to move quickly enough to grab his leg before he fell.*

He rubbed absently at his right shoulder where she had pinned him that evening. "No problem. But I admit I've still got a sore shoulder from that."

"Um, remember the tree branch?" Katrina asked pointedly. In all her years, nobody ever tried to wallop her with a tree branch. Still, she supposed it was amusing from a certain perspective.

He adopted a withering expression and sighed. He felt rather embarrassed by the chain of events in retrospect. "I'm really sorry about that," he insisted. "Please understand. I'm not a violent guy. I was just --"

"Scared?" she prompted gently. She easily recalled the intense fear in his eyes that night and regretted that she had been the source.

He shook his head slightly in resigned fashion and confessed, "Exactly." Following a silent pause, he asked, "How's your arm?"

"My arm?" Katrina replied vaguely, before quickly adding: "Oh, the tree branch. I'm fine, no problem at all."

"Oh, good," he responded as his eyes widened a little with

surprise. "But I swung really hard at you. You know, while hardly major league-worthy, I was a pretty good home run hitter in college. So, I imagined it must have been pretty jarring at least," he prompted.

"Not really," she replied. "Although my jacket sleeve was scuffed up a bit." *I'm a tough little vampire*, she silently congratulated herself.

He considered his evaluation of the tree branch and how it would have injured most anybody else under similar circumstances. "Sorry about the jacket," he apologized. "I'll be happy to replace it."

"No need," she countered quickly.

A few silent moments passed as he mulled her responses over in his head. She maintained an amused expression, having anticipated the tree limb incident must have made an impression on him. *Let him think about that a minute or two*, she mused.

"Okay, so you're telling me you didn't even register the hit?" he pressed a little defensively.

"Look, are you happy I'm not injured or not?" she retorted with a hint of annoyance. "Because it sounds to me like you're more upset your 'little smack' was ineffective. It's going to take a lot more than a swinging branch to make an impact on someone like me."

*Now he's just being egotistical*, she thought irritably.

A shiver went up Caleb's spine briefly as he considered her reply. He held up his hands in a surrendering gesture, realizing his ego needed to take a back seat really quickly. "No, you're absolutely right. I'm sorry, that was way out of line," he conceded earnestly. "I'm very happy you weren't hurt and that you're so durable."

There was another lengthy pause. She smiled with increasing amusement, covering her mouth with her hand as she stared into his gentle eyes.

"Something funny?" he inquired warily.

"Oh sorry," she replied. "I was just thinking back to the

shocked look on your face after you hit me with that tree branch and it broke in half."

His shoulders slumped forward, and he conceded, "Maybe we should just try and forget the whole event."

"Perhaps," she agreed good-naturedly, but with a smug expression.

He sat still for a moment and found he was once again staring into her beautiful green eyes. He looked away suddenly, awkwardly wondering what he should say next.

She considered him for a moment as he stared at her and frowned slightly when he looked away. Katrina realized that she needed to lay her cards on the table so she would know how to proceed further with him.

"Caleb," she began, noting his eyes darted to meet hers at the sound of her voice. "I'm sorry if I scared you, and I know you have a lot of questions for me, which I'll be happy to answer. But I need to know what happened last Friday night. The degree of terror in your eyes looked overwhelming, and I can't think of what I could have done to scare you so badly."

He swallowed hard as the memory of Friday night washed over him again. "It was your eyes. They glowed so brightly," he explained. "And something flashed in my mind, like a memory, but less tangible. Only, I knew at that moment I needed to be afraid -- no, terrified for my life. The emotions came over me like a lightning strike from nowhere, and all I could do was run as fast as possible. I couldn't even think clearly. Everything was like a blur in my mind."

Katrina considered his explanation, which rang true by his body language. She wondered if it were some bizarre reaction related to her hypnotic attempt on him as a child after she had killed his father right in front of him. "Are you scared of me now?" she asked, although she wasn't sensing fear from him so much as nervousness.

"Do I need to be?" he asked cautiously. He really wasn't sure what he was supposed to feel. All he knew was that he very much still cared for her.

"Scared or afraid? No," she clarified. "Careful? Yes."

He nodded. "Well, maybe I am still scared, a little bit. But what do you mean by needing to be careful?"

She considered him for a moment and reached out to touch his hand that rested on top of his knee. He flinched only slightly, but his reaction still saddened her. However, she proceeded to softly cover the top of his hand with hers.

"I won't intentionally seek to hurt you, Caleb," she assured him, "except in the case of a couple of rare instances."

"Such as?" he asked carefully as his pulse increased.

She still gently held her hand atop his and explained, "There are a few important rules if you're really serious about any long-term relationship with me, Caleb. A couple of them are 'deal breakers,' in a manner of speaking."

He thought seriously about her explanation and ventured, "Like when you told me not to tell anybody about you."

Katrina nodded affirmatively. "That's the biggest rule of all, yes," she stated firmly but with gentleness in her eyes.

He took a deep breath. "I suppose I can appreciate the importance of a rule like that," he conceded.

"Good," she explained. "Because that rule is what protects me from humanity."

They fell silent for a brief time before she returned to a previous topic. "This won't work between us if you're always afraid of me," she ventured quietly. "Do you understand?"

He considered her statement carefully. As he gazed at her face, so soft and lovely, he had a hard time imaging being afraid of her, despite his actual feelings.

"Yes," he nodded slowly. "I understand."

"That's good," she said with a hopeful smile.

He considered the statement a moment longer. "But you need to explain things so I'm not afraid. Information defeats fear of the unknown."

She nodded, impressed with his mature assessment. The evening was going about as well as she could have hoped, so far.

"What do you need for me to do or say to help inform you better?"

"Well, I have a few questions, you see," he ventured hesitantly. "If that's not a problem, of course."

*Okay, here come the questions,* she thought with resignation. On the few occasions during her lengthy existence when the few men she revealed herself to wanted to understand her better, they all presented a host of questions, some intelligent, others outrageous. She sighed and nodded. "Ask your questions."

But he sensed something resigned, or perhaps melancholy in her reaction to him. It bothered him, and he realized he didn't want to be a source of unpleasantness to her.

"Never mind, Katrina," he offered gently. "I'll just find out over time. You'll tell me when, or if you're ready."

Her eyebrow arched high. *Nobody's ever responded like that before,* she recalled. *They all had insistent, sometimes insulting, questions in the past. How oddly refreshing.*

Caleb rose, abruptly deciding that he should leave. Their meeting had gone well, but he didn't want to press his luck. Besides, he wasn't sure he could keep from asking a litany questions if he stayed much longer.

"Wait," she said with concern as she rose to stand before him. "Where are you going?"

"Well, home," he replied. "Maybe we could see a movie later tomorrow night or something?"

Her eyes widened slightly and she adopted a slightly confused expression. She was suddenly feeling compelled by some very strong emotions.

"No," she insisted in a non-threatening tone. She was somewhat shocked by the depth of strong feelings washing over her at that moment. She didn't want him to go and suddenly didn't care about his potential questions. She just knew that she wanted him to stay.

"So then, you're busy tomorrow? How about Saturday then?" he persisted.

Katrina blinked and slowly but deliberately stepped towards him.

His eyes widened with surprise, and he asked, "What's wrong, Katrina?" His pulse quickened, and he found an anxious tension rising inside him.

"Don't go, Caleb," she whispered to him softly. "Ask me anything, but don't go yet." She just wanted him to stay with her. She'd been so worried that he wouldn't have wanted even to see her again, but was relieved that he was finally there.

Her left hand reached out to caress his cheek lightly with her fingertips. Her right arm subtly wrapped around the small of his back, and she moved in a fluid blur as her soft lips lightly brushed his.

He drew in a breath from the feeling of her warm lips tenderly touching his skin. He pressed his lips against hers gently, but with more force than she had, and kissed her passionately. The next thing he knew the room spun slightly, and he was lying on the couch with her on top of him. They continued to kiss for a time, and she ran the slim fingers of one hand through his hair and across his scalp, causing him to shiver slightly with appreciation.

She nestled her lips in the small of his soft neck and kissed him there. He murmured with satisfaction as she kissed him again. She felt strong desire rise in her, and her fangs began to extend slightly. The scent of his skin and the underlying blood beneath called to her, and she could feel his strong pulse against her lips as she kissed him.

She abruptly stopped, and her entire body froze in place.

"What's wrong?" he whispered as he turned his head quickly to gaze at her. He saw her eyes glowing green back at him, and he jolted slightly.

"I'm sorry, but it's not safe for you, Caleb," Katrina insisted. It was so long since her last intimate encounter with a man. Her body was suddenly so alive with desire for both his body and his blood, and the dual urges in her threatened to overwhelm her like a tidal wave. It was all too much to process at once, and she feared for his life at that moment, afraid she would lose control.

Caleb's mind raced with confusion. One minute, they were sharing a passionate moment together, and the next minute she suddenly stopped. *And what's with her eyes?* he wondered.

She sensed his confusion and began to push away from him, but he reached out and pulled her against him in a strong embrace.

"No, Caleb," she insisted more forcefully as she began to exert her extraordinary strength to disengage from him. "You don't understand. You're in danger right now. It's too much for me."

But he held on with all of his might and kissed the top of her head. "Then make it safe for me, Katrina," he urged with sudden resolve. "You said that you didn't want to hurt me, so mean it now." His heart was racing at that moment as he wondered if he were about to die or not. He just knew he didn't want to let her go, ever.

She concentrated intently on calming her hunger. At similar moments in her past with other men, a number of them had suffered because of it. For them, it had been the consequence of being with her. With her passion came the desire for blood, and one was rarely relinquished without partaking of the other. But Caleb was different. She needed to protect him.

With him holding her tightly to his body, her face was pressed against his neck, and she could feel his pulse throbbing through his skin. She realized it was so painfully long since she had rested in a man's arms. "I want you so badly," she rasped as her lips found the soft skin of his neck again. "I want you in so many ways."

He held on to her tightly and whispered into her hair, "I want you, and I want you to have me too, Katrina."

She shut her eyes tightly as she tried to focus on remaining calm. *He doesn't realize what he's saying to me. He has no idea!*

"Stop," she protested.

"No," he insisted. "I'm yours."

*Oh Caleb*, she thought powerfully. *So trusting, so foolish.*

Yet his sense of trust in her merely added to her desire for him, and Katrina made the decision to find the balance necessary to be with him safely. She struggled with the bloodlust in her body, fighting to control the feral emotions and urges within her. The self-discipline that served her so well in the past began to reassert itself, and she felt her body respond accordingly. The future was so uncertain, and he might someday die, but not at her hands that night.

"Hold very still," she whispered with resignation as she kissed the soft skin of his neck. "Try to relax, but don't move unless I direct you to."

He swallowed hard and felt her lips move to the opposite side of his neck. She kissed him again on his soft skin. He felt her tongue as it sensually touched his skin, and wanted so very much to please her, to trust her implicitly and totally.

A new sensation occurred, although it was also somehow familiar. It was a numbness that spread on the area of his neck where she kissed him and where her tongue was pressed. He remained very still as she instructed him, and her right hand began to caress him. A satisfying shiver rolled through his body, and the numbness grew in his neck until he couldn't feel her tongue against his skin anymore.

"Now freeze," she whispered into his neck.

He felt a slight prick in his neck, not terribly painful. Her hand continued to caress and massage his body as she ran the fingers of her other hand gently through his hair in a soothing fashion. He felt himself grow slightly light-headed and thought he heard soft slurping sounds. He closed his eyes and patiently waited, while also appreciating the closeness they were finally sharing.

Katrina was in ecstasy. His blood was delicious to her as it flowed down her throat, but she was careful to draw on him gently. She felt so intimately connected with him, having created a life bond between them. She was partaking in much more than mere feeding. It was a form of consummation.

Moments later, he felt the numbness increase against his throat again, and she was once more kissing at his neck. He heard a subtle smacking sound and slowly opened his eyes to find her green gaze illuminated slightly as her tongue ran lightly across her lips.

"Oh, Caleb," she cooed. "I do love you."

She was so very pleased with him. He was so generous, so giving to allow her to do that. She had sensed his reservation, and she had even tried to warn him. But he had persisted, and despite the fact he was unsure of his fate, he still wanted to please her. That meant more to her than anything that evening. She laid claim to him, and in a singular moment of complete clarity she decided that he was to be her mate.

He smiled with a lopsided grin, and she bent to kiss him. He noticed a slightly metallic taste to her kiss. "I'm falling in love with you too," he offered.

He knew that, despite the brief time they had known each other, he meant every word of his statement. He was so happy to have her in his life and didn't care if she were a vampire or not. And most of all, he truly believed she meant him no harm. Everything she had done since he first met her was nothing but caring and considerate towards him. The feelings he felt for her were so much stronger than for anyone else before, and he realized it must be nothing short of love.

"And no need for worry," Katrina offered softly with an amused grin. "You can't be turned into a vampire from what we shared."

She rose from the couch, and he started to join her, but she pressed her hand against his chest. "Stay," she ordered as she slipped out of her shoes. "I'll be right back."

He settled back onto the couch, and she seemed to disappear from view. It startled him, and he saw lights in the hallway and entryway go out one by one.

Caleb heard a quick noise across the room, and the lights all suddenly went out. Only the glow of the outdoor lights filtered in through the windows in the room.

Suddenly, she was standing there before him. However, she was wearing only her silvery bra and panties, and her eyes were glowing slightly. Her hair was undone and hung like a mantle around her head. Her pale skin gave her a somewhat ethereal appearance in the dim light. *Like an angel,* he silently marveled, *but perhaps edgier.*

"Now it's your turn, Caleb," she purred with satisfaction while moving to the couch and reaching to undo the buttons of his shirt. Her eyes narrowed slyly with anticipation.

In the end, she was a beautiful, sexy, green-eyed, red-haired demon that took him on a heavenly, erotic journey for the remainder of the evening.

# Chapter 4

❦

# Rules

*K*atrina lay against Caleb's body on the large, four-poster bed in the second floor master bedroom. It was a bedroom she rarely ever used. Usually, she operated out of a hidden apartment-sized room in the basement portion of the house. The huge bedroom they were in at the moment was primarily for show, but she did keep part of her wardrobe, perfumes, and cosmetics stored there and in the adjoining grand-sized bathroom. And though it was rarely occupied, at that moment she was very happy to be making use of the room.

The darkness was solely broken by the glow from exterior estate lights emanating through the nearby window. It was well past two o'clock Friday morning, and Caleb draped one arm lazily across Katrina's pale-skinned body.

His thoughts were filled with the bliss of being there with her. It seemed like something out of a dream for him, and he wanted it to last forever. She had brought so much happiness to him that evening, and he recalled the intimate closeness and intense passion they had shared twice already. Such closeness of body mingled with the taking of his blood was so foreign to him. It seemed dark and dangerous, and yet laced with affection. He recognized that a significant evolution had occurred between them, both emotionally and intimately.

She listened to the gentle rhythm of his heartbeat, while the sound of blood flowing through his veins generated a type of anatomical song in her ears. She could sense the contentment in him, and it pleased her greatly. She lightly caressed

his face with her fingertips as she considered a sense of pleasure she hadn't felt in so many years with someone. A humorous thought occurred to her, as she realized he knew so very
little about her true nature. She wondered with mild amusement how many odd questions he had left unasked of her. The
edges of her mouth upturned slightly, and she gazed up into
his pale blue eyes from where she laid next to him. They were
beautiful and projected a peaceful, innocent quality.

"That wasn't so scary, was it?" she teased softly.

"You're so full of energy," he murmured.

"You meant to say 'life' didn't you?" she admonished. "I
am alive, you know. You didn't just make love to an animated
corpse. The movies have that all wrong, I'm happy to say. I
breathe, and warm blood flows through my veins."

She heard his heartbeat increase slightly and smiled.
She'd hit the nail on the head, it seemed. She bent her face up
to kiss his neck softly, and he chuckled. He wasn't about to confirm her suspicion regarding his unspoken question, but was
inwardly happy the answer was definitely a positive one. *Alive
is so much better than undead*, he mused, and bent his head to
kiss her softly on the forehead.

"No transforming into a bat, no sleeping in coffins, and I
have absolutely no aversion to crosses," she added for clarification in an amused tone.

"Glad to hear it," he replied with approval. "I left my cruci-
fix at home tonight just in case, though."

She heard a loud growl from his stomach, and she giggled.
"Somebody's hungry," she ventured.

"I was too nervous to eat before I came over," he confessed.

Katrina smiled, and the realization struck her that she had
no human food in the house, other than some Coca-Colas in the
refrigerator and some wine in her basement. He was the first
human guest to visit her home since establishing her residence
in the Atlanta area.

"Hm. We've got a grocery problem here, I think," she announced. "I'll need to work on that sometime soon."

He understood her reference immediately and chuckled. "I have an early class this morning anyway, so I'll just grab something on the way home," he said while stretching his lean, muscular body beneath hers.

"If you must," she accepted with resignation as she rolled off of him to sit on the edge of the bed. She didn't want for him to leave yet, but she understood why.

He propped himself up on one elbow and gently kissed her shoulder from behind. "You're amazing, you know," he offered reverently.

She turned her head to glance at him over her shoulder with a warm grin and saw the look of sincere adoration on his face. She loved it, and it immediately sent a satisfied feeling through her body. With a quick motion Katrina pressed her lips to his and nearly drew the breath from him in a passionate kiss. *So are you, my love*, she reflected.

Minutes later, he gazed at his reflection in a large full-length mirror as he dressed. He glanced at his neck where she'd bitten him, and his eyes widened slightly with surprise. Slowly rotating his neck towards the dim lamp light, he ran his fingertips across his skin as his eyes searched for anything resembling puncture marks, but saw nothing out of the ordinary. *There's no way I imagined that*, he insisted.

Katrina appeared beside him wearing a green fleece robe and a sly grin on her face. "Vampires have a technique that works marvelously. Our saliva can heal wounds."

"That's impressive," he complimented as something else dawned on him. He raised an eyebrow and said, "I remember now the same numbness when you helped me with my cut forehead the night at the apartment. It healed completely in a couple of days. I thought it was the antiseptic."

She distinctly recalled the night in question. "Well, if done properly I could've healed it even faster, but I had to be subtle at the time."

His eyes darted to hers in the mirror's reflection, and he turned to face her directly.

"What else can you do?" he asked.

Her gentle green eyes glinted playfully, and she reached up to caress the side of his face with the back of one hand. "Well, you already know I can move quickly," she said.

"Extremely fast," he agreed in a subdued tone. *Like a bolt of lightning, in fact.*

"And considerable strength," she said slyly. "Acute hearing and a keen sense of smell, which are both helpful."

"And your eyes?" he asked intently. "Tell me about your eyes."

She considered him for a moment. "I can see in the dark for the most part, but I can also focus on distances farther than humans."

"But they glow at times," he whispered.

She paused, kissing him gently on the lips. "It's a reflection of intense emotion, passion, anger, excitement," she explained while wrapping both arms around his waist and snuggling against him as she rested her chin on his shoulder. She wanted to keep her thoughts regarding mild hypnosis to herself for the time being.

He paused to mull over her revelations, and his heart rate increased slightly as he considered an important question. "Can you read minds?" he asked.

Katrina both heard and felt his increased heartbeat and gathered the question was important to him. "No," she replied directly. "But I can read body language extremely effectively."

"Hm," he replied as his muscles relaxed somewhat. "The hearing, vision, sense of smell...pretty enviable qualities."

She leaned into his ear and whispered, "Yes, Caleb, and all designed for hunting prey."

He paused as the gravity of her statement sunk in. "People then," he clarified as his body tensed again slightly. "As prey."

She kissed his cheek to comfort him and sighed. "Anything on this planet with blood is prey," she clarified. "Which, when you think about it, isn't far removed from how most humans see other animals."

"Am I prey to you?" he asked carefully. A small shiver ran

through his body as the thought of being her next prey flashed in his mind. *Am I a mere moth flying into a bright flame?*

Katrina reached up slowly to grasp his chin, turning his face to meet her gaze. Plainly detecting that he was unsettled by the query, she deliberately softened her otherwise serious expression to avoid projecting a threatening image.

"You are *not* prey to me," she stated. "You could never, will never be prey to me."

He was both grateful and relieved. The corners of his mouth upturned slightly as she took his face in her hands and kissed him firmly and passionately on the lips. The warmth of her kiss soothed the tension caused by the dark topics they discussed, and he felt a euphoric wave of affection flow through his body.

"Now go, Caleb," she encouraged as she gently massaged his shoulders with her hands. "Get something to eat and get some sleep. I'll come to your apartment after sunset tonight. We have more to discuss."

Upon returning home, Caleb's tired body slept, despite his mind's lack of cooperation. He awoke on the cool November Friday morning to daylight shining through his sheer curtains. Due to the warehouse directly across from his apartment window, he rarely received direct sunlight until the sun was higher in the sky, but the ambient glow from the new day still filtered in.

The revelations from the previous night filled him with both awe and happiness. But with the light of day, he felt he was returning to an alternate reality. Daytime signaled his life as a college professor, while at night he became a lover, a partner, to a mysterious woman who had captured his heart and perhaps his soul. The surprising revelation was stark in his mind: he was in love with a vampire.

*No,* Caleb corrected himself with a smile. *I'm in love with a beautiful, remarkable, caring woman who just happens to be a vampire.*

It was a typical Friday at the college. He taught two classes and held some midday office hours. He also visited with some of his peers and the division office staff, but his mind was frequently distracted with thoughts of Katrina.

He realized that he was obsessing a little over her. *But then, don't all new couples obsess over each other, at least until they achieve a comfort zone and a routine?*

Katrina spent the day lounging in the renovated basement level of the estate serving as her bedroom, den, and entertainment area. There were no windows breaking up the sheet rock that covered the brick-backed walls, but picturesque tapestries and paintings had been hung, colorful depictions of historical periods from ancient times to the Renaissance, including some outdoor scenes.

She wore comfortable cotton loungewear as she sat before her elaborate computer environment checking email, hoping for some word regarding the sudden disappearance of both Garett and Octavia in Europe. She read a message from Alton stating that his investigations in Paris had come to dead ends. However, he was in Trondheim, Norway, and had found Octavia's estate residence in the countryside burned to the ground. Apparently, it was nearly a total loss to the fire, but no bodies had been found. Alton said that the below-ground safe room Octavia maintained as a sheltered residence during the daytime, much as Katrina did, was the focal point of the fire.

Katrina's eyebrows rose suspiciously, and she replied to Alton's message.

> *Alton,*
> *It's too much of a coincidence, so there's little chance the fire was accidental. Somebody was after Octavia, and I suspect something ill has befallen Garett. We need to determine the commonality between the two events. How can I help?*
> *Katrina*

Her eyes narrowed as she clicked *send. Are we dealing*

*with a kidnapping or a murder?* Either prospect was difficult against a vampire, except perhaps when aided by daylight or other UV-related sources. *That is, unless it were due to another vampire.* She didn't like the idea of that. Twice before a vampire had become a foe to her kind, and it had not ended well on either occasion.

She glanced at the clock, realizing she had to begin readying herself for her evening with Caleb. Given the latest revelations regarding the missing vampires in Europe, she welcomed a pleasant diversion.

By Friday afternoon, Caleb was home and cleaning up his apartment in anticipation of Katrina's visit. He thought about cooking dinner for them, but abruptly realized she didn't need to eat food.

*How odd*, he thought. They'd been to dinner together a number of times. She appeared perfectly ordinary, just like any other person, like any other human. And with the stroke of one revelation, many of the normal mannerisms and views of traditional dating were completely usurped in his mind.

*Okay, so I'll abandon the cooking idea. Should I eat before she arrives? Maybe I should wait and ask.* Finally, he decided to text her. She responded that she would accompany him to dinner that evening and added he should dress comfortably.

Time passed quickly, and before he knew it, dusk transformed to evening. He showered and changed into a new pair of blue jeans and a turquoise dress shirt before slipping on a black leather jacket. He could always change after seeing Katrina's attire.

The doorbell rang after 7 pm, and his pulse quickened in anticipation as he opened the door with a smile. Katrina stood before him wearing a pair of black denim jeans, a black turtleneck sweater, and knee-high black leather boots. Her hair was pulled back into a ponytail like the night before. She was definitely dressed to kill, in a manner of speaking.

She pressed the tip of her finger against his chest as she

stepped forward with a playful grin, demanding, "You didn't even look through the peephole, my love. What if I were a robber?" She handed him a small paper sack labeled with a local drugstore as she walked past him.

He took it from her and glanced at it curiously. One side of his mouth upturned in a partial smile as he shut the door behind her. "Well, if you were a robber, you'd probably be waiting for me in some dark parking lot, wouldn't you?"

"Hm, we're going to have to work on security issues with you, I see," she noted absently before leaning into his lips with her own, kissing him warmly, yet all too briefly.

"I missed you today," he whispered as his hands went to her hips to prevent her from pulling away from him.

Her arms encircled his waist, and she smiled brightly at him. "I missed you too," she confessed. "Daytime is hard when all I want to do is be with you."

He considered that for a moment. "I guess I haven't given it any thought recently. I take both the day and night for granted, I suppose."

"As all humans should," she responded matter-of-factly, releasing him and pulling away to sit on one of his kitchen bar stools.

Something in the way she said that bothered him, but he wasn't sure why. Rather than press the topic, he sat on a stool facing hers as he looked into the drugstore sack she had handed him earlier.

"What's this?" he asked while withdrawing a container of iron supplements and one of a general vitamin supplement for men.

She smiled at him and tapped the end of his nose with the tip of her forefinger. "You'll need to keep your constitution strong if you're going to have a vampire mate drinking from you periodically."

He grinned. "Is that what I'm called? A mate?"

She regarded him fondly. "It's the term my kind likes to use. It's an important position of endearment and commitment."

He smiled with satisfaction at the title as the red-haired vampire observed his reaction closely. He was flattered that he had made such a wonderful impression on her. With a brief glance into her eyes, he noted that she seemed very pleased with him.

"So, just what do you do during the day when the rest of us humans are busy enjoying the sunlight?" he asked.

She sighed at his question, recalling how much she had enjoyed the daytime as a human. But rather than lament to him about that, she replied, "A lot of Internet-related activities mostly: finances, shopping, researching, learning, and there's always email."

"Email? To other vampires?" he ventured with a raised eyebrow. He was so focused just on her that thinking beyond the scope of one vampire was an altogether new concept for him to tackle.

Katrina smiled at his curious tone. "Of course, silly. You didn't think I was the only one, did you?"

*Honestly, I haven't considered the topic much yet,* he thought.

"Do you have very many vampire friends?" Caleb inquired.

She considered him for a moment. "Before I answer your question," she began carefully. "There's something you need to know about your role in my life."

*Uh-oh,* he thought while gazing into her eyes. *Have I already done something wrong?* he wondered.

She reached out, grasping his hands in her own and holding them gently. They were warm to the touch, and she sensed a tension in him.

"It's okay, my love," she reassured him. "It's important that you realize there are certain expectations you need to be diligent about with us. It's a matter of safety for us both."

"You mean something like ground rules?" he asked.

She shook her head at him with a warm smile. "Yes, some ground rules. Now, just relax and stare into my eyes while we discuss this, okay?"

Katrina peered into his eyes intently and held his gaze
while literally willing him to pay attention. He felt compelled
to stare into her eyes, which began to glow slightly with beautiful green intensity.

"Your eyes, they're like beautiful emeralds," he murmured
before recalling her explanation from last night. "You're upset?"

She released his hands and pressed her forefinger against
his lips. "Sh. No, Caleb," she admonished gently. "Please, just
listen."

He fell silent and nodded, still drawn to her luminous eyes.
Indeed, her eyes didn't appear angry at all. In fact, he felt a
peace wash over him, similar to the feeling of relaxation just
before drifting off to sleep.

She had no intention of trying to force suggestions into
his thoughts, merely to compel his attention for the important
information she was preparing to discuss. While she couldn't
read his thoughts, she knew it would be much easier to gauge
his reactions, including any attempts at evasive responses.

Her expression softened, and she studied his features until
her eyes locked onto his. She loved to stare into his pale blue
eyes. She saw a gentleness in them, as if his very spirit were
filled with innocence and sincerity. His eyes melted her prime-
val heart.

She moved her stool closer to his until their knees almost
touched as she sat across from him. She took each of Caleb's
hands in hers and placed them together atop her own knees. "I
don't mean to sound intimidating, but you need to know we're
about to discuss some important matters," she explained, "conditions that are very important for you to honor."

His eyebrows rose with curiosity. *Wow, heavy topics already*, he mused.

He nodded and remained silent as he stared into her eyes.
He was already fully committed to this journey with her. He
cared for her deeply and was quite honestly falling in love with

her. She was so different from other women he had dated. She had a maturity about her, tempered by a sincere, tender nature. But he also sensed an edge about her personality, something beneath the surface that wasn't necessarily threatening to him because he felt safe being with her. *I feel protected and secure around her.* No, it was something else. Something dark. But still, there was no way he was about to turn away from her or the amazing prospects her otherworldly nature revealed to him. He felt that she might be the one for him, if there really were such a thing.

As for Katrina, she committed to the decision that she wanted him in her life. She had been drawn to him for some time, and her love for him already felt firmly entrenched. It was a revelation both stark and strong in her mind. She had lived long enough to know the difference between mere physical blood interests and the feelings of devotion associated with love. Though both were important to her, she felt that Caleb embodied a holistic solution covering all the vital areas in her life. Perhaps she still recalled the innocent, caring child who showed no fear to help her. Or maybe it was all she observed of him when he didn't even know he was being watched or listened to.

*Great, I'm a stalker for sure*, she silently chastised herself before focusing on the task at hand.

"There can be no deviations from these, Caleb," she insisted.

"I understand," he replied simply.

"Are you ready?"

"Yes," he said with a nod.

"First, you must never reveal the true nature of my existence to anyone, no matter the emotions or motivations driving such an inclination."

She paused to ensure that he absorbed the requirement.

"Second, you must reveal to me any knowledge or suspicion of anyone who might have determined my true existence or nature."

Another pause.

"Third, you must never willingly give or submit yourself to another of my kind," she continued. "I tend to be mildly possessive, my love, and I insist on this."

His eyes widened only for a moment as he absorbed what she said. Her words were soothingly melodic as he remained somewhat entranced by her gaze.

"Fourth, you may only have my blood when I offer it to you."

He frowned with sudden curiosity. "But why would --"

Again, her finger pressed against his lips and her eyes flashed momentarily. "Sh, no talking."

He fell silent again and nodded as she removed her finger from his lips, though he marked the topic for future query.

"Fifth, never accept blood from another of my kind."

She held his gaze and noticed no discernible change in his emotions. *So far, so good*, she mused.

"Sixth, you will never ask to become one of my kind," she said with emphasis.

His eyes widened momentarily, and she felt his hands twitch in her own for only a second. *He's going to be really curious about that one*, she decided.

Karina's mind recalled the past experiences with partners in her life as a vampire. In the end, so many were nearly obsessed with the greedy prospect of conversion to her kind. She could see the obvious temptations, but there was more to it than what they each saw. Immortality came with its disadvantages, as she had learned painfully over the sometimes endless stream of years. She recalled the morning she met Caleb as a child, when she had tried to seek her own finality in the morning sunrise and was suddenly happy she had decided to give life another try.

"Seventh and most importantly, never lie to me in matters concerning any of the aforementioned rules, my love," she insisted gravely.

Finally, she blinked, and her eyes returned to their normal

green color.

"You agree to respect and abide by these seven rules?" she asked.

Caleb nodded. "I love you, Katrina, and I'll follow them to the best of my ability."

A feeling of dread began to grow in her, and she insisted more strongly than she intended, "Please, Caleb. I know you can do this for me."

He frowned, urging, "Katrina, what's wrong? I won't let you down."

Her eyes adopted a sad expression, and she sighed deeply. Then her eyes closed, but when she reopened them again they were less morose. "In the past, these rules, though simple, have been breached in one way or another by a previous partner," she explained.

He nodded with understanding. "They betrayed your trust. You had to abandon them?"

But she shook her head negatively while holding his gaze. It was much worse.

"No," she stated grimly. "They died."

His eyes widened slightly with surprise, and he blurted, "Died?"

"They died," she repeated simply.

"You mean died, as in they couldn't bear the pain they caused you? Couldn't bear to live without you?" he insisted urgently, although a sinking feeling in the pit of his stomach suggested a graver conclusion.

"No, I couldn't bear the danger and pain they caused me. They died, and all by my hand, save one. He was a suicide," she explained in a sorrowful tone.

His pulse raced until it felt as if his heart would explode out of his chest. *So, she will kill me if I break one of these rules?*

In the silence around them, Katrina heard his heart pounding and saw his pupils dilate. It was painful to know she was causing him such intense distress.

He swallowed hard, and his mind struggled for something

to say.

"Are you okay, my love? What are you feeling?" she asked carefully as she observed his body language, and she listened to his breathing and heart rate.

"I'm scared as hell, that's what I am," he replied anxiously.

"You mustn't fear me, Caleb." Her eyes appeared softer to him.

"Too late," he replied somewhat shakily, but with a half-hearted attempt at a nervous grin.

"Caleb," she cooed soothingly.

"It's a lot to take in at once. In fact, I'm already worried about making a mistake," he ruminated.

Katrina regarded him with a sympathetic expression. "Don't worry. I'll help you. This will be a learning experience for both of us," she encouraged before adding wryly: "Although more of a relearning experience for me, I suppose."

He regarded her warily. He didn't want to be the next victim in her list of previous failures.

"Here's my commitment to you, Caleb," she offered as she reached out for his right hand.

He allowed her to take his hand between both of hers before she continued.

"I promise to protect you to the best of my abilities," she began. "I will cherish you and all you give to me. I will be respectful of you, and I'll be honest about my feelings."

She smiled warmly at him, hoping to impart a sense of encouragement. After a moment and some effort on his part, he adopted a nervous half-smile, grateful that she was at least trying to be supportive.

"And I will never take blood from you without your consent or offer," she added solemnly. His expression suggested that he didn't realize how major a concession she had just given him. "Traditionally, a vampire takes blood from their mate at their own discretion," she added.

His eyes quickly met hers. Though he knew very little about her kind, he considered for a being that placed a high value on blood, such a stipulation seemed significant.

He considered the roller coaster of emotions and revelations swarming through his head in the past few days, and at times he found everything a little hard to digest at once. Still, he knew he was in love with Katrina. He was smitten with her. But her revelation about previous fatal relationships had certainly instilled a small degree of fear. *Perhaps it's a healthy response by a human to a vampire.* However, he hoped it would dissipate as their relationship grew, because he truly didn't want to fear her.

She regarded him with a hopeful expression, but she could sense, almost feel, the emotions battling inside of him. She realized her stipulations and rules might seem cumbersome or intimidating to a potential partner, but they were in place for a reason. Experience had taught her the importance of the rules for both her and him.

"I accept," Caleb softly agreed as he stared into her eyes. "But you're not allowed to let me down either."

She took his face in her hands and kissed him deeply. His arms folded around her waist, and he pulled her towards his body. As her lips parted from his and she began to release him, his lips pressed against hers again with more passion. A moment later, he reluctantly allowed her to pull away from him. She gazed at him intently as she sat back from him, and her eyes sparkled slyly with approval.

"Done, and sealed with a kiss," she said simply as if some secret contract negotiation had been completed. She recalled his earlier question before she had covered her list of rules.

"By the way, I have a number of contacts who are fellow vampires," she said. "Some I even consider to be close friends, and two in particular are like family to me."

He nodded and fleetingly wondered if he would ever have the chance to meet any of her vampire friends or associates, though the thought also sent a pang of anxiety through him. *Perhaps one vampire is enough for me for right now*, he conceded.

His stomach growled, and Katrina's eyes darted to him before smiling with genuine amusement. It was the second time in less than twenty-four hours that his stomach had intervened on their time together.

"Come on. Let's go get you something to eat," she offered with a smile.

Much to his satisfaction, she agreed to let him drive her Audi sports car. He enjoyed the driving experience, and she reveled in how much pleasure it gave him. She studied his boyish grin, which briefly reflected the child he once was.

Caleb took them to a steak house across town he particularly enjoyed. They were both pleasantly surprised when a table in an uncrowded area was available. Normally, a Friday night would have involved a wait, but fortunately a formerly unused section of the dining room had just opened.

The atmosphere was casual and hosted a variety of patrons ranging from families, to couples, to groups of friends. The room was comfortably lighted, and the tables were covered with simple white linen table cloths. After ordering drinks, Caleb perused the menu, while Katrina sat quietly to his right with her back turned to most of the other patrons and watched him with interest.

He glanced at her and casually asked, "Are you hungry?" Realizing his mistake, his face reddened slightly.

One side of her mouth upturned slyly. "Yes, actually."

"Really? Well, what sounds good for dinner?" he pressed.

"You," she replied almost too quietly to be heard. His scent was tantalizing to her, and the ever-present desire for blood was there. It was a universal desire among all of her kind, and her recent bonding with him only heightened her desire.

His eyes widened, but he grinned nevertheless. "Oh, really?" he prompted with a hint of playfulness as he looked deeply into her green eyes.

Katrina's eyes held his gaze, but with only a hint of amusement. She truly, deeply wanted to press her mouth against his soft neck and partake of him. She didn't want to kill him, but she definitely craved a taste.

The waiter delivered their drinks and promised to return for their entree orders soon.

After another silent moment, Caleb's grin began to fade, and he swallowed a sip of his drink with a single hard gulp as her eyes held his in a near trance. He had the feeling she was looking at him much like a hungry wolf would stare at a rabbit. An uncontrolled shiver ran up his spine, and she broke the trance by looking down at the menu in front of her.

"Perhaps my selecting something from the menu would be safer for you right now," she suggested smartly.

"I'm good with that," he agreed frankly.

"For now," she added almost as an afterthought.

He blinked again and glanced back down to his menu, soberly realizing the double meaning in her comment. Caleb was so used to the playful banter of a conventional courtship that it shook him to realize just how seriously she took the whole blood topic.

"I'm sorry," he apologized without looking up at her. "I wasn't making light of your needs."

Her hand darted across the small table, and her fingers caressed the top of his right hand. The sudden action startled him, and he jolted slightly as his eyes rushed up to meet hers. Fortunately, her expression had softened.

"I didn't mean to be harsh, but there are moments that are actually hard for me," she began. "I'm only trying to protect you while helping you realize how dangerous our mutual interest in one another could become. It takes years to gain control over the constant craving for fresh blood, but even when mastered, the desire for it is always present. Our recent intimacy has heightened a craving in me, and I'll need to be careful."

He nodded and one corner of his mouth upturned slightly. Part of him wanted to ignore the fact she was more than the human she appeared to be before him. However, a momentary doubt ran through his mind as he wondered whether he really were in danger being with her.

"You seem in such control at all times, so measured in your actions," he ventured. "Particularly after last night, it seems almost odd that you could still be dangerous to me."

She sighed gently. "I've attempted other relationships over the years, but I always regretted them. You might recall our earlier conversation this evening?"

His shoulder muscles tensed as the uncomfortable fact resurfaced. *She killed them all in the end, except one who committed suicide.* However, he was resigned to showing her how positive a relationship could be, even for a vampire. *But I wonder how many of her previous partners started with the same positive intentions?*

Katrina raised one eyebrow slightly, fully measuring the change in his body language and sensing some agitation. While it wasn't her intent to intimidate him, she wanted to be open and honest regarding the seriousness of their pairing.

By the time he had resigned himself to asking additional questions, the waiter appeared, and they both seemed relieved by the distraction. She ordered a small garden salad with no dressing, and he ordered a well done steak with twice-baked potatoes and a side salad.

"Do you still enjoy eating regular food?" he inquired curiously once the waiter departed.

"Sometimes," she reflected. "Some dessert items, like chocolate, still hold a certain satisfaction for me, and I've learned to appreciate a few other foods in small quantities. But most of the time it's simply about trying to appear more human to those around me."

"So you can digest food without any problems?" he asked.

Katrina considered his question briefly before responding. "Sort of. I don't get any nutritional value from it like you do. It's much the same way your body would react to eating grass or leaves from a tree. Although liquids are generally fine, my body doesn't digest large quantities of human food very well," she explained.

"I find most dishes revolting, particularly those involving

cooked meat," she continued with a wrinkled nose. "In fact, most of us don't like the smell or taste of cooked meats. Foods prepared with fresh fruits and vegetables or grains are more palatable, although preferably in very small quantities."

He nodded, filing the information away. Following a moment's recollection, it registered on him how little food she actually consumed when they had gone out. As a matter of fact, on all those occasions, he suddenly couldn't recall a time when he saw her eat anything with cooked meat in it either. He had a small epiphany about the steak he had just ordered.

"My meal won't bother you, will it?" he asked while reaching out to the small wicker basket for a roll.

She smiled appreciatively. "I'll endure on your behalf. Just don't ask me to try it."

He smiled back as the waiter briefly reappeared to refill their tea and water glasses and update them on the status of their meals. Meanwhile, Caleb's thoughts composed an entire series of additional questions. She noticed the brightened look in his eyes and anticipated what was coming. Readying herself, she adopted a resigned, yet amused, expression.

"Do you mind?" he asked after noting her countenance.

"Proceed," she replied while gracefully folding her porcelain-like hands on the table before her.

"What year were you born?"

She regarded him with a steely expression and countered darkly, "It's not polite for a man to ask a lady her age."

His eyes widened slightly, and he quickly explained, "Sorry, it's the historian in me, you understand. Just the idea of how much human history you may have experienced could stagger the mind, depending upon when you became a vampire."

She raised a suspicious eyebrow and ventured, "Perhaps. Still..."

He swallowed once and offered, "I respect your reluctance, and I mean no disrespect, Katrina, but how about if I were able to guess?"

One corner of her lip upturned as she considered his suggestion. She could understand his seemingly innocent curiosity and conceded, "Very well, but you only get one guess per day, and I won't tell you if you're close or by how much."

"Hints?" he pressed with a playful glint in his eyes.

"No," she stated in a superior tone. "No hints."

He thought for a moment as he casually munched on the piece of bread he'd just buttered. She had mentioned that she had previous mates, but he had no idea how many or for how long each might have been with her. *Months? Years? Maybe I should shoot for the moon and see what happens.* Somehow, he could easily envision her outfitted in a nineteenth century dress.

"1896," he ventured hopefully.

"No," she stated with a neutral expression before prompting: "Next topic."

He rolled his eyes and insisted, "Come on, at least tell me if I'm in the right century or not."

She adopted a smirk and replied, "Well...no. Next topic."

He shook his head and moved on rather than risk annoying her. "Okay then, out of all the people in this world you could just as easily have chosen, why were you interested in me?" he asked.

Her eyebrows rose appraisingly. That's a question she hadn't expected from him.

"I knew you were special the moment I met you," she stated simply. *Never mind that you were only a child at the time.*

He watched her with a dubious expression.

"You may not realize it yet, but you have an appealing innocence about you. Your heart is in the right place, and you're capable of extraordinary decisions and actions under unusual circumstances," she explained.

"But how could you know all that?" he pressed.

She smiled slyly and assured him, "Trust me. I know."

Caleb considered her response as he absently buttered another roll. She watched him as he prepared his bread and was momentarily intrigued by the delicate movements of his hands.

*An artist's touch,* she observed.

"What do you like most and least about being you?" he asked in a subdued voice as a waiter passed by a little too closely for comfort.

Katrina's eyes darted to the waiter for a split second before returning her gaze to Caleb.

"The best part is the heightened senses that I have now," she explained. "I see, hear, smell, taste, and appreciate so much more of the world from a vampire's perspective. It's as if the finer details are easier to pick out and focus on."

"And the least," he prompted.

She regarded him with sad eyes. "I miss the morning sunrise. It used to fill me with a sense of hopefulness, as if life could start fresh again if yesterday weren't so pleasant."

He nodded, realizing that he hadn't given such things much thought. *Perhaps many of the wonders of life are wasted on humans.*

He munched on his piece of bread and noticed she was studying him with a penetrating gaze. "What's your favorite holiday?" he asked out of the blue.

"I don't mark holidays anymore," she stated absently. She was trying to remember the last time that she actually celebrated a holiday and found herself lost in the recounting.

"Mine is Thanksgiving," he offered with a smile.

She broke from her reverie and regarded him with a curious expression. "Why Thanksgiving?" she asked.

He smirked. "Great food and no annoying gift shopping conundrums."

She grinned and rolled her eyes at him. "I should've guessed," she considered out loud. "A man's answer, for certain."

"Which reminds me, what's our plan for Thanksgiving?" he queried with a smile. "It's next week, you know."

She was at a loss for words, having forgotten about the need to celebrate holidays now that she had a human mate again. It was so long ago.

"Anything you want, as long as you're not expecting me to cook some oversized, dead bird for you," she insisted darkly.

Caleb couldn't help but laugh out loud. "How about a small, dead bird, which I'll be certain to have catered with some trimmings so you won't have the smell permeating the house?" he clarified hopefully.

She smirked despite herself and nodded. *It's hard to refuse him a happy holiday, after all.* "Okay, but we eat at your place," she insisted. "That way you won't stink up my house with dead animal meat scents."

"Done," he agreed with a grin. "Okay, I've got another question."

"Oh no, now it's my turn," she insisted.

He grinned and inclined his head in acquiescence.

"Do you want children?" she asked plainly with slightly upraised eyebrows.

He was surprised by the topic and it registered in his expression.

"Well, sure. Someday," he replied thoughtfully.

"I'm barren now that I'm a vampire," she stated.

"Oh," he replied sympathetically. "Well, that's okay."

"Today it is. But what about a year from now, or five years from now?" she prompted patiently.

"Well, we could adopt," he ventured hopefully.

Katrina rolled her eyes. "Oh, I can't wait to see the expression on the state adoption inspector's face during the daytime interviews when I can't be in the sunlight. It would take mere seconds for sunshine to make my skin sizzle and burn before their eyes."

The grisly vision made Caleb shudder, and he quickly forced it from his mind. "Okay, I see what you're trying to do," he replied evenly. "Next question," he challenged.

She smirked at him, silently admiring his resolve. "Okay. Won't your friends and coworkers find it strange when I can't attend daytime social functions with you?"

"Well, I'll tell them you're feeling ill, or have work obligations, or you're out of town," he stated, proud for having thought so quickly on the fly.

She arched one eyebrow.

"There are plenty of evening events you can attend," he added smartly.

She nodded appraisingly. *Nicely done*, she conceded. "What do you say as you and your friends get older, much older, and I remain young looking?" she asked slyly.

That was something he truly hadn't considered. A sobering expression formed on his face as he mulled the concept over in his mind.

Katrina nodded slightly as she noted his thoughts deepening on the matter.

"Strong genes?" he ventured with a smirk.

She wasn't amused, and a momentary surge of irritability rolled over her. "No, not acceptable, Caleb," she admonished.

He shrugged. "Okay, so you have me there, I suppose. I guess we'll just have to address that later."

"The here and now is always easier for people to indulge in carelessly. But I have to consider the future at all times prior to my actions. The future is always just around the corner for me," she explained. "The concept of eternity demands careful planning at most levels. Small decisions today take on larger impact and meaning tomorrow."

"A butterfly flaps its wings in Japan, and a strong wind blows in China?" he ventured with a raised brow.

His analogy intrigued her. "Well, not always with that impact, but the idea resonates in much the same manner."

He sighed and conceded, "Okay. So I don't have all the answers. But is that a good reason to just walk away and forget the whole thing altogether?"

"Yes," she replied simply. "It is, actually."

He just stared at her and snorted derisively as he shook his head. *Why is she being so obstinate about this?* "I already assured you that I'm fully capable of commitment, and I'm willing to make sacrifices," he retorted defensively.

"And abandon all those you care about or that are an important part of your life?" Katrina pressed evenly.

His expression grew more subdued, and a pained look was visible in his eyes. "There aren't many left to abandon," he replied grimly.

His response surprised her momentarily, and she regarded him thoughtfully. *That was a stupid thing to ask him*, she admonished herself. *I know better than anyone what he's lost in his life.* She found herself wishing she could take back her previous question.

"I seem obstinate and negative, don't I?" she asked. "But I'm not trying to be."

He looked at her with a mix of frustration and helplessness. *Why is she being so serious and contrary all of the sudden?*

Katrina looked at him with compassion and explained, "Please don't be angry, Caleb. I'm experienced enough to know that right now you're feeling euphoric. It's the infatuation phase of our relationship, after all. Right now everything feels new, exciting, and hopeful. It's hard for you to wrap your head around the negative or the challenging."

"Wait, so you're not feeling infatuated about us or me right now?" he asked with a note of concern.

She smiled, realizing how very young he still was, how inexperienced in the ways of the world, even as an adult human. *I feel like I'm robbing the cradle more and more as time passes*, she mused sardonically. The fact that she had known him as a child wasn't lost on her, either. *Then again, I've seen a lot more of the world than he*, she silently conceded, *more than I'm comfortable admitting to him, actually.*

"Of course, I'm feeling quite infatuated with you, my love. I merely want you to see the larger tapestry taking shape before you. Eventually, your feelings of infatuation are going to pass, and you'll be facing the very real and substantive issues we'll be forced to confront as a human and vampire. You can't continue living exclusively in the moment. These issues are serious and complex," she explained. "Time isn't an enemy to me as it is to you, which is why I must be careful today to consider the prospects of tomorrow."

He nodded belatedly and blurted, "But if I were like you --"

Katrina's eyes angrily flashed in brilliant green, and her eyes narrowed to slits as she gestured with her right index finger upraised. "Stop there," she issued with more force than she had intended.

His mouth snapped shut, and his eyes widened with surprise. Some curious diners nearby raised their faces and stared at them from across the room. Katrina quickly lowered her hand and settled back in her chair. Her eyes returned to their normal green hue, but she continued to stare at him.

He started to approach the topic from a different angle, which she anticipated by watching his expression.

"Don't," she ordered. "Remember rule number six. You must never ask to become one of my kind."

He breathed a heavy sigh and nodded in resignation. *Oh yeah, rule number six*, he considered sullenly. *This is a little harder than I thought back at the apartment tonight.*

His reaction was enough to satisfy her regarding the topic, and her disposition returned to its previously relaxed state while he chewed on his lower lip and reached out absently to grasp his tea glass.

"You're pouting," she admonished him.

He took a deliberately long time to sip and swallow his tea and replied, "Hardly. I'm just thinking to myself, that's all." He resented her choice of words in describing his mood and was too proud to admit how correct she actually was.

Katrina, however, was becoming adept at reading his individual traits and body language, and she knew better. Instead, she glared at him from across the table. *Men can have such infuriatingly sensitive egos sometimes*, she fumed.

Moments later, the server delivered their entrees and quickly departed. Caleb ate his food in silence, while Katrina picked at her salad just for show, eating very little in the process. She had become quite an accomplished actress over the years and could blend into a room without raising suspicion.

She fell into a dark mood following the abrupt lull in conversation and fleetingly wondered if their declaration of commitment to each other was a hasty mistake. She considered an alternate reality where she hadn't reached out to Caleb and instead watched briefly from afar before moving on to some other part of the world.

*After all, why should a chance childhood encounter that he doesn't even remember somehow graduate into something tangible between us?* She felt a sense of sadness and loss at the prospect of his not being an active part of her life. The mere thought of severing connections to him caused her more internal conflict than she expected. To her, the impact he had already made in her life was significant, and she was all too aware of how much she cared for him, loved him. She put her fork down silently, stole a glance at him with a dart of her eyes, and noted that he appeared to be as morosely affected as she felt.

"What are you thinking?" she asked gently.

He finished chewing, swallowed his mouthful of steak, and put his fork down. "Why is rule number six so important?" he insisted firmly, though with a respectful tone.

She considered him for a moment before answering. "Becoming one of my kind changes you. You may not think you're different afterwards, but you are," she explained. "I like you the way you are now. You bring a balance into my life. Your innocence and your gentle, compassionate nature are refreshing. Those are rare qualities, even rarer among my kind."

"There's hardly a harsh, cruel woman sitting before me. In fact, you've only been very kind and caring towards me," he countered quietly so as not to make a scene. "And you've displayed a sense of compassion and encouragement towards me. How is that any different from how I might be as one of your kind?"

She glowered at him, giving her face a slightly cruel look to it. "How I feel towards you, how I choose to treat you, that isn't how I generally feel about the rest of humanity," she stated with an edge to her voice. "I'm a predator, Caleb. I'm a great white shark that wants to tear into your flesh. I simply choose not to because of my feelings for you specifically. You're the exception in my life, not the rule."

That was a dose of honesty he hadn't been entirely prepared for, and he felt like he'd just been doused with cold water. His eyes widened slightly with surprise at the vehemence in her voice.

"I don't exactly see you running around town tearing out people's throats," he countered in a low whisper.

"What makes you think I don't when you're not around?" she asked levelly. She had hoped to avoid such a harsh subject with him, but perhaps a dose of honesty was best. She needed him to understand there were few warm fuzzies about being a vampire.

Caleb was speechless as he stared at her. His mind raced to process what she just said. *It isn't as if I heard about people disappearing or turning up mangled and bloodless in Atlanta recently. Is it?*

"Do you remember the mugger in the college parking lot? You let him live. I saw him flee, and he was alive," he insisted firmly.

Her eyes flicked to his for a moment and looked away, as if she were considering what to say next. "Why do you think I left you so quickly that night?" she asked coolly.

He froze and deliberately gazed across the dining room at other patrons so that he didn't have to look her in the eyes.

"Caleb, look at me," she insisted in a whisper.

He kept his eyes averted, so her hand darted to his and squeezed it abruptly to get his attention. His eyes shifted to look at her with a start, and he gazed into her level stare. Her green eyes appeared steely and cold to him all of a sudden and intimidated him.

"I'm not justifying myself to anyone. I kill whenever I deem it necessary. I live as one of my kind, and I relish in it," she stated plainly. "I've left a trail of blood reaching all the way back to my creation. Blood is nourishment, but it's more than that. The taking of it thrills me, as it does all of my kind."

"It has to be more than that," he pleaded. "What we shared the other night, what I gave to you, was gentle, not vile."

"It's true that the taking of blood can be part of an intimate experience for us," she explained as she gently massaged his hand in hers. "It's a higher form of bonding with a mate, versus simply a feeding activity."

"And yet, you make yourself out to be some kind of evil serial killer," he admonished in a whisper. "But you're not that to me."

"Just you wait to see what would happen if my blood supply deliveries ever cease," she warned ominously. "I'm going to feed, one way or another."

"You don't have to kill to feed," he countered. "If that were true I'd already be dead."

Her facial muscles relaxed, and she regarded him with a sympathetic expression.

"My sweet Caleb," she offered as she gently squeezed his hand in hers. "I'm not asking you to hate me. Just don't confuse the facts of what I am with the emotions between us."

He squeezed her hand back and gazed into her eyes affectionately. "Then quit trying to scare me away," he insisted. "I'm not leaving, and you'll only succeed in annoying me."

She smirked at him and rolled her eyes. *He's persistent, at least*, she considered.

"Fair enough. Just bear in mind a little caution is healthy in your life," she said with a note of finality. "But you mustn't be afraid of me."

The waiter came by to refill their tea and water glasses and then departed quickly. Katrina saw that he seemed to gather they were in an intense discussion. "He gets a good tip tonight for being observant," she noted absently.

They sat silently for a time. Caleb finished his meal, and

Katrina picked at her salad while mostly watching him eat. She studied him, observing his individual mannerisms and learning even the small nuances of behavior few people even realized they exhibited. She found him so very intriguing, so unlike the men in her past, save for one, perhaps. *But that was a long time ago*, she reflected. Caleb's professed devotion to her, even after knowing her dark and often violent nature, was so at odds with his reserved, gentle personality. She certainly loved him, but it was simply amazing that he could feel the same of her.

*People are primarily a food source and generally don't mean much to me*, she thought as she watched him finish eating. *However, Caleb matters, and I want to ensure that he remains happy and safe*, she noted decisively.

He flashed a sidelong reassuring smile at her, and she smiled warmly in return. By the end of their meal together, his emotions had moderated somewhat, and he held her hand while droving them to a movie across town. Once the movie was over, Caleb was once again simply happy to be with her and kissed her affectionately on the lips as they walked back to her car.

She made certain not to belabor any further difficult topics with him for some time afterwards, content merely to appreciate his company and garner a continued sense of closeness between them.

# Chapter 5

## Life Anew

Caleb and Katrina continued to spend much of their free time together, though mostly during the evenings. They attended an independent film debut downtown and went to one of the local Civil War museums. But they were just as happy sitting together watching television or talking into the night about a variety of topics, including history, travel, and their likes and dislikes. Much to Caleb's surprise, Katrina seemed quite comfortable spending time at his apartment during evenings that they weren't out on the town together.

The two also shared satisfying intimate time together, and Caleb discovered how passionate Katrina could be. Following those occasions, he usually fell asleep with her nestled alongside his body, though always waking alone the next morning. She was quite stealthy, and he was never sure at exactly what time she departed, but he often smiled upon finding his deadbolt locked with the key on the floor where she had slid it back underneath the door on her departure. *She certainly takes safety seriously*, he mused.

Caleb relished their time together and was pleased she seemed to feel the same. Spending time with her was addictive, and he frequently found his daytime thoughts straying to his new red-haired girlfriend. *No, we're mates now*, he corrected himself on more than one occasion. Still, the word was strange to him, hardly a contemporary term, and he often referred to Katrina as his girlfriend when referencing her in casual conversations with his coworkers.

Another week passed quickly, and the Thanksgiving holiday was soon upon them. As promised, Caleb ensured no "dead birds" were cooked at the apartment. Instead, he bought a precooked turkey and dressing, then prepared some of the side dishes himself, including baking a small pumpkin pie. It was his mother's recipe, which caused him some momentary sadness at the memory of her passing nearly two years ago. Holidays were when he missed her most; recalling the happiness that he and his mother enjoyed. The hours passed as he alternated between cooking and reminiscing.

Katrina arrived at his apartment promptly after sundown and happily watched him eat his meal as the last half of the Cowboys-Lions football game played on the TV. He finally convinced her to try some candied yams and a thin slice of the pumpkin pie he had baked, both of which she actually found quite tasty. She appreciated the flavors of both and was very impressed that he knew how to cook. She was also drawn to the scent of his body and the blood that flowed inside of him.

After dinner, they sat together on his couch to watch *Casablanca* on the classic film channel. She nestled against his chest as he wrapped his arm around her shoulders and pulled her close to him. She took in his scent and momentarily felt her fangs begin to extend in anticipation. Just as she considered requesting a "small snack" from him, he asked her an unexpected question during a commercial.

"So, are male vampires stronger than female vampires?"

Katrina contemplated, "Hm, that's actually an interesting question that nobody's asked me before. I would say, no. There's some sort of leveling of the playing field that occurs when we transform.

"However," she added, "older vampires become more skillful with experience, just like humans do. So an accomplished vampire who spent their life concentrating on fighting would be naturally more accomplished than one who spent their life more sedately."

His eyes took on a spark of renewed interest. "How has my

mate spent her time as a vampire?"

Her eyes narrowed at him before responding, "I've had a variety of experiences in my time as a vampire." She wasn't particularly interested in revisiting much of her history with him on that topic. Suffice to say she had a reputation of sorts, including a number of her life's experiences that were particularly violent and might alarm him.

"And how are your combat skills, Grasshopper?" he teased in a mock-oriental tone.

She grinned at him with a playful look. "Let's say, I wouldn't want to be the vampire who had to find out."

He smiled back with an impressed expression. "So, I'm dating a Jedi master vampire then?" he whispered in a conspiratorial tone.

"Sorry, no light saber," she replied ruefully.

"Too bad."

"But I have fangs," she said hopefully as she turned to face him and deliberately extended and bared her fangs.

His eyes widened noticeably as he suddenly found himself staring into her open mouth at the extremely sharp set of fangs extending down through her two canine teeth. It was a fierce visage for such a beautiful face. "Very sharp and pointy-looking," he observed politely with a tentative smile.

She closed her mouth, adopted a predatory expression, and began slowly leaning towards him. He grinned back at her and leaned slowly away. She launched herself on top of him and pressed him into the couch cushions with her body. Her soft lips pressed to his, and she drew the breath from him as she kissed him deeply. It was at such times that he felt the strength of her body, combined with the sensual nature of her form, and it never failed both to surprise and arouse him.

A short time later, he relented to her wish to partake in the "small snack" she had considered earlier, and though she drew only a minimal quantity of his blood, she relished every drop. She was surprised by how easy it was to accept him into her life and equally amazed by how quickly he seemed to adapt to her vampire nature. But as they sat together on his couch that evening, one thing was for certain: both were quite at ease with each other, and they were growing closer day by day.

It was her first Thanksgiving event in a long time and his second without his mother. But together, they both enjoyed the occasion thoroughly. He only wished she were able to come over earlier in the day. *Maybe next year I could spend the entire day at her place*, he mused.

The week following Thanksgiving, Caleb felt the upcoming end of the semester pulling at his energies and focus. It wasn't a time for distractions. However, on one early Wednesday morning, he knew from the moment he woke up that he was trying to come down with something. All the telltale signs were there: aches, pains, slightly elevated temperature, and runny nose, all the indicators of one of humanity's worst perpetuators of unhappiness, the common cold. To him, it felt like the plague. Worse yet, he had evening plans with Katrina to attend a new exhibit at a local art museum.

He'd been looking forward to the event for a few days. Of course, it seemed any excuse to be with her filled him with anticipation. But his plans came to an abrupt halt as he sneezed and reached for the Kleenex. His head was already in the throes of a throbbing headache. "Crap," he muttered miserably.

First, he called the college to leave word with his dean that he was ill. At least he sounded as convincing as he felt. It was his first sick call, so he anticipated no problems at work. He didn't want to give his illness to Katrina and needed to cancel their plans. *Can vampires even get sick?* he wondered for the first time since meeting her. Before making the call, he staggered into the bathroom to dig out the cold medicines. The only package he had was outdated by more than six months, but he thought the medicine should work well enough. Afterwards, he fell back into bed and felt around for the phone, hidden in the bedcovers following his earlier call.

"Katrina?" he asked as soon as the other end of the line picked up.

She listened for a moment and asked, "Caleb? It almost doesn't sound like you. Are you okay?"

He explained about the head cold, and she asked him a series of questions about his symptoms, making him promise to update her on his condition later in the day.

By that afternoon, his presumed head cold had progressed into something more dire. His fever felt worse, though he didn't bother to try to find his thermometer to take his temperature. The aches and pains in his body were stronger, and he felt miserable.

He failed to call Katrina as promised, having lost track of time as he lay in bed trying to rest. His mind fluctuated between dreams and consciousness. He had waking dreams filled with odd, bizarre scenarios and locations, some from his past and others from his present. At one point, he dreamed he was a switchboard operator at the college, and the phones kept ringing. Jolting in bed, he realized he was home and his phones were ringing incessantly.

Caleb finally managed to grab at the home phone tangled in his bed sheets and tried to speak through chattering teeth. He felt like he was freezing, and yet he could tell he was actually sweating.

"H-h-hell-llo?" he stammered.

"Caleb!" Katrina replied urgently. "Thank goodness you answered the phone. I almost called 911! You didn't call all afternoon, and I've been worried sick." She felt trapped and helpless all day while the sunshine held sway over her life. But the sun was nearly set, and she fully intended to go to Caleb's apartment to check on him in person.

"How are you?" she asked with concern. She determined that he sounded worse just by the sound of his raspy breathing and chattering teeth over the phone.

"S-so-sorry," he stuttered pitifully. "I-I l-lost t-track of t-time."

"Oh, Caleb," she cooed soothingly. "I'm coming for you. Try to hold on just a little bit longer, my love."

"N-no. D-don't n-need you s-sick too," he insisted weakly.

"I'm coming," she insisted, and the line went dead.

He barely recalled setting the phone down before he was wrapped in his sheet and comforter, shivering ceaselessly. He felt exhausted mentally and physically, and his mind wandered through a half-conscious state.

Katrina made it to Caleb's in record time, managing to avoid any traffic stops along the way as her Audi sped through the Atlanta city streets and highways. The gate guard at the apartment garage entrance recognized her immediately, and within minutes she was rapidly knocking on his apartment door.

"Caleb! Caleb, can you get to the door?" she called urgently through the locked door.

She reached an immediate decision to have a spare key made to his apartment at the earliest opportunity just as a safety precaution. She considered, of course, that she could easily force the door open in one swift motion. But that held the added difficulty of explaining the forced entry to the building maintenance people. Still, she was prepared for that if he failed to answer in the next few seconds.

She heard a shuffling sound on the other side of the door with her sensitive hearing, followed by the sound of Caleb's pitiful voice, "K-Katrina?"

She sighed with relief and gently coaxed, "It's me, my love. Just unlock the door, okay?"

She thought that she heard him utter the word "contagious" through chattering teeth.

"I can't get sick," she whispered loudly enough for her voice to carry, but not enough for any neighbors to hear. "Caleb Taylor, open this door immediately, or step away from it in two seconds!"

She heard the deadbolt click and didn't bother waiting as she began opening the door firmly, yet cautiously enough not to catch him with the opening sweep. She was unprepared for what she saw when she slipped inside.

He wore sweatpants and a T-shirt, and both were damp with sweat. His features were very pale, and his hair was a tangled mess. She immediately smelled the tell-tale scents of sickness, sweat, and staleness in the air.

Her hands reached out for him as he leaned back against the wall, and she carried him to the sofa where she placed him gingerly in a reclined position.

"Don't worry. I'll take care of everything," she said soothingly, though as much to calm her own anxiety as to comfort him. She felt his forehead, and it was burning to the touch. His fever was dangerously high, and she immediately knew what to do.

She ran a cold bath for him and glanced at the expired date on the box of medicine that he had apparently taken. "Oh, Caleb," she sighed with resignation while shaking her head. *Typical male*, she chided. She had seen the great influenza scourge of the nineteen hundreds and recognized how potentially lethal the 'flu could be. It was easy to see that his body was in the throes of something very dangerous.

She quickly found a gym bag and began stuffing clean undergarments, socks, T-shirts, and more sweatpants inside. She snatched a better-looking pair of his sneakers and some of his toiletries, as well as his hair comb and toothbrush.

After stripping him, she carried him to the bath and placed him in the water. He immediately began thrashing as the cool water penetrated and shocked his skin, but she firmly held him in place. He was gasping and trying to speak but his words were incoherent.

Eventually, she was able to get his body temperature down enough that he was out of immediate danger. He was unconscious, and she took care to ensure he didn't slip into the water.

She picked him up, laid him on top of his bed, and began drying his body with a towel. She slipped some fresh sweatpants and a T-shirt on him, grabbed his house keys and duffle bag, scooped him up in her arms, and proceeded to take him home with her.

Fortunately, she didn't run into any other occupants on her way down to the garage. That would have been a very difficult sight to explain.

She made an expedient stop by a local drug store on the way to her house to grab some flu-friendly foods, as well as some tissues and other items he would need. They proceeded to her estate, and she was relieved at how much more restful he had become since his fever dropped slightly.

The tall, red-haired vampire laid him on her bed in the subterranean room. She settled him beneath the satin sheets, having removed his clothes completely, and kissed him gently on the forehead. Though she was concerned for his welfare and healing, a maternal part of her was pleased that he was there for her to care for. He brought such a peaceful, important dimension to her life, which filled her with indescribable joy.

She quickly located and unpacked some key items from storage in a separate basement, things left over from one of her many past career experiences, in this case a nurse's aide. Carrying the items back to her room, she laid them out on the nightstand next to the bed where he lay resting.

She placed a hand on his forehead to check his temperature. He was still slightly feverish, which only confirmed her decision. She reached over to the nightstand and retrieved a small syringe. After neatly and effortlessly sticking a vein in her left arm, she extracted a small quantity of her blood. She released the blood into a small bottle of saline solution and shook the bottle to mix the contents, which turned to a reddish hue.

She drew a quantity of the liquid back into the syringe and inserted it into one of the veins in Caleb's left arm. Slowly, she emptied the full syringe into his system.

"This is better than any antibiotics, my love," she murmured softly. *If he were impressed by what my saliva could do, he'll be amazed when he experiences my blood.*

The following hours were a two-fold process. First, Caleb's own immune system was bolstered in its mission to fight off the virus by assistance from the antibodies in Katrina's blood cells. Once Caleb's body was mostly rid of the influenza, his own antibodies began attacking the limited quantity of Katrina's cells, which prevented the transformation process from continuing in his system.

Katrina recollected moments of her own transformation and the angst that still rose in her as she realized the choice hadn't been her own. Add to that, she was feeling selfish regarding Caleb. She liked his human blood, craved his human blood. It wasn't as if that were his primary appeal, for she loved him for who he was. But his blood was just pure ambrosia to her.

She lightly caressed his forehead, and he stirred ever so slightly. The next few hours involved the purging process for her blood cells, and he became more agitated and restless, nearly mimicking the symptoms of 'flu. *Even under the best of circumstances, it's a difficult process*, she mused. She moved to the other side of the grand-sized bed and lay down alongside him to watch him rest, allowing her thoughts to roam for what seemed like endless hours.

Sometime in the early hours of the following day, Caleb began to stir. His eyelids fluttered open, and his eyes tried to focus on his surroundings. He was immediately disoriented. A swift intake of breath was all he managed before Katrina was perched on the edge of the bed, gazing down into his eyes.

He was startled for a moment at her sudden appearance, appearing momentarily confused. "Katrina? Where am I?" he asked.

She smiled down at him. "You're home -- at my home, that is."

His body was sore and still somewhat achy, but he felt a world of improvement over his last memory from the fevered, languished experience at his apartment. His pallor was much healthier looking, and he didn't have the same haggard appearance of the night before. He tried to sit up, but her soft hand fell upon his chest and pressed him gently back onto the bed.

"You need to rest," she cautioned him. "You're still not quite back to a healthy state."

He blushed slightly and said, "Um, I kind of need to –"

Her eyes widened, and she offered, "Oh, of course."

"Hey! I'm naked!" he exclaimed as he started to throw off the white satin sheet covering him.

She smiled slyly at him and muttered, "Just how I like you. And the bathroom is to your left."

He blushed furiously, so she turned her head while he pattered across the plush carpet into the nearby bathroom and quietly closed the door.

She went to his gym bag and removed a pair of his underwear, which she left hanging on the door knob to the bathroom. A moment later, the door opened slightly, and the underwear disappeared inside as the door shut again. *Modest*, she considered with amusement.

She moved like a whirlwind as she changed the bed linens to a clean set of dark blue satin sheets. She also replaced the white comforter with a dark blue one.

Minutes later, an only faintly blushing Caleb pattered back to the bed and stopped just short of where Katrina perched in nearly the same spot as before.

"Weren't those white just a minute ago?" he queried with a puzzled frown.

She smirked while holding the sheet aside as he slipped underneath it, and then she rolled the lightweight blue comforter over him. He obliged her with satisfaction, fully appreciative of her efforts to care for him.

"You look much better," she observed with a gentle smile. "You scared me last night."

He smirked back up at her, appreciating her simple beauty as she gazed down upon him. "Thank you. I'm grateful you were there for me when I needed you most."

"You bring out my maternal instincts, it seems," she replied with a warm smile.

The mention of that word wasn't lost on him, and one eyebrow rose curiously. "I thought you said vampires were barren?"

"Vampires are, but I had two children before I became a vampire," she answered simply. It was a somewhat painful memory for her and one she hadn't mentioned to most of her previous partners.

"And perhaps a husband?" he pressed.

She nodded. "It was a long time ago and a topic I'm not quite ready to discuss, if that's okay with you."

He easily detected her reluctance and merely nodded. "I'll be here when you're ready," he offered as he reached out to grasp her right hand in his.

The edges of her mouth upturned slightly. "Thank you."

Something she had said a few moments prior revisited his thoughts, and he frowned slightly. "Wait, my fever broke overnight? That seems awful quick for how I was feeling."

She paused, silently considering how to respond to him. "Your body had a little help."

He gave it some thought and noticed the syringe and reddish fluid on the nearby nightstand. "Is that your..." he ventured carefully.

"Yes," she interrupted gently, "but you shouldn't need any more of it now." She collected the items into her hand so swiftly that he wondered if they were ever there. "There are strong healing properties to my blood that were just what you needed, but not enough to cause more permanent reactions to your system," she explained with a sober tone.

Caleb felt a momentary pang of jealously run through him. If he were a vampire, he wouldn't need to worry about illness, and they would have lifetimes available to spend together. Aside from the whole "banishment from sunlight for the remainder of eternity" issue, the benefits seemed to outweigh the detriments to him.

She watched his eyes and detected the momentary conflict reflected across his facial features. *I better change the subject quickly.* "Are you hungry?" she asked. "You can probably manage some soup and crackers, if you want."

The topic of food hadn't occurred to him until she mentioned it. As if in response, his stomach growled. She rolled her eyes at him and smiled.

"You and your stomach," she teased. "I'll go prepare something for you."

He watched her walk across the large expanse of room and disappear through a door-sized opening at the top of a small series of stairs against the wall.

*You're just full of surprises, aren't you?* he wondered.

He called in sick the following day, but did so grudgingly because the end of the semester was upon him, and it was a really inconvenient time to be ill. But one thing was for certain, he was very appreciative of Katrina's attentions during his recovery.

"And how is my patient feeling?" she asked with a bright smile as she perched on the edge of the bed dressed in pink cotton pajama pants and a fitted pink cami.

Caleb thought that she had the kind of smile men died for. He considered that perhaps some actually had, in fact. "Much better," he replied. "Thanks, Kat."

She frowned. "Did you just call me a cat?"

"What?" he countered with confusion. "No, K-A-T. You know, a nickname."

Her eyes stared directly into the pillow next to his head with a distant expression, as if fixed upon some other time or place.

"I'm sorry," he insisted. "I wasn't trying to be insulting. It was meant as a term of endearment."

Her hand reached out to stroke the side of his face to still his momentary animation. "My husband used to call me Cath," she said softly, almost too softly to be heard.

His mind raced with this tidbit of information. "Was that your real name?" he asked gently as his hand reached up to hold hers. He recalled that the day before she hadn't wanted to discuss her husband, so he had let the topic drop.

Her eyes looked down into his sadly. "We don't talk about our human lives usually. We try to forget what and who we were then."

He hadn't realized the significance of such information.

"It's something very rare and special when we tell someone our human name," she said.

He started to ask her, but realized that she might not want to tell him. *Perhaps I haven't earned that privilege yet.* "I understand," he replied somewhat sullenly and looked away from her to stare at the other side of the room.

She frowned down at him and asked, "You don't feel special?"

"Not so much, I suppose," he replied absently as he stared across the room. "It's okay, really. I realize that I'll have to earn a special place in your life over time."

Her hand gripped his chin and forced him to look back at her. She stared back intently into his pale blue eyes and pressed her face to within a half inch of his. "Don't ever say that again," she ordered sternly.

His eyes widened with surprise.

"My name was Catherine," she stated quietly. "My husband called me Cath."

She kissed him on the forehead and laid her soft face next to his.

"Thank you," he replied softly. "I'm honored to know that."

There was a pause as she held her face next to his, and her lips touched his ear. "And you can call me Kat," she whispered. She found his nickname for her somewhat endearing, despite never having been a fan of nicknames in her past. *At least, since Cath was last used*, she mused darkly.

He turned his lips into her neck and gently kissed her there multiple times. She giggled at the tickling sensation it caused.

"Somebody's feeling better, I see," she remarked slyly as she bent her lips to his.

They kissed lightly for a few moments before she sat up

and stared back down at him.

"By tomorrow you'll be back on your feet and feeling as good as new," she assessed with a grin.

"Then I hope tomorrow never comes," he muttered with sincerity.

He felt as if he could lay there staring up at her beautiful face and mane of long red hair forever.

Caleb was actually feeling better by that same afternoon, and he slipped into a pair of sweatpants and a T-shirt. He realized that he would be back at the college campus early the next day and considered all the preparations for the upcoming finals. Fortunately, his classes were being tended to during his brief absence by his peers, and he was pleased his division dean was such an understanding person when it came to personal illness.

While Katrina did laundry and other activities, Caleb took the time to walk through the house. There were rooms he actually hadn't seen before, and he felt a stroll would do him some good. He smirked, as the term "stroll" was very appropriate. Katrina's house was a sprawling series of rooms along central hallways on both the first and second floors. The notable exception was how her "lair" was laid out as a large single room, much like an open-architecture apartment where the areas were functionally separated without corresponding walls or partitions. He wondered if all vampires preferred that style of layout.

He made his way down the central hallway on the first floor and walked past the theater room, exercise room, and office study until he reached the end of the corridor. He turned and walked into the small library lined with oak bookshelves packed with volumes of books. A medium-sized window with closed wooden blinds and dark curtains separated the two sides of the room opposite the entrance where he stood.

Beneath the window was a finished oak table and reading chair. But the most notable fixture stood in the middle of the finished wood floor. A rectangular display case containing a simple polished sword sat atop a polished rectangular oak table only slightly larger than the display box it held.

The sword was suspended upon a felt-covered set of wooden blocks. The blade appeared to be approximately three feet in length and was made of a steel alloy of some kind. It was edged on both sides and had a small groove running down the flat length of the blade from the simple crossguard to about six inches before the tip. The hilt was of the same steel construction and included a large rounded pommel set at its base. The weapon appeared to be well-maintained and oiled.

"Nice replica," Caleb noted admiringly.

"It's not a replica," Katrina's voice uttered from the doorway, startling him and causing him a small jolt.

He turned to curiously look at her as she walked over to the display case to stand beside him. Her arm absently wrapped around his waist as their attention returned to the sword inside the display case.

"It was my husband's," she noted quietly.

"He was a collector?" he carefully asked, hoping for additional information about her past.

She quietly considered his question and paused as if deciding how to respond further.

"It was his father's, actually," she added.

He looked at her with an intense, sidelong glance. "Your husband carried this sword?" he asked with more emphasis than intended.

"It was usually above the fireplace, actually," she explained. "My husband was a farmer by trade. Most of his days were spent plowing or tending the animals."

"Katrina, would he have used this sword if he were called to duty?" Caleb gently pressed.

She turned to regard him with a somber stare that revealed nothing of the thoughts going through her mind. *Sorry, but you're going to have to work this one out for yourself*, she considered thoughtfully.

"You know, soldiers regularly carry swords in ceremonies,

even today," she muttered before kissing him on the forehead. She removed her arm from around his waist and silently left the room.

He watched her depart and returned his gaze to the sword before him. *Yeah, but this looks nearly medieval,* he soberly considered.

He wished that he had more depth of knowledge in the area of historic weapons. *Could she be from the medieval period? And how unreal would that be?*

Katrina returned to her computer console, concerned over the growing issue of vampires going missing. First, it was Garett in Paris, and then Octavia in Trondheim, and the past week Wallace from Lima, Peru, had disappeared. She communicated daily with Alton regarding the investigation that he was performing, but so far he had no definitive clues or possible explanations. They were equally uncertain as to whether any of the vampires were still alive, though Alton was inclined to think not. The question as to the common thread associating them was still elusive, as well.

Caleb returned to work the following day, borrowing Katrina's car to get home just after dawn in order to change into dress clothes and grab some revised lecture notes. His coworkers were relieved regarding his quick recovery, though his strength was still slow in returning. His dean was particularly happy to see him at such a late stage in the semester. Katrina texted him twice that day to check up on him, and he called her once at midday.

That evening, Katrina came by his apartment following a quick detour to pick up dinner for him. He marveled at how caring and attentive she was with him, and she even departed early so that he could get some additional rest. He didn't want her to go, but was in bed scarcely ten minutes before falling asleep. He was also none the wiser as Katrina watched him for a short time from outside on his fire escape through the sheer curtains of his bedroom to ensure he settled in nicely. *Old habits*, she quietly reflected before stealthily departing to drive home.

As the week of finals finally came to an end, Caleb had a strange visitor to his office Friday afternoon. A tall, dark-haired man appearing to be in his late thirties and wearing a navy blue suit introduced himself as Harry Maddox, personal aide to Ms. Alondra Vargas, the President of Corporate Research Enterprises. The company had recently located in the Atlanta area and was seeking talented people with strong research skills to apply for part-time corporate research projects, which their company performed for client businesses.

According to Maddox, as he spoke with some of the faculty at Robert Fulton Community College, Caleb's name was recommended more than once, so Maddox wanted to make a special effort to reach out to him. Maddox searched for prospective talent at local colleges and universities because professors often had spare time available in their teaching and off-semester schedules to perform the needed research. Also, their professions were geared around the collection and dissemination of information, which made them ideal as part-time contract staff for the company. Caleb was informed that the salaries for such research projects were substantial and worth the time spent on them.

He considered the offer and quickly decided a little extra money would be welcome for gifts during the upcoming holidays. *Besides,* he considered, *there's somebody important in my life now that's worth showering gifts upon.* He agreed to fill out one of their online applications and submit it by the end of the week.

Maddox seemed confident an interview would be forthcoming soon after sending his resume, and he thanked Caleb for his time. Later that day, Caleb was feeling hopeful for a little reprieve from his constant penny-pinching, and it boded well that he might be able to pay for more of the activities in which he and Katrina took part. Despite Katrina's recent assurances that her wealth was more than enough for them both, he still felt self-conscious about the topic.

It was a sunny but chilly afternoon as Caleb drove his car across town to the office complex in Atlanta's business district. He was happy the fall semester was over, and he was dismissed from college-related duties until mid-January. And as promised by Mr. Maddox, Caleb had an interview scheduled less than a week after emailing his resume to CRE. Rather than risk disappointment, he decided not to tell Katrina about the opportunity unless he was actually offered a position.

The building was a four-story, modern-looking structure composed of glass facade housing a variety of commercial offices. He parked in an outdoor visitor's spot and went in through the main building entrance.

The interior lobby of the first floor was professionally decorated and sported some comfortable-looking chairs and office sofas interspersed with small metal-framed glass end tables. In lieu of a receptionist, a large LCD display presented a listing of all the various office names and corresponding room numbers. The business owned and operated by Ms. Alondra Vargas was Corporate Research Enterprises, LLC.

"Room number 404," Caleb muttered as he spotted the office listing.

Inside the elevator, he used the closed shiny doors to double-check his appearance. His conservative black suit and starched white shirt was complemented by a splash of color in his bright red tie. He was trimmed in power colors and exuded confidence from the realization.

He absently wondered how many people would be competing for the position. He exited the elevator into the plain-looking hallway and noted the variety of door plaques as he passed by. Some doors were glass and had the name of the business etched into them, while others were solid wooden doors relying on the small plaques next to them to denote the business name. As one might expect, the more social-oriented businesses used the inviting glass door methods, such as the two doctor's offices and one family planning office.

CRE's door was one of the solid oak wood doors utilizing a plaque. It wasn't surprising, since their business mission was geared around research and likely wasn't intended for the general public. He opened the door to the office and immediately noticed the sweet scent of fresh-cut flowers in the air.

The room was painted in rich earth tones and sported a couple of outdoor, Central America-themed pictures. Two large, wooden lateral filing cabinets were against the wall to the left, and a set of office-styled guest chairs were next to them with a small table between the chairs. One chair was occupied by a blonde woman in her mid-forties wearing a light-colored business suit.

Harry Maddox rose from a desk to the right of the door entrance. Maddox's desk was flanked by smaller filing cabinets and a bookcase filled with binders and reference materials. A telephone, computer, and laser printer were sitting atop the desk, and stacks of folders covered most of the remaining area.

Maddox smiled in a friendly manner and walked around the desk to greet Caleb. "Good afternoon, Mr. Taylor. I'm so glad you agreed to attend the interview with Ms. Vargas."

"Nice to see you again, Mr. Maddox," Caleb replied crisply as they shook hands.

Maddox gestured to the empty seat next to the lady to the left and offered, "Please have a seat. I apologize, but we're running a little behind this afternoon. Ms. Spencer is next, and your interview will follow hers."

"Thank you," Caleb replied and took a seat next to the lady, who smiled pleasantly at him in passing.

He watched Maddox return to his desk and begin preparing printed materials and placing them into a manila folder as he glanced at Caleb and inquired, "Mr. Taylor, we have your online application and references, but is there any additional information you would like to add before the interview today?"

Caleb shook his head and smiled, and the phone on the desk came alive on loud speaker. A female voice with a Hispanic accent announced, "Harry, I'm ready for the next applicant. Please send in Ms. Spencer."

"Yes, ma'am," he replied and nodded to the lady sitting next to Caleb.

As the woman rose from her seat, the door to the inner office opened and someone who Caleb recognized from the college exited from the office. It was Jason Newman, a middle-aged professor of English with whom Caleb had chatted on two or three occasions.

A woman with jet-black hair wearing a dark business suit and conservative high-heeled shoes stood slightly behind the man exiting the room.

"Thank you for coming in today, Mr. Newman," the woman issued in a professional tone. "We'll be in touch if you're selected."

Newman thanked her and nodded to Caleb with a friendly expression as he exited the office.

Ms. Vargas smiled at Caleb in an appraising manner before greeting Ms. Spencer and closing the door behind them.

*Wow, my prospective employer is beautiful*, Caleb reflected. He sighed, glanced over to the desk where Maddox was busily typing away and resigned himself to reading a news magazine on the table next to him.

Within half an hour, the office door opened and Ms. Spencer departed. Caleb rose from his seat and swallowed a little nervously as Ms. Vargas appraised him briefly.

"Caleb Taylor, I believe?" she ventured after considering him for a moment.

*Well, that's a good start, I suppose*, he thought hopefully as he reached out to shake her hand. "Yes, ma'am," he replied politely. "It's a pleasure to meet you."

"Likewise," she responded pleasantly. "Please come in."

The room was moderately sized, though at least twice as large as the reception area out front. The furniture in the room was all matching walnut, with a large executive desk, behind which were twin bookcases flanking a curtained window. Two comfortable-looking reading chairs sat in front, with a small sitting area with a couch and coffee table to the left, and a small conference table with seating for six to the right. The window behind the nearby couch was open, though the tinting subdued the light levels.

Ms. Vargas gestured to one of the elegantly finished leather reading chairs, while she orbited the desk to sit in the high-backed leather chair before Caleb. She touched the tips of her fingers to one another on the desktop while considering him, as if studying him. He swallowed once and smiled back pleasantly.

"Mr. Taylor, thank you for coming in this afternoon," she began. "Please tell me a little about yourself."

He related his experience as a history professor at Robert Fulton Community College and his graduation with a master's degree in history from Georgia State University. He explained his interest in history was both professional and personal. He smartly tied that into the benefits such skills brought to a research position like the one he was applying for.

Ms. Vargas listened with interest, only interrupting once to ask him to describe in further detail his college thesis on the role of women and minorities during the American Civil War. After he finished speaking, Ms. Vargas nodded her head and adopted an introspective expression.

"We're an international group, with research offices located throughout the world. We locate in areas of customer need and relocate where necessary on short notice," she explained. "Please be aware the position is only part-time and temporary, but we're happy to work around your available hours, so long as we receive your research reports back in a timely fashion based upon the communicated deadlines."

Caleb nodded, "Yes, ma'am."

"Our clients are companies preparing for a host of activities, including possible takeovers, market expansion, and reorganizations," she stated. "They appreciate discretion and expediency."

He nodded his head in understanding.

She asked him about his organizational skills, research experience, and a host of other questions about his interest in the position, as well as how much time he would have to devote to performing the research. Finally, she sat back in her chair and smiled at him. It wasn't unnerving, but more in the manner of being appreciative. "Mr. Taylor," she began.

"Please, call me Caleb," he offered.

She appeared to be momentarily caught off-guard, but quickly recovered. The corner of one side of her mouth upturned slightly. "I must confess, Caleb, as I performed some research on your background prior to your interview today, I wasn't precisely sure what to expect," she offered candidly.

His eyes widened slightly, but he remained silent for the moment.

"However, I'm intrigued," she noted appraisingly.

He smiled in a hopeful manner.

"Having heard my expectations and a little more about the nature of the position, are you still interested?" she asked.

He nodded. "Yes, Ms. Vargas. I'm very interested."

She smiled in a satisfied manner and rose from her chair. "Congratulations, Caleb. You're hired," she offered while reaching out to shake his hand.

He smiled brightly and shook her hand. "Thank you, Ms. Vargas," he offered sincerely. "I won't let you down."

She smirked and replied, "Somehow, Caleb, I don't think you will."

As she moved to guide him back to the closed office door, Caleb turned to her and noted the curious rise of her eyebrow in response.

"One question," he ventured. "When do I start?"

"How about tonight?" she asked.

He was caught off guard, and his eyes reflected surprise. "Tonight?"

"Certainly. We can discuss the research in question over dinner tonight. You can even claim the time on your timesheet as a required business meeting," she offered with a confident smile. "Let's say eight o'clock at Tomasso's Peak?"

He smiled nervously, realizing it was one of the city's more elegant and exclusive restaurants. He was also suspicious of such an invitation over merely a part-time research position.

"Is everything okay, Caleb?" she inquired carefully.

"Well, yes. I mean, I'm flattered," he began uncomfortably. "It's just very unexpected, and I'm only a part-time employee."

She barely seemed to contain her amusement. "I appreciate the contributions of all of our staff, no matter the position. And one hardly requires major occasions to be celebratory, Caleb. Let's just say I have a positive feeling, and high hopes, for how helpful your contribution is going to be to my ventures here."

He frowned slightly but managed an appreciative expression at the same time. "That's very kind, thank you," he replied. *This is very strange.*

Ms. Vargas opened the door and stated emphatically, "It's settled. Eight o'clock, then."

He shook her hand once more, and she looked to Maddox with a bright smile.

"Harry, I'm pleased to say that Mr. Taylor -- Caleb is joining our Atlanta venture," Ms. Vargas announced.

Maddox smiled congenially and reached out to shake Caleb's hand again. "Congratulations, Caleb," he offered. "You just can't know how much we're going to appreciate your assistance here in Atlanta."

Caleb smiled and left the office feeling somewhat relieved and surprised at the same time. *That was the strangest interview I've ever attended,* he thought as he drove away. Halfway home, he changed his mind and decided to go directly to Katrina's to share the good news with her firsthand.

When he arrived at Katrina's estate, he realized that it was one of the few times he had visited her during the daytime. As he stood outside ringing the doorbell, it occurred to him he hadn't called ahead to let her know he was coming.

"Caleb?" came Katrina's voice over the speaker at the front door next to a small video camera.

"Hi, Kat," he greeted into the camera lens with a smile. "I hope you don't mind my coming by unannounced. I've got great news!"

The front door clicked, and her voice replied, "Come in, my love. I'm in the lower level."

"Ah, you're in the 'lair' again," he quipped with a grin as he opened the front door and entered.

The blinds and curtains in the house were shut, but some emanations of sunlight still glowed around the windows. He shut the front door, headed past the stairs leading to the upper level and into a lengthy hallway to his right. He heard the front door lock itself before he turned the corner.

The hidden sliding door to the lower level was open, and he immediately spotted Katrina sitting before her massive computer hutch where multiple computers were set up. He referred to the giant room as her "lair" because it was essentially a small windowless apartment, capable of supporting all primary living functions. He thought of it as a subterranean bunker, of sorts.

She smiled at him as he appeared in the doorway, and he practically glided down the short flight of carpeted steps to the floor level.

She took a moment to admire his sharply dressed appearance and rose to hug him as he approached her. She planted a kiss firmly on his lips once he was in her arms. "Somebody looks very sophisticated," she complimented with a twinkle in her eyes.

"Thank you," he replied, his arms still wrapped around her slim waist. "And this sophisticated gentleman in your arms has excellent news, I might add."

She smiled, appreciating the upbeat tone of his voice surrounding the mysterious news.

"I just landed a potentially lucrative part-time consulting job," he announced proudly. "Best of all, it works around my available hours."

She frowned, suspicious about how good it sounded. "And what's the catch?" she insisted. "You have to leave town? You have to pay some money up front? What?"

He looked slightly taken aback and retorted, "I applied online and just finished my interview across town."

"Okay, you've piqued my curiosity," she admitted as she led him by the hand into a side alcove set into one corner of the room.

Caleb observed that the alcove contained a fully equipped wet bar and a leather couch set before a large-screen TV and multimedia surround sound system. *Impressive*, he admired.

She stripped his suit coat from him, laid it across the back of the couch, and pulled him onto the couch with her. Rolling him onto his back, she lay slightly atop him, staring at him with an amused expression.

"There, you're trapped," she said smugly. "Now tell me what this is all about, because it sounds too good to be true, my love."

He smiled and recounted how he met Harry Maddox and interviewed with Alondra Vargas. He also related what he discovered about Corporate Research Enterprises, LLC.

She seemed intrigued, but frowned slightly when he got to the part about dinner with his new employer that evening.

"That's one of the best restaurants in town, Caleb," she said with a frown. "Just what is she expecting from you in return for dinner?"

His complexion flushed slightly at the thought. "Hopefully, just a 'thank you' for the dinner and the promise of hard work on some research project for her company."

"Is she attractive?" she asked with a raised eyebrow. "Be honest with me. I can read you like a book."

He stared into her eyes and answered sincerely, "Actually, she is a beautiful woman."

"Hm," she replied somewhat evenly. "I want you to come by and tell me everything after dinner. And remember, if I detect anything more than the scent of her on your shoulder from a discreet hug, I'm going to kill her and likely bite you, but without the nice numbing sensation."

His eyes widened slightly, and he swallowed hard.

Her eyes softened, and she smiled slyly. "Got you," she teased.

He exhaled a breath he hadn't realized he was holding and rolled his eyes. "Aw, Kat!" he breathed with exasperation.

"I'm only partially kidding, however," she clarified mildly. "I want you to call me after dinner. I'm curious to hear if there's more to this than meets the eye."

He bent his head up to kiss her quickly on the lips and admonished, "There isn't a woman in the world that's enough to compete with my beautiful vampire."

She kissed him warmly, sensing the actual sincerity in his voice and expression.

"Good boy," she teased him. "I see the potential for continued survival in your future."

He smirked, shook his head at her, and suddenly glanced at his watch. "Ohmygosh," he muttered. "I have just enough time to go home, shower, change clothes, and meet Ms. Vargas at the restaurant."

She let him off the couch with a sigh and managed to get a last quick kiss from him before he raced back up the stairs to leave.

"I'll call after dinner tonight," he promised as he reached the hallway.

"You better!" she yelled back at him as she went to the computer and began pulling up any information she could find related to Corporate Research Enterprises, LLC.

# Chapter 6

&#x25AA;

# The Restaurant

*T*omasso's Peak was located at the top floor of the down-town Atlanta Hilton Hotel. It was a tasteful gathering place for the leaders in business and politics. As the elevator doors opened to the top floor, Caleb's view opened into a grand waiting room that could hold upwards of fifty people. The lighting was subdued and presented an aura of cultured elegance.

He was amidst the movers and shakers of the day, those he had little chance of meeting under everyday circumstances. He felt out of place dressed in his off-the-rack, yet perfectly matching, royal blue Ralph Lauren dress slacks and blazer. It was the second best outfit he owned. After interviewing in his only suit earlier that afternoon, he was too ashamed to wear it again that night for the dinner with Ms. Vargas. He sighed as he made his way to the maitre-d's podium. *I need to purchase another suit*, he realized.

"Good evening. May I help you?" asked a tall, middle-aged man dressed in a traditional black tuxedo with an air of superiority. He was obviously unimpressed with Ralph Lauren.

"Hello, my name is Caleb Taylor, and I'm expected at a table for Mrs. Vargas," Caleb responded politely with a friendly smile.

The man looked down his nose at him and glanced at a small LCD screen set into the facing of the elaborate walnut finished wood podium.

"*Ms.* Vargas' table is expecting you, Mr. Taylor," he said, placing specific emphasis on her title.

Caleb winced inwardly at the oversight and responded, "Thank you." *Great start,* he thought. *I can't even announce myself properly.*

"Ms. Adams will escort you to Ms. Vargas' table," the stuffy gentleman added.

A young woman in black tuxedo slacks and ruffled shirt accented by a simple black bow tie appeared seemingly from nowhere to escort him into the dining room, which was not quite as dimly lit as the entrance, but equally elegant. The rich scents from a host of finely prepared foods permeated the room. Crystal flower vases filled with varieties of freshly cut flowers adorned fine white linen table cloths. The elaborately designed crystal glassware and elegant fine china on each table was impressive. The silverware was the finest he'd seen, and, of course, everyone seated at their tables were dressed very dapperly. It was the second time in less than ten minutes he felt inadequate to his surroundings.

His silent escort led him to nearly the middle of the large dining room where he saw Alondra sitting patiently in an elegant red silk dress. Her neck was adorned by an elaborate cascading platinum necklace inlaid with an array of diamonds. Her hair was elegantly raised in a style that must have taken hours to arrange. She looked completely exotic, like someone out of another time and place.

Alondra smiled at him as the escort announced simply, "Ms. Vargas, your guest has arrived," before smiling and smartly departing.

Caleb noted absently that he hadn't even earned the announcement of his name, but he smiled brightly as he greeted his employer, "Ms. Vargas, you look amazing."

*I should've rented a tuxedo,* he silently lamented.

"Please, sit, Caleb," she offered with a flourish of one hand as she held a small menu in the other. "And please call me Alondra."

As he sat, a young waiter appeared to fill one of the crystal glasses at his place setting with water. "May I offer you something more to drink, sir? Perhaps some wine or a cocktail?" asked the waiter politely.

"Iced tea would be fine, thank you," Caleb replied simply before turning his attention back to Alondra. He was once again struck with how beautiful and elegant she appeared. After perusing the options on the menu, he shook his head at all of the tasty selections. He was having a hard time deciding.

Alondra regarded him closely and asked, "May I recommend something?"

He smiled and politely nodded as she gestured by holding her hand up slightly to signal the duty waiter across the room. The man smartly nodded and gestured sharply to the waiter who had served them their drinks earlier.

Caleb sat his menu down onto the table as his cell phone vibrated. He slipped the phone out and glanced at his text message. It was from Katrina.

*Call me. Now.*

"Um, I really need to call my girlfriend," he explained. "Do you mind?"

He started to rise from the table, but Alondra's eyebrows twitched ever so slightly, and she inclined her head and offered, "Of course, but please stay for your call. There's no reason to leave on my account."

He smiled at her and muttered a quick, "Thanks," as he casually scrolled down to Katrina's directory entry.

She picked up after only one ring.

"Caleb?" she asked intently.

"Yep, it's me," he replied. "We're at the restaurant, and I just got your text message."

"I'm concerned, Caleb," Katrina urged.

He heard keys being clicked furiously on a keyboard. *She spends a lot of time on the computer*, he noted absently. "Oh?" he asked. "Um, perhaps we could talk about this later tonight."

"How may I serve you, madam?" the waiter queried Alondra as he appeared beside their table.

"We're ready to order. He will have the Mediterranean

Chicken Pasta," she responded.

"CRE has only been around for a short time as a company," Katrina quietly muttered. Something suddenly triggered in her mind, though subtly, but she couldn't quite place it.

"Oh, and please add some garlic-sesame bread for him as well," Alondra added.

"And yet they're international already," Katrina muttered absently, and her typing fell silent. She frowned while listening to the background noise at Caleb's end.

"And for you, madam?" the waiter inquired.

"I'll have the Mandarin Jade Salad," Alondra replied. "But please, no dressing."

"Very good, madam," the waiter replied.

"Hello?" Caleb asked as the silence drew out on the other end. *Maybe the connection dropped.*

"And an appropriate vintage of your best wine, please. I'm feeling particularly celebratory tonight," Alondra announced.

Katrina nearly gasped as she realized what was bothering her. It was a voice from her past. "Caleb, listen to me very closely," she stated in a hard, flat voice.

He struggled not to let his surprise show as his eyes darted to Alondra's face. His heart skipped a beat, and his mind was immediately racing. *Why is she sounding so strange all of the sudden?*

Alondra's eyes darted to his face for only a fleeting moment, but he noted it nevertheless.

"Yes, madam. I'll see to it immediately," the waiter replied crisply before departing.

There was prolonged silence on the phone, and Caleb pressed it to his ear so firmly he thought it might meld to his skin.

"I'm going to be very unhappy when we see each other again," Katrina informed him in a level, hard, and lethal voice. Then the line went dead.

Caleb's eyes widened with complete surprise, and Alondra's eyes momentarily narrowed before returning to a more sedate state. *Could she have heard somehow?* he wondered. He swallowed hard as his hand dropped away from his ear, and he almost dropped the phone as he missed the cell phone pouch at his hip trying to put it away. He glanced up at Alondra somewhat tentatively. *Was there the hint of a smile on her lips?*

"Everything okay?" she asked gently, but with an amused smile that didn't match the look in her eyes.

"I-I think my girlfriend is a little upset with me," he replied quietly. His mind raced for answers to numerous questions at once.

"Why? Whatever's happened?" Alondra inquired.

"Well, she's really big on rules," he mused absently with a frown.

"Really?"

"Yes," he stated simply while glancing into her eyes. "But I'm not sure which one applies in this instance."

"Sounds a little harsh, if you ask me," she observed with amusement.

Caleb just sat there with a bewildered look on his face.

"Tell me about her," she pressed. "You haven't mentioned her yet."

"Well, it started with a history class I was teaching," he began and proceeded to relate what he thought were the safe parts of his past with Katrina. He conveyed the benign aspects nearly anyone would talk about when discussing their partners or spouses. Alondra seemed to hang on his every word, which made him feel more comfortable. She smiled mildly at some points and nodded at others, portraying the consummate good listener.

The waiter returned with the garlic-sesame bread and poured the wine for them as Caleb described his teaching position at the college, as well as the way he looked forward to being a researcher for Alondra's company. Still, in the back of his mind he was mulling over Katrina's earlier reaction over the phone.

Alondra took a small sip of her wine as Caleb reached for

additional bread and noted he had consumed half of it.

"Wouldn't you like some?" he asked. He felt guilty for being such a bread hog.

She merely smiled and replied, "No, thank you. I'll wait for my salad."

Something seemed familiar, but he couldn't quite put his finger on it. His thoughts were interrupted by the arrival of their food. His pasta smelled delicious as the plate was placed before him. He glanced over to her salad. While fruity looking, it nonetheless looked rather plain.

She smiled at him and insisted, "Go ahead. Try it."

He smiled back and eagerly sampled his entree. It tasted as amazing as he hoped. He must have been hungry because he suddenly realized he'd taken numerous bites before looking up to reach for some more bread.

"How's your salad?" he politely inquired.

She regarded him with an amused expression. "Actually, I'm more excited about dessert."

His eyes glanced down at her salad. It had barely been touched. He frowned, and the waiter interrupted the silence by suddenly appearing at the table. Alondra looked up with a displeased expression, apparently not welcoming the interruption.

"Ms. Vargas," began the head waiter apologetically. "There's someone waiting at the front desk who seems insistent to see you."

Katrina, wearing a pressed black pantsuit, appeared to stand beside Caleb, and his head whipped to the right to stare up at her with surprise. Her long red hair cascaded around her shoulders like a mantle. But most notably, her face looked particularly displeased, almost stony. Her left hand fell firmly onto his right shoulder and gripped it like a vice. His eyes widened with alarm from the anger her strong grip implied.

"Kat?" he asked dumbfounded.

Alondra's eyes narrowed to slits, and she glared up at Katrina while muttering to the waiter, "That's fine. She won't be any trouble at all."

The head waiter observed the exchange with a note of surprise. "Of course, madam. I'll set another place." He retreated in an almost eager manner.

"Hello...Katrina, isn't it now?" Alondra offered with a narrow-eyed expression. "It's been a long time."

"Not long enough," Katrina muttered through clenched jaws.

Caleb was confused. "You two know each other?"

Katrina growled slightly and ordered, "Later, Caleb."

"Still possessive about your pets, I see," Alondra observed pointedly. "You haven't taken one in for a while, and I'd almost grown tired of waiting...almost."

His eyes shot up to look at Alondra with a startled expression, but her eyes remained focused on Katrina's face. The woman's manner had changed completely from a few minutes ago.

"The last one committed suicide, as I recall," Alondra said absently. "He preferred not to betray you. And something tells me this one has a similar quality about him."

Caleb's eyes widened at Alondra and darted to look at Katrina's face, which displayed a momentary expression of pain before turning stony again.

"So...Alondra, isn't it? You've been doing a lot of international traveling lately," Katrina noted. The explanation for what had happened to other vampires around the globe was suddenly becoming clear to her. Unfortunately, the common thread among all the missing vampires was also clear, and Katrina was part of that commonality.

"Just visiting old friends," Alondra said.

A different waiter appeared with a chair while another held items for a new place setting, but Katrina waved them away with her right hand while ordering, "Take it away. We're not staying."

The waiters exchanged confused glances and withdrew. Nearby patrons observed the exchange with curiosity.

Caleb felt Katrina's grip shift to his upper right arm and barely had time to engage his legs before he was being hauled upwards out of his chair.

"Caleb is tendering his resignation, effective immediately," Katrina stated flatly.

Alondra's eyes were filled with amusement. "Fine, but such a shame." She looked at Caleb with an empty stare and added in the same quiet, flat manner Katrina had used, "Don't worry about your severance. I always square my debts in the end."

A shiver went up Caleb's spine at her threatening tone. Alondra didn't seem to be the same person he had met that afternoon, or this evening, for that matter. His mind was racing, and his pulse quickened noticeably.

"Leave the city tonight," Katrina ordered in a lethal voice. "While you still can."

"Forget about me," Alondra demanded quietly. "Keep an eye on your pet."

The threat was implicit, but Katrina didn't reply. Instead, she turned Caleb around by the upper arm, and they quick-stepped out of the dining room and to the lobby elevator. For the time being, she needed to secure Caleb.

For Caleb, everything was happening too quickly to process. He had no idea what was going on and had never heard Katrina sound so lethal before. His mind swam with chaotic thoughts.

When the elevator doors opened to an empty car, Katrina half-pushed him into the elevator and quickly turned to depress the button before anyone else could enter. She pressed the parking garage button so quickly that all he saw was a blur of movement.

After a moment, he reached up to remove her left hand from his shoulder because the pressure from her grip was becoming uncomfortable. She removed her hand with an irritated expression, but said nothing.

"Kat, what's going on?" he asked as the elevator descended.

"Later," she insisted firmly.

"No, I want to know now!" he demanded, but her eyes flashed bright green as she glared down at him. He jumped slightly and fell silent beside her. His mind was still racing furiously at what had just taken place, and now he felt a little wary of Katrina's mood.

The elevator doors opened to reveal the parking garage. Though it was full of cars, he managed to recall where he had parked. He started to turn left, but she grabbed his right arm, pulling him in the opposite direction.

"Kat, my car's this way," he insisted as he tried pulling from her vice-like grip. He was momentarily pleased nobody else was nearby because he felt embarrassed by the way she was manhandling him.

"Forget it," she replied evenly. "You're riding with me."

"But --" he tried to object, but she jerked his arm while walking away. It seemed like his arm was destined to be elsewhere, so he tagged along with it.

"We'll retrieve your car later," she offered after a lengthy pause.

Within moments, they were standing beside her Audi. She clicked the remote and pulled the passenger door open at nearly the same time with her free hand, while tugging at him and practically pressing him into the passenger seat with the other.

"Buckle up," she ordered before slamming the door shut.

He was stunned as he buckled himself in. She was already in the driver's seat beside him before he had even latched the buckle.

She backed out of her spot and whipped through the parking garage far quicker than seemed safe. They were at the exit booth in what seemed like a blur. Her window was already rolled down to present a larger bill to the attendant than was necessary.

"Keep it," she stated flatly while revving the engine.

"Thanks," the attendant muttered as the gate began to rise. But their car was already pulling away, the top of the car barely missing the bottom edge of the rising wooden gate.

Katrina found an immediate opening in traffic and gunned the motor as they sped forward.

"Kat!" he exclaimed in a worried tone. He had never seen her act in such a reckless manner before. She was normally such a cautious driver.

"Hush, I'm thinking," she insisted without even glancing at him as she weaved in and out of traffic. She swiftly reached over to the radio and initiated a CD selection. "Map of the Problematique," by Muse, began playing loudly. *Hopefully that will distract him from asking too many questions right now*, she thought fleetingly. She was trying to think steps ahead of Alondra Vargas, although she knew her by a more ancient name.

Caleb thought it was simultaneously breathtaking and terrifying watching cars and lights flash by them. He glanced at the speedometer, which reflected nearly twice the legal speed. He was surprised the police hadn't already fallen into a pursuit behind them. Within minutes, they were on the I-20 heading across town.

"Am I going home?" he asked tentatively.

"Briefly," she suggested. "You have to pack."

"For what?" he insisted. "Where are we going?" At least he was finally getting her to talk to him.

"You'll be staying with me for a time," she answered.

"Because of Alondra?" he asked simply.

"Yes."

His mind raced with his adrenaline rush. He paused briefly before asking, "You heard her voice over the cell phone, didn't you?"

"Yes," she replied.

"She's a vampire?"

Katrina didn't answer.

He replayed the interview with Alondra Vargas that afternoon. *She was in an office with the window open to the sunlight streaming in, wasn't she?* He recalled the window was covered with a filter of some kind. *Perhaps an ultraviolet filter?*

His mind quickly reflected on the exchange between Alondra and Katrina. He recalled Alondra's comment regarding anticipating dessert, and a chilling thought ran through his mind.

"She intended to kill me tonight," he ventured as tightness formed in his throat.

"Probably," Katrina replied between clenched teeth as she tightly gripped the steering wheel.

He recalled something Alondra said about one of Katrina's previous mates. "Was she responsible for one of your mate's deaths?" he asked over the loud music.

"Not now, Caleb," she barked harshly.

He flinched as if she had slapped him. "Really, I'm sorry," he muttered somberly, his meaning two-fold. Her right hand reached out and caressed the side of his face as her left hand gripped the steering wheel.

He took a deep, even breath as she reached over and turned up the volume, continuing to blare music as they sped along the highway. Obviously, he was going to have to wait before pressing her for additional information.

Katrina hovered over him like a second shadow in his building's parking garage. Inside his apartment, she seemed very impatient as he shoved a variety of clothes and toiletries into the small suitcase he kept in the coat closet. He added shirts and pants into a hanging garment bag. To him, the whole situation was unfolding in a preposterous manner, but Katrina didn't seem in the mood to entertain any disagreements.

"Kat, how long am I packing for?" he asked. He tried focusing on immediate tasks to avoid dwelling on his growing sense of anxiety. He'd never seen her so agitated and distracted before. And if she were that agitated, then he was scared as hell.

She seemed deep in thought as she stood like a statue in his living room staring at the window leading out to the fire escape. "Just fill your suitcase," she replied absently.

He stared back at her as he tried to make sense of everything. "Look, Kat, I don't appreciate the way you're treating me right now," he insisted irritably.

Her head whipped around to look at him with a piercing stare, and he froze where he stood, transfixed by her predatory gaze. It wasn't a very pleasant visage.

"I'm sorry," she offered in a milder tone of voice as she realized that he was unnerved by her behavior. "I'm merely trying to put a plan together while also making sure I take you somewhere safe until we can sort this out properly. Please, try to trust me, my love."

He sighed. "Okay, I can do that."

"And please, try to pack more quickly," she urged after only a moment's pause.

He nodded while grabbing whatever seemed logical, including his laptop and a couple of books he had purchased recently. He marveled at how hard it was to pack accurately under stress and on a moment's notice.

A few minutes later, Katrina appeared in his bedroom doorway. He stopped and glanced into her green eyes. *At least they aren't glowing at me*, he noted.

"Ready?" she pressed.

He nodded, and she raced in a blur to his bed to grab his suitcase. He gaped at the speed of her movements, but grabbed his laptop case and the hanging garment bag and followed her out the front door. He wondered when he would see his apartment again as he turned the key to lock the deadbolt. He turned around, and she gestured with her head for him to lead the way back down the quiet hallway to the elevator.

The elevator doors opened to reveal Harry Maddox standing inside holding a silenced automatic pistol. Caleb's eyes nearly popped out of his head as Katrina's body thrust past him while pushing him backwards.

Caleb's body impacted the wall with a thud, and the suitcase Katrina was carrying hadn't even hit the floor before she slammed into Maddox like a speeding train, knocking him backwards against the far side of the elevator. Maddox's handgun silently discharged multiple times as the elevator doors slid shut behind them.

"Oh, God!" Caleb exclaimed as he rushed forward to punch frantically at the elevator door button. He felt stunned and watched in horror as the elevator descended despite his efforts. He ran back to his apartment, fumbled frantically with the door lock, and grabbed the metal baseball bat that he kept in the coat closet.

Racing to the stairwell door, he noticed the elevator was returning to his floor. He positioned himself to the side of the elevator doors so he could swing onto the person exiting. He prayed silently it would be Katrina, but was ready in case it wasn't.

"Oh please, Katrina," he muttered as the doors swished open.

He glanced inside to emptiness. The faint scent of gunpowder played in the air. "What the –" he whispered.

The stairwell door behind him burst open, and he whirled in horror to face the sound as he raised the bat overhead to strike.

Katrina towered before him and neatly jerked the bat from his grasp, her eyes blazing green. "Miss me?" she asked with an almost devilish grimace.

He was speechless, but so grateful to see her.

"What is it with you and batting at people?" she demanded.

He nearly fell over with relief and joy as he gasped, "Kat! I thought --"

"I know," she interrupted him as she grasped him by the arm and dragged him back to his open apartment door. The painful realization solidified that if she had moved a second slower, he might be lying dead in the hallway. She tossed the baseball bat into his apartment and closed the door.

"Hey, I might need that," he retorted.

"You won't need it where I'm taking you," she countered darkly.

He didn't care for the way she said that.

"Keys," she insisted. He dutifully handed her his house keys. She hadn't considered grabbing his spare apartment key before leaving her house, being more worried about getting to him in time.

They gathered up his belongings and got back into the elevator just as one of his neighbors peeked out of their front door to see what the commotion was about.

"What happened?" Caleb demanded anxiously once the elevator doors shut.

"That guy," she began.

"Maddox, Harry Maddox," he explained. "He's Alondra's personal aide."

Katrina gritted her teeth and growled, "It figures."

"What did you do --" he began before letting his words trail off.

They exited the elevator into the nearly deserted parking garage and headed to Katrina's car. "He's not going to be a problem anymore. He went dumpster diving," she seethed.

Caleb was taken aback at the level of anger in Katrina's reply as she quickly and effortlessly propelled each piece of his luggage into the back of her car. He almost felt her warm breath on the back of his neck as he opened the passenger door. She hovered over him until he was buckled into the passenger seat, after which she rushed around the car and into the driver's seat with blinding speed.

Moments later, they were accelerating out of the parking garage and onto the city streets. Once on the highway, they headed in the direction of Mableton.

Caleb was either going into shock or starting to feel the adrenaline abate slightly in his system. In fact, he felt an intense weariness spread throughout his body. It was then that his stomach growled with hunger. He realized that he had only managed a few bites of his food and some of the bread before the evening went to hell.

He glanced over to Katrina who merely sighed and demanded, "You're hungry? Now?"

"I'm sorry! It wasn't my idea!" he exclaimed as the stress of the evening began to fray the edges of his nerves. His body was placing metabolic demands upon him that weren't necessarily his invention.

She considered her available options. They were very close to the estate where she could secure Caleb, but she realized there was little if any food in the house. *Yet another variable I'll have to contend with soon*, she realized. The situation was ludicrous, but she was committed to meeting his needs, no matter the circumstance.

She shook her head with frustration as she exited the freeway near her estate. Fortunately, there was a fast food restaurant nearby, and she quickly pulled up to the drive-thru speaker. Turning to stare at him with only a slightly exasperated expression, she gestured silently but sharply with a pointed finger towards the menu sign.

He leaned across her lap to stare at the sign for mere moments before she growled, "Faster, please."

"Double cheeseburger, large fries, and Coke?" he asked tentatively with an upraised eyebrow.

She winced at his horribly unhealthy selection, but he merely shrugged in response. She used her hand to press him back to his side of the car and relayed the order to the disembodied voice at the other end of the speaker. She ordered a Coke for herself as well. After paying and handing the food off to him, she revved the engine and swiftly proceeded down the road to her estate as "Angry Johnny," by Poe, played on the stereo.

Katrina activated the driveway gate before reaching the actual entrance, and she sped up to the garage as Caleb shut his eyes tightly. The door no sooner opened just enough for the car to clear before the vehicle screeched to a halt inside as the door closed behind them. Caleb opened one eye as he heard the driver's side door open. A split second later, his door opened and he handed Katrina's Coke to her. He followed with his own drink and bag of food.

"Inside the house, please," she ushered while leading the way into the sprawling house and deactivating the alarm system.

He entered the large kitchen and laid his food on the nearby counter. He turned to go back out to the car for his luggage when Katrina reappeared carrying all of his items. She sped past him and disappeared somewhere into the house.

He began to make his way through the kitchen to follow her when he heard her shout from somewhere in the house, "Eat your burger!"

Caleb sighed, shrugged out of his sport jacket, and sat down at the counter to eat. His hands didn't manage to stop shaking for some time, and his mind was reeling from everything. Worst of all, he had never seen Katrina so angry and upset before. And despite the fact she was very protective of him, her behavior still unnerved him.

# Chapter 7

⚭

## Trapped in a House

Caleb finished eating in silence while Katrina leaned against the kitchen counter, watching him with a blank expression, as if she were a million miles away. Each felt the quiet oppressively building between them. After throwing his food wrappers in the trash, he puzzled over what to do next. He suddenly felt spent as his earlier adrenaline high faded, and he barely stifled a yawn.

"You're exhausted," she observed in a detached fashion.

He walked over to her and wrapped his arms around her waist, feeling the taut muscles through her blouse as he hugged her. He inclined his head to press his warm lips to her neck, noting her skin felt rock solid as well.

"Thanks for being there for me," he offered genuinely. "Once again."

Katrina deeply breathed in his body's scent, letting the air escape in one long sigh. He smelled tempting to the part of her nature that craved his blood, but she pushed the thought away and returned his embrace in earnest. It was then Caleb felt her body relax somewhat in his arms.

"Tired?" he asked sleepily. It seemed impossible to him that he could feel remotely sleepy after all that had happened. However, he anticipated part of the reason was that he finally felt safe at Katrina's estate with her.

"No, I'm not tired," she replied absently.

"How is that even possible?" he marveled out loud.

"Strong stamina," she commented distractedly. Her

thoughts were focused on Alondra Vargas. The woman was a very old and dangerous vampire and had her sights on Caleb. The notion was entirely unbearable for her. *Just as she must have targeted those other vampires, and their mates,* she mused ominously.

It was obvious to Caleb that he had lost her full attention. He realized she'd surrendered herself once again to more pressing thoughts.

"Sometimes I don't sleep for days," she added with a distant look in her eyes. *Particularly when I'm worried.*

She gently disengaged from his embrace and moved down the short hallway near the kitchen to lock the door leading into the garage. Next, she walked to the security keypad near the kitchen door and entered what seemed like a fifty-digit code. Caleb heard a series of motorized whirring sounds and noticed heavy metal panels sliding downwards from out of the framing of the house on the outside of each of the windows.

"What the --" he muttered in amazement.

"Security panels," she replied. "They'll help keep intruders out. Or at least, give me more time to prepare for them. It keeps sunlight out, too, allows me to roam the house freely in daytime."

"Yeah, do you think?" he retorted at the pronounced understatement. Not only was everyone else held at bay outside, he was shut away inside, locked in a giant, oversized box. *A very regal, comfortable box nonetheless,* he reflected.

She stared at him in an expressionless, penetrating manner. He noticed her gaze and silently stared back. She seemed to come to a decision, and her eyes sparkled with renewed life. She reached out to take his right hand in her own, beckoning him to sit on a nearby kitchen counter stool. Once seated, she stood before him and tried to offer a supportive smile.

"Caleb," she began tentatively. "I realize everything that's happened this evening has occurred very quickly for you. This must be very unsettling. It must seem as though I've turned into a crazy woman and whisked all control from you suddenly."

He responded with a half-smile, but nodded his agreement. She seemed suddenly very assertive and insistent that evening, which was somewhat unnerving.

"I don't have the right to proceed any further until I ask you something," she said. "Do you trust me?"

He silently considered that for a moment and squeezed her hand in his. "Yes, I do," he offered sincerely.

"I'm glad. All I've done so far has simply been to try and protect you, but the final choice has to be yours. Do you approve of my trying to protect you from the dangers Alondra Vargas presents to you?" she asked pointedly. She hoped with all her heart he would say yes.

He considered that at length. It wasn't as if he had any experience with the sort of threats presented by a vampire. Other than hole up in his apartment, he lacked any plan of what to do next. But his apartment didn't seem like the safest place in the world anymore, either. However, he didn't know what to expect from Katrina, who seemed to have become awfully quiet, dark, and dangerous the past couple of hours, almost like another person.

Finally, he ventured, "Am I going to be a prisoner here?"

She smiled thoughtfully at his question, and brought his hand to her lips and kissed his palm reverently. *He looks so innocent, just like the eight-year-old boy from so many years ago.*

"No, love," she reassured him. "You're not my prisoner. I merely need to be the guide for your activities for a time until we're able to stop Vargas. But you may have to show some patience with me and be prepared to relinquish some control in your life for a time. Rest assured, I have your best interests at heart and would never do anything deliberately to harm you. I've had a lot of experience with combat, including against vampires, so I'm prepared to do what's necessary to protect you against a host of potential threats."

"I have to stay here for a time?" he probed. He didn't like the idea of being shut away from the world, if even for sound reasons.

Katrina features turned serious. "Honestly? Probably, at least until I formulate a plan of action and take steps to eliminate threats to you."

He sighed. "And this would begin when?"

"Well, the moment you give me your approval," she explained. "The sooner the better, unfortunately."

He nodded and pondered.

A pang of worry ran through her as she wondered if he were preparing to decline her offer. The thought of relinquishing him to the outside world unprotected broke her heart; his chances of survival would plummet soon afterwards. He already meant so much to her, and she only wanted the opportunity to try to help him.

He stared into her green eyes and glanced down at her soft hands. They appeared so gentle, and yet he recalled how they became the hands of a killer back at the apartment, albeit to defend him. *But then, isn't that what vampires are good at: killing?*

As the silence grew, she repeated, "Caleb, will you let me try to protect you?"

He never broke his stare with her. "Okay."

Katrina raised her eyebrows curiously. "Okay?"

"Please protect me, Kat," he requested. "If you think that's possible."

She smiled and felt a heaviness lift that she hadn't fully realized was hanging over her. She would do her best to help him, even if it meant her own death.

"Please, trust me and try to be patient," she implored. "I know it's a lot to ask under the circumstances."

He nodded and smiled as she craned her neck down slightly and kissed him lightly on the lips.

"We begin," she said. "Why don't you take a shower and try to get some rest?" she suggested. *I'll try my best for you,* she resolved. Her thoughts returned to the actions that she needed to take in the immediate future. She had the feeling it was going to take most of the night just to put together a preliminary plan of action. Alondra Vargas had caught her completely by surprise.

He nodded and turned to leave the kitchen, but realized he wasn't sure what part of the house he was expected to go to. He looked at her with a questioning expression, causing her to break from her self-imposed reverie.

"Oh, sorry," she replied to his unspoken question. "Your things are downstairs in my room, and I didn't cipher lock the door, so you can just walk right in."

He was happy that she still wanted him to sleep with her. She seemed so distant, and it unnerved him almost as much as Alondra had.

"And I can get out also?" he asked gently, not wanting to sound ungrateful for her efforts to protect him.

"You have unfettered access to anywhere inside the house," she replied matter-of-factly.

He nodded, noting "inside the house" with a nod. He hesitated, not sure if he should say more after all that happened.

She raised an eyebrow in silent query.

"I know I'm sort of a shut-in now," he began carefully. "And I realize that you have a lot on your mind, Kat. But I hope you won't shut me out. Okay?"

Katrina nodded slowly before he turned to leave the room. She watched him depart and sat quietly on a stool at the kitchen island counter in the middle of the room. She remained statue-still, thinking about what had happened, analyzing all the variables and processing how she should proceed. Even from where she sat, she could hear his subtle movements deeper in the house. Under different circumstances it might have filled her with happiness, but was instead tempered with concern for his continued safety.

Caleb finished his shower, pulled on some dark sweatpants, and brushed his teeth while reflecting on all that happened that day. His memories quickly returned to the moment when the elevator doors at his apartment building had opened to reveal Harry Maddox standing there with a handgun. It sent a shiver up his spine.

He marveled at how fast Katrina had reacted. She'd been a blur of movement that seemed impossible for any being. He was suddenly very relieved that she was so quick to respond, or he wouldn't be alive.

He turned to leave the bathroom and walked right into Katrina. Her hands immediately grasped his upper arms and stabilized him as he lurched with surprise.

"Jesus, you startled me!" he exclaimed as his heart raced.

"Sorry," she muttered while gazing into his eyes with concern. "How are you doing?"

He was instantly encouraged that she seemed much more like the Katrina he knew and loved, rather than the angry, distracted Katrina from earlier that evening. "Better, thanks to you," he mumbled as he inclined his head to kiss her lips.

She gently kissed him back and wrapped her arms around him, squeezing and pinning his arms to his side. With a sudden exhilarating whirl, he found himself lying on his back on the bed with her next to him.

He kissed her passionately, thankful to have her so close to him and wanting to impart some form of thanks for saving his life. His right hand crept up to massage the back of her scalp gently.

She enjoyed his affections, equally relived that he was alive and well, but concerned for the coming days. The process of formulating a plan of action involved the two beings other than Caleb who she could trust the most. There were genuine logistical issues to confront, as well as a proper plan for securing him in the safest manner possible.

He sensed her distracted mindset, noting her lips stiffened as he kissed her. He stopped kissing her and removed his hand from behind her head to let his arm drop onto the bed beside him. Her eyes darted to his, and she frowned slightly.

"You left me again," he commented wryly.

"Sorry," she muttered. She stretched alongside his body while perching on her left arm to look down onto his face. "Tell to me again about Alondra Vargas," she probed gently. "Both the interview and the dinner."

He sighed and related all that had happened or was discussed. She prompted him occasionally, asking for clarifications, but mostly listened intently as she stared into his eyes, almost as if studying him.

"I didn't break any rules," he said finally. "But you were very angry, and I couldn't figure out what I did wrong."

She frowned and whispered, "I know. You didn't do anything wrong, my love." She took a moment to kiss him affectionately, not wanting him thinking that the situation was his fault. They were both being targeted by a lunatic.

"At the restaurant when you were on the phone with me," Katrina recalled, "it was Alondra's voice in the background I recognized. But I knew I had to guard what I said to you because, as a vampire, she could hear my conversation with you just as easily as I heard hers. I couldn't say anything directly that might have tipped her off, or who knows what she might have done in desperation. I tried to hint to you that I'd be upset when I saw you next, but you thought I was angry with you. I'm sorry about that."

He smiled supportively. "I understand that now. Thanks."

She was inwardly pleased that he was so forgiving. It was another aspect of his kind nature that she loved so much.

"So, just who is this woman?" he insisted.

Katrina sighed and stared across the room with a distant expression. "The woman who calls herself Alondra Vargas is actually known to my kind as Chimalma. It's Aztec and means 'shield-bearer.'"

"Aztecs?" he muttered with recognition. His Central American history text described the Aztecs as a warrior people who controlled the area around Mexico until the early 1500s, when the Spanish under the leadership of Hernán Cortés conquered them during explorations of the New World.

He frowned as a realization struck him. "The Aztecs haven't been around since the 1500s," he murmured. "She's over five hundred years old." *The woman looked stunning for five hundred years old.*

Katrina noted his surprised expression and was simultaneously impressed with the depth of his historical knowledge. "My little historian," she noted with a brief smile and a quick kiss to his forehead. "But she's actually closer to six hundred years old. She was turned in the early 1400s."

His eyes widened at the revelation. "But why is she trying to kill me?"

Her expression turned grim again. "You're just an outlet for her revenge against me," she explained. "In fact, I'm just the latest on a list of targets of my kind, apparently."

She surmised that Chimalma must have started with Garett in Paris and moved to Octavia in Trondheim, to Wallace in Lima, and finally to her in Atlanta.

"But why?" he demanded incredulously.

"It's a long story," she said with a sigh.

"Well, are you planning on letting me leave the house anytime soon?" he asked pointedly.

Katrina frowned, and her eyes swiftly darted to glare at him, "No, I most certainly am not."

He sighed. "Thought so. Then I guess I have time."

She rolled her eyes at him and began to recount events from the past. "There was a time in the late 1940s in Central and South America when a battle raged between vampires of two opposing ideologies. A vampire named Quintis began building his own personal Central American empire reflective of the crime syndicates of Sicily and Italy. At first, his endeavors gained him a reputation among nearby governments as a sort of mafia leader. But eventually, he sought to coerce vampires from the area to join him or succumb to his will, including a requirement for tithing to him. To make matters worse, Quintis proposed a plan to turn loyal human commanders into vampires in hopes of creating a vampire-supported leadership structure."

She explained that Chimalma and her vampire consort, a Brazilian named Davi, approached a number of fellow vampires in the region, which included Katrina, to rise against Quintis before further damage could be done.

She continued, "Our efforts served two equally important agendas. First, Quintis' actions were threatening the group of us directly, which none of us would tolerate. Second, it would serve as a message to the rest of the vampire world that overt actions that were in disregard to a path of secrecy would be dealt with."

Caleb found the history that Katrina described both compelling and remarkable. Best of all, she revealed a little more about her past to him.

"Ah, so if that took place in the 1940s and if you were in your late twenties when turned, then I know you were born at least by around 1900," he ventured with a half-grin at the revelation.

"This is hardly the time, Caleb," she admonished with a tight-lipped expression. She hoped he would stay focused on what she was telling him because it would help him to understand why all of what she was doing was necessary. Perhaps he wouldn't feel resentful of his circumstances so much if he understood more clearly.

"Sorry," he murmured.

"Unfortunately," she continued unabated, "while Quintis was ultimately dealt with by a number of us acting as a team, Chimalma's consort, Davi, was killed in the explosion with Quintis. He sacrificed himself because the detonation had to be done manually following a malfunction in the arming and timing mechanism. A number of us were severely injured in the fighting, including Chimalma, and he bought us the time to depart to safety. Davi was a hero that day, and we owe him our lives. The problem is that Chimalma lost a long-time mate, and she eventually held us responsible, blaming each of us for allowing him to die."

Caleb said nothing as the somber nature of the story fully registered.

Katrina got up and went to her computer across the room. She sat down and began typing and clicking on various windows on the desktop in a furious manner. The screen flickered and flashed like a lightning storm from the speed with which she changed screens and selections. She reached over to another smaller computer screen, which looked like it was attached to a laptop, and clicked some options. The lights in the room went out, save for the illumination from the screens before her. "Try to get some sleep," she instructed distractedly as she continued to type.

He sighed and slipped underneath the bed's satin sheets. At first he was too keyed up to rest and kept wondering what she was doing on the computer. But as he lay there, the sound of her clicking and typing eventually lulled him into an exhausted, dreamless sleep.

Caleb awoke with a start, not knowing what time it was. The room was silent, and the glow of the computer monitors was subdued by screensavers. Katrina was nowhere to be seen, but he heard the sound of a shower running in the bathroom off to his left. He illuminated his watch face and noted that it was nearly seven in the morning.

He stretched in bed and was instantly inspired to determine what Katrina was up to on the computer screens. He listened to make sure the shower was still running and gently slid out of bed.

His bare feet were quiet across the thick carpet as he tiptoed over to the computer hutch. He pressed the shift keys on both keyboards and noted the smaller screen session that controlled the house security systems was password locked, but the large flat panel display session to the right went immediately to the Windows desktop.

He looked at the list of minimized applications, recognizing some as being financial, while a couple of Internet brows-

ers had headings related to European travel. He frowned and
started to click on the travel topic browser, but then heard the
shower stop.

He froze and quickly tiptoed back over to the bed to lie
down. Realizing his mistake, he hoped the screensavers would
come back on before Katrina exited the bathroom. He momentarily considered going back to the larger console and forcing
the session into screensaver mode, but the bathroom door quietly opened before he had time.

He closed his eyes and tried to lie quietly on the bed as if
asleep. Yet another mistake. *Katrina's a vampire with excellent
senses. Oh crap*, he cursed silently as his heart began beating
more quickly.

Breathing in, he smelled the sweet fragrance of cherry blossoms, which was her favorite. Following the sound of a quiet
sigh, the bed shifted as if someone were lying down, and he felt
Katrina's warm body press against his.

He dared not open his eyes, despite the fact that he probably wasn't fooling her. He focused on trying to calm himself,
but was having trouble concentrating.

Her warm breath tickled the side of his face as she whispered to him in a steely tone, "What am I going to do with you,
Caleb?"

While partly annoyed, another part of her found his curiosity endearing. Unfortunately, she didn't have the luxury of
encouraging him under the circumstances.

He swallowed hard and his heart raced loudly in his ears.
Keeping his eyes shut, he murmured, "You mean, in a rhetori-
cal way?"

"Open your eyes," she commanded quietly. *You're not fooling anybody*, she thought with amusement at his antics. Still,
she was determined to take a stern approach with him.

He slowly opened his eyes. Her stoic expression spoke volumes. He hated the thought of her being angry with him. "I
just want to know what's going on, okay, Kat?" he replied defensively.

She regarded him with a tight-lipped expression, though she inwardly understood his curiosity.

"I didn't see much," he reassured her. "The windows showed financial information and travel to Europe."

"What online activities did you perform?" she asked pointedly. *Hopefully he didn't try to do anything rash like initiate online communication with anyone*, she appraised. *Chimalma's a shrewd hunter who'll make use of any resources to scope out a target, even online.*

His confused expression showed plainly in the room's dim lighting. "Nothing. I only looked at -- listen, what were you expecting me to do, exactly?" he stammered.

"Good," was her simple reply before disappearing from beside him with a lurch.

He heard clicking sounds, and his gaze darted to the computer hutch where she closed applications and locked the keyboard. She muttered something under her breath about being more careful. Seconds later, she moved in a sudden rapid motion, only to reappear beside him again.

*At least her eyes aren't angrily glowing at me*, he considered.

Katrina gathered him in her arms and pulled him to her, melding her lips onto his and kissing him warmly. He gave up trying to make sense of the exchange a few moments ago and focused on her immediate attentions.

*You dear young man*, she thought. *How I adore you, Caleb.*

He managed to part his lips for an instant to whisper, "I don't understand what's going on, Kat. Help me understand."

She paused, still holding him in her arms, and replied, "I'm taking care of things in my own way, Caleb. Let me do what needs to be done, and try to be patient with me."

Her soft lips found his again, and his mind became pleasantly distracted.

"Why won't you tell me?" he pleaded between another series of kisses.

"Because it would only upset you," she answered before

rolling on top of him and nibbling at the soft skin of his neck.

The blood desire was rising in her quickly as she took in his body's scent, and she both felt and heard the powerful pumping of blood through his veins. She craved the distraction, as well as the opportunity to share herself with him before initiating her plans. She needed to savor the moments with him and didn't want to waste precious time in conflict with him.

"I'm not going to just sit around helplessly while you take care of everything," he objected gently.

"Oh yes, you are," she stated in a tone harboring no further argument. *You agreed to this, remember*, she mused.

"We're partners, Kat," he insisted. "We help each other when times get tough."

Katrina paused, her lips nearly touching the soft skin of his neck. "This is way out of your league, my love. Your expertise is history," she explained softly as her breath almost tickled his neck. "Mine is hunting and killing. Leave this to me."

*And let me return to that tasty neckline of yours*, she added as her feeding urge increased. She returned to nibbling at his neck and kissing his lips. He wanted to argue further, but his mind was effectively distracted by both her body and his own desires. Still, he had no intention of letting the matter drop for long.

He felt a set of razor sharp fangs touch the skin of his neck and froze like a statue.

"I'm partaking unless you say no," she rasped into his neck with hot breath.

She had surprised him, being so forward about taking his blood. But in the span of two heartbeats he knew his answer. "I wouldn't dare," he managed to gasp as he felt the immediate numbing sensation from her tongue against his skin. *I owe her my life. What price then is a little of my blood?*

Later that morning, after they both roused from dozing in each other's arms, Caleb slipped into jeans and a T-shirt and went to the kitchen for something to eat.

Fortunately, Katrina still had leftover food from his recent 'flu recovery. He heated some soup in the microwave, opened a package of crackers, and removed one of the Cokes that Katrina kept stocked in her refrigerator. While making a mental note to ask her about groceries, he wondered if she could hear him from the sub-level room.

"Kat?" he whispered as he pulled the soup bowl from the microwave.

He sat down at the island counter with his cola and crackers. A minute later, he called in a normal tone of voice, "Kat, I need you."

He smiled while stirring the bowl of hot soup. "Not such good hearing after all," he mused quietly.

"Really?" queried her voice at his left ear.

"Crap!" he yelled as he nearly flew from his chair.

"You called?" she asked, completely satisfied at his surprise. *I just love doing that to him.*

His heart raced as he realized how close he'd come to dumping hot soup in his lap. "Jesus, Kat," he muttered as he shook his head, trying to catch his breath.

"So you're passing your time by testing my hearing?" she asked with an amused expression.

He blinked at her with bewilderment. "Just curious."

"Try to remember that vampires have excellent hearing. Your life may depend upon it someday," she admonished mildly.

Suddenly his little boon wasn't so amusing anymore.

"Eat your soup before it gets cold," she suggested as she moved to lean against the counter.

He reseated himself and recalled what he meant to tell her earlier. "Oh, yeah. I noticed we're low on food, human food, that is. I suppose a trip to the grocery store is in order tonight, under your watchful protection, of course."

"Cabin fever already?" she teased. *I suggested this might not be easy.* She smirked, almost impressed with his artful attempt to gain some outdoor freedom even under the current dangerous circumstances. But she had already considered the issue and had a solution well in hand. "No need," she said.

His expression soured.

"I already found a local grocery store service that delivers at night. After you finish your soup, come down to my room, and you can order what you want."

He sighed, aggravated she was so determined to keep him under lock-down conditions. He was used to open windows, open doors, and free passage at a moment's notice. Now he didn't even get the benefit of the sunlight through a window. Night and day were meaningless under his current circumstances. But at least he welcomed some Internet distractions. *Maybe she'll let me surf the Web.*

"Sure," he replied. "Thanks."

She turned as if to leave, but he hastily swallowed his mouthful of soup and waved at her.

"Wait," he urged. "I misplaced my cell phone last night. I had it when we got to the house."

"It's safe," she said dismissively. "You can have it back when this is all over."

He frowned, wondering what his cell phone had to do with anything. But before he could inquire further, she sped down the hall back to her lair. He groaned as he returned to his soup.

A short time later, he sat beside her clicking on the various food items for sale on the grocer website, while she intently observed his selections.

"If you have something else to do, it's perfectly okay with me," he offered.

"Nope, I'm fine. Your product choices are intriguing."

He rolled his eyes and continued shopping. It felt more like she was monitoring his activities.

"Don't forget toiletries," she prompted.

He clicked on a number of relevant items.

After twenty minutes, he finished his selections. He had covered all of his favorite foods, as well as other necessities he'd need for a couple of weeks' stay. He had no idea how long his current isolation might last. The final price of shopping cart selections with the delivery charge was a small fortune, but Katrina seemed unconcerned.

As he clicked the order button, he opened up a new window to do some surfing. However, her hand darted out to cover his on the mouse and locked his hand firmly in place.

"Okay, thanks," she offered. "We're done here now."

He gave her a vexed look, but she merely stared back at him with a polite, resolute expression.

"I'd appreciate some surfing time," he suggested. "It would be a great way to occupy myself, and it'll keep me out of your way."

She merely smiled slyly and politely countered, "Oh, then you'll love my movie collection in the theater room. I have hundreds of titles covering numerous genres. And if nothing strikes your fancy, you can order as many movies as you want via cable. Either way, it's a great way to pass the time and still be out of my way."

He started to click the mouse to open a new window, but her grip tightened around the bones of his knuckles. It was firm, but not enough to cause him pain...yet.

"I'll play nicely if you will, my love," she offered in a friendly voice, though her eyes were steely.

It was the most pleasant-sounding warning he had ever received. He gave her a dirty look as she allowed him to remove his hand from atop the mouse.

"So, what if I decided to retract my agreement to let you protect me?" he asked pointedly.

She paused, letting him stew a moment before replying, "Sorry, but my plan is in action now. I'm afraid you missed your window of opportunity. But trust me, you'll thank me when all this is over, my love."

"I'll be upstairs if you need me," he said flatly as he got up to leave.

She watched him depart with a sigh, knowing full well he was upset. Certainly, what he was going through was difficult. But for the first time since events unfolded, she felt comfortably in control. Unfortunately, she also sensed that he was nearing a boiling point soon, and she wasn't looking forward to the confrontation.

The boiling point came sooner rather than later.

Caleb spent part of the early afternoon loading a computer game on the notebook he had brought from home, but the software wanted to perform a hardware update for his video driver to work correctly. Unfortunately, Katrina locked him out of the wireless Internet access throughout the house. That nixed checking both his personal and work email and killed Internet surfing, as well. So he ultimately turned off his notebook.

Instead, he decided to pass the time playing a game on his cell phone. That is, until he recalled that she had taken his cell phone from him. He growled under his breath and barreled through the house to stand at the top of the stairs leading down into her lair.

"Kat, this is crazy," he complained. "No phone or text messaging, no Internet access, no email, no outdoors access, not even an open window during daytime!"

"It's for your own protection," she countered with an even voice as she typed on her keyboard. *He has no idea what lengths Chimalma will go to in order to get to him*, she considered.

Her patience was running a little thin, but he apparently failed to pick up on that. *Doesn't he realize I have important preparations to make?*

"I just don't understand," he persisted irritably. "I think I have at least some say in this."

Her patience level weakened, and she flew from her computer console in a blur to tower before him at the top of the stairs. She grabbed him by the shoulders and instantly placed her face less than an inch from his. His head darted backwards as if he'd been struck.

"No, you don't have a say," she said in a cold, level voice. "I'm the vampire here, the one with the important skills and experience that are going to keep you alive. That makes me the alpha in this partnership right now, understand?"

"I won't be bullied, Kat," he snapped. "Not by you and not by some rogue maniac vampire."

"I'm not concerned with your male ego, Caleb," she countered heatedly. "I'm worried about saving your life!" *You overly sensitive man*, she fumed silently. *Can't you see I love you and can't have a future with you if you're a corpse!*

He had no response to her outburst. Instead, he merely glowered at her.

She rolled her eyes in disgust. "Listen to me, Caleb. Chimalma's an expert predator and loves to use cruelty and intimidation as part of her arsenal. She'll butcher some innocent person just to send the images via cell phone or email. She'd issue threats to you, some very creative in their imagery, to work you into a scared frenzy. All simply to unnerve you before moving in for the kill. She takes terror to new levels for humans. And she's very good, too good."

His muscles tensed as the chilling nature of her explanation hit home. But another thought at the forefront of his mind bothered him. "Exactly how do you know so much about her techniques, Kat?" he insisted in a rough voice.

Katrina loosened her grip on his shoulders and moved her face away from his slightly. She gazed right past him as her eyes took on a distant stare.

"I've been a violent creature at times, but never like that, Caleb. And fortunately, my last mate was spared such treatment," she continued grimly. "But after Chimalma's mate died, she changed. She became cold and cruel. Her bitterness towards me slowly grew greater over time because she was closer to me than to the others, so I watched much of her cruelty develop firsthand. Before we severed all ties, she left a path of butchery and intimidation in her wake through Central and South America. There were letters, pictures, films, and a sordid host of other horrors with her calling card on them. The authorities thought it was the work of death squads or crime lords, but others of my kind knew the truth, and some of us tried to reason with her. She went after a number of our human associates and their loved ones to send a message that she felt betrayed. Some of my peers and I hunted for her, but she disappeared with no trace.

"We thought she went into the sunlight for a final time to end her pain or simply went underground into isolation. The killings stopped, so those of us searching for her returned to our own lives. That was maybe fifty years ago. A number of weeks ago, some of my peers who participated during that horrible time suddenly and mysteriously disappeared. Then she showed up here in Atlanta to come after you. That's my first contact since she dropped off our radar all those years ago."

He thought that she was recollecting the script of some horror film rather than reality. He was dumbfounded as he stared into her eyes. She slowly pulled him into a firm embrace, which he didn't resist, and held him against her body for a few silent moments.

"When Chimalma suddenly reappeared with you in her sights, almost in her grasp, I had to hide you, Caleb, immediately isolate you from any access to her or the world in general until I have the opportunity to deal with her once and for all," she explained.

"I apologize. I didn't realize any of those things," he whispered as his arms wound loosely around her slim waistline.

They stood silently embracing each other for a time before he let his thoughts turn to an equally dark topic. "How do you fight a vampire, exactly?"

She sensed his heartbeat increase slightly, and her expression grew hard as she considered his uncharacteristic topic of interest. She pulled away from him to look into his eyes, but still encircled him in her arms. "I don't think that's something you need to worry about," she replied carefully. "Leave the vampire fighting to me."

"I think it's good for me to know," he insisted. "Just in case, you understand."

Katrina's expression turned grim, and she released her hold on him. She took him by the hand and half-dragged him out into the hallway. *Fine,* she thought, *you want to see how to fight a vampire? You may reconsider once you see this.*

"Come here," she insisted as she pulled him behind her. She led him through the house to the exercise room. When they entered the large wood-floored room, Katrina rolled a ten-foot-square, heavily padded crash mat to the center of the floor. She removed her sneakers and socks and told him to do the same.

"Come on, Kat," he pleaded with annoyance. "Look, don't beat the crap out of me just because I asked –"

"Shoes!" she ordered again as she moved to stand near the center of the mat she had laid out. *I have no intention of abusing you,* she fumed silently, *much less try to take out my frustrations on you. You're my charge, after all.*

He sighed, slipped off his sneakers and socks, and joined her at the center of the mat. When he was in place, she stood with her feet slightly apart and her arms relaxed to her side and instructed him calmly, "Now, just touch me."

"What do you mean, 'touch'?" he asked warily.

She sighed with exasperation. *I forgot how much patience it takes with new students in the realm of combat techniques.* "Just try to touch me anywhere," she clarified. "Use your finger, a hand, a foot…"

He shrugged and whipped his hand out to swipe at her arm. But she was no longer standing there and instead was just inches out of his reach. He groaned.

"Again," she prompted.

He focused on relaxing his body so that he wasn't tensing. He moved close enough to her to be able to reach her without extending himself. And he repeatedly tried lashing out to his left, his right, straight ahead, and even stomping at her toes or foot with his own. But each and every time, she either moved backwards or to one side.

She remained very calm as he worked himself into a sweat. After nearly ten minutes, he felt like he'd gone through an aerobic workout, while she appeared completely relaxed, almost bored.

"That's all?" she asked incredulously.

He bent over at the waist and grabbed his knees with both hands to stretch his back and catch his breath. "That's ridiculous," he panted with frustration.

"Hm," she replied in a displeased tone. She was hoping to impart firsthand just how fast vampires could move, but it seemed like he wasn't getting the picture.

"You don't have very good long-term memory, Caleb," she admonished. "Remember the night at the park, the attack at the college parking lot, and Maddox in the elevator? Didn't any of those events impact you somehow?"

"Yeah, they scared the hell out of me. So, show me what to do so I'm better at this," he insisted irritably.

She shook her head and growled in frustration. *Patience and practice is what you need*, she thought. "I can't teach you to be faster," she explained. "You have to practice that yourself."

"Fine," he retorted. "You try touching me this time."

She shrugged as he put his arms out to his sides and adopted a balanced stance like he would in baseball, allowing quick movement in either direction. *Just like stealing bases*, he silently affirmed. He nodded and relaxed his muscles to react faster. His eyes concentrated on her center mass so that he might have some warning to telegraph her movements easier.

Katrina whipped her hand outward and gently poked his chest with her fingertip before he could even react.

"Damn!" he cursed. "Try again."

The same scenario repeated itself for many minutes, only she varied the locations of her pokes: once again on his chest, on each of his arms, on his forehead, then tapping the top of his foot, and finally pinching his earlobe.

"Ouch!" he yelped. "No pinching!"

She sneered at him, and he grumbled under his breath. *This is actually kind of fun*, she mused, *I forgot how satisfying teaching can be!*

"What am I doing wrong?" he insisted. He had been pretty fast both in running and reacting in baseball just a couple of years ago in college. And he was still very fit.

But she merely shrugged and replied, "You're too slow." *Don't take it personally*, she reflected. *Not everyone is Bruce Lee.*

A sudden rush of frustration rose in Caleb, and he growled. He lunged out at Katrina to grasp her with both hands. She was slightly surprised, but reacted by pushing her right hand forward towards his chest as she swept his foot with hers. His left hand deftly managed to slap her on the right arm as the flat of her right hand pressed into his chest, forcing him backwards. His knees buckled from underneath him as his body shifted backwards from the force of her hand. With a swift pressure, her hand redirected him onto the crash mat to land flat on his back, knocking the breath out of him.

"*Oof,*" came the rush of air from his lungs as he impacted the mat.

"Temper, Caleb!" she chastised him sharply as she pressed her hand onto his chest to pin him in place.

*Losing control is the fastest way to get hurt*, she considered silently. "Unlike me, another opponent will use the opportunity to hurt or kill you," she warned.

But he was ecstatic and began laughing as he struggled to gather his breath again.

She stared at him with a mix of confusion and irritation.

"I touched you!" he rasped.

She regarded him with a wry expression. "Yeah, a glorious defeat." *Is he crazy?*

Caleb continued to chuckle despite himself. He caught his breath and asked with as much sincerity as he could muster, "Kat, can you please show me how to do that?"

She shook her head, removed her hand from his chest, and muttered, "Oh, brother." *Yep, he's giddy-crazy*, she confirmed.

"Please?" he begged. "Just some things in case I run into angry humans?"

She pursed her lips as she considered his request, conceding it wasn't such a bad idea. "No vampires," she insisted, silently reflecting on how *Buffy the Vampire Slayer* was a good show, but hardly presented the challenges of fighting real vampires.

"Just for humans," he assured her.

She shook her head, sighed, and proceeded to instruct him in basic falling techniques so he wouldn't hurt himself. She covered balance and throw techniques, as well as fundamental punching. They practiced for a couple of hours, and Katrina conceded he was an attentive student.

By the end of the third hour, he was comfortable with some of the most basic moves. Katrina enjoyed the time spent with him, despite the martial nature of their focus. While not encouraging him to turn to violent behaviors, she also didn't like the idea of his being totally defenseless. Most of what she showed him was defensive in nature, anyway.

As for Caleb, he felt empowered to protect himself for the first time in his life. He realized that Katrina was the best body guard he could dream of, but he still felt more independent and self-sufficient knowing some basic moves.

Following a short break, he insisted on demonstrating what he had learned. She only made a couple of small corrections to his techniques and was for the most part quite impressed with his mastery. She explained that it would take hours of practice to become competent, but he was well on his way. In an odd way, she appreciated sharing the experience with him since it was his first exposure to such knowledge. She felt comfortable knowing he was learning from an appropriate source, at any rate.

After practicing his routines twice more with her, he asked, "How long did you train in your fighting skills?"

She considered his query, recalling the years of experiences related to such mastery. "Many years, my love. I lived under the tutelage of a martial arts expert for a time before gaining enough competence and expertise to be lethal. Even then, it was through many more years of practice that I perfected those skills. Plus, I trained with other vampires when possible and adapted new techniques that worked for me. I added firearms training, as well as swordsmanship and fencing."

He regarded her with awe as he considered the experiences she must have had over the years. It also suggested her possible age. Surely she was more than a century old. "You were born in 1856," he guessed.

She frowned at him. "No. Next topic." *Give him credit for trying.*

He sighed with resignation. "How do you hurt a vampire?"

She regarded him with narrowed eyes and a grim expression. After traversing the short span next to him, she pressed the tip of her finger to his forehead. "By using this, Caleb. You can't outrun or outfight us, but you can hope to outthink us."

He frowned with a dejected expression, countering, "I didn't mean you, Kat, never you. Don't include yourself with other vampires like that."

Her expression softened, and she snaked her right arm around his waist as she pulled his body against hers. Her green eyes stared into his as she reassured him, "I know that."

*I adore you, Caleb.* She kissed him lightly on the lips. "Killing a vampire requires that their body experiences extreme damage in a very short period of time," she said. "Much more than you could deliver without assistance, my love."

He considered the grave information carefully and nodded.

"Beheading works fine, of course," she explained. "As does prolonged exposure to sunlight. And there's always abrupt corporeal obliteration, such as a massive explosion or immolation in fire."

He blanched at the grisly nature of what she described to him. He didn't mind watching such violence in horror films because that was just special effects, mere fantasy. But the idea of graphic violence against someone in real life sickened him.

"I know I'm not a pacifist, but I don't know if I could deliberately kill anyone either, Kat," he offered as he kissed her neck and hugged her against him tightly. "At least, I've never tried to kill anyone before."

He appreciated their embrace, loving the feeling of her body against his. He had never felt so closely and intimately bound to someone as he did to Katrina. The experiences they had shared in their short time together were amazing and occasionally terrifying. And the affectionate manner in which she treated him was remarkable. Even her taking of his blood felt intimate, as if he were truly offering something valuable of himself to her.

She held him closely and whispered, "I suspected as much, but there's no shame. You're a gentle spirit, Caleb. It's a blessing, not a curse."

Katrina sighed, equally enjoying their embrace. *Besides, I have enough violence inside for both of us*, she thought grimly.

That night, the groceries delivery arrived. However, Caleb was forced to remain in the kitchen unloading the bags. He made only one attempt to peer around the corner and out the front door, at which time Katrina turned to glare at him with both hands placed firmly on her hips as she guarded the front entry. Scowling, he quickly skulked back into the kitchen to continue unloading groceries.

"...like a drill sergeant," he muttered irritably as he put things into cabinets.

"I heard that!" she snapped from the front area, causing him to wince slightly.

Fortunately, the remainder of the evening was uneventful, and she sat with him on the couch in the living room watching a movie. As if sensing the tension that had formed between them earlier, she snuggled next to him in bed until he fell asleep.

Caleb slept fairly late the next morning and, upon waking, immediately heard Katrina typing on her computer. He glanced over to see her already dressed in blue jeans and a sleeveless tank top. He stretched, yawned, and got up to wish her a good morning.

Though not as distracted as the day before, she still only kissed him cursorily before returning to her Internet activities and messaging. He gave up asking what she was doing and quit trying to read over her shoulder after a few pointed admonishments from her. Instead, he slipped on a pair of jeans and shaved.

As he pulled on a dark T-shirt, a sudden idea occurred to him based upon something she had said earlier about using his head against vampires. Maybe if he could prove his ability to be resourceful, she'd consider how useful he could be to her in whatever plans she devised. He grinned as he ate breakfast and considered the matter further.

After taking his vitamin and iron supplements and washing the dishes, he made his way up to the first guest bedroom at the top of the stairs and moved to stand with the window closely at his back. "Calling all vampires," he announced in a raised voice.

It was only a few seconds before Katrina appeared in the doorway to the room wearing a perplexed expression. She regarded him curiously and asked, "Is something wrong?"

He smiled playfully and mock-complained, "You know, I really didn't approve of that half-kiss this morning."

She smirked and retorted, "Oh really? And what do I get for a do-over?"

He turned his head slightly to expose the soft skin of his neck to her and teased, "Maybe a little nip?"

She immediately crossed the distance between them, wrapping one arm around his waist. She leaned into his body to brush her lips against the exposed side of his neck. *That's my kind of reward*, she relished.

The blinds flew upwards as he jerked on the cord behind him to reveal the glass window and solid metal shutter on the outside of it.

"Could've had some sunlight for you," he teased with a smirk.

She smiled slyly. "Nice try. But that's definitely using your head."

"Caleb Taylor, world famous vampire hunter," he crowed with satisfaction.

"Cute," she replied with a wry smile.

"It's all I had. I left my vampire mace back at my apartment," he replied dryly.

She smiled with sly approval. "Very good. Now you're thinking."

His smirk faded. "Vampire mace?"

She shook her head and explained, "Well, not vampire mace, but mace or pepper spray nonetheless. My kind has very sensitive senses, and mace would provide an abrupt overload to our sense of smell, as well as causing our eyes to tear momentarily. It might not be a very powerful defense, but it could gain you enough time to escape."

"I know it's daytime right now. But maybe tonight we could run out to the sporting goods store for some mace," he offered hopefully.

She saw right through him and countered mildly, "Or we could just get some from out of the storage cabinet in the basement."

"What if yours is too old? It's newer and fresher at the store," he challenged.

"Caleb," she warned him with narrowed eyes.

"Well, crap!" he exclaimed with aggravation.

She considered him with a frown, but her expression grew mischievous again. "We need to work some aggravation out of your system, my love," she suggested and gently kissed him on the lips. Her eyes flashed seductively as she stared at him with slightly upturned edges of her mouth.

He noted her expression and leaned his head to the left, neatly exposing the soft skin of his neck to her. "I apologize, Kat," he offered gently. "How about a small, quick nibble as a peace offering?"

"Now that's what I'm talking about," she whispered as her fangs extended slightly in anticipation, and the strong blood craving surged through her system.

*He deserves a little something special afterwards too*, she considered generously as her tongue found the soft skin of his neck in preparation for her bite. She had to be careful, though. Despite the small amounts of blood she was partaking in, she didn't want to strain his system before he regenerated more blood. She just couldn't resist warm, fresh human blood when offered so freely. The sense of intimacy she shared with him was addictive. *Still, this will have to be my last indulgence for a little while,* she considered as her fangs broke the soft skin of his neck.

# Chapter 8

### ༄

# Visitors

Caleb spent the better part of the next two days trying to occupy his time. He read part of a novel he brought from his apartment. He also camped out in the theater room watching cable television and movies from Kat's expansive DVD collection. Caleb counted no fewer than six hundred films from all different genres and periods dating back to the 1930s. It was definitely an eclectic collection, which generated a pleasant distraction.

Katrina felt much less distracted the past couple of days and wasn't even irritated when he periodically interrupted her at the computer console in her room. They hadn't argued, and she had deliberately been more attentive towards him. She peeked in on him as he watched television in the living room or a movie in the theater room. Once in a while she wandered in to watch him prepare a meal and eat or slumped into a chair near him as he read.

The one thing she didn't do was explain any of her preparations, activities, or possible plans. She remained silent, often going out of her way to change the conversations back to safer topics when he tried to make unwanted inquiries. That infuriated him, but he refrained from debates or disagreements with her.

Katrina insisted that he continue sleeping in the large bed in her sublevel room and usually curled up with him until he drifted off to sleep, though she was rarely beside him when he awoke. He typically found her sitting at the computer console

either typing or switching rapidly between a cascaded series
of individual windows. Other times she stared at the screen
blankly, as if deep in thought or in some kind of trance. On rare
occasions when she spoke on the telephone, she whispered, often leaving the room to continue the conversation elsewhere.
On two occasions, Caleb found her in the study at the far end
of the first floor. He wasn't sure what she was doing, but it involved some paperwork and manila folders. She often shut the
door, leaving only a sliver of light, and he respected her subtle
signal for privacy, even though he peeked in to confirm she was
at her desk.

Of all the challenges facing his unusual circumstances, the
most annoying was losing a visual sense of night or day. His
only determinants of the passage of time was his watch and the
clocks in the house. He discovered that watching the local news
at various times helped deter his sense of detachment from the
world around him. When watching the local weather coverage,
he craved a walk outside to experience the mundane conditions
being described or shown. Granted, he wasn't really missing
much, as Atlanta's mid-December weather was usually sunny
and in the upper forties to mid-fifties.

What impacted him most was that Christmas was less
than three weeks away, and this was the first time in his life
he might miss the holiday season entirely, unless Alondra Vargas -- Chimalma -- was dealt with soon. Given the gravity of
their situation, he was too embarrassed to ask Katrina about
her thoughts on or plans for Christmas. It was to be their first
together. Though the way things were going, it was likely to be
dark, ominous, and foreboding. He wondered what the rogue
vampire had in store for them. It would be horrific if something
happened to Katrina while she was trying to protect him. Anxiety coursed through him as his overactive imagination plagued
him with violent imagery.

*What would I do if something happened to Katrina?* he morosely wondered.

In the short whirlwind of falling in love with Katrina, Caleb had become completely smitten with her presence in his life. Her very existence fascinated him, although her vampire nature sometimes unsettled him. The strength of the attraction that he felt for her frightened him somewhat. She was everything he could hope for in a lover, friend, and companion.

Most recently, he discovered that Katrina had an occasionally short temper coupled with a propensity to be somewhat authoritative towards him. And while those were annoying qualities, she seemed to have his best interests at heart so far. Despite that, he knew that he loved her. He owed his life to her a number of times over already. *Who else can I say that about in my lifetime?*

He mused over those thoughts while leaning against one of the large, spiral-fashioned oak columns flanking the entry of the oversized living room at the back of the house. The room was comfortably furnished and sported a large, widescreen television inset into a niche above the fireplace.

For no discernable reason, Caleb glanced to his left towards the partially visible front entry area. Katrina stood at the foot of the stairs leading to the second floor. She leaned against the banister railing, watching him with a penetrating expression. The shaft of light from the front entry room cast a strange glow on her pale complexion. The shadows around her caused his vision nearly to glance over her, if not for her striking long, red hair cascading around her shoulders.

"You look deep in thought," she observed.

*Actually, you look lonely and forlorn, my dear*, she thought. It was painful to be so secretive with him the past few days, but it was better he wasn't involved in her plans to address Chimalma. Likely, he wouldn't approve of her plan or her methods, leaving silence the better part of valor.

He folded his arms across his chest. "How long have you been standing there?"

"A while," she responded casually. "Long enough to see a host of emotions playing across your face." *I want to assuage your negative thoughts and feelings and return to happier times as soon as possible*, she mused as a pang of sorrow swept through her.

He nodded while moving into the living room and taking a seat on the large leather couch. Leaning back into the cushion, he stretched his legs out in front of him, crossing his feet at the ankles. He stared at her, gesturing with his hand for her to join him.

She floated gracefully across the distance, studying him intently as she walked. He said nothing to her, instead watching her graceful transit towards him. He marveled at her body's fluid, rhythmic motion, and wondered why he hadn't paid more attention in the past. Perhaps because he was usually so focused on what they were doing or where they were. *Would anyone who took the time to look at her see her like I do?* he wondered.

She sat down beside him, curling her body alongside him. He draped his right arm lazily across her shoulders as her head rested against the inside of his shoulder.

"What were you thinking about?" she asked softly. *Maybe me*, she mused humorlessly.

"Many things," he replied vaguely. "You seem much more settled the past couple of days."

She smiled slyly and clarified, "You mean, much less angry and irritable."

He smiled at her quick interpretation of his evasive comment. He angled his face to meet hers and quickly kissed her on the lips. "Sorry, but yeah," he confirmed.

"I'm not as angry, it's true," she explained introspectively. "I'm more determined and resigned than angry. And I'm not angry with you, my love." *But let's not dwell on that topic, shall we?* she mused. "Have you eaten yet?"

"Huh? No, not yet," he answered with a glance at his watch. It was nearly 6 pm. The day had passed, and he had barely noticed.

"Come, I'll watch you make something," she offered and rose to help pull him to his feet. "We can chat while you eat."

Actually, the truth was she practically pulled him up from the couch, and he marveled at her controlled use of strength. "Did you ever have trouble adjusting to your increased strength after becoming a vampire?" he asked on their way to the kitchen.

Katrina considered his query with the hint of a smile. She recalled the number of times she had accidentally broken fragile items. She had also injured some men during intense acts of passion, which was a shocking wake-up call that she needed to learn control at an early stage of her vampire nature. "Hm, yes, I did," she replied as he removed a pizza from the freezer.

He set the oven to preheat and went about removing the pizza from its packaging.

"I broke a number of things," she replied with a smirk. "There were a number of accidental injuries inflicted on others, as well."

Caleb retrieved a pizza pan from the cabinet. Oddly, Katrina had a fairly well-stocked set of dishes, cookware, assorted cooking utensils, and basic kitchen appliances. He wondered why she had originally gone to the trouble, but he was grateful for her foresight.

"Over the years, I adjusted to my body's new attributes," she continued. "But it took a great deal of patience and practice."

He sat on a kitchen barstool to wait for the oven to heat. She wandered over to the cabinet, removed a drinking glass, and proceeded to fill it with ice cubes and water from the refrigerator dispenser.

"Now I act and move with precision unless I'm extremely angry," she added as she placed the glass before him on the kitchen countertop.

His eyebrows rose curiously. "Why water?" He preferred colas.

She frowned slightly. Water was important for the health of his body and his blood. "I don't like the amount of cola you've been drinking lately. You've looked a little dehydrated. Do me a favor and try to drink more water in the near future."

"Right you are, Mom," he answered smartly while raising his glass in salute.

She lightly smacked him on the back of his head with the flat of her palm and threatened mildly, "Don't even go there." Her limited experience with motherhood as a human was a topic she avoided almost as an emotional defense mechanism. Perhaps someday she would feel comfortable discussing it with him.

He sipped from his water glass. "So, when angry, you might still lose control of your strength sometimes?" he asked carefully.

Her lips curled into a devilish grin. "I try to show restraint, but you might not want to do anything to make me enraged." She almost felt guilty for taking advantage of his innocent nature to unnerve him, inwardly aware she'd never do anything deliberately to harm him, even if angry. But she had a good poker face. The truth was she loved catching him off-guard like that. She sensed in his reactions that he enjoyed it on occasion as well.

He shivered involuntarily at her sadistic visage, which thankfully was an uncommon facial expression for her. A part of him felt another emotion flash across him. *Is it simply intrigue or perhaps something more erotic?* He gave her a sidelong glance as her features relaxed. The preheat warning went off, and he placed the pizza in the oven.

They talked about how he spent his day and about a film he had watched in the theater room. That led to a discussion about Katrina's favorite films. Not surprisingly, she had a diverse interest in film genres, including foreign films. When asked if the language barrier in foreign films bothered her, she explained that she spoke a number of languages fluently besides English, including French, Italian, German, Spanish, and some forms of Chinese. He was truly impressed by the revelation and realized he felt fortunate just to know some Spanish.

By the end of their conversation, his pizza had finished

baking, and he dished out some slices onto a plate. Despite his offer, Katrina declined a slice.

"There's something I want to chat with you about," she ventured. "You may be interested to know vampires have as diverse a set of personalities as humans. They're often a reflection of their former human selves."

Caleb nodded as he munched on his first slice of pizza.

"But a common variable among vampires is that the older ones tend to have lofty self-images," she continued. "They often see themselves as elevated far above the status of humans and expect both respect and deference from them. Naturally, the world's full of people who feel they're so much better or more worthy of privilege than their fellow humans. It's the same with a number of older vampires."

He frowned, wondering why she chose that topic. He reached for his water glass and realized it was empty.

She picked up his glass and went to the refrigerator to refill it. "I like to associate with vampires who don't have such lofty self-images. But they're still worthy of respect, if only because of the positive, respectful manner in which they conduct themselves among humans."

"Thanks," he muttered as she placed the glass of water before him. He took a sip of water and munched on another slice of pizza while considering what she said. After a few moments, she continued.

"But never forget they're vampires," she warned gently. "They crave blood and see humans as food as much as companions, peers, or fellow beings. And while you may not necessarily need to fear the vampires I associate with, you always need to respect what they are. Never forget that their appreciation for you will never match what I feel for you. Though other vampires could eventually befriend you, always bear in mind I already love you. I'm the mate, and no vampire relationship is stronger. Does that make sense?"

"Kat, why are you telling me this?"

"Because visitors are coming," she offered with a supportive smile.

"Visitors?" he asked intently as he slipped another slice of pizza onto his plate.

Katrina paused. "Some friends, fellow vampires."

His eyes widened slightly at the revelation. "When?"

"They're on their way now," she replied softly. "They'll be here any time."

Caleb's heartbeat quickened, and his appetite suddenly abandoned him. He pushed his plate away and reached for his water glass.

"Go ahead. Finish eating your pizza," she offered supportively.

His eyes flickered to hers. *Oh hell, more vampires*, he lamented.

Around nine o'clock that evening, Caleb was cleaning up the kitchen when he heard the faint ringtone of Katrina's cell phone. As he finished rinsing the remaining dishes, she walked through the kitchen with the phone to her ear.

"I'm going to the garage now," she noted before flipping the phone shut. She stopped by Caleb, neatly using her arm to corral him around the waist, and ushered him to walk before her. "They're here," was all she said as they headed for the small hallway near the garage.

A feeling of nervous anticipation passed through him as she gently urged him further down the hallway to the garage door. She punched in a series of codes on the wall's security panel faster than he could gather the sequence. He heard the garage door opening beyond, and the lock on the small door leading into the garage clicked twice. She opened the door and followed him inside.

A late-model black sedan with tinted glass and a car rental vanity tag on the front bumper pulled into the empty garage bay closest to where Katrina and Caleb were standing. A man appeared to be driving.

Caleb noticed that it was dark outside and felt the cold night air tickle his bare arms and begin to permeate his cotton

T-shirt. It was a very tempting sight being just a few feet away from access to the driveway.

Katrina immediately noticed his body language as he looked outside. "Don't even think about moving," she stated in a flat, commanding voice from behind him as she tapped the garage door button to close the bay door. *If who I think is watching is out there, you need to stay where you are, Caleb*, she thought. But rather than explain herself, she decided her gruff command would have to do. *He probably thinks I'm a real bitch.*

The car's engine shut off, and the driver's side door opened as Caleb gave a heavy sigh. He turned to give her a dirty look over his shoulder as the bay door closed fully.

"Be nice. We have company," she whispered with a brief poke in the small of his back with the tip of her finger.

A dark-haired man over six feet tall who looked to be somewhere in his late thirties to early forties exited the vehicle. He was of solid build and wore dark gray casual slacks and a white, long-sleeved dress shirt. His pale complexion matched Katrina's.

"Katrina!" he exclaimed with a bright smile that displayed his perfect white teeth. He walked around the back of the car to the passenger side.

Katrina moved past Caleb and hugged the man warmly. "It's good to see you, dear friend," she greeted him in a brighter mood than she had displayed recently.

"It's been too long, my dear," he replied in a rich English accent.

Caleb felt an immediate pang of jealousy as he watched the exchange, though he kept his facial expression pleasant and respectful.

The man glanced at Caleb with bright hazel eyes and appeared somewhat amused. He disengaged from the embrace with Katrina and immediately moved past her to reach out his right hand to Caleb.

"Alton, I'm pleased to introduce you to my mate, Caleb," Katrina offered from behind the man with a smile and a gleam in her green eyes.

Caleb took his hand and immediately noticed the man's firm grip. He also carried himself with an air of authority. Caleb momentarily wondered if he were titled or not. "Pleased to meet you, sir," he greeted the man.

"Alton," the fellow offered congenially.

"Sir Alton," Caleb ventured formally.

"Just Alton," the man corrected him in the crisp British accent with a disarming smile. "It's a pleasure to meet you, Caleb. I've looked forward to meeting the man who stole Katrina's heart."

Caleb grinned and glanced at Katrina, who winked at him.

The moment was broken suddenly by a loud banging sound coming from the truck, which startled Caleb enough that his body physically jolted with surprise. His heart skipped a beat, and he stared at the trunk warily. Both Alton and Katrina looked sharply towards the rear of the car, but neither seemed surprised.

"Alton, open this trunk right now!" came a muffled female voice from inside.

Alton moved past Katrina to the rear of the car and activated a button on his key remote, and the trunk lid snapped open. Caleb moved closer to where Katrina stood, keeping well away from the trunk.

A short, blonde-haired woman appearing to be in her mid-twenties gracefully slipped out over the edge of the roomy car trunk and frowned up at Alton sourly. "It's about time, Alton," the young woman snapped. "Next time you can ride back there."

Her face was beautiful, and her hair was straight and trimmed at jaw level in a bob reminding Caleb of a Charleston dancing girl from the 1920s. She was approximately five feet and a half, and her petite body was hugged by a pair of denim blue jeans and a dark, snug Alice Cooper concert T-shirt. Her general appearance was like one of the young college students Caleb taught in his history classes, except for the unusual hair style. But she didn't appear much younger than he was, actually. Following a moment's reconsideration, Caleb noted that her T-shirt seemed out of tempo for her age. Still, he found her to be striking on a number of levels.

The young blonde's bright blue eyes seemed to gleam as her attention was diverted to the sight of Caleb standing awkwardly before her. He was still trying to ascertain why she was in the trunk.

"Hi. Caleb Taylor," he offered a little nervously while extending his hand to shake hers.

"Hi." She returned his handshake and offered an appraising grin. "I'm Paige, Paige Turner."

The pun almost made him chuckle. "Heavy reader, are you?" he quipped with a smirk.

Paige's eyes widened brightly at the reference, and her pearly-white teeth gleamed at him as she grinned broadly. "Oh, I like you already."

Though she was friendly, Caleb was unsettled by the view of her glinting teeth. It made her look almost sinister. In addition, Paige's eyes were a penetrating blue and appeared to target Caleb as she stared at him.

Katrina smiled subtly at the exchange between her friend and her mate. Her eyes darted to Alton speculatively, and she noticed that the corners of his mouth were upturned in a subtle smile. She was pleased everything was off to a good start.

Paige moved quickly to Katrina to embrace her energetically. Katrina smiled brightly as her arms warmly enveloped the shorter woman.

"Missed you," Paige muttered as she popped a kiss on Katrina's cheek. "Been too long, Katrina."

"You too, Paige," Katrina replied warmly with a quick, sisterly peck to Paige's cheek.

A quiet moment passed before Katrina and Paige released from their hug, both still smiling appreciatively. Caleb wondered what the back story was with them.

"Let's get everybody settled inside," Katrina suggested,

breaking the momentary silence as she noted Caleb's reaction.

Caleb moved immediately to the car's open trunk and removed two large leather duffle bags. Alton opened the rear car door and effortlessly pulled out two large black suitcases from inside. He followed Katrina into the house. Caleb shouldered both duffle bags, one over each arm, and headed through the garage.

"Very gentlemanly," Paige observed as she followed Caleb. "But I can carry my own bags, thank you."

Caleb smiled. "I'm happy to oblige."

At the doorway leading into the house, he thought he heard the sound of Paige inhaling deeply from behind his head.

"Hm, nice vintage," she whispered.

A small shiver went up Caleb's spine as Paige playfully giggled.

Caleb took Paige's luggage to one of the guest rooms upstairs. The youthful blonde vampire silently followed Caleb into the room and stared at him intently with a smile on her face as he placed her bags on the bed. Her expression was both appraising and unsettling, and he only briefly made eye contact with her to smile in a welcoming fashion before quickly departing.

"Thank you, Caleb," Paige called in a remarkably upbeat tone of voice that contrasted to her intense gaze.

"You're welcome," he replied before barreling downstairs.

Katrina directed Alton to a guest room next to Paige's, but further away from the stairs. She smirked and shook her head upon hearing Caleb's quickly retreating footsteps down the stairs.

"He doesn't know what to make of Paige," Alton surmised with an amused expression.

"It took me years. How about you?" Katrina countered with an upraised eyebrow.

He chuckled deeply. "She's really quite charming once you get used to her dynamic personality."

"Oh, I can appreciate her fully now," Katrina countered.

"But it wasn't immediate," she recalled with a smile.

"Part of that's because you were always so serious," Alton noted pointedly. "But I sense that Caleb has tempered that somewhat."

Her smile faded slightly as she admitted, "We were doing fabulously, but we've been arguing a little bit since Chimalma made her appearance."

He nodded supportively, but said nothing.

"I mean, I've tried to be especially patient with him," she continued. "I've really been more openly affectionate and understanding than in the past."

"And he makes you happy, I suspect," he suggested. "His personality likely encourages you to feel that way."

She smiled shyly. "Yes, I'm very happy. I haven't felt this in a long time, Alton. I'm in love, after such a long time."

"He's very different from the others," Alton noted. "I could tell that upon first meeting him."

Katrina smiled while reflecting on Caleb's many appreciable attributes. He was very different from the men in her past, except perhaps for one.

"And what's been his reaction to our little plan?" he asked.

She frowned and replied in a cooler tone of voice, "You know there's nothing for him to react to. We're going to do what needs to be done, what we should have done half a century ago."

He raised an eyebrow in surprise. "You mean, you haven't told him anything?"

"He knows what he needs to know," she countered evenly. "Nothing more."

Alton's eyes narrowed suspiciously. "That's a little overprotective, even for you. No wonder you've been arguing more lately."

Katrina scowled. "I tried that with my last mate, and he committed suicide. You know that, Alton, and I'm not making the same mistake twice."

Alton remained silent.

"Caleb's a gentle soul," she explained with some exasperation. "And he's experienced enough violence in his past already. Chimalma's not going to get to him, much less warp his mind and emotions."

Alton sighed softly and raised both eyebrows appraisingly. "I respect that, Katrina. But I recommend caution. Such isolation could breed resentment, as well."

Katrina shook her head in resignation. "I'm trying my best here."

He considered his former pupil and reached out to embrace her, causing Katrina's former irritation levels to subside somewhat. "Come on," he offered. "Let's go chat a little bit with Caleb before the night gets away from us."

After a moment, Katrina pulled away from him with an appreciative smile and turned to lead the way downstairs.

They were no sooner downstairs when Caleb's nervous voice could be heard in the kitchen. Both vampires exchanged curious glances and hastened in that direction. Upon arrival, they saw Caleb backed up against the kitchen counter bar while Paige stood before him with her arms crossed.

"A Coca-Cola?" she asked cynically. "I said thirsty. Hello? I'm a vampire. Maybe the next time you say you're thirsty, I'll bring you a glass of soapy water."

"I'm really sorry," he apologized.

Alton covered his mouth with his hand to hide the smile forming, while Katrina's expression became steely.

"Problem?" Katrina asked pointedly.

"Maybe just a little," Caleb answered nervously. "It seems I'm not quite certain where to find some blood for our guests."

"Oh, I already found some blood, all right," Paige noted with a sly expression as she smiled at him.

"Paige," Katrina chastised her in an ominous tone.

The young vampire adopted a sour expression and looked up at the ceiling with her arms crossed.

"He doesn't know where I keep the blood yet," Katrina informed Paige levelly. "I don't feed in front of him."

Caleb had never observed her while she consumed blood,

except from him, obviously.

Paige's eyes reflected sincere surprise, and her eyes darted to look at Caleb before turning to stare at Katrina with a puzzled look. "You're kidding," she scoffed incredulously. "There was a time when you used to drink before other humans as you drank from the human serving as the donor."

Caleb's eyes darted to stare at Katrina with a degree of silent shock. But his mind began to work over what was just said, and he blinked slowly as his gaze drilled into Katrina's with intensity.

"That's enough, Paige," Alton warned in a harsh voice.

"I bet he feeds in front of you, Katrina," Paige ventured with mild annoyance.

"How many hardy men balked at discovering your true nature?" Katrina demanded.

"None that lived," Paige countered. "However, he already knows you're a vampire."

Caleb turned his level gaze upon Paige as his body's muscles tensed. "I apologize for my ignorance," he stated flatly. "I'm not allowed to offer you my blood, but I'll be happy to retrieve some for you, if Katrina would just point me to the proper location."

Alton's expression reflected momentary surprise, but then he gazed upon Caleb with approval. However, Katrina's face grew concerned as she saw the tense series of emotions playing across her mate's face.

"I'll show them –" Katrina began.

"No," Caleb interrupted coldly. "I want to take care of it."

Katrina said nothing, but reached out for Caleb's hand, which she grasped gently in hers, and led him through the kitchen to a nearby door leading down into her small wine cellar. A long series of descending concrete steps led to a concrete room surrounded by storage shelves, a couple of workbenches, and a portion of the far wall containing a series of wine storage shelves stocked with a variety of bottles of wine. Immediately at the bottom of the stairs and to the right was a medium-sized white refrigerator.

Katrina opened the refrigerator to reveal shelves lined with a large variety of plastic bags of human blood. There were a variety of blood types, and each was labeled in the same manner one would see in a hospital or surgery center. Caleb estimated the combined total of blood would likely constitute a sizable quantity of human bodies.

"Each blood type has a somewhat different flavor to a vampire, but just like wine, each packet of blood may have a unique taste all its own," Katrina explained softly. She glanced at his face to find him just staring and taking the information in.

"Its own vintage," he ventured quietly, recalling the word Paige's earlier comment.

She nodded after a brief pause and agreed, "Yes, something like that."

"Which ones do I take?" he asked.

"Just randomly pick one of each for them," she stated with a sigh. "They'll let you know if they want something specific."

He grabbed two of the chilled pints of blood before pausing to ask, "Do you want one?"

"No," she replied quietly. "Thank you." She shut the refrigerator door, and he turned to walk back upstairs. But she reached out and pulled him into her arms protectively. He seemed so vulnerable to her, just like the little eight-year-old boy she remembered.

"It's okay," he muttered absently. "I'm okay with this." He sounded as if he were trying to convince himself. *Is this like a cow who's been asked to bring a steak to a human?* he wondered.

She shook her head slightly. "It's my fault. Perhaps I've sheltered you too much. But I was afraid."

It dawned on him what she was getting at. "You were afraid I'd be too unsettled by all this?" he asked.

"Yes," she said and kissed the top of his head. "So many new things are coming at you quickly. How much is too much for you?" *I don't want to frighten you away, my love.*

He formulated an answer as she stood with her arms

wrapped securely around him. "You scare me. You all scare me," he replied earnestly. "But I love you, and I'll do what I have to do."

She silently considered him and sighed. She was relieved to hear his resolve. "Then I suppose you can stink up the house with a cooked dead bird or pig at Christmas, if you want," she conceded.

He smiled wanly. "Deal, but it's going to be a big, dead bird this time."

She chuckled and released him from her grasp, and they walked upstairs together.

Paige and Alton sat in chairs in the spacious living room drinking warmed blood from tall glasses while Katrina and Caleb sat together on the couch. Caleb leaned back, stretching his arms across the back cushions as Katrina curled up next to him. She wrapped one arm behind him while the other lazily draped across his waist.

"Alton's my oldest friend," Katrina began. "He was also an important mentor in my life. He helped me better understand and adapt to my vampire nature after being abandoned by the one who turned me. Alton shaped my understanding of financial matters and expanded my fighting skills. I'm forever indebted to him."

Alton nodded his head appreciatively, but corrected her with a smirk, "Hardly. Forever is too long. Perhaps for another century or two."

Paige and Katrina both grinned.

"Well, I could never abandon you, Kat," Caleb proclaimed, cognizant of how strongly he was drawn to her.

She smiled and warmly kissed him on the cheek. *I hope not. It's more than I could bear.*

"It happens from time to time," Alton noted absently before sipping blood from his crystal glass.

Caleb was hungry for more details, hoping to understand Katrina and her background better, but she seemed satisfied to quit the topic. Alton seemed to notice as well, because he subtly raised a curious eyebrow.

"As for Paige," Katrina explained with a smirk. "She happened into my life purely by accident. I helped to mentor her in her vampire nature at an important time in her life. My experience with Alton came in quite handy, it seems. Paige and I became quite close friends, almost like sisters, and we've remained close ever since."

Paige smiled with satisfaction.

The conversation turned to the journey to reach Katrina's estate for each of the visiting vampires. Alton came directly from his investigations in Europe once he learned Chimalma had surfaced in Atlanta. Paige was in Los Angeles and made the journey once Katrina decided how to proceed.

"I'm surprised really," Paige admitted with an amused glance at Caleb. "He hasn't even asked about my arrival in the trunk."

Caleb regarded the vampire briefly and turned to look at Alton.

"Katrina's idea, really," Alton said to Caleb, noting pointedly: "She does everything for a reason."

Caleb's mind began considering all that happened in the garage that evening. Two things stood out. "You were trying to hide her," he ventured. "Nobody would see her, only Alton."

Katrina smiled as she listened to Caleb's assessment.

"Way to go, Sherlock," Paige complimented with a smirk.

But Caleb frowned and continued, "Wait. She also let me go into the garage with the door open when you arrived. Yet she hasn't even allowed me to open a window."

Alton raised an eyebrow, while Katrina's expression turned introspective.

"So?" Paige countered.

Caleb looked at the youthful vampire. "So, she does everything for a reason, just as Alton said, which means she wanted someone to see me in the garage with her. And that's why she was so irritable when she saw me considering a short walk out to the driveway. I was only to be seen briefly and with a minimum of exposure. So Katrina thinks someone's probably watching the house."

"Most likely," Alton offered.

"Katrina wants our numbers to be underestimated so we have a stronger balance of power," Caleb ventured with a small grin. "Or so she can act with Paige and hold an element of surprise."

Katrina smiled and muttered, "Well done." She was very impressed with Caleb's deductive reasoning skills, particularly why she was stern with him in the garage. *Perhaps I underestimate him at times*, she considered thoughtfully.

Paige's expression brightened for the first time since meeting Caleb in the garage. "Katrina said you're pretty intelligent."

Caleb inclined his head in silent appreciation.

"And," Paige hesitated, "though I don't know why I'm bothering, I suppose I should apologize for the whole blood episode in the kitchen. I obviously didn't fully realize the situation with you two."

The edges of Caleb's mouth upturned slightly. "Apology accepted."

Katrina inclined her face up to Caleb's neck and placed a delicate kiss upon his soft skin. She was very proud of him. His first exposure to other vampires wasn't entirely without issues, but things were working out nicely.

Alton noted Katrina's action with approval, while Paige grinned mischievously.

"Congratulations, Caleb," Paige offered in a perky tone. "You've made the feral tiger purr."

Caleb blushed, while Katrina glared at Paige with a withering expression. *That was in the past. I'm trying to change into something less feral lately*, she resolved. *But it's hard for me after so long.* She quickly changed the subject.

"It's getting late, and I think Caleb and I will turn in," Katrina suggested. "Please make yourselves comfortable, and let me know if you need anything. And help yourself to the blood supply. Otherwise, I'll rise early, and we can discuss plans and arrangements."

Alton offered, "Good evening to you both."

Paige nodded with a smirk.

Katrina rose and took Caleb by the hand to lead him from the room to the sublevel and manually shut the hidden door sealing off the room from the rest of the house.

Once they were close to the bed, she pulled him onto it, kissing him warmly on the lips. He appreciated her display of affection, but his mind still yearned for more information about her after having been baited earlier.

"Why won't you tell me more about yourself?" he urged between kisses. "I'm dying to know all about you and your past."

*I love you, and I'm building my trust with you, but please be patient with me*, she wanted to tell him. *I've already been hurt and betrayed by too many in my lifetime.* But something vulnerable kept her from revealing even those thoughts to him at the moment. Instead, she smiled slyly and muttered, "In time, my love. A girl can't give all of her secrets away at once."

*Hardly a girl, but a powerful feminine force of nature*, he silently countered. He sighed with resignation that more of her background wasn't forthcoming that night, although she effectively distracted him again with additional slow kisses.

"I'm proud of you tonight, my love," she complimented.

"Well, I'm trying," he replied sincerely.

"Better yet," she noted presciently and with a satisfied smile. "You're succeeding."

The next morning, Katrina rose well before Caleb woke. She showered, dressed in jeans and a black sweater, and quietly left him sealed in the room by himself as she met with Alton and Paige concerning their final plans.

Later that morning when Caleb finally stirred, he noticed with a start that Katrina was gone. He yawned and looked over to find a glass of ice water on the nightstand, along with a note from Katrina.

*Dearest Caleb,*

*I didn't want you to be disturbed while you
slept. I'll be back to check on you before breakfast. Please drink the glass of water. Remember
what I said about hydration.*

*Love,*

*Kat*

He sighed with resignation, put the note back on the nightstand, and drank the glass of water, leaving only the unmelted
ice. He immediately realized his thirst once the first gulp of
water had gone down his throat.

He stretched and went into the nearby bathroom to shower,
shave, and brush his teeth. Afterwards, he slipped on a pair of
jeans and a Georgia State sweatshirt. Forgoing shoes, he padded up the stairs to the sealed exit door leading into the rest of
the house. He was unable to slide the door open and looked at
the keypad next to the door frame to see a red LED marking
the door as locked.

"Oh, for Pete's sake," he mumbled, realizing that he couldn't
even use a phone to call her for help because the phones were
disabled by a code. And Katrina still had possession of his cell
phone.

He irritably smacked the door with the flat of his palm
and proceeded down the stairs over to the couch set before the
large, wall-mounted TV. He plopped down to contemplate how
frustrated he was getting with the whole security arrangement
he had endured lately. He felt a little like a prisoner in a gild-
ed cage. Finally, he lay on the couch and channel-surfed for a
time.

Within an hour, he heard the door at the top of the stairs
behind him slide open, but nothing more. He frowned and sat
up on his knees to look over the high back of the couch. Seeing
nobody, he tilted his head slightly.

Strong arms enveloped him from behind, and he jolted
with surprise. The arms quickly tightened around him and he
saw the profile of Katrina's face peer around from his right. He
turned his face to hers, and she kissed him warmly.

"Good morning," she greeted in a slow, sweet voice. "Sorry it took so long, my love."

"Good morning," he replied as his irritation subsided from the warm greeting she gave him.

She effortlessly pulled him from the couch and onto the floor so that he stood before her, and he turned towards her and kissed her again.

"Did you have to lock the door?" he asked suspiciously.

"I didn't want you to be disturbed," she said smoothly.

He narrowed his eyes, not believing a word of it. "Why won't you just tell me what you're doing?" he murmured with exasperation.

She regarded him sympathetically before her smile faded somewhat. "I was merely trying to be nice, but fine. We were discussing some important matters that I didn't want you overhearing or getting involved in. Does that make you feel better?"

He considered her explanation and conceded, "No, not better. But at least it's an honest answer."

She nodded, and asked, "Are you angry with me?" *Please don't be mad. I'm really not trying to aggravate you*, she considered silently.

He folded his arms before his chest. "I'm not angry, just a little disappointed, that's all."

"We talked about this once before, Caleb," she gently tried to remind him. *I understand how hard it is to give up control, but you have to trust me.* She felt a small degree of guilt as she realized that trust was hard for her as well.

He recalled the conversation, or rather confrontation, Katrina referenced all too well, having been on the losing end of it. "I know, I know," he retorted offhandedly while walking past her to go upstairs to get breakfast. "Alpha vampire running the show right now. Got it."

She smirked as she watched him depart. *Well, at least he's learning.*

He walked into the kitchen and noticed Paige standing at the kitchen counter making a cold cut sandwich. It appeared a very normal-looking scene as she stood in her khaki capris, floral cotton shirt, and sandals and cut the sandwich in half. The fact that she had seemed to be an edgy vampire the night before suddenly seemed odd to him.

Paige pulled a handful of potato chips from a foil bag and casually dropped them onto the plate, which she set on the counter near him. She licked the stray salt from her fingers as she walked to the refrigerator and filled a glass with ice water.

She sat the glass near the plate of food and offered with a sly smile, "Morning, kiddo. It's close enough to lunchtime, and since I don't cook, I hope you won't mind the sandwich."

He stared at her with near shock at the completely unexpected circumstances. She seemed to appreciate the expression on his face because her smile brightened noticeably.

"Well, dig in," she suggested.

He raised an eyebrow as he sat on a barstool at the counter. "Thanks, but to what do I owe this particular honor?"

She smirked with genuine amusement. "Peace offering. Besides, Katrina said you'd probably be hungry because she left you for longer than she intended. It was her idea, really."

His eyebrow rose curiously.

"Honestly, I think she's just trying to kick-start things with us a little bit," she added with a conspiratorial whisper.

"Nice start," he replied with a smirk. He picked up the ham and cheese sandwich and took a bite, noting that it had his favorite garnish, mustard, on it. After realizing how hungry he really was, he began alternating between bites of sandwich and potato chips. He was particularly aware that the short, blonde-haired vampire seemed amused watching him.

"Wow, you can really put it away, can't you?" she noted with a grin.

His face flushed a little as warmth rose to his cheeks while he chewed. That seemed to amuse her even further. He decided to break his silence by asking how she liked Los Angeles. He had never visited the west coast himself.

"I like the people well enough," she answered fondly. "It's a place where both the strange and unusual can feel at home. I fit right in! Way too much sunshine out there, though."

He almost chuckled, but was politely mindful of the mouthful of sandwich that he was chewing at the time.

She described the wonderful scenery and plethora of diversions that she enjoyed in southern California, including rock concerts, parties, clubs, shopping, and a host of other activities that he hadn't considered, such as motorcycle rallies and nighttime surfing parties.

As he finished eating his sandwich and chips, Alton cleared his throat from the kitchen entrance behind him. The sound warned Caleb of his presence without startling him, which he appreciatively noted as he glanced over his shoulder.

"Oh, hi, Alton," Caleb greeted as he reached for his water glass.

The tall vampire moved to sit on a stool next to him and asked, "Would you mind if we had a brief chat?"

Caleb shrugged and took a final bite of his sandwich. He was beginning to like the stately vampire. Alton sounded like a member of the English gentry, those aristocratic gentlemen of property from Jane Austen novels, but without the characteristic air of superiority. He fleetingly anticipated that his English accent was likely popular with the ladies. "Sure," he agreed amiably.

Paige nodded to Alton and moved to depart.

"Thanks for lunch, Paige," Caleb said.

"Aw, you're welcome," she replied with a smile before disappearing from sight.

Caleb was happy for his pleasant reintroduction to Paige. He liked the version that he had started getting to know that morning.

Alton silently paused for a few moments to observe the young man. "So, Katrina told me about your brief experiences with Chimalma, but I'd like to hear your recollections firsthand. It may provide helpful insights that may have been overlooked initially."

Caleb nodded and recounted his experiences, including any dialogue with Alondra and Maddox, to the best of his ability. The process took a little longer because Alton interjected occasionally to ask for clarifications and further details. Caleb noted once again how politely and congenially Alton presented himself. When he had finished, Alton sat silently for a few minutes in contemplation. But Caleb had a question of his own to ask.

"I'm a little curious about when Alondra, um, Chimalma mentioned that Katrina was possessive in her past," he ventured carefully.

Alton murmured, "Mm, yes. Well, vampires are possessive at times with their mates, particularly the human ones."

Caleb nodded.

Alton stared at him intently. "But don't confuse possessive with protective, Caleb. Katrina cares for you more than you likely realize. And as a human, you're particularly vulnerable if another vampire wanted to target you."

A thought occurred to him as the restaurant conversation between Katrina and Chimalma replayed in his mind. "I told Chimalma about how much Katrina meant to me before she arrived to retrieve me," he absently recalled. "Then Chimalma told her to 'keep an eye on her pet.'"

Alton nodded. "She was deliberately pushing Katrina's buttons," he ventured. "The more Katrina has to focus on protecting you, the less she can focus on Chimalma directly. It's good that Paige and I arrived when we did."

Katrina and Paige silently appeared in the kitchen entryway from the main hallway, though Caleb realized that he probably wouldn't have noticed if he hadn't already been facing in their direction.

"I'm glad you're here to help protect Katrina in all of this," he commented to Alton with a note of appreciation as he caught Katrina's eyes.

But Alton's features reflected amusement, and he actually chuckled. Paige also smiled slightly, while Katrina arched an eyebrow at her former mentor. Caleb looked at Alton with a puzzled expression.

"My dear boy," Alton corrected him, "I'm not here to protect *her*. She's more than capable of protecting herself. She's the heavy artillery in this mission. I'm merely accompanying to aid in directing the hunt, as well as to provide assistance where needed."

Caleb turned to stare at Katrina and demanded, "What's he talking about?"

But Alton spoke up before she could respond. "Your mate happens to be one of the most lethal vampires I've ever known. She's earned quite a remarkable reputation among our kind, actually."

Katrina frowned. She was uncomfortable discussing the levels of violence that she was capable of. She didn't want Caleb to be afraid of her, either. *What can I say?* she wondered.

Caleb's eyes widened as his gaze shot back to Alton, and he recalled, "But you're her mentor. Katrina said that you taught her how to fight. And you just said that you and Paige arrived at just the right time."

One of Alton's eyebrows arched as he explained, "You misunderstand, Caleb. I was her mentor in showing her the safest practices of a vampire, and I helped shape her mastery of financial matters. But I only taught her the art of sword fighting to broaden her skill set. She was an expert in her own right in other forms of melee combat when I first met her. She's an efficient killing machine, even for a vampire. And as for arriving on time, I merely meant that Chimalma's trail will be easier to follow since her appearance was so recent."

Caleb wasn't sure how to react to Alton's revelations.

"What we plan to do is find Chimalma and bring an end to her rampage," Alton continued.

"You're going hunting," Caleb ventured with chilling insight.

"A predator seeking a predator," Alton ventured as he glanced at Katrina. "And the fiercest one I know is your mate.

Having seen her firsthand with Maddox, you should realize just how deadly she really is."

Caleb shivered slightly while looking at Katrina, and his heart rate increased noticeably.

"Alton," Katrina sharply interrupted. "That's enough." *Damn it, you're scaring him,* she tried to convey with a steely expression at her former mentor.

*My God,* Caleb thought as the recent steak house conversation with Katrina resurfaced in his mind. *She really is a great white shark among sharks then.* He thought that she had been exaggerating when she made that comment, or was simply analogizing the dangerous nature of vampires.

Katrina was concerned as she took in his expression.

All three vampires in the room stared at him, having heard the noticeable increase in his heart rate. He swallowed once and decided to leave the room rather than be the center of such rapt attention. He slid off the stool and started to walk into the hallway leading to other parts of the house. But as he began to pass Katrina, she extended one arm and caught him at the waist, leaving her arm in place as a bar rather than drawing him to her.

"Remember what I said about fear, Caleb," she muttered very softly as her green eyes gazed into his pale blue ones.

"A little fear is good," he replied, having recalled their past conversation at the steak house.

"But not from me," she amended, "or this won't work between us."

As a matter of fact, he did recall that point having been made.

"Come here," she whispered, "but not in fear." She removed her arm from barring his passage, dropping it to her side.

He paused before slowly moving to wrap his arms around her slim waist. He felt her arms gently enfold him in response, and she bent her head downwards to nestle her nose into the side of his warm neck.

*Thank you, my love,* she thought with relief.

His eyes scanned the room to look at Alton and Paige, but they had already quietly disappeared from view.

Katrina breathed in his scent, heard his heartbeat, and felt his pulse against her soft lips. She kissed him softly once, twice, a third time.

He considered her affectionate nature, coupled with her propensity to be somewhat authoritative recently. He also recalled the light-hearted times they had shared together with both of them laughing and appreciating each other's company. His memory went back to the night at the restaurant with Chimalma and the attack from Harry Maddox. There were so many dichotomies in Katrina's personality. The distance between her caring nature and her violent nature seemed threadbare at times. But he loved her nevertheless and was beginning to realize just how much she loved him as well.

The two of them stood in each other's arms as time seemed to stand still.

But time was cruel, and their embrace didn't last long enough for either of them before she reluctantly released him to attend to additional preparations for what lay ahead.

Eventually, the afternoon gave way to evening, merely the turning of a clock from Caleb's perspective. He tried distracting himself with a film in the theater room. He absently watched the imagery from the ceiling-mounted projector play across the screen, his thoughts focused on what Katrina was planning to do next. To his aggravation, the three vampires overtly left him out of those conversations. The event led to another brief, heated exchange with Katrina earlier that day after his lunch chat with Alton, resulting in his current sulk in the theater room.

"Hey, kiddo. Alton's in the front sitting room and wants to chat with you," Paige issued from the doorway before she disappeared from sight.

He stopped the movie and proceeded down the hallway to the front of the house.

"You rang?" he quipped from the doorway. Alton gestured towards the couch. He plopped down and stared inquisitively at Alton, who sat in a high-backed reading chair with one leg crossed over his knee.

Alton steepled the fingertips of opposing hands against each other while gazing at Caleb with an introspective expression. "How to begin," he muttered.

Caleb sat patiently, trying not to feel unnerved by the sober-looking vampire's close inspection of him.

"You're an unusual selection for Katrina," Alton commented absently, as if speaking more to himself than Caleb.

"How so?" Caleb asked as his eyes darted to the vampire's.

The corner of one side of Alton's mouth upturned slightly in a wan smile. "She was surprised by her attraction to you, actually," the vampire commented before adding with a raised eyebrow, "But then, the manner of your meeting was rather unusual, so she had more time to be intrigued with you at another level."

Confusion immediately spread across Caleb's features as his mind raced to decipher the vampire's vague commentary. It didn't make sense to him. *Why is meeting through a college class so unusual?* He was likewise jealous of Alton's more complete knowledge of Katrina.

"Typically, Katrina has selected mates more closely matching her own disposition," Alton observed with a distant expression, as if recalling events long since past. "But they were inevitably a poor fit for one reason or another," the vampire continued before Caleb could inquire further. "They challenged her authority or tried manipulating her for their own agendas."

"Katrina mentioned that eventually she killed them all," Caleb supplemented, recalling her brief revelation.

Alton's eyebrow rose. "That's true in all but one case."

*Of course, the suicide.* Caleb remembered what Alondra, or rather Chimalma had said about that, as well. "Katrina's had rotten luck picking mates," he muttered. *Then again, I've had rotten luck picking girlfriends in the past,* he considered. *Katrina broke that streak for me, though lately our relationship seems strained at times.* He wondered if they were operating under unique circumstances, perhaps even for a vampire.

Alton frowned as he watched emotions play across the young man's face. "Granted, her suitors were ill-fated. Yet her past selections were based upon understandable criteria for a vampire: blood, sexuality, wealth, influence, and power. These were all qualities that brought something to the table that she either craved or needed for her own agenda. Quite similar to other vampires, really."

Caleb's expression grew troubled while considering those criteria, realizing that most didn't qualify for him. He was living a very humble lifestyle financially and had no important political or social connections to bring to the table. He certainly wielded no power as a faculty member of a small community college. However, he had blood to offer and felt that he was a good sexual partner to Katrina. At least, *he* thought so.

Alton seemed almost amused by Caleb's introspective manner. "Caleb," he quietly interjected.

The young man's eyes darted back to the vampire.

"It's possible that you're a better fit for her," Alton offered with a hint of encouragement. "You bring a more peaceful, sincere element into the mix. You're a new dynamic for her, Caleb."

Caleb's facial expression became more hopeful.

Katrina's icy voice suddenly announced, "New dynamic? Not entirely true. My human husband was similar to Caleb."

Caleb's eyes darted to the room's entrance to see her leaning against one side of the door frame with her arms crossed before her and looking particularly displeased. However, Alton failed to seem surprised by her appearance and acknowledged her with a partial wave of one hand.

"Alton," Katrina warned. "I don't appreciate you airing my past so openly without my consultation." *Please don't push my life story on him before I'm ready*, she silently willed.

"He deserves to know something," Alton replied crisply. "It might have saved needless bickering between the two of you recently."

"There hasn't exactly been time," she retorted with annoyance.

"You should've made time. That is, if you want someone left to care if you return home or not," Alton retorted with a momentary flash of his hazel eyes.

Caleb viewed the exchange with some concern. But he was too riveted to say anything, feeling that important details were finally coming to the surface.

"And why are you suddenly so interested?" she demanded hotly. "You've never bothered before." *Where were your concerns years ago when all the other men in my life were taking advantage of me?* she fumed. *Now, when I finally have someone sincere and caring in my life, is when you want to get involved?*

"This one's different. He actually makes you happy," Alton noted pointedly. "And you haven't experienced happiness in some time, I recall."

"I'll thank you not to play matchmaker in my mate selections," she admonished.

"Oh, I don't know why I bother," he noted while throwing his hands in the air.

Katrina's expression softened somewhat, and she took a deep breath. She appeared by Alton's chair in a blur to lay a hand across one of his shoulders. "Because you care," she offered with resignation. "And I appreciate your efforts." *It's hard to hold a grudge against you, dear friend,* she conceded. *Good friends are hard to come by for a vampire.*

Alton smiled and reached back to pat her hand with his own.

Caleb relaxed as he mulled over everything from the past few minutes. Things were beginning to make more sense to him.

"The young man has promise," Alton noted, as if he weren't in the room.

Katrina perched on the edge of the couch next to Caleb and wrapped her arm around his shoulders affectionately. "I know," she said while smiling at him warmly. *He shows more than promise*, she thought. *I love him.*

Alton glanced at his wristwatch. "Time is short, Katrina. If you're going to have him, you need to make haste."

*Have him?* Caleb wondered.

Katrina noted his confused look and leaned over to whisper in his ear, "I want you now."

Caleb's eyes darted to hers, focusing on the sly smile and playful sparkle in her green eyes that he loved so much. "Are you still angry with me?" he asked softly. It hadn't been long since their most recent argument.

"There's no time for anger between us," she quietly replied. Soon, they would be engaged in a venture from which she might not return if things went badly.

Caleb swallowed hard, and his eyes darted to see Alton staring at them with an amused expression. His eyes darted back to Katrina in time to see her face hovering before his. He felt her soft lips touch lightly upon his own.

He pulled away from her, and she tentatively gazed back at him. He smiled slyly while rising from the couch and backing away from where she still perched on the cushion.

She began to frown with a degree of uncertainty. *Where are you going?* she wondered.

"If you can catch me, you can have me," he stipulated before turning and running out of the room and up the stairs to the upper level of the house with all of his speed.

Alton laughed in the background as Caleb was almost halfway up the stairs.

"Run, kiddo!" Paige yelled from somewhere nearby.

Caleb felt an arm around his waist, which spun him around as he was propelled up the stairs in a blur. The breath was nearly taken from him as he felt his body flung against a bed in the first guest bedroom nearest the stairs.

Katrina's lips pressed against his in a warm, passionate kiss before pulling away. He stared up at her slightly glowing green eyes and grinned.

"Caught you. You're mine," she whispered slyly.

"Well, a deal's a deal," he muttered and felt her lips press against the soft skin of his neck. What he really wanted to say was, *I'm glad that I'm yours.*

She kissed him affectionately, savoring his taste and scent.

He felt her warm, moist tongue against his neck and the beginning of a numbing sensation there. As Caleb turned his neck slightly for easier access, he felt Katrina's fangs extend to his skin.

The bedroom door gently closed behind them, followed by the sound of soft giggling. "Crazy kids forgot to close the door behind them," Paige muttered with a smirk while floating down the staircase to the first floor.

The time with Katrina passed quickly for Caleb. One moment they were sharing each other, and then it was the next morning -- that was, at least according to his watch. He was even more oblivious to the passage of daytime and nighttime since Paige and Alton's arrival nearly two days ago. It was morning, and he woke with a start as Katrina pulled away from where they lay together in bed.

Caleb's hand darted out at her from underneath the covers to grasp at her, and he managed to catch her arm in his hand.

"Somebody's getting faster," she noted slyly.

"Don't go yet," he pleaded in a sleepy voice.

She sighed and leaned over to kiss him briefly on the forehead. "I've got to shower, and then it's time to pack," she whispered before slipping from the guest bed and into the nearby bathroom.

He watched her beautiful, pale-skinned body depart and muttered, "Me too."

Katrina spent most of the morning packing. Caleb began packing things too and was surprised that nobody was trying to stop him. Once again, the clock seemed to take on a life of its own, and it was early evening again. But unlike the earlier part of the day, there was a palpable tension in the air. It was nearly time to go.

Alton and Katrina staged their luggage near the front entry area, while Caleb brought his suitcase to the sitting room immediately adjacent to the front door.

Both Alton and Katrina were dressed in business casual attire, and each wore sober expressions. Caleb looked down at his blue jeans and blue denim shirt and considered changing clothes. However, he was afraid that if he left the room things would proceed without him, and he wasn't ready to concede.

Meanwhile, Paige stood nearby in a pair of black jeans and a red turtleneck sweater. While her face was neutral, she was nervously nibbling at the tip of one fingernail.

Caleb stood defiantly before Katrina, squaring his shoulders, and staring up into her green eyes. One corner of her mouth upturned slightly with amusement, though her eyes were steeled with determination.

"You're staying here," she said flatly before he could say anything.

"You're not leaving me behind," he insisted with narrowed eyes. "I'll only end up following you once you've left."

Her eyes flashed green for only a moment before returning to their normal state. She took in his defiant stance, as if ready to take on all three vampires single-handedly. Her eyes played across the determined, set look of his eyes, and she felt a surge of admiration for him. At that fleeting moment, Caleb reminded Katrina of her human husband of so many, many years ago. All of the qualities were there: a gentle nature, caring and compassionate, determined, honest, intelligent, and utterly handsome.

A satisfied expression played across her face, and Caleb frowned with momentary confusion before setting his jaw firmly again.

Alton watched with a semi-amused expression, while Paige appeared somewhat sad. They both knew that his battle was lost before he ever fought it.

"That's why Paige is staying behind with you," Katrina issued plainly. "She will keep you here and keep you safe."

"Operation Babysitter ready for action," Paige offered with

a playful grin.

A split-second look of surprise crossed Caleb's face. He frowned with confusion, unaware that all three vampires weren't going together. And it was then he belatedly realized that Paige didn't have any luggage prepared. He exchanged quick glances between Paige and Katrina. "Babysitter? No, you need all of us for this. You can't afford to leave anybody behind."

"Katrina and I can handle this," Alton reassured in a steady, convincing tone of voice. "We're well suited for this task."

Caleb's pale blue eyes were immediately determined again, but Katrina had noticed his flash of confusion from a moment ago.

"We'll have a great time, Caleb," Paige offered with a hopeful expression. "We can watch movies, play some chess, and maybe even toast some s'mores over the fireplace together!"

Caleb just looked at Paige as if she weren't in her right mind. Refusing to be distracted by the short, blonde-haired vampire, he shook his head and returned his complete attention to Katrina. "I'm going with you," he issued slowly and deliberately in a steady, confident voice as he folded his arms before him.

Katrina's expression softened, and she felt a surge of adoration flow through her. "I love you too much to let that happen," she whispered.

His eyes widened slightly as she wrapped her right arm around his waist and reached around with her left hand to grasp the base of his neck. She pulled him tightly against her in a warm embrace and began to kiss him deeply.

He was surprised by her sudden kiss, but eagerly returned it. He felt the breath practically being drawn from his lungs as her lips locked onto his mouth. Immediately realizing what was happening, his hands hastily tried to push her away, but she held him like a vice. He struggled furiously against her grip, drew a frantic breath in through his nose, and tried to break the seal of their kiss. She pinched his nose closed between her fingers while making a sharp intake of breath over his mouth, and within seconds it was all over. His body went limp in her arms as he fell into unconsciousness.

Katrina gathered him up and laid him gently on the nearby couch. It pained her to have to do that to him, but she couldn't allow him to be endangered by accompanying them. *Perhaps someday he'll understand*, she hoped silently.

She took a moment to take in Caleb's peaceful features as he lay unconscious on the couch. "Take good care of him, Paige," she insisted quietly as her fingers affectionately caressed the side of his face.

"You know I will," Paige promised.

"He's going to be upset when he rouses," Katrina warned. "So, please don't hurt him."

Paige grinned. "I'm a good babysitter, and I'm great with problem children."

Katrina regarded her with a slightly amused expression and momentarily marveled at how upbeat and light-hearted a personality the vampire seemed always to embody. Despite Paige's difficult beginnings as a vampire, she always maintained such a youthful, energetic quality about her. It was one of the reasons that Katrina mentored her when her vampire creator died not long after her turning. She smiled at Paige and bent down to kiss Caleb on the forehead.

"It's time to go," Alton offered with a hand on Katrina's shoulder.

Katrina nodded, and they turned to depart.

# Chapter 9

## Hunting

**C**aleb regained consciousness while lying on the couch and immediately lurched into an animated state. The sound of his heartbeat pounded in his ears. "Don't leave me behind!" he shouted as he sat bolt upright.

Paige suddenly appeared at his side, perching on the edge of the couch. Her right arm stretched across to the back cushion before him in a corralling fashion. "Whoa, tiger," she crooned. "They're already long gone."

"Damn it!" he cursed.

She smiled supportively. "You may not believe it yet, but you're a hell of a lot safer in here with me than you'd be out there with them."

He didn't want to believe that at the moment. All that mattered was they had left without him, left him behind. "I just want to help somehow," he lamented. "I know I'm not much of a threat to a vampire, but I could've done something useful."

"Listen, don't take this the wrong way," she said matter-of-factly, "but if you had gone along, they would've spent more time looking after you than they would hunting Chimalma. As it stands now, they can concentrate fully on what needs to be done."

"Yeah, sure," he sighed with exasperation. *Maybe Paige is correct*, he considered. *At least, it sounds logical.* However, it still didn't change how he felt about the matter. His eyes focused on the pale arm before him barring his way.

Paige narrowed her eyes and regarded him warily. "Are

you going to play nicely?" she asked.

His pale blue eyes darted to her deep blue ones with a degree of surprise at her question. It was similar to a recent comment made by Katrina.

"What's wrong?" she asked.

"Do all vampires ask that?" he demanded irritably. "Seems like I've heard that a lot lately."

Surprise and curiosity showed simultaneously on Paige's face as she slowly removed her arm, allowing him to sit up. The vampire considered him for a quiet moment with a peculiar expression. "Listen," she offered in a cordial tone, "Katrina asked me to keep an eye on the surveillance system in her room. That's where you've been staying, but I don't want to make you feel uncomfortable or anything. And since you're already packed..."

It made sense that Paige might want to stay where she was close to the computer and monitoring equipment. "Oh, sure," he responded casually. "Yeah, I can move my things into another bedroom." He recalled the smaller bedroom at the top of the stairs where he and Katrina shared their most recent, and hopefully not last, intimate time together. "I'll move into the one at the top of the stairs," he offered. "Of course, if it's okay with you."

"Sure, that's fine," she agreed with a slight nod as she moved to let him stand up.

He rolled upright, rose, and realized that his belongings still sat in a suitcase in the middle of the floor. The final minutes before his blackout replayed in his mind as he ran one hand over his scalp and through his hair.

"Caleb," Paige gently prompted.

He turned to her, once again marveling at how she looked like a young college student from one of his history classes, barely old enough to be called an adult, though not much younger-looking than himself in reality.

"I don't know you very well, and I'd like to avoid any misunderstandings between us," she explained carefully. "So, I'm here if you want to talk about anything, okay?"

"I understand," he replied congenially. "And thanks. That's very kind." He quietly moved to take his suitcase upstairs with a somber expression.

"Yeah, I can see we're going to have a barn burner of a time," Paige muttered under her breath as he left the room with suitcase in tow.

Alton drove himself and Katrina across the darkened city of Atlanta to the four-story, modern-looking structure that housed the Corporate Research Enterprises office. Upon their arrival, the nearly empty parking lot suggested that most of the building's offices were closed.

Alton parked their car at the rear of the building, where the only other vehicle was a cleaning service van. He and Katrina exited the vehicle wearing long black winter coats and black leather gloves. Alton reached into the back seat and withdrew a small black briefcase, which he laid on the trunk to open. He removed a small plastic-encased device and slipped it into his coat pocket. Placing the briefcase back in the car, the two of them proceeded to the building's service entrance.

The night air was crisp as a cold front entered the city from the northwest, and Katrina took a moment to appreciate the feel of the cool breeze against her pale skin. She felt her senses sharpening and honing their sensitivity and was especially happy to be in the field actively doing something rather than just sitting and waiting. She momentarily considered how truly desperate Caleb was to escape his own in-house captivity. Still, she felt better knowing that he was tucked away safely with Paige.

"Cameras?" she asked while scanning the area for the second time since their arrival.

"None on the exterior," he noted. "But there will likely be some inside."

Alton reached into his coat pocket and withdrew the plastic case with lights and a few small buttons on it. He began pressing buttons until two green lights on the device lit up. "This will jam all electronics when we enter," he stated quietly. "That should take care of alarms and camera systems. But because of the power consumption, we'll only have about ten minutes before the battery goes dead."

She quickly glanced at the device and asked, "Where did you get that?"

He smiled and muttered, "British intelligence toy. Somebody owed me a favor."

Her eyebrow shot up, and she adopted an impressed expression. *His device is going to make things much easier.*

They entered the building, and, as expected, there was nobody around. They avoided the elevator and made their way to the stairwell. It took only a few seconds to race up to the fourth floor, where they exited into the main corridor. The offices on the floor appeared to be closed already, and they heard no activities from within any offices they passed.

They arrived outside Room 404 and noted the company sign for CRE was still on the plaque. Katrina tried the door handle and to no surprise found it to be locked. Alton reached into his pocket and pulled out some lock picks, but she held up her hand.

"We don't have time," she noted before stepping back and swiftly kicking the door near the locked door handle. The lock broke away as the door slammed inwards and open. He shut his eyes tightly at the momentary crashing sound.

"Are you going to kick in all the doors we run into?" he asked sharply.

Katrina scowled. "Only the ones that get in my way."

Alton shook his head, but followed her into the dark offices. The lack of lighting was no problem for the vampires, though there wasn't much to see really. The furniture was bare, and only a few empty cardboard boxes remained in the area. Katrina walked into Chimalma's office and scanned the room. She noted the two chairs placed in front of the desk and imagined Caleb sitting in one of them as he interviewed for the supposed part-time position not long ago. *It was a rather elaborate ruse to get Caleb closer to them until Chimalma was ready to spring a trap. I'm so grateful that they didn't kill him once he was here.* The mere thought repulsed her.

Katrina gritted her teeth angrily as she shuffled through the abandoned desk and nearby filing cabinets. She found nothing of interest remaining related to either CRE or Alondra Vargas.

"Well, it was a long shot," Alton muttered.

"Agreed," she stated before turning to depart the office.

He pulled the door to on their way out, although its damaged lock mechanism failed to hold the door shut. "What next?" he whispered under his breath so only she would hear him.

"Follow the money trail," she muttered. "She'll have to purchase something either where she's at or where she's going next." *Somehow I'm going to find her*, Katrina vowed.

Alton made an agreeable grunting sound as they reentered the stairwell and sped downstairs to the ground floor. They failed to notice anyone in the building, except for a janitor inside one of the supply closets gathering his tools and supplies. The janitor was oblivious to either of the vampire's presence. Seconds later, they were walking outside.

"Finances are your bailiwick," Katrina announced while entering the passenger side of the vehicle.

"Of course," Alton agreed brightly. "And I happen to have a contact at Interpol who can help us."

Caleb unpacked his suitcase, placing his clothes in the guest room dresser and storing his toiletries in the adjoining bathroom. He felt somber and tired, but most of all lost. *What do I do now?*

"This must be what it feels like when a spouse goes to off to war and leaves the other behind," he mused darkly while perched on the edge of the bed. The minutes seemed to last forever as he sat in virtual limbo.

He heard a light tapping noise and looked up to see Paige

leaning against the door jamb looking thoughtful.

"You don't know what to do next, do you?" she ventured softly.

"No, not really," he replied glumly. *This is the most useless I've felt in a long time.*

"Now, we get to do the hard part. We wait," she replied soberly. "They'll check in regularly to let us know how things are progressing. In the meantime, we keep you safely occupied and as happy as possible."

He adopted a wry expression. *Safely occupied and happy as possible,* he thought. "Yeah? Like what?" he asked aloud, not necessarily directing his question to Paige.

"We need some 'getting to know you' time, I think," she suggested.

"Okay," he replied absently, if only for the sake of something to do. "You start." His thoughts were still focused on Alton's and Katrina's departure, but he didn't want to get on a bad foot with Paige. Being locked in a house with a hostile vampire wasn't an enviable prospect.

"So," she began with a charming smile, "have you memorized all of Katrina's rules yet?"

He looked up with surprise. "You know about the rules?"

"Of course, silly," she chuckled. "I lived with her for quite a few years. We've talked about her partners in the past. I'll admit she has quite a few rules compared to other vampires."

"There's normally fewer?" he inquired.

She looked at him sharply. "Yes, but that's not important to you, Caleb," she clarified tactfully. "What matters is that you learn and follow her rules."

He rolled his eyes.

"So," she continued while sitting next to him on the bed, "you've memorized them then?"

"Um, I'm working on that," he hedged.

"When you can recite them backwards, she'll be much easier to live with," Paige mused thoughtfully.

"You had to learn them?" he inquired.

"Me?" she asked. "My only rule is not revealing the true nature of our kind to humans."

"Great," he groaned. "I feel like I'm in grade school again with these rules."

"You have to realize it's hard for us to trust you humans," she explained diplomatically. "Our anonymity is all we have to protect us from the danger humanity poses to us."

"I suppose I can understand that," he conceded. "My initial reaction to her secret wasn't exactly noble."

She giggled as if remembering something funny. "Oh yeah, the tree branch guy."

Caleb turned what seemed like three shades of red simultaneously and felt the heat quickly rise to his face. "I see my storied reputation spread fast."

"Yep, old Tree Branch Caleb," she said grandly in her best southern drawl. "That's how you're known in these parts."

"Great," he said wryly. "Just great." *It wasn't the proudest moment in my brief history with Kat*, he admitted.

She grinned at his reaction before adopting a more sympathetic expression. "I'm sorry about teasing you. She actually thinks it's pretty amusing now," she said. "I can tell she adores you, Caleb."

His thoughts went immediately to Katrina. He worried for her safety and wished she hadn't left him behind. *Trapped in a grand-sized box, complete with closed lid and all the amenities.*

Paige seemed to detect where his feelings were going and reached across the short distance between them to pat him on the back lightly.

"I could've helped her," he muttered dejectedly. "I can go out in the daylight when vampires can't, for example."

She raised one eyebrow and granted, "That's helpful, I admit."

"And before you arrived, Katrina drilled me in some potentially handy martial arts moves," he added optimistically.

Her smirk faded as she withdrew her hand from his back and chastised, "Okay, now you're just being delusional. A few 'moves' doesn't make you combat-ready."

Caleb held up his hand in an apologetic gesture. "Fine, I'm saying I'm not in bad shape, that's all."

Paige adopted an incredulous visage. "And I thought you were actually smarter than the average guy. Listen champ, you may think you're in pretty good shape, but you're no match for us on your best day. Any one of us would wipe the floor with you. Trust me."

He considered her thoughtfully as he stared into her blue eyes. It was difficult to envision her as overtly dangerous.

"You humans are far more fragile than you think when it comes to us," she insisted.

He recalled being sore for days after being tossed around by Katrina that evening in the park. "She did throw me around like a rag doll the night of the branch incident," he reminisced.

"And I bet she wasn't even trying to kill you," Paige ventured with a grin.

"It sure felt like it at the time," he muttered, wide-eyed.

She was introspective as if deciding what to say next, or how best to say it. "Katrina's like a sister to me, and I respect her probably more than you realize," she began slowly. "And I can tell you that she wouldn't go to this much trouble if you didn't matter a great deal to her. You and I both know she loves you, kiddo."

A warm feeling passed over him, and he started to smile.

She grinned at him as if reading something in his expression. "And I'm willing to bet you care enough about her to trust her to have your best interests at heart," she ventured quietly.

He nodded and smiled back wanly. *Yes, I trust Katrina and feel deep appreciation for what she's doing to protect me. I just yearn to be with her, maybe try and help her somehow. Instead, I'm left to sit around and hope that I have enough patience to make it through the waiting and worrying part.*

Katrina and Alton checked into a hotel on the outskirts of Atlanta. They needed a temporary base of operations until de-

termining Chimalma's location. Rather than returning to the
estate and further agitating Caleb, the hotel allowed them immediate mobility to act or relocate as warranted. Once settled
in the room, Katrina's thoughts immediately turned to her
mate. She dialed her cell phone and only waited two rings before Paige picked up. After giving her a brief update, she asked
about Caleb.

"Just as you predicted, he was irritable initially, but he's
doing much better now," Paige reported in an upbeat tone.

"Where is he now?" Katrina asked.

"He's in the shower in a guest room upstairs," Paige explained. "He's sleeping there while I'm in the sublevel. Do you
want to chat with him?"

Katrina considered it and declined, "No, it's probably better if I don't just yet. He'll likely still be upset with me for leaving him. Just tell him that we checked in and are working on
tracking Chimalma further. We'll call when we know more."

Paige paused, prompting, "And?"

Katrina sighed and added, "Tell him that I love him, Paige."
She could almost hear Paige grinning on the other end of the
phone.

"Now, that's what I'm getting at," she responded brightly.

Katrina shook her head with a smirk and instructed, "Say
goodbye, Paige."

"Goodbye, Paige," the spritely vampire replied before hanging up.

Alton walked in from one of the two bedrooms asking, "Why
do I feel like we're two parents who just left the teenagers in
charge of the house while we're gone?"

Katrina chuckled. "Good thing that one of the teenagers is
a vampire."

He nodded agreeably as he powered up his laptop on a
nearby table.

The first night without Katrina was difficult for Caleb. After his shower, he received an update from Paige on Katrina's

phone call. She spent the evening sitting in front of the computers and security surveillance system in Katrina's lair, leaving him the main part of the house to himself. He lay on the main living room couch watching television until nearly 1 am before making his way up to the guest room.

Once asleep, he had restless dreams that eventually turned into a nightmare. Katrina and he happily strolled though a moonlit night at one of Georgia's numerous Civil War battlefield parks. One moment they were walking hand in hand, and the next Katrina disappeared. He called her name while running through dense trees, across battlefield cannon emplacements, around old stockade fencing, and across open stretches of grassy fields. But his voice was barely a whisper even though he yelled at the top of his lungs.

He finally heard snarling and growling sounds and made his way towards the source. Upon entering an eerie-looking graveyard among a copse of thick pine trees, he saw Katrina facing off against Chimalma. Both looked fierce, and their eyes were ablaze with fury. He noticed that each combatant had a set of jagged claw-like fingernails, which were dripping blood. By the moonlight, he saw dark stripes covering the clothes of each woman. *Those have to be blood streaks*, he realized.

Katrina's face turned towards him, and she hissed. In that same moment, Chimalma's right hand darted out and plunged into Katrina's rib cage. With one swift, terrifying movement, Chimalma's hand exited Katrina holding her still-beating heart while blood dripped thickly to the ground. The Aztec-descended vampire screamed in exaltation. Katrina's eyes flashed and went dark as her body slumped lifelessly to the ground. He was stunned, and watched with horror while shouting, "Katrina! No! *No!*"

Then there was nothing.

He awoke in nearly total darkness, the only light emitting from the dimly glowing numerals of a digital clock sitting atop the dresser across the room. He was breathing in short gasps and broke out in a cold sweat. "Oh God," he muttered, putting one hand to his forehead while propping himself in a sitting position with the other arm.

Seconds later, the door to the bedroom swung open, and Paige was at his bedside. He felt a brief rush of air wash against his slightly damp face as her bright blue eyes illuminated in the darkness.

"Are you okay, kiddo?" she asked with her cool palm pressed soothingly to the side of his face.

"Yeah," he breathed. "Just a nightmare."

"Wow, you really broke out in a sweat," she remarked absently. "Want to talk about it? I heard you shout Katrina's name."

He nodded in the darkness and began to recount the brief nightmare as Paige turned on the small lamp on the nightstand. It didn't take long for comprehension to dawn on both their faces.

"Well, I don't have to be a dream therapist for that one," she noted sagely.

"Yeah," he remarked darkly. "Keep your useless butt at home so you don't distract Katrina and get her killed."

"It's probably best," Paige agreed. "But she knows how badly you want to be there with her. It means a lot to her, Caleb."

He nodded and slipped over the opposite side of the bed. He was thankful for having put on a pair of men's pajama pants earlier as he walked towards the adjoining bathroom. He needed to towel off and didn't want to parade around naked in front of her.

"Nice-looking useless butt you've got there," she nevertheless teased while observing his lean, shirtless figure.

He grinned and felt a growing appreciation for her company. But his thoughts quickly turned back to Katrina, and he prayed that everything would turn out completely differently from his nightmare.

It was mid-afternoon the following day as Katrina and Alton stayed safely behind the dark curtains of their hotel room that the first major break occurred in their hunt for Chimalma. Alton used his laptop while Katrina reclined on the room's sofa drinking blood from a hotel glass. She had brought a lockable cooler with packets of blood.

"Chimalma made her first mistake," he observed with satisfaction.

She sneered and countered darkly, "Her first mistake was coming after Caleb and me."

He ignored her and continued, "She must be using disposable cell phones to avoid being traced. But she's also still trying to run a small international company. My Interpol contact acquired her corporate cell phone records, and guess what?"

Her interest was piqued, and she listened closely to her friend and mentor.

Alton noted her focused attention with a grin. "She's still accepting calls on the corporate cell phone she carries," he added with satisfaction. "I've got her latest location from the coordinates forwarded to me."

"Just how did you get Interpol to help us?" she asked.

He smiled. "Simple. Chimalma's crimes qualify her as either a serial killer or domestic terrorist."

"Hm, helpful," she admired. "Would there be someone of interest there, as well?"

"Perhaps," he replied with a smirk. "But I'm not quite ready to say just yet."

"I'm happy for you," she offered sincerely.

Alton continued to smile as he retrieved a satellite image, which he zoomed in on progressively. It was of an area near Warren, Pennsylvania, in the far northwestern corner of the state close to the southern border of New York. He brought up MapQuest and focused on the city of Warren. Katrina appeared at his shoulder to peer intently at the screen.

"Why there?" she asked as her mind began organizing information and assessing variables.

"It's only a small town, barely eleven thousand people as of the last census," he noted as he searched the Internet for additional information. "Established in 1796, its main claims to fame were oil and lumber. The town went through hard economic times, with only a few companies serving as primary employers. But look." He pointed to the screen.

"CRE has a small corporate retreat just outside of town," Katrina observed.

"Great location," he mused. "Lots of forest and hills and very few people."

"But why there?" she insisted with a frown. "She's hiding from us? That doesn't make sense."

Alton murmured his agreement. "Unless she wants us there. In which case, she's picking the battle ground."

Katrina scowled. "Fine with me."

"Okay, destination known. Now what's our plan, besides you tearing her to shreds?" he asked pointedly.

She glared at him, but admitted that he was correct. Her anger would only be useful if channeled properly. "I see explosives in her future," she said coldly.

"Quite an extreme attention grabber, don't you think?" Alton queried. "Perhaps a simple beheading would be better and far less dramatic?"

"Immolation eliminates evidence," Katrina countered.

"Are you suggesting we blow up a lodge full of potentially innocent people?" he insisted incredulously. "That's pretty bloodthirsty, even for you."

She gave him a withering expression and snapped, "Of course not. Rather, we set up a kill zone near her and draw, or drag, her into it."

He considered the idea and conceded, "Hm, seems plausible and direct. If you'll arrange for a charter flight, I'll make a few calls to some contacts that can help outfit us with helpful tools."

"We'll need a place to stay affording both privacy and some degree of safety from sunlight," she added.

Alton searched the Internet further as Katrina retrieved information related to corporate charter flights from a folder in her luggage. She had used Sunset Air a number of times. The company was owned by a fellow vampire and was well-known among her kind for both its discretion and safe, reliable service.

"Got it," Alton said. "There are cabins not far from the town of Warren. I'll reserve one for us."

"Fine," she warned. "But we're picking up some dark sheets and duct tape somewhere because I'm not about to spend the day with you hiding from sun rays in a cramped cabin closet."

He chuckled and shook his head.

It was early evening already, though it felt to Caleb that time had practically stopped. He spent most of the day reading a biography on Theodore Roosevelt that he had brought from his apartment. Later that afternoon, he had talked Paige into connecting his laptop to the Internet long enough for him to update his video drivers so he could play a computer game he'd tried loading a few days prior. However, she was attentive to his activities, and once he was finished, she disabled the wireless access in the house, much to his chagrin. Still, it allowed him to pass a few hours getting lost in the game. However, he felt guilty for being able to sit casually playing while Katrina and Alton did all of the dangerous work on his behalf. *Once again, I feel useless*, he fumed.

Paige showered, changed into some black cotton lounge pants and a baby blue T-shirt, and sat barefooted at the computer hutch in Katrina's sublevel room. Caleb made his way down the steps and plopped down on the nearby bed. He was going stir-crazy and was prepared to do just about anything to get out of the house, even if it were just for a few minutes. He couldn't recall a time in his past when he had endured the kind of isolation that he was experiencing.

"Hey, any chance I could talk you into deactivating the front door code for about ten minutes?" he asked in a pleasant, innocent voice.

She smiled politely. "I seem to recall Katrina's saying something along the lines of 'Caleb stays inside the house, period.'"

He glanced at her with a speculative expression, hoping she wouldn't notice. Much to his chagrin, she did.

"Come on, just a brief evening walk?" he pleaded hopefully. "I'll only walk to the end of the driveway and back. That's all. You can go along with me for protection, if you like."

She smiled. "Well, sure. I can do that."

He gave her his best appreciative-looking smile.

"But it's going to be awful hard for you to take that walk with two broken legs," she amended with narrowed eyes and flat voice.

His eyes widened momentarily with surprise, and his smile disappeared entirely.

She shrugged. "I have my orders, and they don't include either of us leaving the house."

He folded his arms across his chest and sighed derisively.

"For any reason," she said forcefully with a raised eyebrow. "Remember, nobody's supposed to know I'm even here."

"Paige, please," he pleaded in an urgent voice. "I'm going stir-crazy in here."

"I sympathize with you Caleb. I really do," she said. "But it's for your own safety, after all."

"Listen, I've never felt so bored and useless in my life," he complained.

She regarded him coolly before smiling back at him. "Well, we better find something for us to do then."

That caught him off-guard. "Like what?" he asked carefully.

She grinned menacingly. "You could show me some of those handy vampire combat moves that you said you learned from Katrina!"

He gave her a dirty look as she walked past him with a smirk over to the nearby sitting area to turn on the wall-mounted television. "You're just plain sarcastic. You know that, don't you?" he called after her irritably. *She seems to enjoy toying with me*, he noted irritably.

Paige forced a laugh. "Be nice. Don't make me stand you in the corner."

He hurried to the couch and found her already lounging on the cushions methodically surfing through cable channels. She didn't even glance up as he glared at her over the back cushion.

"Oh, really? Stand me in the corner?" he pressed with a hint of incredulity.

"Well, despite my appearance, I'm a lot older than you," she ventured. "And you're only in your mid-twenties as a human, so I guess that makes you the spoiled youngster here."

He folded his arms before him and asked, "That so? Well, just how old are you then?"

"My vampire life?" she asked. "Oh, I'm around the century mark now."

He hadn't expected her to be quite that old. Her youthful appearance and manner led him to believe she might have only been a vampire for a short time. "A century?"

To him, she seemed like a peer, someone he could have known through college. She had a very modern attitude for someone from her time period if she were truly a century old. "I'm finding that hard to believe," he muttered while taking a seat in an open spot at the end of the couch near her pale feet.

Paige ignored him and continued to channel surf.

"You're so...modern," he added, grasping for the right word.

She glanced at him curiously, considering him at length. "Really," she replied thoughtfully. "Well, you apparently don't know much about the early 1900s then. It was a wild time, not much different from today really, other than the technology."

He felt the history teacher persona rising in him to take over. "My specialty is really more the pre-twentieth century, but my impression is everyone was much more conservative in the early 1900s compared to today," he ventured.

A smirk formed on her face and she corrected him, "Ah, that may have been true in some of the small towns or as reflected in public photographs, but I can tell you that people in the cities threw some really good parties behind closed doors in those days." Her eyes grew distant, as if she were seeing another time. "Oh yeah, some really wild parties behind closed doors, especially in the 1920s. We did things that would put even cable TV shows to shame. You see, people aren't all that different, really, just the facades of what they want to show outwardly."

"Well, but there was barely women's suffrage," he countered.

"Women's suffrage," she scoffed. "I'm talking about the essence of what makes men and women tick inside, Caleb. The emotions, the passions, the sex!"

He blushed slightly, which she regarded with a grin.

"Oh yeah, that's right," she teased. "You're the history professor. Well, take it from me, professor, it's one thing to read about it and another thing to live it."

Her statement struck him like a cold splash of water to his face. *It was a pretty good response*, he admitted and noticed how very different Paige seemed from Katrina.

She observed his expression out of the corner of her eye while changing the channel to a romantic comedy. "So, spill," she insisted simply.

*Spill?* He shook his head at her strange term and offered, "You're just so different from Katrina, that's all. You're a lot less serious, for example."

She paused while staring at the television, as though not fully focused on the movie before her. She cast him a sober expression. "Katrina's serious for a reason. I'm pretty young as a member of my kind. You don't survive as long as Katrina or Alton without time and events taking some toll on you, I think. So, I may not be like I am now when I'm their age," she explained. "That is, if I make it to their age."

"What do you mean by that?" he asked.

She considered her words carefully as he patiently waited.

"Before Katrina left, she warned me," Paige said while staring into Caleb's eyes. "She told me not to leave the house if at all possible. She said that Chimalma is very old and powerful for a vampire because of how long she's been honing her skills. And if Chimalma manages to elude Alton and Katrina somehow...well, we don't want to confront her out in the open."

"But you're a vampire too," he countered.

"I'm a teenager among my kind," she explained in a quiet voice. "Chimalma, Katrina, and Alton, they're serious adults, the veterans."

He frowned at her ominous tone and everything implied in her explanation.

She noticed his reaction and offered a hopeful smile. "But hey, I'm a tough teenager," she reassured him. "I've never lost any kids on my watch."

Caleb rolled his eyes with a smirk, and she giggled at his reaction.

"So, I wonder know how old Katrina is in vampire years?" he asked nonchalantly.

She gave him a wary sidelong glance and retorted, "Oh no, you don't. You're not getting that out of me if Katrina hasn't told you. You take that up with her. Though more than likely, she'll tell you when she's ready."

He sighed with resignation.

"So, what do you say? How about a horror film?" she prodded playfully. "There's a good vampire movie on the Chiller Channel."

Katrina and Alton took a small charter flight from Atlanta to Bradford, Pennsylvania, to the east of Warren where they last placed Chimalma. Despite the waning hours of night, they were able to take possession of a Jeep Cherokee they had arranged from Atlanta.

On their way to Warren, they stopped at an all-night discount store to stock up on the various supplies that they needed for the cabin. They also acquired an adequate supply of both regular and dry ice for their blood supply. Upon arriving at the campgrounds, they managed to wake the manager, who was staying onsite in a cabin next door to the main office. After hasty, sincere apologies to the semi-retired fellow and a large sum of money to help assuage his irritation, Katrina and Alton arrived at the small, non-descript log cabin.

Even at night, when darkness softened the edges of everything, the cabin was both modest and antiquated. The interior was fairly small, consisting of one main central room with a small stone fireplace, a small kitchen-dining area with a wooden table and four plain wooden chairs, two small bedrooms with wooden framed double beds, and one central bathroom. Katrina noted a small closet next to the front door, which brought to mind her quip to Alton back at the hotel regarding hiding from sunshine in a closet. The few windows in the cabin were thankfully small, and they came well-prepared to cover them for the coming daylight.

As they hauled their supplies into the cabin, Katrina smirked.

"What's so amusing?" Alton asked while carrying an armful of baggage.

"I was just thinking about Caleb and how he complained so much about being locked indoors," she recalled. "I should've brought him to a cabin like this for one day, and he'd be on his knees begging me to return to the estate."

He raised an amused eyebrow and teased, "Tsk, tsk, Katrina. You'd actually torture poor Caleb like that? Such vengeful thoughts towards your mate."

An idea settled into her mind as she considered the matter further. "Actually, it's kind of quaint. Being sequestered in a cabin with Caleb for a weekend might actually be romantic. We could spend our days inside and walk through the moonlight appreciating the outdoors from a completely different perspective from what he's used to," she ventured thoughtfully. "He might enjoy that."

Alton raised a curious eyebrow in response and offered with a mock-mortified expression, "Okay, now you're scaring me. Since when did you become such a hopeless romantic?"

She frowned and stuck her tongue out at him, but he merely grinned and chuckled.

He pulled out his notebook computer and established satellite communications for Internet access. He received an email from a clandestine contact regarding some specialized equipment and explosives they needed for the battle with Chimalma.

Katrina watched him for a moment and glanced at her watch. It was nearly dawn.

"I'm going to unpack some things and call Paige to check up on everything back home," she stated while carrying her luggage into one of the bedrooms. "They should be up and around before long."

Caleb woke not long after seven o'clock, unable to sleep beyond that. He had trouble falling asleep the night before, though thankfully had no further nightmares. Standing before the bathroom sink wearing a pair of men's pajama pants and gazing into the mirror, he scraped the blade of his straight razor against his face to attack some remaining stubble. His thoughts were distracted by ruminations on how Katrina was doing. On his last pass with the razor, he abruptly cut his chin.

"Damn!" he cursed as he rinsed the blade in the sink.

A few droplets of blood fell onto the front of his bare right shoulder. He cursed again when he realized how deep the cut went. He toweled the remaining shaving cream from his face and noticed Paige standing next to him, still dressed in some comfy-looking dark blue cotton pajamas. She seemed to appear out of nowhere.

"Are you okay?" she queried. "I thought I heard you curse."

"Sure, I'm fine," he replied. "Cut myself shaving, that's all,"

She moved her body closer to Caleb's and looked up at his chin. She licked her finger to moisten it and pressed it against his skin. He remembered how a vampire's saliva helped close wounds and felt a momentary numbing sensation. After a minute or so, she withdrew her finger to inspect his chin. Paige licked her finger absently as if sampling the flavor and took a deep breath of the air between them. Her blue eyes glowed as she focused on the small droplets of blood on his shoulder.

Caleb's eyes widened as her body lurched closer to his bare chest. The muscles in his body immediately tensed, and his heartbeat began to increase slightly.

"Mmmm," she murmured from deep in her throat as her nose touched his right shoulder, and he felt the side of her soft face against his skin.

Placing both of his hands carefully and respectfully on her slim waist, he tried to push her away, but immediately froze when one of her razor sharp fangs touched the bare skin of his shoulder. He held his breath and remained statue-still.

Paige parted her lips slightly and her tongue flicked out to lick the drops of blood from his skin. Her fang suddenly retracted, and she pulled away from him with a start. "I'm so sorry," she apologized in a rough voice while stepping back from him a few feet.

Her eyes still held a deep blue glow as he gazed into them. "Are you okay?" he asked tentatively.

"That was close," she offered shakily. "Katrina would tear me to shreds. You're forbidden fruit, my friend."

He stared at her uncertainly.

"But sweet fruit," she added with a smirk in a whisper almost too soft for him to hear.

His eyes widened at her comment.

"Sorry. Control is still hard at my age when I haven't fed and fresh blood is present," she explained with a nervous chuckle.

Before he could say anything further, she darted from the room in a blur. He released the breath that he didn't realize he was holding. *That was close*, he silently agreed to her earlier comment.

Upon hearing a phone ring downstairs, he raced from the room and down the stairs.


Katrina glanced around the dimly lit cabin with a grim expression and momentarily worried as she counted to the fourth ring while calling the estate from her cell phone. Alton scrutinized the front window in the main room, making sure no sunlight would break through the combined drapes layered with dark sheets they had put up.

He had rented a cabin in a more remote area of the scenic, wooded park hoping to deter unwanted visitors or passers-by. They also placed a vinyl cover over their rented Jeep parked in front of the cabin.

"Hello?" came Paige's tentative-sounding voice at the other end.

Katrina breathed a sigh of relief before demanding, "Paige, is everything okay there?"

Following a pause, Paige replied innocently, "Just fine here. Are you two all right?"

Katrina immediately picked up on Paige's hesitant reply and didn't like the tone of her voice. It sounded as if her calmness were somewhat forced. *Something's wrong*, she thought. *Just what have they gotten themselves into?*

"Where's Caleb?" she urged. "Is he well?"

"He's fine, Katrina," Paige assured her sedately. "He's just fine. In fact, I hear him racing down here now."

A few seconds later, Katrina heard Caleb's voice in the background demanding, "Is it Katrina? Is she okay? Let me talk to her."

Her face immediately relaxed. *Same old Caleb*, she thought with a relieved smile.

Meanwhile, Alton smirked at Katrina knowingly. She caught his expression and frowned back at him.

"Just a second, Katrina. I'm putting you on speaker," Paige said at the other end.

The phone crackled, and Katrina also put her cell phone into speaker mode for Alton's benefit. He moved to sit in one of the plain upholstered reading chairs across the room.

"How are you two?" Katrina asked.

"Us?" asked Caleb somewhat anxiously at the other end. "We're fine. Nothing going on here."

"Yep, we're both getting by," Paige agreed a little too convincingly.

Katrina frowned, but Alton remained silent as he peered at her from across the room. However, his expression seemed almost amused by the exchange.

"You're not very convincing," she insisted suspiciously. "As Paige so often likes to say, 'spill.'"

Paige and Caleb winced nearly simultaneously at the tone of Katrina's voice as they stood in the middle of the sublevel room near the computer hutch.

"Well," Paige hesitated. "You see, Caleb cut himself --"

"What?!" Katrina demanded over the speaker.

"Shaving!" they yelled in unison.

Paige continued, "He cut himself shaving, but he's fine now. No problem."

She waved her hand in the air at Caleb in a calming motion. There were a few seconds of complete silence at Katrina's end, and they thought they heard a slight chuckle from a male voice in the background. *That had to be Alton*, Caleb considered.

"Then why do you sound so nervous?" Katrina asked in a quieter, calmer voice.

Paige shut her eyes tightly and Caleb waited for a moment before answering, "Everything's fine, Kat. I'm fine. Paige has been wonderful, and I believe absolutely no rules were broken. I promise."

Katrina's eyes flashed bright green, and Alton's expression turned momentarily serious.

"Rules? You don't believe any were -" Katrina pressed in a stern voice. "Do you mean my parting instructions or The Rules?"

There was silence at Caleb and Paige's end of the line.

Paige's eyes snapped open and glared at Caleb as she

mouthed the words, "Oh, shit." Caleb's eyes widened to the size of saucers, and he felt like an idiot for not censoring himself more closely.

"Either, really," he replied weakly.

Paige heavily massaged her fingertips against once-again closed eyelids and emitted a somber groan. There was complete silence Katrina's end of the line.

Caleb sighed in a resigned fashion, walked over to the handset lying on Katrina's desk, picked it up, and turned off the speaker mode. "Kat, it's just me," he said while glancing up to motion for Paige to leave, but she was already closing the room's sliding access door behind her as she hastily departed.

Katrina stared at the cell phone in her hand and turned off the speaker option. She noticed Alton closing himself into one of the cabin's two bedrooms with a noticeable click of the door mechanism.

"I'm alone, as well," she said softly. However, she knew full well that her voice was still detectable by another vampire's sharp hearing, particularly in the small cabin they inhabited. Still, she appreciated Alton's respect for her privacy.

Katrina calmed herself while listening to Caleb's steady breathing at the other end. She thought she heard faint traces of his rapid heartbeat, which was somehow soothing to her. *Perhaps it's just the satisfaction of knowing he's alive and well.*

"I miss you so much," Caleb breathed into the phone. He hadn't felt this way about anyone's prolonged absence in his life, except following the death of his mother.

"I miss you too," Katrina agreed at the other end in a low, but gentle voice.

"Listen, I've had some time to think," he began quietly. "About me, about us. And I think I understand something."

He paused, but only heard silence.

"I'm sensing -- hoping how much you must care about me to do what you're doing," he continued. "And for that, I'm sorry that I've made you so angry with me lately. I don't like it when we argue with each other."

"Caleb," she tried to interrupt him gently.

"I've been selfish about my own wants and needs, not really appreciating what lengths you're going to for me," he persisted. "And if Paige would open the front door for me, I'd rather stand outside to accept whatever fate I'm due than cause you continued grief, no matter the fear I'm feeling."

"Stop," Katrina ordered firmly.

He ceased speaking at once, not wanting to irritate her. *I'm just trying to be honest with her.*

She didn't speak immediately, but paused a few seconds more in silence.

"Caleb, I'm not angry with you," she explained in a soft voice. "I've been upset that someone so innocent and dear was targeted for revenge against me. Granted, my patience hasn't been at its usual level of tolerance, but don't turn this onto yourself. I won't allow it."

He started to open his mouth, but then stopped and just listened.

"You mean so much to me now," she conceded earnestly as much to herself as to him. "I want you in my life and safe. There's so much I want to share with you, so many things I want to tell you."

He smiled a little, and his heart soared with a liberating feeling.

"So don't even think about walking anywhere into danger," she warned. "I truly can't abide that."

He paused and smiled at her open, caring words. *She's the most amazing woman*, he considered. "I feel the same about you, Kat," he replied gently.

His heart felt like it would burst with happiness despite the darkness of the current circumstances. "And Kat," he added quickly.

"Yes?"

"There's no need for concern. Nothing bad has happened,"

he explained. "I was bleeding from a razor cut, and Paige...
well, I'm not bleeding anymore."

There was a pause, and she surmised quietly, "She tasted
you, didn't she?"

"Yes," he admitted. "But nothing more. She even sealed the
cut nicely."

Silence.

"I understand," she said finally. "And I appreciate your
honesty. Now, please put the speaker back on and call Paige
into the room again."

Feeling strangely vindicated, he put the phone back in
speaker mode and shouted, "Paige, telephone!"

A few seconds later, the sliding door opened abruptly and
Paige traversed the distance down the stairs in what seemed
like a blur. She stopped just two feet from Caleb, who marveled
at her speed. *Hell, you might even be faster than Katrina.*

"I'm back, Katrina," she offered in a friendly voice.

"Good," Katrina began in a casual tone. "Everything's fine,
Paige. Caleb explained the situation. And thank you for taking
such good care of him."

Paige's eyes widened, and she flashed an appreciative
smile at Caleb.

"Are you feeding regularly?" Katrina asked.

Paige paused, her smile fading somewhat, and replied in a
circumspect tone, "Maybe not as often as I should."

"I've mentioned before that there's about a three-month
supply of blood stock in my wine cellar refrigerator," Katrina
explained evenly. "Please feed as often as you like. But please
stop tasting my mate."

Then Katrina added gently, "And Caleb, try to curtail any
further 'bloodletting' on your part until I return."

He rolled his eyes, and Paige winked at him with a renewed
grin.

"And as to some brief outdoor privileges?" he ventured
hopefully. "Daylight is safe for me, no vampires."

"Well, since you mentioned it, not on your life," Katrina

countered emphatically. "Not until we return. I don't trust Chimalma not to hire humans to wait for you during the day when you would normally think that it's safe from vampires."

That made sense to him. *I should've expected as much*, he supposed. *Even vampires can hire hit men. After all, that has to be what Harry Maddox turned out to be in the end.*

"We should be back no more than two days from now. We found Chimalma and plan to move as soon as possible," Katrina informed them on a new train of thought.

Caleb's relaxed manner became tense at hearing the revelation from Katrina. Paige's eyes turned serious as well.

"Both of you be careful," Paige urged.

Caleb's heart was racing by that point, and his heart was in his throat. He felt helpless being stuck in a veritable bunker and wished he were able to be there with Alton and Katrina. Paige moved closer to him, placing a supportive hand on his shoulder.

Alton's deep voice broke the silence at Katrina's end of the line, "She's coming back soon, Caleb. Trust me."

Then they said quick goodbyes. After the phone went off, Paige pressed some codes on the handset in rapid sequence and gave Caleb the best reassuring smile that she could muster.

"What if they try to breach the house during the day?" he speculated darkly. "You can't go outside in sunlight, so you're vulnerable during daytime."

"We've already prepared for that," Paige said simply.

He stared at her as if waiting for additional information, but she said nothing more.

"So, is it on a need-to-know basis only too?" he pressed.

She sighed and nodded. "Sorry, better you don't know. Suffice to say, plans are in place."

Caleb was hardly encouraged.

"Katrina's a great planner," she reassured him. "Remember? She's one of the veterans."

"I know," he conceded.

"One of the adult vampires," Paige added with a growing

smile.

"Yeah," he replied absently and moved towards the stairs to leave.

She followed him with a playful grin. "She knows what to do. She's the alpha in your partnership."

"All right," he muttered darkly as he reached the top of the stairs.

"Of course, I'm the alpha in the house right now," she teased as she walked just behind him down the hallway.

"Bad vampire, no more nibbling," he teased back while entering the kitchen to get a Coke from the refrigerator.

"Don't push my buttons, Tree-Branch Boy," she warned with a sly smirk.

"Whatever," he muttered with exasperation as he popped the can open.

"Am I bugging you yet?" she asked as she leaned across the island countertop to poke him in the back repeatedly with her fingertip.

He deliberately sighed loudly before taking a drink from his cola can.

It was night again, and Alton drove the Jeep while Katrina sat in the passenger seat with a steely expression. They were on their way to meet with an arms dealer Alton had used before. The dealer was providing a couple of weapons they would need, including the explosives they planned to use to kill Chimalma. The route to their destination was aided by a dash-mounted GPS with coordinates provided by the dealer. Fortunately, the location was only a couple of hours away from their cabin, so they could easily navigate to and from the transaction on the same night.

*I just want this over with quickly*, Katrina thought. *I have a vampire to kill.* "Are you sure about this dealer?" she asked for the second time that evening.

He restrained a sigh and replied, "Don't worry, Katrina. I've dealt with the man on two previous occasions, and both times he provided the items as promised."

"So, what precisely did you need an arms dealer for in the past?" she inquired.

"Oh, just a couple of past favors for some acquaintances," he replied vaguely.

She glanced at the GPS and noted that their destination was only a few miles away. She pulled on a pair of black leather gloves and absently noticed that he was already wearing some.

As they neared a turn-off comprised of a narrow dirt road leading through dense trees, Alton muttered. "Remember, let me do the talking. You're my silent business associate."

"Fine," she agreed neutrally. *It's not like I'm here for a conversation.*

They pulled up in front of a large, sheet metal barn with a curved canopy roof. The poorly maintained building had peeled silver paint interspersed with rust along its façade. Two large metal sliding doors remained wide open, but Alton stopped their vehicle outside the entrance and cut off the engine.

Just inside and to the right was a white panel van parked to the side of the large bay area. A number of battery-powered spotlights placed inside the barn in various locations provided ample illumination to the interior.

Wearing their long, black leather coats over dark jeans and sweaters, they exited the vehicle into the cold night air. Katrina had suggested that the subdued wardrobe might be useful at night, and power colors were always helpful for business meetings. Alton had merely chuckled and acquiesced.

Two rough-looking men, an older man with a graying beard and a clean-shaven younger man, were pointing small submachine guns in their direction as they walked towards the barn entrance.

"Please, come in," came a man's gruff voice from inside. "But I'd appreciate your removing your coats and leaving them outside."

Alton's eyes darted to Katrina long enough to see her shrug, and both of them removed their coats to lay them on the hood of their Jeep.

"Much better," the man said congenially.

They entered the barn and counted four other men inside. Each was a hard-looking figure with his own gun, and they wore a mixture of hunting clothes and military camouflage. A person stood at each interior corner of the barn, and two more men stood at the middle of the dirt floor towards the back.

Katrina glanced around the room as they entered and saw no additional people present.

Before they were halfway into the building, a tall, middle-aged man with a cropped haircut and faded U.S. Army Special Forces emblem on his camouflage jacket spoke up. "Please stop there so we can perform a quick search for weapons."

Alton and Katrina silently stopped, and the younger of the two men flanking them shouldered his submachine gun and patted down Alton. He moved to Katrina, but took a noticeably protracted time to pat her down, his hand lingering at her hips and thighs longer than she was willing to endure.

"Move them or lose them," she growled angrily. *If this goes badly, you get to die first*, she silently promised the fellow.

The man quickly stepped back and nodded briskly to the man at the center of the room.

"Mister Alton," the middle-aged man greeted with a northeastern accent. "So good to do business with you again. Please approach."

Alton gave Katrina a motion with his head to indicate that she should stand where she was while he neared the dealer.

"Mr. Preston," Alton greeted with a slight nod as he halted approximately two feet from him.

Within a span of a few seconds, Alton's eyes observed a small table to Preston's left sporting a large plastic container left open to reveal small wrapped packages of plastic explosives. There were detonators and priming wires visible as well. To the side of the container, Alton noticed a small, handheld crossbow with a quiver of wood-shafted and metal-tipped arrows.

Preston took notice of Alton's glance to the table before he offered, "If you look at the table, you'll see that everything you asked for is there."

Alton nodded. "I'm confident that's the case."

Preston raised an eyebrow, but his expression returned to a more neutral manner as he ventured, "Despite the small order and manageable quantity of explosives, they were difficult to acquire on short notice. I'm afraid there's going to be a slight price mark-up."

"How much of a mark-up?" Alton asked evenly.

Preston exhibited a calculating expression and stipulated, "Fifty."

"Another fifty thousand," Alton muttered irritably.

Katrina's jaw tightened at the exchange taking place between the two men. She just wanted to get the transaction over with because they still had key items to acquire for their mission, although from more conventional sources.

"That's fine," she snapped impatiently.

Preston looked sharply across the length of the large area to Katrina before focusing on Alton again. "The lady has good hearing," he observed with a frown, adding pointedly: "And appears to be in a hurry."

The man nearest to Katrina made an effort to point the barrel of his gun at her menacingly, but she merely ignored him.

"Fifty thousand will be fine," Alton remarked levelly.

"Ah, no. I'm afraid you misunderstood. That's fifty percent," Preston explained with a straight face. "Not fifty thousand."

Alton's eyes narrowed. "That's not at all what we agreed upon."

Preston merely shrugged. "Like I said, it was hard to come by on short notice. And from the lady's comment, you appear to need these items in a hurry. Just business, nothing personal, you understand."

Alton started to reply, but Katrina's cold, hard voice cut

him off. "That's too bad for you then," she stated lethally. "Because my business is personal this time."

Preston's eyes narrowed, but Katrina was already in motion. She grabbed the younger man standing next to her by the neck and swung him around, so when the older man next to her fired, the bullets impacted the younger man's back. He screamed, and she grabbed at his waistband with her free hand to seize a combat knife from a leather sheath.

She simultaneously snapped the younger man's neck with her left hand while deftly slashing at the neck of the older man before her. The older man's neck was nearly severed in half as his body fell to the ground, and blood spurted around his fallen form.

Alton slammed his right fist into the side of Preston's head, knocking him to the ground as the vampire lunged at the man standing behind Preston. The guard started firing in Alton's direction, but the tall vampire sidestepped the firing arc and lashed out with his hand. It took only one swift motion to break his neck, and Alton snatched the submachine gun from the dead man's hands.

The two men at the back corners of the room were firing at Katrina, but she had already dropped the body of the younger man and moved in a blur across the room towards the man in the rear left corner. It took only a second to cross the distance, her eyes blazing bright green with rage. She stepped past the man while holding the combat knife outwards slightly with her arm to catch him in the chest with the blade. The force of her impact knocked the man to the ground with a gasp, and his body thudded heavily to the dirty floor.

Alton swiveled the dead guard's gun in his gloved hands to the remaining guard to his left and behind him. The guard was firing across the room at Katrina as Alton aimed and fired two quick belches of gunfire. Bullets riddled into his neck and head, and the guard spun to the ground in a bloody arc.

Katrina glanced over to Alton and noticed Preston lying on the ground but bringing an automatic pistol upwards in an aimed arc towards Alton, who was still torso-twisted away from the arms dealer. Her hand swooped down to pluck the knife from the chest of the guard at her feet, and she hurled the blade at Preston just as Alton was turning back to face him. The blade imbedded in Preston's arm, causing his gun to fire wide and to the side of Alton.

Alton snarled angrily and jammed the butt of his gun into Preston's forehead with brutal force, causing the man's cranium to be shattered by the impact. His body hurled back to the ground with a bloody thump, and Alton discarded the gun absently as he glanced towards Katrina.

"I was right. You're the heavy artillery, just like I told Caleb," he quipped darkly. "But your negotiation skills could use some work."

She scowled as she walked over to her former mentor. "I thought I did pretty well, actually. We get the merchandise and keep our money."

He smiled grimly as he moved to the small table to close the fabricated case containing the explosives and detonators. He glanced back long enough to see Katrina standing over Preston's body and glancing down at his crushed skull.

"You don't overcharge a vampire," she muttered lethally before moving to the table to pick up the crossbow and selection of arrows.

Katrina looked over at Alton and demanded with a note of incredulity, "Are you sure that you actually dealt with these people before?"

Alton shrugged. "As I said, I conducted two successful transactions with them in the past. I suppose they simply don't treat repeat customers very well."

She gave him a withering look as they loaded the items into their vehicle, and both turned back to gaze at the old sheet metal building.

"Should we use some of the explosives?" he asked absently as he considered their options.

"No, it will tip the authorities, as well as associate this

scene with Chimalma's fate," Katrina estimated. "Load the bodies into the van and set fire to the gas tank. It should be just enough to cover our tracks. We won't worry about their blood around the building because there's nothing left to tie it back to us."

Alton raised an eyebrow at his former pupil. "You're good."

She smiled back with a menacing grin. "Killing is a specialty of mine."

He frowned and warned, "Fine for now, but I want you to let go of this when you get back to Caleb."

Her facial expression fell slightly as the vision of Caleb appeared in her mind's eye. She knew that he brought out the best in her and realized that he might be the only one who could tame her renewed savagery in the end. *At least I hope that he can.*

"I'm going to try," she replied quietly.

She steeled herself for the task ahead and walked deliberately back into the building. Alton followed quietly behind her.

Within twenty minutes, they had stacked the bodies and firearms into the panel van. Katrina punctured the vehicle's gas tank and drained a large amount of fuel to spread underneath it and onto the bodies using an old bucket she found inside the building. She used a match to ignite the spilled fuel as Alton watched from near their Jeep. Afterwards, she sped from the building as the fire erupted throughout the interior of the van.

Katrina slid the two main doors closed and walked calmly back to where Alton stood. She picked up her coat from the hood of the vehicle and tossed his to him. Moving to the passenger door, she suggested, "Still lots to do tonight. We better get going."

He watched her for a moment, marveling at her initiative and efficiency, and then slid into the driver's seat. They pulled away into the night, leaving the abandoned building behind.

"Where to next?" he asked as she selected various options on the GPS.

"The nearest all-night department store," she replied. "We

need some heavy length of chain."

Alton frowned and looked at her curiously.

She noted his expression as she looked up from the GPS. "Well, Chimalma's not going to just walk into a booby-trapped kill zone, is she?"

Alton raised both eyebrows and considered the idea for a moment.

"There," she offered in a satisfied tone. "I found a store not far away from our route back to the cabin."

He glanced at the GPS and headed in the designated direction after they returned to the paved roadway.

# Chapter 10

❦

# Nighttime Guests

*A*lton focused on preparing and rechecking the equipment and supplies intended for their night-time assault. They also studied the satellite images of the area around the retreat facility, as well as maps of the area roads and designated points of interest within miles of their target.

When evening finally arrived, both vampires felt as prepared as possible for their endeavor. As Alton helped load their implements into the Jeep, he took note of Katrina's focused manner.

"I've seen that look on your face before, you know," he observed as she closed the back door of the Jeep with a resolute push of her hand.

Her piercing green eyes probed into his as she inquired, "And when was that, exactly?"

"Decades ago, actually. Around the time of your last hunt for Chimalma," he recalled.

She arched an eyebrow. "Yes, but this time's different."

"Really? How so?"

Her expression was stony. "Last time was a fruitless hunt. This time, I plan to be successful and perhaps gain a little closure."

Alton nodded silently as he walked around to the driver's side of the Jeep while Katrina secured the cabin's front door.

*This time, Chimalma, I'll commit you to dust*, she vowed coldly, *and you'll never threaten Caleb or me again.*

The night was cold and clear, with a crescent moon shining

among the array of stars blanketing the sky. They arrived outside the retreat facility close to ten o'clock and parked the Jeep
some distance away. Exiting the vehicle, they each wore black
jeans, sweaters, leather gloves, and hiking boots. They dabbed
black shoe polish on their faces to subdue their pale skin, confident they would blend into the night quite effectively. Additionally, Katrina tied her long, red hair back in a single, tight
ponytail.

Alton secured two combat knives to his web gear and was
armed with a small automatic pistol with silencer. They were
his weapons of choice for the type of activities they planned.
Though fighting wasn't his preferred activity, he had experienced enough in his time on Earth that he was no stranger to
various forms of combat and violence.

She adjusted her black leather harness gear that held a
number of knives and throwing stars. They served her well
when she performed stealth work. Wrapped across her shoulder and extending to her hip was a long coil of steel cable, which
he had convinced her was superior for carrying in a stealthy
situation and was almost as strong as the logging chain she
wanted to bring. She admired his forethought on the matter
and silently berated herself for not having thought of it first.
She also sported the repeating combat crossbow with a leather
sheaf of the wood-shafted, metal-tipped bolts.

Both vampires slipped small tactical ear bone conduction
microphone/receivers into their right ears, which would allow
them to stay in relatively silent communication with each other so long as they remained in close proximity and away from
sources of interference. The devices were highly effective and
commonly used by military and police tactical teams.

Alton handed her a small handheld detonator. "I have one
just like it tuned to the same frequency. That way either one of
us can trigger the explosion when we're ready."

Katrina nodded, and he handed her the small electronic
jammer they used at the downtown office building in Atlanta.

"Do you remember my instructions regarding its use?" he

asked.

She nodded.

"Don't forget you only have ten minutes of power once it's activated," he added, "during which time our communications will go dead."

"Got it," she replied while slipping it into a holder attached to her leather harness. "I'll try not to use it, if possible."

"Let's go then," Alton suggested.

Both vampires moved out silently into the nearby woods in the direction of the retreat facility.

The area was hilly and packed with dense trees interspersed with hiking trails. Small creeks throughout the area emptied into a large river running directly below the small meadow intended for use as the kill zone. Both of them kept to the trees, though their skilled vampire bodies were adept at moving silently through the dense coverage. They moved a short distance apart, so they were approaching the retreat grounds from slightly different angles. Katrina intended to approach somewhat from the front, while Alton would approach from the back because it was closer to the area where he needed to set up the kill zone.

Alton made his way up the facing of a steep, tree-covered hill and soon came upon one of the small hiking trails. He avoided the trail because it was more easily watched or booby-trapped and remained in the trees as his acute senses tuned to any unusual sounds or movements.

After ten minutes, he detected the sounds of a human moving around in the dry leaves covering parts of the ground. He approached to within twenty feet of the guard, who wore hunter's gear and carried a rifle with a night scope. The guard smoked a cigarette near one of the small hiking trails and appeared somewhat bored. He stamped his feet to generate warmth, obviously having been standing in the cold night for some time.

Alton retrieved his silenced pistol and managed to creep to within four feet of the man and slightly behind his area of vision. He raised his pistol and fired once at the base of the man's head, affecting an immediate kill. The figure slumped to the ground, and Alton stamped out his lit cigarette and pulled the figure into some dense bushes nearby. Then he moved silently onwards to seek additional guards.

"One down," he whispered.

Katrina heard and smiled grimly as she made her way through the trees. Her senses felt attuned to the natural environment around her, and she reveled with the thrill of the hunt. Yet another part of her was anxious for it to be over. The sooner she finished, the sooner she could return to Caleb.

Still, she shamefully admitted that the renewal of violence of the past few days had rekindled a sense of pleasure. She loved to stalk prey, regardless of whether it were humans or animals. It was a vampire attribute she relished and warmly embraced, even though in recent years, she sought more sedate and reclusive feeding habits. Now she felt the call of the hunt, though for serious reasons and much higher stakes than her personal pleasure. *Now it's for my mate.* Just the thought of Caleb and the manner in which he fulfilled the role of mate supplied her with renewed vigor for her task at hand.

Before long, she heard the sound of a person some distance ahead coughing in the night. Her hearing zeroed in on the man's location, and she began the stealthy endeavor of stalking him. He was dressed in traditional hunter's garb, but held an assault rifle with infrared scope. The man was looking through the infrared sight, but was looking to his right and sweeping left in her direction.

She increased the speed of her closure to the man's position and moved more to the rear of him so his scanning arc wouldn't point in her immediate direction without his turning around. Even in the dry winter conditions, she avoided noise that would alert someone to her presence. The breeze caused tree limbs to brush together, generating some ambient noise as her footfalls fell relatively silently one after another.

Once she arrived to within thirty feet of the man, Katrina

aimed her combat crossbow at the figure and carefully locked him in her sights. After accounting for the minimal wind, she let loose a bolt that caught the man squarely in the mid-left quadrant of his back. He fell to the ground with little struggle, and she closed the distance to him to slash swiftly downwards across his throat with one of the combat knives sheathed in her web gear.

"One down," she whispered.

She continued on her way, once again scanning the distance with her keen senses to detect another guard.

Within an hour, both of them had taken six more guards out of operation. Alton moved towards the designated kill zone to start distributing his explosives in an even, circular pattern for the most efficient detonation.

Meanwhile, Katrina moved closer to the retreat facility, a medium-sized, two-story conference center with built-in suites of guest rooms. There was also a small restaurant built into one end of the facility, along with a small boat house skirting an oversized pond just behind the main building. The only other major structure was a large storage building positioned well away from the conference center to the east of the boat house.

Katrina was struck by how the entire compound seemed to be closed. There were only half a dozen vehicles in the parking lot, which likely belonged to some of the guards on duty. She had expected to encounter a contingent of guests who would pose an additional impediment to their plans. The Website for the facility didn't indicate any specific closure periods during the winter months, although it was only about two weeks from Christmas. Whatever the reason for the abandoned facility, she found the development encouraging.

She made her way towards the storage building, the nearest structure to her position, allowing her the opportunity to examine further the central complex grounds from a relative degree of cover. As she hugged the building, she wondered how Alton was coming along with the explosives.

"Alton?" she whispered. "Status?"

There was a silent pause.

"Nearly halfway complete," Alton replied finally.

"I'm at the storage building just east of the boat house to survey the grounds further," she whispered. "Then I'll move into the facility for Chimalma."

"Right," he replied. "Be careful. I'll head for the storage building after I'm done here."

"Copy that," she whispered. She permitted a small smile to cross her lips as she moved forward.

Alton completed the configuration of explosives and double-checked the array. While working, he reflected on his experience with demolitions, honed during clandestine operations that he performed for the British Secret Service during World War II and again during brief periods of the Cold War. Of course, he had conducted the operations under separate names and identities, but the cumulative experience had proven handy at such times.

He returned to the retreat grounds, being careful to ensure that no additional guards moved into the area. After arriving effortlessly at the storage building near the boat house, he failed to see Katrina in the immediate vicinity.

"At the storage building," he whispered.

There was a pause, and Katrina replied, "Area surveyed. Moving into the main facility."

"I'll stage near the facility to watch for guards and respond as needed," he whispered.

"Copy," she replied.

Katrina completed her survey of the main grounds of the retreat complex, but found no other guards outside. She moved towards the rear entrance of the building where there was less direct lighting from exterior sources. Most of the interior of the building was dark, except for main hallways and some offices, which appeared vacant.

She tried the rear entrance and was wary when she found it to be unlocked. Abruptly, she heard the sound of Chimalma's voice from within the lower level near the main office area. She reached to her web gear, extracted the small jamming device, and activated it. Unfortunately, her communications with Alton would be suspended until she turned it off again or until the ten-minute battery expired.

After only a moment, Katrina no longer heard the sound of Chimalma's voice as she entered the open area, which appeared to be a gathering room for socializing and mingling near the registration desk. She peered down the length of a long hallway as she made her way to the front entry area and on to the main offices where she originally heard Chimalma's voice.

A guard wearing a woodland camouflage uniform and carrying a silenced submachine gun appeared at the very end of the hallway and pointed his weapon at her. In a blur, she grasped three throwing stars from her web gear and flung them at high velocity down the length of the hall towards the guard as he was pulling the trigger. Two rounds passed in front of Katrina's body. The others went wild into the ceiling when the throwing stars impacted the man's upper chest and throat. He spun to the ground clutching at his neck, and in a matter of seconds, fell silent.

She proceeded towards the main offices.

Alton was preparing to move around the storage building to head for the front of the facility when he heard a small sound behind him. He swiftly turned with pistol in hand and saw the long, curvy blade of a knife already speeding towards him. He barely had time to swivel his body to avoid being hit in the chest with the blade, instead imbedding firmly into his stomach with a meaty thud.

He grunted from the impact and saw a blur of movement as the dark-clad figure of Chimalma kicked him in the chest with a booted foot, knocking him to the ground as his pistol spun off into the night to land on the ground nearby.

"Well, if it isn't Alton," she offered with a dark expression as she hefted a short-bladed machete in her right hand. "Ever the foolish chevalier, I see."

"Go to hell," he muttered through clenched teeth as his hand went to the hilt of the blade buried in his stomach.

"You first," she seethed back at him with scowl as she moved towards him with the machete raised.

The day passed rather quickly for Paige and Caleb. They performed a number of mundane domestic tasks, including laundry, vacuuming and mopping the floors, and cleaning the bathrooms. He was less than enthusiastic about the chores, but she quickly convinced him that despite the anticipation of word from Katrina, daily life had to continue. Paige emphasized that Katrina was particularly orderly and would be very appreciative for their efforts upon her return. That finally convinced him to put some vigor into his endeavors. She was additionally pleased that it kept him occupied during the day, leaving less time for boredom or feeling listless.

Once evening arrived, Paige showered and changed into fashionable blue jeans that fit her perfectly and a Goth black Garbage concert T-shirt bearing a picture of Shirley Manson. After Caleb showered and cleaned up, he slipped on a pair of jeans and a T-shirt and went looking for something to eat.

As he finished eating a single-sized, oven-baked lasagna, Paige walked by the kitchen counter where he sat. She shriveled her nose and frowned unpleasantly as she glanced at him.

"What's wrong?" he asked while chewing the last bite.

"Dude, there's way too much garlic in that," she noted with disgust.

He raised his eyebrows curiously. "Oh yeah, vampires are allergic to garlic, aren't they?"

She gave him a withering expression. "No, Van Helsing, vampires aren't allergic to garlic," she teased. "There's just way too much in that dish. Remember? Keen sense of smell?" She paused and added, "Besides, garlic alters the appreciable flavor of your blood for a time after you consume it."

He grinned. "Sort of curdles the milk?"

She considered that and smirked. "Yeah, something like that."

"I guess I'm safe for tonight then," he quipped with a smile. "You nibbler!"

She stuck her tongue out, countering, "Not funny, Tree-Branch Boy."

He washed the dishes as she perched on a kitchen stool casually watching him.

"So," Paige ventured. "What sounds good for tonight? Movie, TV, or maybe a game of cards? I'm a pretty mean poker player."

Caleb rinsed the dishes, placing them in the drain board next to the sink. "How about chess?" he suggested.

She considered his offer. "Ok, kiddo. But I hope you won't feel too bad when I kick your butt at it."

"We'll see," he mused with a sly grin and headed to the living room where Katrina kept a chessboard.

"Hey, hold up, tiger," Paige interjected. "Go brush your teeth and use some mouthwash to get rid of the garlic breath. No chemical warfare allowed in the chess game!"

He chuckled and headed upstairs. Ten minutes later, the two were playing chess while Paige sipped at a glass of warm blood that he had prepared for her.

"No sympathy points for the blood offering," she warned. "But thanks, much appreciated."

He smiled as they exchanged a series of rapid moves and counter moves, trading some pawns in the process. Caleb began thinking more thoroughly about his strategy. The spunky vampire proved to be quite an accomplished chess player. It surprised him, since she always seemed more the party-girl. But then, he considered there was likely much more to her than he suspected.

Paige alternated tapping two fingernails of her right hand on the coffee table as she stared across the chessboard at him.

"Hey, quit cheating," Caleb mock-complained as he carefully studied the variety of pieces remaining across the board.

"That's not cheating," she retorted as she continued the strumming while staring at him intently. "It relaxes me."

He glanced up at her, noticing her intent stare. "What?" he pressed with a frown.

"Are you sure you're up to a game of chess with a vastly superior being?" Paige asked with a grin.

Caleb grinned back and challenged, "You know, humans are far better chess players than vampires."

She frowned suspiciously. "How do you figure?"

He smiled. "Because vampires can only make effective use of their 'nights.'"

Paige shook her head with a sour expression and retorted, "Ew. I'm so gonna bite your neck over that one."

Their game continued at a more sedate pace, with each of them taking a deliberative period of time to consider their respective options quietly before moving.

As Caleb pondered his next move, Paige suddenly cocked her head to one side and froze in place. He looked up curiously and started to ask her what was wrong, but she held up her hand for silence.

Her eyes widened, and in a blur of movement she lurched up from her chair to grab him by his upper right arm, jerking him to his feet abruptly. "Crap! We should've played in Katrina's room. We've got visitors," she snapped as she dragged him into the kitchen and threw open the door to the basement before pulling him down the stairs.

"Who? What's going on?" he demanded as his pulse rate soared.

At the bottom of the stairs, she pointed to the far corner of the room towards a stack of crates and boxes and ordered, "Hide behind those crates and keep quiet, no matter what. And stay put! I'm coming back for you!" Then she bounded up the stairs, closing the door to the basement behind her.

He glanced frantically around him and started for the stack of crates when he paused and looked at the nearby workbenches. *Need a weapon,* he resolved.

Spotting a medium-sized steel crowbar, he grabbed it and hefted it in his right hand. The lights abruptly went out, but instead of heading for the crates, he moved back towards the foot of the stairs and felt his way to the side of the concrete steps. He stood along the lower side of the stairs in front of the refrigerator so he could get a clear swing at someone who might descend to the floor level. It also provided a small degree of visual shelter for him until someone descended to the bottom.

His heart felt like it was going to explode as he listened intently for any noises from above. He thought he heard a small popping sound followed by a door crashing into a wall. There was the muted sound of boots scuffling upstairs.

Caleb jolted as he heard the song "Temptation Waits," by Garbage, begin to blare above from house's speaker system.

*I'll tell you something*

*I am a wolf, but*

*I like to wear sheep's clothing*

He heard muted gunfire followed by a blood-curdling scream and a thunderous crash upstairs.

*I am a bonfire*

*I am a vampire*

*I'm waiting for my moment*

Another muted scream came from above followed by two successive shotgun blasts.

*I just can't get enough*

*I'm like an addict coming at you for a little more*

An abrupt rumbling crash sounded upstairs, followed by some muted gunfire and more crashing sounds. Then there were no further noises, save for the loud music.

*I'll tell you something*

*I am a demon*

*Some say my biggest weakness*

Caleb was shaking slightly, but his jaw was set as he heard the door open at the top of the stairs. He saw a red light appear on the steps and walk its way down to the bottom of the stairs next to where he was standing in the pitch blackness. He raised the crowbar with his right arm and prepared to swing as the music blared from above.

The red laser dot swept forward and to the right as it made its way around to him. Silenced gunfire erupted, and he swung the crowbar with all his might. In the quick successive flashes from the weapon's muzzle, he saw a hooded figure in goggles wearing body armor as the crowbar connected with the figure's head with a dull thud.

Caleb slipped on something under his feet and plummeted downward as he heard the whizzing of bullets while the figure's assault rifle continued firing, even as the figure sprawled onto the floor near him. A cool fluid penetrated through his jeans and he reached up to rub his forehead with his hand, smudging himself slightly with the substance.

*You are a secret*

*A new possession*

*I like to keep you guessing*

He heard another sound at the top of the stairs followed by footsteps. Raising the crowbar where he sat panting, he planned a desperate strike at the figure's kneecap.

Katrina made her way into the main office area and approached a short hallway leading back to small offices. In the hallway she noticed letter-sized pieces of paper lying on the floor approximately two feet apart from each other. Each sheet bore the phrase *Keep Reading* in large black letters.

She frowned and followed the trail of papers while brandishing her crossbow, ready to fire at any immediate target. Her keen hearing registered only silence, reassuring her nobody else was in the immediate area.

At the end of the hallway was a small clerical office, including a small conference table with the repeating message of papers leading across the floor towards it. On the tabletop were a small digital recorder and a white piece of paper, which read

*ALTON IS ALREADY DEAD.*

Katrina turned off the jamming device and snapped, "Alton! Alton, can you hear me?"

But she registered no response in her com link. She heard the small digital recorder lying on the table reactivate and begin playing its looping message in Chimalma's harsh-sounding voice. "Katrina, Caleb is dead. Mercenaries texted me to say they just entered the house. Too bad. It seems humans just don't take bullets very well, I'm afraid."

Katrina gasped as if her heart were being stabbed repeatedly by a knife. She wanted to scream out loud and barely managed to contain herself. *Damn it, Paige, you better have saved him!*

Whirling around, she ran through the facility towards the nearest exit in a blur. Her eyes were blazing green, and she felt like a maelstrom of anger and bitterness. She had one immediate focus: *kill Chimalma.*

Her only hope was to locate Alton's last position and expect that Chimalma was still there.


The cool, sticky fluid he sat in rendered standing too risky, so Caleb crouched on the floor. He nervously held the crowbar like a baseball bat, hoping he might have one more swing to someone's kneecaps left in him. As he heard the tentative footsteps above, he hoped his luck would hold out as it did with the first attacker.

"Caleb?" came Paige's tentative voice.

The crowbar clattered to the concrete floor, and he muttered, "Thank God."

"Caleb!" Paige gasped from somewhere in the darkness before a flashlight snapped on to flash down at him. "Oh hell! Where are you hurt?"

His eyes widened and he glanced down in the flashlight's glow to see he was sitting in a pool of blood. "Jesus!" he cried with shock.

"Crap, crap, crap," Paige chanted as she dropped the flashlight into his lap and began feeling around his body with her frantic hands. She sniffed suddenly and stopped running her hands over him. "Wait," she snapped and bent her face close to his.

Her tongue quickly darted to the blood on his forehead. "Good, good. Not your blood," she uttered. "Stay here!"

Then she was gone, and the assailant's body next to him seemed to leap off the floor and up the stairs with a scraping, dragging sound. Within moments, the loud music stopped, and the lights snapped back on.

"Ew, gross," he muttered as he stood shakily and stared at the red, slimy liquid covering his hands and the floor where he stood.

He heard a brief footstep on the stairs above, but when he looked up, Paige was already standing before him. There was blood smeared around her mouth, and he stared at her with wide eyes. Her youthful and playful appearance had turned macabre. She frowned at him.

"Oh, sorry," she apologized while wiping her mouth with the back of her hand.

"Are they gone?" he asked.

"We got them all," she responded. "And nice job, by the way."

He started wiping his bloodied and still shaking hands on his jeans. *No harm in that now*, he thought absently. "You kill to a soundtrack?" he demanded.

"Throws the attacker off," she replied with a shrug. "Even the military uses music to get inside an enemy's head."

He stared blankly at the blonde vampire, quite unsure what to say.

"Well, that explains the blood," she mused while gazing at the plasma seeping freely from the bullet holes in the refrigerator behind Caleb.

"I've never killed anybody before," he absently muttered as his mind replayed events from the past few minutes.

"I figured," she smirked. "And you still haven't. That thug

is unconscious, but he's still alive."

His eyes darted to hers, and panic began to rise in him. "Where is he?"

"Yeah, I need to go take care of that now," she interrupted with a glance upstairs. "Take off all of your clothes and leave them on the floor. Then go upstairs and take a shower."

"My clothes?" he challenged.

"Uh, yeah!" she retorted sharply. "I don't want any more blood tracked through the house than necessary. We've got a lot of it to clean up as it is."

"Wait, won't we need to worry about the police coming soon? Somebody must have heard what happened," Caleb asked.

Paige scowled. "Around here? Nah, the house's insulation and security paneling on the windows would've muffled some of it, and there's too much distance between properties, as well as dense forest obstructions creating a sound buffer. Besides, the types of people living in neighborhoods like this care more about how nice your landscaping looks than whether or not they heard a noise from your property. Just try letting your lawn grow out of sorts. That's when they'll come looking for you."

"Oh," he replied blankly. He noticed that her T-shirt had two small holes across her midsection, and there was blood staining through the fabric. "You're hurt!" he barked with alarm as he pointed to her shirt.

She glanced down at her midriff. "Nah. Just a couple of shotgun pellets. I'll be fine."

His mouth fell open in shock.

Paige tilted her head slightly and held up her hand for silence. "Gotta run," she said.

She darted up the stairs, and Caleb was left standing alone. He sighed, stepped over to a dry portion of the floor away from the growing pool of blood, and started stripping off his clothes. Once finished, he felt extremely vulnerable as he tiptoed up the cool concrete stairs and through the house until reaching the stairway leading up to the bedrooms. He peered around carefully and crept up the carpeted stairs and into his bedroom, closing the door behind him.

Caleb finished showering and slipped on fresh jeans and a snug black T-shirt. Fortunately, he had grabbed a set of athletic shoes when hastily packing back at his apartment. He considered how it felt like weeks since he'd seen his own place. As he exited the bedroom and proceeded cautiously downstairs, he noticed occasional blood spots on the carpeted floor, but no bodies.

He heard muffled sounds coming from the garage beyond the kitchen. Frowning, he quietly moved in that direction.

When he arrived at the door leading into the garage, it was hanging wide open and barely suspended from its hinges. The door handle section was merely a jagged hole, as though something had taken a half-moon bite out of it. There were five black-uniformed bodies wearing body armor lying in a heap in the far corner of the garage to his right. Caleb swallowed and scanned the room until he saw Paige holding one of the attackers against the far wall by his neck. The man's face was contorted in a look of rage laced with pain. His left arm was limp to his side, as if it were a hanging fixture from his body, and his right hand was grasping with futility against her hand as it held him in place.

"How many more of you are there?" Paige asked coldly. "Or shall I break the other arm too?"

"No more...none," the man gasped in strangled fashion.

Caleb froze in place as he watched the event with horror. Ever since meeting her, Paige had reminded him of a sweet, mischievous, and spritely young woman. She still looked the same, save for some blood streaking her bob-cut blonde hair, but her visage was completely vicious instead of playful. It sent a shiver up his spine, and yet his eyes were unable to look away.

Part of him felt that what the assailant was receiving was well deserved, and part of him was disgusted by Paige's violence. Somehow the middle-aged assailant with graying mustache seemed far less threatening, completely vulnerable, in fact. However, another part of Caleb wanted to be the one strangling the assailant instead of Paige. It was that thought that chilled him to the core.

As she maintained her strangle-hold, the man struggled with another emphatic response: "Just us!"

Paige froze in place and continued pinning the assailant to the wall as her head slowly turned to gaze back over her shoulder at Caleb. Her eyes were a blazing bright blue color, and their baleful appearance simultaneously filled him with both awe and terror. He felt frozen in place by her gaze, like a deer standing in the headlights of a speeding, oncoming train. At that moment, she emanated and embodied the visceral, terrifying power of a vampire.

"Caleb," she spoke in a lethally calm voice. "You need to go back into the house now."

"Let me go. You promised!" the man sputtered in a strangled gasp as he flailed in place with his legs.

"Oh, I'll keep my promise," she assured him calmly while still looking directly at Caleb, but there was something cruel in her expression.

Caleb became aware of a slight, uncontrolled tremor passing through his entire body as he stared wide-eyed at the scene before him.

"The house, Caleb," she repeated calmly. "Please."

He kept nodding his head up and down and stepped backwards until he felt his back hit the wall behind him. He managed to stumble down the short hallway into the kitchen only after Paige's full attention returned to the assailant. Caleb's breath was coming in small, ragged gasps as control slowly returned to his body.

He was barely across to the other side of the kitchen when he heard a loud cracking sound, followed by the dull thump of something hitting the garage floor.

"There," Paige's semi-distant voice carried to his ears. "I let you go, as promised."

Caleb absently walked through the house without really seeing where he was going until he reached the farthest room on the lower floor, which happened to be the study. It was dark, save for the glow from the small desk lamp dimly illuminating the large oak desktop. The window behind the desk had a heavy metal plate in place blocking visibility to the outside world, and he silently stood staring at it. He was feeling a little distant from his body, as if seeing himself in a dream. And yet he realized that he was still standing before the shuttered window.

He stood silently for what felt like forever.

"Caleb," prompted Paige's quiet voice from the doorway. She had showered and changed into some new black jeans and a plain white T-shirt with a pink Hello Kitty on the front.

Caleb shut his eyes tightly and didn't turn around. He wasn't sure how long he had been standing before the study window, but noticed that the earlier tremor in his muscles had dissipated. However, his entire body was rigid, like a brick wall. A small hint of terror began to creep back into his mind, like a bad memory resurfacing.

"Are you okay?" Paige asked gently.

He was thankful that her voice had lost its quiet, lethal edge. "Yes, fine," he replied quietly, carefully. *Please go away.*

She silently considered his response, as if studying him. "It had to be done," she offered. "You realize that, don't you?"

He nodded. Yet something still bothered him about his reaction earlier, something new and terrible.

She frowned and approached him from behind in a very deliberate, human way. Her bare footfalls made noticeable sounds on the carpeted floor, which he was able to detect with his own hearing.

*Is that for my benefit?* he wondered.

Very gently, yet deliberately, she placed her right hand on his shoulder and immediately noted the hard tenseness of his muscles as he remained statue-still.

"You and I are okay then?" she asked softly, but with a hint of uncertainty in her voice.

He nodded. "Yes, we're fine."

She stepped closer, and her right arm wrapped underneath his arm and across his lean chest muscles to rest flat against his ribs. She elevated herself up on her tiptoes and kissed him on the cheek ever so softly. "I'm your babysitter, remember?" she asked gently. "Your guardian. I'm here for your benefit, nobody else's."

His body relaxed a little, and he opened his eyes.

"I scared you, didn't I?" she surmised easily.

He nodded. "Somewhat." *No, you scared the hell out of me!*

"Well, I'm not going to hurt you," she reassured him soothingly. "I wouldn't dare, even if so inclined. You're not like other humans anymore. You've been claimed as a mate by a vampire. You were special before, but you're very special now."

Paige hugged his back snugly against the front of her body, and Caleb felt her warmth penetrate soothingly through his T-shirt and into the cool skin of his back. He hadn't realized he was feeling chilled until her body was against his. She flexed her right arm gently to pull him against her and used the fingertip of her left hand to trace the outline of his left ear.

She felt his pulse and his heartbeat and studied his breathing pattern. "Something more is bothering you."

He considered her statement, and the source of his feelings dawned on him in its entirety. "It's me," he replied faintly. "I saw you strangling the man in the garage."

She frowned. "Yes. And?"

"I wanted to be the one strangling him."

Her eyes narrowed as she considered his revelation and ran the fingertips of her left hand gently across the left side of his face. "Unusual for you, I think, given your disposition," she ventured. "But understandable."

"I've never felt like that before." He frowned. "It's not like me."

His entire life had been a struggle for composure and avoidance to open hostility. He had feared his father as a child,

feared the anger directed at him at such a powerless age. He
never wanted to convey such violence against anyone else, so
he avoided aggression altogether. But something had changed
in the past couple of hours. Somehow the idea of violence didn't
seem so abhorrent anymore.

"Something bad has awakened in me, I think," he whispered. *What's happening to me?*

Paige considered his response. "Well," she whispered soothingly into his ear. "I guess we'll have to help you tame it. Avoidance is dangerous, but control is useful and healthy."

A silent moment passed.

"I appreciate it," he responded numbly.

She gently pressed her lips to the back of his neck and
lightly kissed him.

"What was that for?" he asked.

"Because I'm proud of you, kiddo," she whispered soothingly. "You did very well today."

He smirked. "Thanks, babysitter."

She patted his chest lightly with her right hand. "Come on,
tiger. Let's try to get this house cleaned up again. And we've
got a door in the garage to repair, as well."

"Wait," Caleb said suddenly.

She kept her arm around him and asked, "Yes?"

He reconsidered asking his question, but curiosity burned
in him to know the answer. "Earlier, when I was in the basement, and I heard you fighting those men," he began.

She waited for him to continue.

"Where the hell did you learn to fight that many people at
once?" he asked intently.

Paige paused, patted him absently on the chest a couple
of times with her hand and finally responded in a quiet voice,
"Katrina taught me while I apprenticed with her. I honed my
skills with her for a few years, occasionally joining her to do
mercenary work in unpleasant parts of the world."

He let that sink in for a moment.

"No human's going to harm you while I'm here, Caleb," she

reassuringly whispered in his ear. "I learned from the best. So, come on. You can help me now."

Paige pulled away from him and turned to lead the way from the room. He turned to follow her and detected a more hopeful sensation beginning to replace the dread that had permeated his earlier feelings.

"You were pretty scary today. I didn't expect that from you," he said. "And you seemed prepared, just like you said a couple of days ago."

"Well, not totally prepared, really," she replied sourly as they proceeded down the hallway.

"Yeah? How so?" he asked.

"I forgot to pack more than one Shirley Manson T-shirt," she replied glumly. "The one I was wearing was ruined, of course."

The recollection about her stomach wounds resurfaced suddenly, and he reached out to grasp her shoulder from behind. "Oh crap, the gunshot wounds!" he exclaimed. "Are you okay?"

She stopped, turned to him, and lifted the lower portion of her T-shirt to reveal two small, faded scars slightly reddened against the pale, smooth skin of her stomach. "Healing up fine," she replied happily.

He gaped at her. "You heal fast, but what about the bullets?"

She smirked, reached into her pocket, and revealed two large shotgun pellets in her open hand. "Vampires are resilient, Caleb," she offered with a smile. "Aren't we amazing?"

He frowned, briefly recalling the earlier scene in the garage between her and the assailant and replied darkly, "Amazing and terrible all at the same time."

"Maybe a little of both," she agreed in a subdued tone as she lowered her T-shirt.

Katrina raced from the interior of the facility, trying to maintain a degree of stealth as she gave the storage building a wide berth in favor of approaching from the opposite direction.

In the end, it was a sound decision.

She saw Chimalma's dark-clad form standing over Alton as he lay on the ground and quickly realized that he was seriously wounded. She unraveled the steel cable wound over her shoulder and raced towards her target from behind. Anger flared like a volcano inside her as she closed in.

Chimalma raised her machete to strike down at Alton when Katrina deliberately hissed. The renegade vampire's head twisted to glare at her with an incensed expression.

Alton used the split-second opportunity to stab at Chimalma's calf muscle with a combat knife unsheathed from his web gear. The short blade impaled her leg seamlessly, and the Aztec vampire screamed in pain.

Katrina immediately took advantage of the situation to lasso Chimalma's neck with the steel cable and jerk with all of her strength, causing the injured vampire to choke and grapple at her neck while dropping her machete. Katrina hauled on the steel cable with a swift ferocity, fueled by the severe angst and anger welling up inside of her. She was nearly feral as she pulled the renegade vampire to the ground.

Katrina moved in a blur to punch at Chimalma's face, stunning her so she could wind the steel cable around her arms and chest, effectively rendering her temporarily immobilized. The vampire gnashed her fangs and hissed in anger and pain as Katrina repeatedly and ferociously slammed her gloved fist into the woman's head until Chimalma's head was severely bloodied.

The pain that Katrina felt in her hand was nothing compared to the agony of the idea that Caleb might be dead, combined with the concern she felt for her wounded friend. Alton lay on the ground on his back, clutching at the hilt of the knife protruding from his abdomen.

"Go!" he yelled in a raspy voice.

Katrina wasted no time, and hauled the still-hissing vampire over her shoulder and sprinted into the woods like a demon-possessed rocket heading straight towards the kill zone.

"Kill me, but your human pet is dead forever!" Chimalma seethed in an agonized voice with Alton's blade impaling her calf.

"Die, you bitch!" Katrina yelled as she swiftly arrived in the designated clearing overlooking a large river near a sheer cliff.

She threw the ancient vampire into the clearing and grabbed at the combat crossbow at her waist. Katrina fired two bolts into the vampire, who howled with pain and thrashed on the ground. One of Chimalma's feet caught Katrina's legs, and she fell to the ground, dropping the crossbow. Rather than continue the melee, Katrina turned to flee as she grabbed for the detonator on her web gear.

She glanced back only momentarily to see Chimalma already hobbling and disentangling herself from the steel cable that encircled her body. Rather than wait any longer and risk her escape, Katrina pressed the detonator button and fell face-first onto the ground as simultaneous bursts of individual explosions erupted. She squinted into the maelstrom and saw Chimalma's body engulfed in a fiery inferno.

It was an explosion of fantastic proportion and would likely usher people to the area in a short time. Katrina rose to her feet once the initial heat wave passed her, and as she stumbled away from the area, her thoughts were immediately of Caleb and Paige.

Her fingers fumbled with her cell phone as her hands trembled with a mix of nearly overwhelming anger and fear. She shakily scrolled through the auto-dial until arriving at the estate number, hesitating a split second before pressing the call button as fear welled up in her chest and throat to nearly uncontrollable levels.

The phone rang five times before she heard Paige's voice.

"Katrina?" asked Paige anxiously.

"Caleb," was all she managed to say without her voice's collapse into wails of tears and anguish.

There was a momentary pause, and then Paige answered

reassuringly, "Caleb's fine. We were attacked in force, but we managed to stop them."

Katrina immediately sank to her knees onto the cold, hard ground as her arms fell to her sides, and she began sobbing uncontrollably. A raw cascade of stressful emotions from the thought of Caleb's potential death came crashing out.

"Katrina?" came Paige's concerned voice. "Katrina? Are you okay?"

It was a number of moments before relief took over and she was able to speak again.

Katrina managed to tell Paige that Chimalma was dead, and that she was returning to aid Alton. On her way, she spotted two guards dressed in hunter's camouflage who had apparently been patrolling the other side of the grounds until the explosions sounded. She took the time to stalk them until she could get close enough to strike.

Knowing Alton was injured, she realized that he would need fresh blood if healing were an option. To save time, she flew out of the darkness at both men, and before they could react, knocked one to the ground with a swift kick and smashed the other man in the face with a high-velocity punch of her fist. The latter man hit the ground in an unconscious state with a thud. The other guard was attempting to recover when Katrina swiftly jabbed him in the throat to disable him. He began gasping for air, and she punched him on the side of the head to render him unconscious.

She immediately gathered up the two men and carried them back to where Alton was still lying on the ground. He pulled the wavy-bladed knife from his abdomen, and blood flowed out of the wound. Katrina dropped the two guards to the ground and bent down to begin licking at Alton's abdominal wound. After some time and effort, she was able to seal the laceration partially. However, her friend had lost a lot of blood and was barely conscious.

She grabbed the nearest guard and deftly used her knife to slice into his throat so the man's blood began flowing from the cut. She held his neck over Alton's mouth, and the vampire began drinking. His hands flew up to the man's body and held it in check as he continued to feed. It took only a short time to drain the man of his easily acquired blood, and Katrina moved to the second guard in the same manner. Alton only needed half as much blood from his body and lay on the ground as Katrina cast the guard aside.

"We have to go soon," she insisted as she inspected Alton's abdominal wound.

"Go," he insisted. "I'll catch up. You need to get to Caleb."

She smiled warmly at her friend. "I called them. Everything's fine. And I'm not leaving you."

He managed a wan smile. "You did very well, Katrina. I'm proud of you today."

Katrina cracked a grin. "You better be proud of me every day." She bent down and kissed him warmly on the lips. "Thank you," she muttered gently. "For everything."

"You're always welcome, my dear," he said with a smile and cautioned with a raised eyebrow: "Best be careful. Caleb would be jealous if he saw that kiss."

She smiled slyly. "He won't mind. He'll get much more than that from me once we return home."

Given the DNA evidence on the two guard's bodies, Katrina took the time to break into the storage building and procure some gasoline. She doused the bodies thoroughly and set fire to them. She also threw Chimalma's blade into the fire and burned the ground where Alton's blood had spilled. By that time, he was in good enough shape for her to help usher him away from the location. She was suddenly happy that the facility was so far removed from the nearby town.

They returned to the cabin, where Katrina loaded the vehicle with their remaining belongings. She drove them to the nearby private airport, where another chartered aircraft was waiting to take them back to Atlanta. Fortunately, their flight schedule suggested that they would arrive back at the estate in the waning hours prior to dawn.

And while Alton seemed anxious for their return to Atlanta, Katrina was beside herself with anticipation.

# Chapter 11

## The Return

**C**aleb thought that he heard voices as he stirred from his dreamless sleep, not the distorted kind of voices that might plague the mentally ill or addicts, but rather a series of muted tones speaking in hurried and urgent fashions. His eyes opened slowly, revealing not pitch blackness, but illumination from a dim glow through the sheer curtains of the bedroom window. While it was still nighttime, moonlight emanated into the room from beyond.

Sitting up in bed, he slipped from beneath the sheets and into his blue jeans. He didn't bother with a T-shirt and went to the open doorway. Caleb no longer bothered shutting the bedroom door unless he was changing clothes. A friendship had formed between him and Paige, bonded forever through a shared sense of survival and the battle for it.

He stood listening in the hallway. The voices came from the downstairs sitting room, across from the foot of the stairs. He could see the open French glass doors leading in, though not the interior of the room itself more than a few feet, and he strained to understand the voices as his heart raced.

Alton's voice registered in his mind. *They're back already!*

Caleb tip-toed to the top of the stairs and stood statue-like, gripping the banister with his right hand for balance in the darkness.

"...watching him closely after that..." Paige noted.

"...seems like a normal reaction...changes to be expected..." muttered Alton's voice.

"...changes? Don't know the half of it..." Paige countered.

Caleb frowned, trying desperately to hear more.

"...kidding?!...attacked a gunman with a crow bar?" Katrina demanded incredulously.

Upon hearing Katrina's voice, his pulse increased, and his heartbeat pounded in his chest. The anticipation of actually taking Katrina in his arms built.

All conversation downstairs abruptly stopped.

Katrina appeared, staring up at him from the foot of the stairs outside the sitting room. She wore black denim jeans that fit her like a glove and a royal blue, loose-fitted, sleeveless blouse. She stood with her bare feet slightly parted and set, and her arms were folded across her chest. Her shock-red hair was pulled tightly over her head into a ponytail.

Caleb gazed upon her face, wholly unprepared for what he saw. Her pale features were hard, and her green eyes were glowing heatedly. They were angry eyes. She was still a vision of beauty, but her visage was tinged with both fierce and predatory qualities. She stood resolutely, appearing fully as the image of a classic vampire, both beautiful and terrible at the same time. Any normal person would have fled running in terror, but he held his ground.

His heart almost stopped as he gazed fully upon her feral beauty. He felt butterflies in his stomach, and his breath caught in his lungs. Despite her intimidating appearance, she was still the focus of his only desire.

Katrina's features softened slightly, but her eyes still glowed green. Caleb somehow sensed that she was moving quickly from anger to desire. The differences were subtle, but somehow he just knew.

He wanted to leap down the stairs to tackle her, but instead mustered his willpower. He steeled his expression with a frown and crooked his finger at her in a slow, beckoning motion as he tightly held onto the banister railing with his left hand.

"You left me, and I was so angry, but I missed you so much that I wanted to die. Then I almost did," he whispered in a choked voice.

A fleeting moment of anguish crossed Katrina's face as her sharp vampire hearing registered his comment. The corner of her mouth upturned in a feral scowl. Her fangs were already extended, making her look terrifying.

Something blared in his mind like a siren. *She looks angry -- and hungry!*

Katrina heard his heartbeat thundering in his chest from where she stood at the foot of the stairs. In fact, she could smell him from where she stood: his body, his blood.

Caleb swallowed hard once and whispered hoarsely, "Am I worthy of you?"

Her green eyes flared brightly before she launched upstairs at him. He had seen her move fast, but was wholly unprepared for the rapid velocity that she displayed, or for the impact of her body plunging into his at the top of the stairs, causing the air to rush from his lungs. He lost his grip on the handrail, and his body spun clockwise before abruptly stopping, only then able to inhale air sharply.

It was a miracle that he was still standing upright, but he quickly realized why. She held him like a vice around the waist with her left arm while cradling the back of his head with her right hand. Her lips pressed into his as she almost drew the breath from his lungs.

He grasped her shoulders, pulling her to him. They kissed passionately and desperately, savoring the moment. He was both relieved and ecstatic to have her safely in his arms again... finally.

Caleb felt his excitement increase as his heart thundered, and he dug the toes of his bare feet into the carpeted floor and pressed against her with all of his strength, trying to push her towards the wall behind them.

She pulled away from his lips slightly with an entirely surprised expression. Her mouth upturned in an amused manner as she allowed her body to be pressed against the wall. Her lips quickly found his again. *I can be gracious*, she conceded.

Time seemed to stop as the heat passed to his bare skin in waves from her still-clothed body. Using all the strength in his lean form, he urged her to move sideways until she was in the doorway to the bedroom and then urged her backwards towards the bed. They fell onto it with a bounce. A feverish excitement rose in their bodies, but hers held an additional insistence of thirst.

Their faces parted by mere inches as they lay side-by-side across the bed.

Caleb frowned and asked in a slightly insulted voice, "Why didn't you wake me when you got back?"

"I looked in, but you were fast asleep. You looked exhausted, and I wanted to let you rest," she replied sympathetically. "I knew you were safe, and that was enough at the time."

"Well, it's not enough for me," he endearingly chastised her.

"I'm sorry," she apologized with a smirk.

"Apology accepted," he said before softly kissing her lips. He pressed the right side of his face towards the bed linens, leaving his neck completely exposed for her. Saying nothing, his intentions screamed, *I'm yours.*

She bent to kiss him softly on the throat. She kissed him again harder before realizing that her thirst was an intense, animal craving. He felt one of her razor-sharp fangs scrape menacingly across his skin.

"You're insane," she harshly whispered against the skin of his neck. "I can't."

"Why not?" he insisted with confusion. "You're hungry. I can tell."

"It's too much. I'm so hungry. I just want to tear your throat out right now," she rasped. "I have to feed first, or you're going to die."

A pang of shock ran through him as he realized just how close he was to being a meal instead of a mate. "Okay, but hurry back," he urged.

She stared at him with intense, glowing eyes, promising

pointedly, "Oh, I will."

The bed lurched, and she was gone.

Caleb lay there listening to his heartbeat racing in his ears. He was filled with elation that Katrina was finally home and safe.

As he sat up, he heard lighter conversation and some chuckling coming from downstairs, though primarily in Alton's and Paige's voices. He moved to the attached bathroom and flipped on the light. He washed his face, brushed his teeth, and massaged his fingers back through his hair. After turning off the light and returning to the bed, he lay down in the moonlight and waited. His thoughts drifted aimlessly when he heard Katrina's voice downstairs followed by Paige's giggling.

"I'm waiting, Kat," he teased.

Katrina appeared at the doorway with glowing green eyes, though lit with passion rather than hunger. Her red hair spilled down, framing her face like a mantle, and she held an amused smirk on her lips. "Demanding, aren't we?" she commented while closing the door behind her.

He started to rise from the bed, but she lifted her right leg and used the ball of her bare foot to press against his muscled chest, nudging him back onto the bed before her.

"Lose your clothes," she quietly ordered.

He smiled while reaching for the buttons on his jeans. "The alpha vampire returns, I see."

"Oh, you have no idea," she muttered as she slid seductively from her jeans and blouse in the moonlight.

A shiver ran down his spine as he lay naked before her. His eyes locked onto the beauty of her body as the excitement rose in his.

She moved slowly and deliberately until she was lying atop him. Her lips met his, kissing him hard.

Then time stood still as their bodies conveyed mutual love and longing.

Later, she lay across his body lazily, her hand caressing his face. "It's nice to feel how much you missed me," she murmured with a smile and kissed his chest. She was truly happy for what felt like the first time in an eternity.

He ran the fingers of his hand soothingly through her long hair and across her scalp. "I can't believe you're finally here," he murmured. He was filled with so many emotions: relief, joy, but most of all love.

They lay together in silence for a period of time before he decided to revisit something. He started to sit up, and she moved away from him slightly with a curious expression. Realization played on her face as she watched him turn his face to the right, leaving the other side of his neck exposed to her.

"Safer for me now?" he whispered.

Her eyes flashed brilliant green for a split second, and she kissed him on the base of his exposed neck. She parted her lips, and he felt her razor-sharp fangs press lightly against his skin. He shivered only once before relaxing the muscles in his body as he leaned against his right arm, which propped him up slightly. She made a small murmuring noise in her throat.

"Somewhat safer, perhaps," she said.

Guiding him to lay back down on the bed, she sat up and straddled his body with hers. She bent down to kiss him lightly on the neck, and he turned his face to kiss her. She kissed him on the lips only once and used her left hand to rotate his face to the right again, facing away from her. She gently pressed against his face, holding it in place.

"Kisses later, my love," she whispered wickedly. "Blood first."

Her lips touched the supple skin of his throat before parting slightly. She pressed her tongue against his skin and held it there until the surface of his neck began to feel slightly numb. Meanwhile, the sound of his own pulse raced in his ears.

Seconds later, Katrina's fangs pressed against his skin, and he felt a slight prickling pressure into his neck. He remained completely still and breathed shallowly as her lips sealed against his throat. Then he heard, and felt, tiny suckling sensations as small moans of pleasure reverberated through her.

*I love him, and his blood*, she thought while drawing his sweet blood into her mouth. He tasted perfect to her.

Caleb noticed that she was pressing into his neck with more pressure than she had used on prior occasions. And while not particularly painful, it was uncomfortable, and he felt stronger nudges of her mouth pressing against his neck. Time seemed to stop again as his thoughts drifted aimlessly. He felt strangely satisfied as he lay completely helpless before her, knowing it was his blood being so casually drawn by her. And yet he felt safe and loved.

She pressed into his neck with a renewed pressure, and he felt an aching sensation where her fangs penetrated for a second time. She had never done that to him before, and his muscles tightened with concern. "Sorry, my love," she murmured as she retracted her fangs and slowed the suctioning of his blood into her mouth.

After a time, he felt her tongue pressed against his throat again, which she held there at length. The numbness spread soothingly through his neck once more, and he welcomed it after her more aggressive feeding. Finally, she kissed him on the neck and moved to lie along his body with her face against his chest.

He turned to stare at the ceiling and whispered with complete sincerity, "I love you so very much."

She smiled, kissed his chest, and replied in a wholly satisfied voice, "And I love you, completely."

They lay together quietly in genuine contentment, both reveling in their reunion. But eventually, his physical and emotional exhaustion took over, and he fell peacefully asleep.

However, while tired herself, Katrina remained awake, just cradling him next to her. She felt so satisfied just being there alongside him, and she wanted nothing more in life than to hold him in her arms.

*He means everything to me*, she mused while listening to the rhythmic sounds of his heartbeat and breathing.

When Caleb finally stirred, groggily realizing he was alone, he opened his eyes but immediately blinked to make sure that what he was seeing was real. The room was brightened by the growing light of morning emanating through the sheer curtains of the bedroom window. He rolled out of bed and sat on the edge of the mattress for a moment. Getting up, he made his way to the window, parting the curtains to see outside for the first time in days. The sun had only partially risen. Since the room was on the front, western side of the house, he wasn't able to receive any of the direct eastern sunlight. Still, he sighed while appreciating the simple ability to gaze outdoors at the glow of dawn.

For a few minutes, he stared out the window as the morning sunshine spilled onto the far side of the front lawn, well beyond the shadow of the large estate's roofline. He had almost forgotten how bright the outdoors appeared in the morning. He stretched, recalling the reunion the night before between him and Katrina with a giddiness that made him feel like a child on Christmas morning.

He wandered into the bathroom to shave and use some mouthwash before pulling on some blue jeans and a T-shirt. Then he recalled something from before Katrina's and Alton's departure. He went to the nearby nightstand, picked up an ink pen and notepad, and began scribbling down some information. He tore off the sheet, folded it in half, and slipped it into his back pocket. *I need to remember to give this to Katrina.*

Not bothering with shoes or socks, he made his way to the bedroom door. "Warning, daylight in doorway," he announced.

He waited, but heard nothing and carefully opened the door to slip from the room. He pulled the door shut behind him out of both courtesy and concern for the vampires in the house. One vampire in particular came to the forefront of his mind, and he smiled as his hand released the door handle.

It took only a split second to realize the hallway was pitch black, and he started to fumble for the hallway light switch when he thought he heard something on the stairs. Before he could react, he felt strong arms envelop him, and soft lips passionately kissed him. He recognized those lips and was only too happy to return the affection in kind.

Finally, he forced himself to draw in a breath, and the sweet scent of cherry blossoms filled his nose. It smelled wonderful and instilled happiness because it was Katrina's preferred fragrance.

"Good morning, my love," she breathed wistfully.

"Good morning, Kat," he replied with a smile, knowing full well that she saw it in the darkness.

Her fingertips lightly caressed the left side of his neck where she had bitten him twice the night before. "How are you feeling this morning?"

He understood the implied meaning in both her action and question and replied, "Never better. Very little soreness, actually."

"Good," she replied happily before kissing him again. "I'm sorry for the aggressive feeding on you last night." She made a mental note to be more careful with him until she had firmer control of her recent violent emotions.

"I enjoyed every minute," Caleb replied sincerely.

She started to release him from their embrace, but he tightened his arms around her waist and just held her against his body. He realized just how much he had missed her for those few days. But then, at the time, he hadn't been certain that he would ever see her again. He swallowed hard at how vivid those thoughts were until mere hours ago.

"I know," she said, seeming to gauge his embrace and body language. "I missed you desperately." A warm feeling flowed through her as she relished his body against hers. *This is exactly what I've been fighting so hard to return home to.*

His embrace slackened, and they slowly unwound their arms from around each other. She turned to lead him by the hand towards the stairs in the darkness, but he immediately tugged against her. "Hey," he quipped nervously. "I can't see in the dark like you, remember?"

"This is a trust-building exercise," she replied slyly.

She pulled on his arm to draw him to her side. Wrapping one arm around his waist like a vice, she lifted him up slightly, and they plunged down the stairs, though to him it felt more like a plummet. Before he could blink, his bare feet touched the cool tile at the bottom, and his heart was racing.

"Do we have trust issues?" Caleb asked carefully.

Katrina's lips once more found his briefly. "Just playing with you," she whispered. She hadd been craving some of the excited feelings of her recent hunt and longed to share some of the tamer sensations from that experience with him.

"Hey, no playing on the stairs," scolded Paige from the kitchen down the hall to their left.

"Um, adults here. Babysitter not needed anymore," chided Katrina.

Caleb adored Paige. He chuckled as Katrina held onto his hand while leading him through the dark to the glow of light radiating from the kitchen area.

"They grow up so quickly," Paige muttered mock-forlornly as they approached the entrance to the well-lit room.

"Too true," Alton agreed solemnly.

Katrina and Caleb appeared in the doorway and released hands.

"Feelin' a quart lower this morning, kiddo?" Paige inquired playfully as she perched on a stool at the breakfast bar wearing faded blue jeans and a black Ramones T-shirt.

He merely grinned back at her.

Alton sat on a stool near Paige and chuckled. He wore casual slacks and a cotton golf shirt and was sipping blood from a crystal goblet. Caleb momentarily marveled how little it bothered him to see that now.

"Good morning, you two," Caleb greeted with a smile. He reached for Alton's hand to shake it, and the vampire returned his firm grip with a perplexed expression.

"Alton, I want to thank you properly for helping Katrina, for helping me," he began earnestly. "I owe you a debt of gratitude, and I don't know to repay you. But if I can ever do anything for you..."

Katrina's eyes narrowed suspiciously as she viewed the exchange with intense interest. Alton smirked, and his eyes darted to Katrina before Caleb noticed.

The stately vampire considered Caleb introspectively. "I've known Katrina a long time, and I hope you realize just how much you mean to her."

Caleb nodded his understanding while glancing up at Katrina. "I think I do."

"Then I charge you with doing something for her each day to make her happy," Alton bequeathed to him. "And in doing so, you can repay a little of your debt to me one day at a time."

Caleb smiled and promised, "I can do that."

Katrina flashed a relieved smile and winked at Alton. She hadn't been certain how he was going to respond to Caleb's offer.

"Hey, what about me?" Paige demanded in a mock-huffy tone.

Caleb grinned, smoothly crossed the short distance to her, and hugged her. "Thanks for taking such good care of me, babysitter. What can I do to repay you?"

Paige hugged him back warmly. "Aw hell, just go out clubbing with me sometime."

"But not by yourselves," Katrina interjected with a raised eyebrow at Paige, who merely stuck her tongue out in response.

As Caleb pulled away from her, Paige nailed a lightning-fast kiss on the side of his cheek and grinned brightly.

"So, Caleb, what are you going to do today?" Alton asked curiously.

"Well, I --" he began before stopping in midsentence to stare curiously at Katrina. "I suppose it'll be up to Kat."

Katrina raised her eyebrow at him, and the beginning of a grin formed on her face. *That was unexpected.*

"Oh, and I almost forgot," he offered while reaching into his jeans pocket to retrieve the folded piece of note paper he'd scribbled on earlier. "These are my email logons for both home

and work and my cell phone and home phone voicemail pass-
words, so you can review anything that Chimalma may have
sent me."

He handed the paper to Katrina with a sincere expression
on his face, and she looked back at him with a degree of satisfaction.

"What have you done to Caleb while I was away?" she
asked as her gaze shifted to Paige intently.

"Oh, didn't I mention?" Paige asked with a smirk. "In addition to babysitting, I mentor as a big sister now, too."

Caleb's first request that morning was to go outside and
stand in the morning sunshine. Though he enjoyed the estate,
he was desperate to be outdoors again. Katrina considered his
request as she looked to Alton for his initial reaction. The tall,
dark-haired vampire shrugged noncommittally.

"Okay," Katrina agreed in a cautious tone. "But we'll go out
through the front side of the house, and I'll stand in the shade
to watch. However, once the sunlight becomes too strong or
directly prevents my observation, I expect you to return inside
when I give the word."

Caleb nodded. "Done."

"I want to go too," Paige insisted.

Katrina frowned and asked, "Really? When was the last
time you braved a daylight excursion?"

Paige considered her question and conceded, "Been a long
time."

"Get our coats," Katrina prompted the younger vampire.

Caleb ran back upstairs to grab socks, shoes, and a jacket
and returned to the front entry area just as the two women
were slipping into leather winter coats that fell to well below
their knees. They buttoned their coats to their necks, wrapped
black scarves around their hair, and put on dark sunglasses
and leather gloves. Together, the two vampires looked like they
were attending a funeral.

Caleb shrugged into his black leather jacket, though he
didn't button it. He looked to Katrina, who nodded for him

to open the front door. A fairly cool, crisp December morning breeze pressed inside upon the door's opening, and Caleb stepped eagerly outside and took a deep breath. The fresh air was cool to him, but hardly cold, so he didn't bother zipping his jacket. The sky was clear blue without a cloud to be seen, a very welcome sight, to say the least.

He stepped out onto the lawn and made his way to the south side of the house where the sunlight was already shining brightly onto the dormant, brown grass. Katrina and Paige hugged the wall, well in the shade, as they slowly walked to within fifteen feet of the edge of the house where Caleb stood. He closed his eyes as the sunlight shone upon his face, and he smiled with pleasure at the feeling of the heat on his skin.

Meanwhile, Katrina whispered to Paige softly, "How does it feel?"

Paige looked up at Katrina and muttered, "Just like standing on the edge of a volcano and watching it erupt."

Katrina smiled and sympathized with the description. Even standing in the shade of the house was uncomfortable with the growing sunlight bathing the world around them in a bright glow. To their eyes, the ultraviolet radiation from the sunlight seemed to cast a colorful aura all over Caleb's body, particularly where it shined on his exposed skin. It looked to them like he was being irradiated in a fiery glow.

"I'd be a cinder by now," Paige muttered darkly.

Katrina just nodded her head, recalling her experience in the sunlight that day when she first met Caleb as a child. It wasn't a pleasant memory. "Caleb looks beautiful, almost like a shining angel," she whispered in an admiring tone.

Paige looked up at her friend, then back at Caleb. "Yeah, I guess I can see that."

He slipped out of his jacket and let the sunshine rain down upon his T-shirt clad torso. He stretched his arms out from his sides as he slowly turned. It felt exquisite because the house blocked most of the cool breeze, leaving only the direct sunlight to warm him. *This feels amazing*, he mused appreciatively.

He paused and turned to look with concern at the two bundled vampires standing in the shade of the house. "Are you two okay?" he asked with a frown.

"We're fine," Katrina answered neutrally. "For now."

Paige said nothing but seemed to be looking around somewhat anxiously as she stood in the relative safety of the shade. "If somebody shows up with a mirror, we're toast," she mumbled irritably.

Katina felt the small area of exposed skin on her face begin to prickle uncomfortably with the increasing UV in the atmosphere. She gauged from the youthful vampire's comment that Paige must be feeling the same thing. One glance at her pensive-looking friend confirmed that. She looked back at Caleb and could almost feel the happiness and satisfaction emanating from him in waves. It made her smile, despite her growing discomfort.

After a time, which Caleb lost track of, the sun began rising to a point where it was overtaking the formerly ample shade of the front yard. The light began moving closer and closer to the west of the house, which only increased the anxiety that both vampires were feeling. He continued to stand in the sunshine, taking his time to look around at the outdoors he had taken forced refuge from for so many days. *This is freedom*, he thought happily.

A few minutes later, Katrina instructed in a firm voice, "Caleb, please return inside the house now."

His smiling face turned to Katrina, and he nodded his acknowledgement.

The women began backing away as Caleb picked up his jacket from the ground and walked towards them with a curious expression. As he got closer to them, they increased their retreat towards the front porch. Paige quickly led the way back through the front door with Caleb close behind. Katrina remained at his back once he approached the steps and followed him inside the house, firmly closing the front door behind them.

"That was fantastic!" he exclaimed as he tossed his jacket

onto a nearby chair. "I almost forgot what the sun looked like."

Katrina smiled as she shrugged out of her coat and removed her scarf and gloves.

"You looked like a miniature Chernobyl standing out there," Paige muttered whimsically to him. "Meanwhile, I felt singed just standing in the shade watching you."

"It was so nice to be outdoors again. I bet you two were glad that I didn't decide to go on a jog out there," he quipped with a mischievous grin.

Paige rolled her eyes and retorted, "And you'd be on your own, Mister Blowtorch."

But Katrina simply gave him a wicked smile, pulled herself to her full height to tower before him, and replied ominously, "The sun would set before you knew it, and you'd be free game for me, my love."

His smile faded quickly, and he adopted a more humble expression as he folded his arms across his chest. "Sorry, Kat," he muttered with a tone of respect evident in his voice. "Thanks so much for letting me outside this morning."

"That's what I thought," she replied smoothly with a sly smile. "And you're welcome."

Alton chuckled as he walked into another room.

By late morning, Alton told Caleb that Paige wanted his help in the garage. On his way there, he reflected on his most recent visit there when Paige was interrogating one of the assailants who had attacked them. He wondered why Paige wanted his help and momentarily considered the pile of dead bodies that she had stacked on the floor following the attack. He shivered, anxiously hoping he wasn't going to be handling corpses.

As he slowly peered into to the garage from the hallway near the kitchen, he heard someone pulling something heavy across the garage floor. His vision into the garage increased, and he saw Paige placing a broken china cabinet against the wall. It was one of the larger pieces of furniture damaged in the house during the assault. He let out a sigh, happy it wasn't something of a more grisly nature.

Paige looked up with a smirk and teased, "Hey there, kiddo. Where've you been hiding? I need help clearing some space for all the junk we have to stack out here for disposal."

Caleb gave a nervous grin and asked, "Oh, that. Where's all of the, um, you know?"

Paige adopted a perplexed look and smiled at his intended reference. "Oh, so that's why you had that look on your face," she offered with a knowing tone. "Alton and I disposed of those thugs last night after he and Katrina returned. We found their panel truck and hauled them off in it."

He frowned. "But how did you dispose –"

"We buried the weapons and ammunition in a rural location and burned the bodies inside the truck some distance from the weapons. It's not very tidy, but should be far enough away from Atlanta that our tracks are covered. We returned just before dawn, not long before you came downstairs this morning."

Caleb's eyes widened. "Well, that's impressive."

"Thanks," she replied with a smug expression. "Now, let's clear some space out here."

The perky vampire tossed some gloves to Caleb, but he had to step back to get a good catch angle on them. As he did, he abruptly backed into Katrina, which startled him as he staggered slightly off-balance. Katrina chuckled at his surprised reaction while her left arm instantly wrapped around his waist to steady him against her. She fluidly presented him with his cell phone in her right hand.

"Vampires are too stealthy for their own good," he mumbled with a degree of embarrassment.

"Your voicemail is clean, and there are two messages from coworkers you'll want to listen to. Also, your work and home email inboxes are cleaned out. Again, you'll want to read a number of new messages," she informed him while ignoring his comment.

He leaned his head back against her shoulder as he retrieved his cell phone from her hand. Its return lightened his former irritation at having been caught off-guard by Katrina's sudden appearance. "Thanks," he offered appreciatively. "And was there anything bad?"

She paused and draped her right arm across his upper chest to hug him for a moment. Paige watched the two of them with a curious expression.

"Yes, my love," she replied in a displeased tone. "Three very bad voicemails and some rather unpleasant, graphic emails with gruesome attachments of some unfortunate victim."

He nodded. "You know, it's macabre, but I'm dying of curiosity. Maybe you could just describe one or two things for me?"

She kissed him on the back of the head while considering his request. *He's an adult after all*, she mused, although she would have preferred not to give Chimalma the satisfaction, even belatedly, of even a cursory level of awareness on Caleb's part. She sighed and offered, "A man was beheaded, and she wanted to share the experience visually. There was screaming from the victim before he succumbed to either death or unconsciousness."

He considered the brief description and quickly decided that he wasn't more curious. "Oh," he replied. "You were probably right not to let me see that. Pretty disturbing stuff. Any idea who the victim was?"

"None."

"And the voicemails?"

Her facial expression turned stony. "Well, Chimalma had some cruel and grisly ideas on which body parts she wanted to remove from you while you were alive to experience it first-hand. There were other messages, but you get the idea."

He tensed and was almost sorry he asked. Pulling away from her slightly, he bent his head up to kiss her soft lips. She happily responded in kind, appreciating the feeling of his lips against hers.

"Thanks, for everything," he murmured.

"Glad to be of service," she replied with a smirk.

"Okay, love birds. Catch-up kissing later, moving stuff

now," Paige insisted as she rolled her eyes at them. She told Katrina, "You're distracting my worker-bee, Red."

Katrina released Caleb from her embrace and countered, "Oh, dry up."

He slipped the pair of gloves on and shook his head with a smirk as Katrina stuck her tongue out at her short friend.

Part of the day involved Paige and Katrina's surveying and recording the damage caused from the incursion of the mercenaries the prior evening. Caleb quickly joined in, if only to spend time being around Katrina. Following their forced separation and the dangerous events of the past few days, he was feeling more thankful for her presence in his life.

Katrina looked around the basement area, noting a bucket containing some broken bottles of wine on the floor near the wine racks. As her eyes quickly scanned the room, she stopped and stared at the steel crowbar that Caleb had used lying on the workbench table. She moved towards it and hefted it in her hand.

"Ah, yes, the crowbar," she muttered darkly. She recalled Paige's quick summary of his confrontation at the foot of the stairs. Her gaze swept across the room until stopping on the refrigerator, which was riddled with bullet holes. She noted the scrubbed area of the floor where the spilled blood was cleaned up for the most part. Tightness formed in her chest as she realized Caleb's final moments could have been on that very spot. She shuddered and tightly closed her eyes for a moment. She was grateful fate wasn't cruel on every occasion. However, she also didn't like the idea of the risk he had taken by doing what he did. She sighed as Paige watched her reaction intently.

"That was dangerous," Katrina chastised as she put the crowbar back on the table and turned to look at Caleb directly.

"I refuse to be helpless for the rest of my life," he said as he stood with his arms folded before him.

She reached out to grasp Caleb's chin firmly in the fingers of her right hand and rotated his face slightly upwards towards hers. Her green eyes gazed down into his pale blue ones in a penetrating fashion with an expression that Caleb thought was part disapproving and part contemplative. After a few silent moments, she slowly moved her face to his and kissed him warmly on the lips. He gratefully responded in kind, thankful she had determined not to be cross with him.

"Perhaps being helpless is indeed bad. After all, I can't be everywhere at once," she agreed. "But I encourage sensible caution in the future versus reckless risk-taking. Understood?"

An approving smile formed subtly on Paige's face as she stood behind Katrina, though in clear view of the exchange with Caleb.

He smiled. "Understood." *I'm more than willing to concede that.*

Her eyes seemed to lighten somewhat as she briefly kissed him again and whispered, "Thank you."

Her attentions returned to the ruined refrigerator next to the concrete stairs. Caleb reached out and entwined the fingers of his left hand into Katrina's right, and she grasped it gently in return as she shook her head.

"I suppose we have shopping to do sometime soon," she noted absently. "New furniture and a new refrigerator."

"And a new garage side entry door," Paige reminded the tall, red-haired vampire.

"I'd love to do some shopping," Caleb remarked brightly. He realized that he must have been dying to get out of the house for a while, because shopping wasn't actually one of his favorite pastimes.

Katrina raised an eyebrow and regarded him thoughtfully. "I'm sure you would."

"There's bound to be a home improvement center nearby," Paige muttered off-handedly.

"We'll make a trip out this evening then," Katrina decided.

Caleb smiled brightly, pulled on Katrina's hand as he moved towards the stairs, and urged, "We'd better start making a list then. I can do some price comparisons on the Internet and check out product reviews, as well."

She smiled with amusement as she allowed him to draw her back upstairs in a hasty manner. Paige snickered as she trailed behind them. *I just adore you, Caleb*, Katrina thought happily.

"This house is too quiet," Paige complained as Caleb and Katrina began their list of items, tools, supplies, and furnishings needed for repair or replacement in the house.

Alton looked up thoughtfully from reading *King Lear* in the main living room recliner. "Some music might be nice," he agreed.

Paige grinned. "Katrina's computer has volumes of music on it. I'll pick out something and pipe it thought the house speakers."

She bounded out of the room as Alton shouted, "Pick a variety, at least!" He shook his head and returned to reading.

A few minutes later, The Who's "Baba O'Riley" began to stream over the speakers. Paige danced up the hallway, looking spritely in her jeans and Ramones concert T-shirt as she swayed her arms and hips to the beat.

Katrina and Caleb walked through the house with a clipboard inventorying the furniture, carpeting, and walls for damage assessments and soon found themselves tapping or swaying to the music. It was an odd sort of setting, three vampires and a human going about various seemingly-domestic activities in the window-shuttered house. And while Katrina and Caleb were more obvious about their mutual happiness, it would have been surprising to all that each member in the household was feeling rather contented as time passed.

It became sort of a game, as each person made their way down to Katrina's computer throughout the day to add their own preferred songs into the playlist. Together they made for an eclectic series of selections. Alton chose arrangements by Chopin, Clause Debussy, Mozart, and Vivaldi and then surprised everyone by including popular cuts from Al Green and the Rolling Stones.

When "Let's Stay Together" played by Al Green, Katrina took Caleb in her arms and began to kiss him warmly. He dropped the clipboard to the floor and wrapped his arms around her waist as they began swaying to the music.

Paige selected songs by The Clash, the Ramones, Coldplay, Johnny Cash, and No Doubt. When Garbage's "Temptation Waits" played, Caleb explained to Katrina how she had played that as a diversion technique during the mercenary incursion.

Katrina scowled and commented darkly, "I approve."

As "Train in Vain," by The Clash, played, Caleb was surprised by how well Katrina could dance. He joined in to the best of his ability and realized it was the first time they had danced together as a couple. He happily noted that she seemed to enjoy it as much as he and made a mental note about that for the future.

As "Just a Girl" played by No Doubt, Paige suddenly appeared upstairs and danced past Caleb as she sang the song out loud and abruptly began to tickle him in the ribs. He flailed on the floor, laughing and writhing as he struggled against her swiftly moving hands and fingers digging at his ribs. Katrina giggled contentedly as she watched the display. By the end of the song, he was laying face down on the floor, trying to catch his breath, and Paige strutted away as she danced to another tune.

When Katrina stole away from Caleb briefly to make her own music selections, she queued up some operatic renditions by Luciano Pavarotti, jazz from Miles Davis, and popular tunes from Bob Dylan, the Beatles, and U2. But she also surprised him by selecting some songs from Jem and Fiona Apple.

The entire affair was very enlightening for Caleb, providing additional insight into the personalities of each vampire. He hooked his Apple iPod to Katrina's computer and made selections from his own library. He played a number of tunes from Silversun Pickups, as well as some popular songs from Our Lady Peace, Foo Fighters, and Greenday. However, he surprised the vampires by also selecting a few classic cuts from the 1960s and '70s. When "Golden Years," by David Bowie, played, Paige returned to dance with him some, admiring his sense of rhythm.

"You, me, clubbing, soon," she demanded at the end of the song while holding her thumb and forefinger to her ear, making the universal hand symbol and mouthing the words: "Call me."

Katrina rolled her eyes and smirked at the playful vampire, while Caleb looked up at Katrina with a silent inquiry in his expression.

"Not anytime soon," Katrina chastised mildly as she made a final pass over the list of items they would need to shop for that evening.

As the last of the music played, Caleb snuck down into Katrina's room to make one more selection. Coldplay's "Green Eyes" sounded through the house, and he momentarily paused at the computer as the lyrics began. As the song continued, he turned and walked to the top of the stairs to exit into the main hallway. He felt a sudden presence behind him, and Katrina's arms enfolded his shoulders. Her body pressed against him from behind as she held him closely and quietly while the song continued.

He felt her lips at his ear. "Is that song about me?"

"Yes," he murmured as her lips softly touched his neck.

"A declaration, perhaps?" she whispered.

"Just that I love you," he thoughtfully replied as the song continued. "And that I need you."

Her lips lightly kissed at his supple neck and soft cheek as she reveled in his reply. "You don't know how happy that makes me," she beamed as she turned him towards her and passionately kissed him.

They embraced each other until the tune had nearly finished and then walked with their arms wrapped around each other's waists into the main living room as the song ended. Paige looked up at Caleb with a wistful expression as she lounged on the couch, while Alton continued to make some notes in a small daily planner perched on his crossed leg.

"A romantic selection of music, young man," Alton noted without looking up. "I approve."

Caleb smiled at the dark-haired vampire as Paige popped up on the edge of the couch with an excited grin. "Okay, enough crooning. It's almost dark, folks. Time to put our shopping groove on!"

Alton stopped writing in his planner long enough to look over at the blonde vampire with a withering expression. "I'll stay here, thank you," he insisted calmly. "I have some phone calls to make, as well as some Internet activities to tend to. I may take a stroll later this evening, as well."

Paige merely shrugged as she took Caleb by the arm and dragged him towards the front of the house. "Ditch the T-shirt, you hobo," she urged as she dragged him with her. "We're going out tonight!"

Katrina just shook her head and raised an eyebrow as her mate was taken in tow by the perky vampire. She glanced down at her own faded jeans and sweatshirt with a sigh and departed to change clothes.

After changing into fresh jeans and shirt, Caleb grabbed his leather jacket. Paige changed into a denim skirt, blue satin blouse, short denim jacket, and black leather boots. Katrina appeared from the sublevel room wearing black, low-rise knit slacks and a stylish, burgundy, long-sleeved, cowl neck top with a long, trendy leather coat. They all piled into Katrina's Audi, and Paige was kind enough to allow Caleb to sit in the front next to Katrina. He anxiously anticipated his first journey away from the estate in what seemed like forever, and the two vampires easily detected the excitement rolling off of him.

"Please grab him if he tries to flee from the car at any intersections," Katrina dryly instructed Paige.

Caleb just shook his head as the car pulled from the garage and down the driveway. He stared appreciatively out the window at the night-laden surroundings as the vehicle made its way to the front of the edition. As soon as they pulled out onto the city streets, Katrina gunned the engine for his benefit, and they sped down the road as alternative rock music played. He certainly appreciated being out in the real world again.

Paige swayed to the music in the back seat as Caleb's mind began to wonder about the information that Katrina had shared with him about their journey to stop Chimalma. The idea that the renegade vampire had hired so many mercenaries between the retreat facility and the attack against him and Paige at the estate caused him to wonder about plans she may have arranged that simply hadn't been activated yet.

Then again, perhaps his imagination was simply running away from him after all the pent-up stress from their experiences. He sighed quietly as the music played and tried to gaze absently out the car window while appreciating the feeling of traversing the open road. He failed to notice that both vampires were observing him closely.

"I bet that our boy's hungry. He didn't eat much for lunch today," Paige ventured from the back seat.

Katrina glanced over at his subdued manner and frowned slightly. "What do you think, Caleb? Hungry?"

He smiled at her and replied, "Sure. How about –"

"And what is it we're avoiding tonight?" Paige interrupted.

He appeared momentarily perplexed, but smiled as he recalled a previous topic with her. "Garlic: no Italian."

"Good boy," she complimented with a quick pat on his head.

Katrina narrowed her eyes while driving as she tried to determine the nature of that exchange and glanced over at Caleb.

"Um, how about a steak house?" he ventured, changing the subject.

"Done," she replied simply. "But after the home improvement store." She quickly pressed some buttons on the GPS and called up the nearest location.

At Builder Mart, the three grabbed a shopping cart, and Katrina read from the list of items they needed. She pushed the cart to the aisles with the larger items, while directing Caleb and Paige to grab smaller things as they passed. He found it amusing that both Paige and Katrina were getting a number of interested looks from a variety of men they passed by, and he adopted a proud expression as he walked with the two beautiful vampires. His manner and expression weren't lost on the two women, either.

"How about if I paw at you a little bit, kiddo?" Paige teased. "That'll really get those guys stirred up."

He grinned, but Katrina frowned and countered darkly, "Yeah, and I bet half the women in here will throw tools at us too."

Paige chuckled as she called off more items for retrieval.

As Caleb went up a small aisle to get rolls of masking and duct tape, he saw a group of people at the back of the store watching an in-store how-to seminar. He looked away, grabbed the rolls of tape, and rounded the corner to head back to their cart. Suddenly, he heard a series of quick popping noises sounding like small gunfire and jolted in place as he ducked down abruptly. Then he realized the in-store demonstration was showing how to use a nail gun, and he sighed irritably.

"Crap," he muttered with a sheepish expression as he turned to walk to the shopping cart, noticing both vampires staring at him intently. He approached the cart feeling a little stupid at his reaction and dropped the items into the cart without looking at either of them.

"It's okay," Katrina offered gently with a gentle brush of her hand on his back. "It's normal given what you experienced."

Paige glanced up at her with a narrow-eyed expression before he noticed, and she smiled while demanding in a mock southern drawl, "Come on, old lady. Keep rattling off that list. My boy's hungry over here."

Katrina rolled her eyes and called off more items as she steered the cart down another aisle. However, she watched Caleb more closely while they were in the store.

Paige suddenly appeared at her side, dropped some paintbrushes into the cart, and whispered, "Between the two of us we can keep him in sight at all times. But just what are you thinking?"

Katrina considered her answer carefully. "Let him know

you're there, but give him some space. I want him to feel safe
without being smothered."

Paige nodded. "Will do."

They continued to fill the cart with a series of home improvement supplies and proceeded to the appliances area.
Caleb pulled a small list from his back pocket containing preferred models of refrigerators and began trolling the refrigerator aisle. Eventually, they selected a standard white model as
a replacement for the damaged one at the estate, and Katrina
arranged for a delivery at the sales desk.

"And what time is best for delivery?" the sales clerk asked.

"Evening would be best," Katrina replied.

Caleb spoke up, "Hey, I'm not teaching until next month.
I'll be available for daytime deliveries."

Katrina wanted to avoid his being the person answering
the door at daytime when vampires were most vulnerable,
but she allowed it. "Fine," she replied. "Daytime will be fine."

They arranged for a morning delivery in two days time.
*At least it will be on the shady side of the house during the
morning*, Katrina mused as she finalized the arrangements.
She would be able to maneuver tactically if needed and still not
catch the sun fully.

After they loaded the items into the Audi's small trunk and
packed one side of the back seat with the remaining packages,
they were on their way to the nearest steak house.

"Kind of cramped back here now," Paige complained as she
shoved a plastic bag of items away from her and leaned forward between the driver and passenger seats.

"Better than the trunk," Caleb quipped and glanced over to
smirk at the petite vampire.

"Go ahead and laugh, smarty pants," Paige teased with a
playful smirk. "I'll shove your butt back here on the way home."

By the time they arrived at the steak house, Caleb's appetite was considerable. His mouth watered at the scent of grilled
steak as he exited the car and held the seat forward for Paige to
exit. Paige squeezed past him and quickly swatted him on the

butt.

"Time to round up some beef for my man," she drawled and scanned the parking lot while he shut the door.

A pickup truck parked in front and to the left of their vehicle had a rough-looking man sitting in the driver's seat, and Caleb noticed the fellow staring at him in the side view mirror as he shut the car door. His eyes strayed to the shotgun hanging in the back window of the pickup, and he paused as Paige slipped her arm around his.

Paige's eyes focused on the man in the truck, while Katrina had already noticed Caleb's stare and stood at the front of their car in a relaxed stance. They gave the truck a wide berth as Paige placed herself on the side towards the truck, and Katrina followed behind them both.

"Hungry, tiger?" Paige asked as they strode across the parking lot.

"Sure," Caleb replied in a distracted fashion as he started to glance back over his shoulder.

But Paige leaned up and kissed him on the cheek to keep his head from turning around, and she felt the muscles stiffen in his arm. "No problem there, kiddo," she reassured him with a smile. "People in the south just love their shotguns."

He did his best to chuckle off-handedly and lied, "Hey, I'm not worried. I mean, that'd be silly and kind of paranoid anyway, right?"

A young man appearing to be a restaurant employee stood finishing a cigarette not far from the entrance next to a decorative ashcan and nodded politely as they passed. Caleb reached out to open the front entry door to the restaurant and courteously let Paige enter before him, but Katrina placed her hand behind his back to usher him before her.

As they stood amidst the crowd waiting in line to be seated, Katrina bent down to whisper in his ear, "You're not silly, Caleb. And don't forget a little fear can be healthy sometimes."

He smiled slightly and nodded as she quickly kissed him on the cheek from behind and placed her hand on his shoulder.

Paige looked deliberately back over her shoulder at Caleb and flashed her bright blue eyes and a white-toothed grin.

"Ditto, kiddo," she whispered. "Your babysitter's always on duty."

An older woman standing next to them glanced at Paige with a frown. But Paige gave her a level, unfriendly stare, and the woman quickly looked the other direction as she stepped closer to the man appearing to be her husband.

After a short wait, they were seated at a table in the corner of the large dining room, with the vampires placing Caleb between them so they could see anyone approaching the table. After a few minutes, he relaxed somewhat. It helped that his hunger advanced to the point that his anxiety was outweighed by his desire for caloric intake. He also appreciated the light-hearted southern hospitality of the waitress and the seemingly upbeat customers around them.

Katrina and Paige both ordered salads, while Caleb ordered a large sirloin steak with baked potato and side salad. He also preordered a piece of the restaurant's signature blackberry cobbler. In addition, they each nibbled at the complimentary rolls, though he ate three of them while the women each picked at their roll without actually consuming much of it. As they sat at the table, Caleb noticed the ladies were receiving some tentative glances from nearby male patrons.

"I'm the luckiest guy in this place," he commented earnestly with a proud tone as he buttered one of his rolls.

"We're just happy to make you look good," Paige offered with a smirk as Katrina grinned.

Both women were happy that his mood had improved significantly.

Very soon, their meals arrived, and Caleb dug into his with a vengeance. Katrina shook her head while Paige's eyebrows rose with some surprise.

"Don't forget to chew, kiddo," Paige teased as she smiled over at Katrina, who merely shrugged.

After about twenty minutes, Caleb decided to ask something that had been on his mind all evening. "So, are we really in the clear now?" he asked. "I mean, Kat killed Chimalma, and only one attack on the estate was actually mentioned on the digital recording at the retreat facility. Are we getting back to normal now?"

"I consulted with Alton about this, and I think we're probably okay. But it's best to exercise a little caution for the time being, just to be on the safe side," Katrina offered with a supportive expression.

"Hey, it's not like someone's going to walk up and just shoot you in public anyway," Paige teased with a smirk.

A moment later, two men wearing Atlanta Police Department uniforms walked into the restaurant and scanned the dining room. The taller officer smiled and spoke briefly to the employee who had smoked a cigarette outside earlier. The young man looked around and then pointed to where Caleb and the two vampires were seated. Paige and Katrina took notice almost immediately and exchanged eye contact with each other while appearing to remain relaxed.

"On second thought, just forget what I said," Paige murmured flatly.

Caleb noticed Katrina's and Paige's expressions were pleasant but guarded, and he stopped chewing his steak. He looked up slowly as the officers proceeded across the room towards them. He felt Katrina's hand touch his thigh lightly underneath the table.

She smiled, bent over to kiss him on the cheek, and whispered, "Keep eating, and whatever happens, just don't move from your seat."

He didn't think that sounded very encouraging, but continued chewing his mouthful of steak. He deliberately looked away from the officers towards a tableful of kids and parents sitting at the larger booth across from them.

The two officers stopped short of the table and smiled. The taller officer, whose nametag read Purvis, offered, "Evening folks. We're sorry to bother you, but we were wondering if you'd

mind helping to settle an argument my partner and I were having after we pulled up next to your Audi."

Katrina smiled pleasantly and replied, "Sure, how can we
help?"

The shorter officer, named Evans, spoke up, "Well, I think
you have a 3.6 liter engine, but my partner says that's it's at
least a 4.2. I bet him dinner that he's wrong. Who's correct?"

Katrina smoothly replied, "Funny you should ask. It's a 4.2
liter V-8 turbo. So I suppose Officer Purvis gets a free dinner
tonight."

Purvis smiled proudly while Evans placed his hands his
hips, though his right hand landed at the front of his firearm.
Paige shifted subtly in her seat and reached up to brush her
hand across a strand of hair at her temple with a smile.

An older waitress approached the taller officer from behind
and said, "I've got your booth ready now, gentlemen. I'll take
you to it."

"Well, hell," Evans replied amiably. "Thanks for settling
things, anyway. You folks have a good evening."

Purvis rubbed his hands together with a smirk. "Thanks so
much, in fact. Y'all take care."

The officers followed the waitress across the dining room
towards an empty booth against the far wall. Caleb's eyes darted between Paige and Katrina, and he noticed both vampires
staring at each other for a moment before looking at him with
knowing smirks on their faces.

"I think we're all probably just a little on edge with everything that's happened in the past few days," Paige offered.

Katrina nodded as she reached down to pat Caleb's thigh
and muttered, "See? Even vampires get edgy sometimes."

Caleb smiled and felt the butterflies in his stomach start
to subside a little bit as their waitress walked up to the table.
"You about ready for blackberry cobbler, darlin'?" she asked
with a wink.

"Maybe I'll get that to go," he replied.

"Sure thing. I'll be right back with the cobbler and your

check," the waitress countered. "Is it together, or will I be split-
ting it up?"

Katrina neatly handed her a credit card and replied with
a possessive arm around Caleb's shoulders, "We're definitely
together. Thanks."

Once the three of them exited the restaurant, Paige led
the way through the parking lot while Katrina walked beside
Caleb with her arm draped around his waist. He carried the
fairly sizable container of blackberry cobbler in both hands, but
leaned into Katrina for a moment with his shoulder.

"Thanks for dinner, Kat," he offered appreciatively.

"You're welcome, my love," she replied.

Paige teased, "That's a honkin' slab of cobbler you've got
there, tiger."

He grinned, but Katrina remarked a little sarcastically,
"Yeah, I think our waitress liked him...darlin'."

"You can't be jealous of the waitress. There's just no comparison," he admonished her mildly, before adding with rever-
ence: "You're like an angel compared to human women."

Katrina slowed to bend down and kiss him appreciatively
on the lips. He had no idea how happy she was to hear him use
that reference. *You were only eight when you last referred to me
as an angel*, she mused.

"We can sometimes become possessive about our mates,
Caleb," Paige offered in a serious tone after making certain
there was nobody else in hearing range.

"I prefer to think of it as protective," Katrina muttered
with a frown as she deliberately tightened her grip around his
waist.

Caleb silently considered the brief exchange between them
as they approached the car. Paige stopped to walk with him
around to the passenger side as Katrina slipped into the driver's seat. Paige opened the door and slid the passenger seat
forward as she took his cobbler from him.

"Hey, I thought I was riding shotgun tonight," he pointed
out.

Paige smirked and used her free hand to hustle him into
the car. "You don't like shotguns, remember? Into the back
seat, lover boy. And buckle up, while you're at it."

She handed his cobbler back to him with a grin and hopped
into the passenger seat as Katrina smiled and started the car.
To everyone's satisfaction, their return journey to the estate
was pleasantly uneventful.

Back at the estate, Katrina took Alton aside in the sitting
room to relay their evening's experiences while Paige and Caleb unloaded the car. Alton listened thoughtfully and paused
for a few silent moments before commenting.

"I think your approach is prudent for now," he agreed. "But
it's important to begin moving back to a state of normalcy as
soon as possible. Being overprotective will likely just encourage unhealthy behaviors and reactions. And I mean for both
Caleb and yourself, you understand."

She narrowed her eyes slightly. "Fine. I understand."

"You can't just hide the two of you away from the rest of
the world and expect anything healthy to come of it," he challenged. "Besides, I seem to recall there's much of the world you
want to share with him. Remember the cabin?"

She smiled slightly. "Yeah, I remember," she replied. *I
want to show Caleb so much of the beauty the world holds and
share each moment with him to renew the experiences for myself, as well.*

Caleb popped his head into the room and said, "I'm going to
take a shower."

He bounded halfway up the stairs, but Katrina barked,
"Caleb!"

After a moment, his head peered back around the corner
with a grin. "Yeah?"

"Move your things to the sublevel room first," she instructed him with a satisfied smile. "I want you in my bed tonight."

He winked and quipped in his best southern drawl, "You
got it, darlin'!"

He disappeared, and Katrina shook her head as her eyes

looked to the ceiling.

"Darling?" Alton asked curiously.

"Just never mind," she responded flatly.

By later that evening, everything seemed to have gone well. The house was in an improved state of order, and Katrina placed some calls to an out-of-town firm to perform maintenance on the more substantial damage inside the house sometime before the end of the year. Having utilized the company on a number of occasions, she appreciated their sense of flexibility and discretion to accommodate special requests or nighttime working hours, which were handsomely rewarded with high bonuses upon completion.

Caleb slept soundly in the sublevel room snuggled in Katrina's arms when he abruptly awoke sometime after 2 am to the sound of growling. His eyes popped open, and he quickly realized that she was the source of the growls behind him. *Must be having a bad dream*, he thought sleepily.

Katrina's body abruptly lurched, and she made a harsh snarling sound as her arms tightened around him. He felt the sudden clamping of fangs into his upper left shoulder and yelled out in pain. It felt like someone had jammed two spikes into his flesh, and the pain seared through his shoulder and neck. He automatically tried to thrust himself away from her, but realized too late that her teeth merely tore at his flesh, causing him to gasp for breath before shouting in agony.

# Chapter 12

## Being Observed

*K*atrina abruptly awoke and felt flesh and blood in her mouth, instantly recognizing Caleb's flavor and scent. Her fangs retracted, and with horror she saw blood beginning to seep from the vicious wounds that her teeth caused.

"Holy shit, Katrina!" Caleb yelled furiously.

She screamed in anguish as the door to the sublevel room slammed aside and lights flashed on.

He was half out of the bed, and she was reaching for him as Paige and Alton appeared at Caleb's side.

"Oh God, Katrina," Paige gasped. "What the hell did you do?"

"She bit me!" Caleb shouted, not realizing the extent of the damage, but feeling warm fluid spreading down his back and shoulder.

Alton moved in a blur and reappeared holding a bath towel from the nearby bathroom to press it against Caleb's back. He was still trying to rise from the mattress, but Paige held him down.

"Stay put, Caleb," Paige urged as her eyes were illuminated in deep blue from the tempting lure of his blood.

Katrina's eyes were full of horror and shock as she tried to move towards Caleb, but his right arm lashed out against her as he stared at her in contorted pain and utter shock.

"Just stay the hell away from me!" he shouted vehemently.

"Sh, Caleb," Alton issued soothingly while pressing the towel against his bleeding shoulder. "Be still. Be still." He moved the towel away for mere seconds to glance at the wound. The flesh was torn around both punctures, though one slightly more than the other. Blood poured from the wounds, and he pressed the towel against them again. "We have to close the wounds, now," he insisted urgently.

Katrina made a move towards Caleb's back, but her lover's right arm flashed up against her.

"No!" he resisted angrily. "Not her!"

Paige's eyes darted at Caleb and then Alton. "Well, I don't think I can do it, Alton," she offered shakily. "You'll have to do it. I've never even tried healing anything like that before."

"Katrina will do it," Alton insisted darkly. He continued to press evenly against the wound with the bloody towel and pointed the index finger of his free hand at Katrina. "You did it, so you fix it," he demanded.

Alton pointed his finger at Caleb where it could be seen by the young man and ordered, "And you, lay still and let your mate help."

The pain was greater than Caleb's angst, and he silently lay there, gripping the pillow beneath him in his right hand. His left arm was drawn down against his body after being placed there by Alton, while Katrina slid over to him and took the towel in her own hand.

"I'm so sorry, my love," she muttered with a near whimper. "I'll make everything okay again. I'm so sorry."

"You'll have to stick your tongue in the deeper wound, or it won't close properly," Alton instructed as he loomed over them. "He's not a vampire, so there's nothing to start immediate healing from the inside."

Katrina removed the towel and pressed her tongue into the deeper gouge on Caleb's back while also pressing her fingers against the shallower puncture. Her red hair fell like a tangled mantle across her lover's back. Caleb felt immediate pain flash through his shoulder and upper back. He gasped and sucked air in through his clenched teeth.

"Easy, son," Alton said as his hand lay against the top of

Caleb's head. "It'll be over soon."

Paige covered her mouth with one hand and tried not to breathe too deeply in the blood-scented air. Her eyes were still glowing bright blue as the blood urge grew inside of her. Her free hand reached out to grasp Alton's shoulder, and he glanced back to note her own struggle.

Katrina sucked on the blood flowing from Caleb's wound while also pressing her tongue into his shoulder and forcing her saliva into the wound area. As she did so, tears fell across her cheeks for the second occasion in only two days. And after nearly a quarter-century since her last crying spell, both recent instances related to Caleb. It was a clear indication of how much he meant to her, but she hated the feeling of vulnerability accompanying the emotional display.

Caleb felt some relief as a numbing sensation began to spread across and through his shoulder, and he was able to breathe a little easier. However, he was still shocked by the event.

"Try to relax more, Caleb," Alton encouraged. "Your lack of tension will curtail the blood flow."

Katrina removed her tongue and began pressing it against the surface of both puncture mark areas, tears still flowing across her cheeks. Within minutes, the blood flow stemmed, and she licked Caleb's shoulder to remove excess blood and maintain the numbness around the wound area. She was mortified at having bitten him, despite its being an unconscious act.

Her thoughts pointedly recalled waking from having a nightmare. She had been attacked by faceless assailants and was defending herself. In her dream, her defense turned into attack as a bloodlust overtook her, and the attackers became the prey. She recalled feeling elation as she lunged at each faceless figure. When she turned around to confront another attacker, it was Chimalma standing before her. She lunged, sinking her teeth into Chimalma's shoulder. And though Caleb thankfully hadn't been part of the nightmare, another reality-based nightmare began when she woke to find her lover beneath her fangs. She shivered momentarily at the horrific recollection.

Alton frowned as he watched his close friend and former pupil wrestle with the emotions washing over her.

"What the hell happened?" Paige pressed while stroking Caleb's head and running her fingertips through his hair.

"I heard growling and snarling, and suddenly Katrina's fangs were tearing into my back," Caleb recalled numbly. "I didn't do anything."

Alton glanced down at Caleb, and his eyes flashed to Katrina. "A dream? A nightmare?"

Katrina ceased her ministrations on Caleb only long enough to say, "Nightmare, no idea I was hurting him."

"Hm," Alton responded as he glanced pensively at Paige. She shook her head back at him and shrugged.

By the time much of the blood was licked away and Paige had retrieved a damp washcloth to clean Caleb's back further, conditions had improved significantly. Both of the wounds were sealed closed, though they were red, swollen, and ugly-looking.

"I need a needle and syringe," Alton requested.

"In the nightstand," Katrina instructed as she gazed helplessly down at Caleb.

Alton found a fresh needle and syringe, as well as the small bottle of reddish looking saline solution in the nightstand drawer. "How old is this?" he asked while holding up the bottle of red-tinged solution.

"Last month," Katrina explained. "Caleb had the 'flu."

"Good enough," Alton replied. "Give me your arm."

She held out her left arm and hardly winced as Alton slid the needle into her skin. After withdrawing some blood, he injected it into the saline solution, and shook it to mix the contents. Finally, he filled the small syringe with the blood and saline mixture.

"That's probably too much," Katrina noted, but Alton's eyes flared with momentary irritation.

"I've been doing this a lot longer than you, thank you," he

admonished the red-haired vampire.

He moved to Caleb's side of the bed, kneeling down beside the young man. "Caleb," he explained gently. "I'm going to apply some of your mate's blood inside your shoulder so it will heal more quickly. I promise you'll feel no pain."

"O-Okay," he mumbled softly.

Alton looked sharply at Katrina, who stared back with a sad expression. "Well? Don't just sit there. Numb his shoulder so I can apply this," he snapped irritably.

Katrina nodded and bent over to press her tongue gently against Caleb's shoulder. He soon felt the pleasant numbing sensation. Alton effortlessly injected the mixture. He withdrew the needle and motioned with his finger to the shoulder. Katrina pressed her tongue against the skin to seal the injection point.

Finally, Alton said, "You need to lie here and rest, Caleb. By morning you should feel better. However, I'm afraid you may have a small scar on your shoulder where Katrina tore the flesh."

"Okay," he offered numbly. "Thanks for helping me."

Alton placed his hand on Caleb's head again and patted him softly. "No thanks needed, lad," he assured. "Rest well." He turned his attention to Katrina. "Make sure he rests easy. See that he falls asleep," he instructed.

"No," Caleb objected. "I don't want to sleep next to her tonight."

Katrina's mouth dropped open in shock, and her eyes welled with fresh tears. "Caleb."

"Stop talking!" Alton snapped authoritatively. "Both of you!"

Both fell silent, and Paige stepped back slightly.

"Caleb, how long did you pray to have her back safely in your arms the past couple of days? How many times has Katrina saved your life since you've known her? Has she shown you anything but love and concern since declaring herself to you?" Alton insisted. "And Katrina, how many times have you assured Caleb that you were protecting him? How many times have you proclaimed your love to him?"

Silence.

"Both of you think about those questions before blame or anger is issued any further," Alton instructed. He took a deep breath and let it out slowly as Paige remained silent behind him. "Caleb, you're to lie in this bed and try to get some rest. Remember Katrina is your mate, and will care for you," he instructed. "Katrina, you will care for Caleb to ensure that whatever is required is done to help him sleep. And until we get this sorted out, you are *not* to fall asleep next to him. You will stay awake to watch over him until he wakes up, and only then will you sleep alone. Understood?"

Katrina appeared sullen as she stared up at Alton and answered, "Understood."

"Caleb?" Alton asked pointedly.

"Yes, sir," he replied.

"Good," Alton replied with aggravated satisfaction before turning to Paige. "And as for you, get out. We're leaving them in peace for now." He harbored no argument as Paige glared at him and followed him from the room. His hand flipped off the light as he departed, sliding the door closed behind him.

Katrina silently stared down at Caleb in the darkness, seeing every detail of his form before her. She felt intense sadness at what happened and was at a loss to understand it. "I'm so sorry, Caleb, my love," she muttered sadly as her voice nearly cracked.

"What did I do wrong?" he asked in a tight voice.

"Nothing, my love, nothing," she reassured him. "It's all my fault. I don't understand. This shouldn't have happened..., ever." She bent down and kissed his bare back numerous times as a tear rolled down her cheek. "I love you," she whispered forlornly. "I just want to die."

He remained silent and tried keeping his breathing even. He felt just as confused as she sounded. *Everything was going so well, and I've been so happy to have her back.*

"Don't die," he said finally. "That won't help anything." It was the best reply he could muster in his current state of mind. He just kept thinking to himself, *Katrina attacked me like an animal!*

She lay against him and ran her fingers soothingly through his hair as she stared blankly before her, going over her nightmare imagery again and again. "Sleep now, my love," she cooed to him soothingly after a few minutes. "Sleep, and we'll make all this go away somehow, I won't let this happen again...never again."

His left shoulder became soothingly numb as her tongue pressed on his skin.

It seemed like forever before he finally drifted off to sleep. During the remainder of the night, his body went through the semi-fevered reactions from his immune system.

Katrina dutifully remained awake to watch over him. She committed herself to understanding what happened that night and to making sure it never happened again. It seemed as if some evil curse Chimalma conjured from the grave were haunting her.

Hours passed without incident.

Caleb woke with a start, quickly sensing Katrina lying next to him in the darkness, propped up on her right arm and staring down at him as he lay on his back. After shifting slightly, he felt a strong soreness in his left shoulder and neck area, although he was surprised it wasn't worse than that.

"Good morning," she whispered, gently caressing his forehead.

"Morning, Kat," he muttered as he lifted his arm to glance at his watch. He winced slightly as a small ache ran through his shoulder. The glowing numerals indicated it was nearly 9 am, and he marveled at being able to sleep soundly given the previous night's disturbing experience.

He felt her soft lips touch his forehead in an affectionate kiss. "You're angry with me, aren't you?" she asked softly.

He rubbed at his eyes with his fingertips, wincing slightly

as he felt a pain shoot through his left shoulder again. Though still irritated and bewildered, he didn't want to cause her mood to dampen further when she was already trying to be so kind.

"I'm okay," he replied evasively. He yawned and stretched his legs in bed.

*He's lying*, Katrina observed morosely.

"So, you were awake all night?" he asked carefully.

"Yes," she patiently replied. "I didn't want risk another accident."

"Alton seemed pretty insistent about things last night," he ventured cautiously.

"What are you trying to say, Caleb?" she asked levelly.

He paused, trying to determine how to broach the subject without being insulting. "Is he a leader or some kind of figurehead among other vampires?" he asked, his body tensing slightly.

She easily detected the tension in his muscles and made an effort not to be upset. "He was my mentor, of course," she reminded him. "Naturally, there are times when I choose to defer to his wisdom."

"Oh," he responded in a casual, but vague manner.

"There are times when he defers to my expertise, as well," she added, recalling their recent exploits together tracking Chimalma.

"Okay," he accepted. *Alton's take-charge attitude was intimidating last night.* "Please don't be angry if I ask this, but should I also be deferring to him?"

Her soft left hand pressed lightly against the right side of his face and pivoted his face to hers. He felt her breath on his skin as she spoke to him, her mouth merely inches from his face. "My rules are the ones that apply to you, nobody else's," she explained slowly. "But you should also defer to him, as well as to Paige, where your safety or well being is concerned."

"I wasn't trying to imply –" he apologized.

"I know," she interrupted him with a slight edge to her voice. "I realize these otherworldly conditions and semantics may seem confusing to you."

"Don't be upset. I already understand you're my alpha vampire," he conceded gently. "I just didn't want to encounter any misunderstandings in the future." *Vampire socialization sure can be complex*, he thought irritably.

Katrina said nothing but kissed him warmly on the lips in reply. *He understands better than I thought*, she mused appreciatively as she removed her hand from the side of his face.

He sighed. "I better get up so you can sleep." The truth was he wanted to have some time to himself to think about all that happened the night before.

"No hurry," she muttered as he pulled his body away from hers and rolled his legs over the edge of the bed.

He held his breath as a fresh pain and subsequent achiness shot through his left shoulder and into his lower neck. He tried not to make a point of his pain to Katrina, despite his continued irritation over the event. He picked up his cell phone and flipped it open to use the ambient light to negotiate the dark to the bathroom. Even the monitors on the computer hutch were in power saver mode.

She watched him gather jeans and a sweater on his way to the bathroom. She could easily tell his discomfort was still considerable, despite her ministrations the night before.

"I'll try to leave quietly when I'm done," he offered congenially.

"That's fine," she muttered as the bathroom door closed. She laid her head down on the pillow and sighed forlornly. *Why did last night have to happen things were getting better again and returning to normal?* she thought bitterly. And yet she realized that in addition to this new matter, she was still wary about his safety. All of the events from the past few days were still so prevalent in her mind, and Katrina didn't want to leave her guard down. *Or am I just being paranoid?*

She had to find some way to return things to the way they were before Chimalma's interference in their lives. She lay in the bed listening for Caleb's quiet exit from the room before closing her eyes and drifting off to sleep.

Caleb sat in a deck chair on the back porch sipping hot Darjeeling tea from a ceramic mug as the winter sunshine beamed down upon him. While his shoulder still ached, he was becoming accustomed to the feeling and adjusted his arm and shoulder articulations to compensate.

After he ate breakfast, Alton and Paige had agreed to let him sit outside in the morning sun on the back porch only if he kept close to the doorway leading back into the house. The door remained open, and he knew that Paige was sitting just inside reading a book, but away from the threat of the sun.

"Feel good out there, Mister Sunshine?" she asked.

He smiled as the warm sun beat down upon him. "Never better." The house sheltered him from any direct breeze, so he felt quite content sitting outside on that cool December morning. Winter in the south didn't always mean cold, even as close to Christmas as it was.

"Stupid sunshine," she muttered darkly. "Half my productive time is wasted hiding from it."

He stifled a chuckle and was struck once again by the memories from the previous night. *What happened?* If it were a nightmare, it was definitely nothing he had experienced around Katrina before. He recalled the snarling in her sleep and the sudden bite on his shoulder. He'd been stunned by how utterly horrible the pain had been. Being bitten by an aggressive neighborhood dog as a child paled in comparison. It was no wonder the legends about vampires struck fear into people's hearts.

"I can't believe how sharp vampire fangs are," he muttered numbly as his mind retraced memories of the attack. "I've never felt pain like that before."

Paige teased, "No-duh! Fangs!"

"Come on. I'm serious," he stated flatly.

She sighed. "It's hell being bitten without the numbing effect, Caleb. I mean, I've fanged a few guys before, but nothing like that. Vampires only do what happened to you when they're in battle, trying to maim or kill an opponent."

He frowned. "What do you mean by 'fanged'?"

"We do that for intimidation or punishment to our human partners sometimes. You extend your fangs and just lightly prick someplace sensitive. It's quick and relatively harmless, but makes a point you're very displeased with someone," she explained. "And if you're really pissed, you usually don't numb or seal the area. It bleeds a little bit, gets sore, and has to heal on its own. Sends a real message."

He didn't like hearing that very much. It made him feel resentful towards vampires given his current situation.

"I probably shouldn't have told you about that," she conceded as an afterthought.

"Thanks for being honest, at least," he replied. *Better forewarned than blatantly surprised like last night. But last night wasn't supposed to have been intentional*, he rationalized.

"She'd never actually want to harm you, Caleb," Paige offered. "It's got to be killing her inside right now. You mean everything to her."

"But she might fang me sometime," he ventured irritably.

"Hey, it doesn't mean she doesn't love you," she countered. "Hell, I'd fang you in a minute if I thought you deserved it."

He shook his head and cursed under his breath.

The silence grew between them, and Caleb's mind wandered as he sipped his tea. After a few minutes, his thoughts drifted, and it occurred to him Christmas was less than a week away. It was strange because Christmas didn't have the same meaning for him after his mother died. While he had friends and girlfriends, it wasn't as if he had anyone truly special to spend the holiday with. Now that he did, the prospect was tainted by the previous night.

Of course, he hadn't done any shopping yet, either. First, there had been the preparations for the end of the semester and finals, and then Chimalma intruded into their lives. Despite what happened the night before, he wanted to try to find at least a little something to give Katrina for Christmas.

"As if I could think about Christmas shopping," he muttered absently.

"Did you say Christmas?" Paige asked. "I haven't celebrated Christmas in years."

"Maybe Chanukah?" he ventured, unsure if vampires even believed in religion.

"I'm not Jewish, Caleb," she retorted. "Most vampires don't celebrate holidays, that's all. It's just another day for us. Oh sure, we might show up at a party or function, but that's about it. I suppose some of us with human companions and mates might take part."

"You don't have a companion?" he asked, somewhat surprised he hadn't thought to ask until then.

Paige paused. "I'm between companions, actually. I don't want to be tied down right now."

"You should try it sometime," he quipped with a suggestive tone.

She chuckled. "Ha, although I bet I could talk Katrina into loaning you out to me on both counts!"

He laughed and choked on his tea as it went down his windpipe, and Paige giggled with satisfaction at his response.

"It's good to hear you laugh again so soon, kiddo," she whispered.

As Paige watched over Caleb, Alton met with Katrina in her sublevel room with the door closed. She was unable to sleep more than about an hour before she got up to shower, and had just finished pulling on jeans and a turtleneck when Alton showed up to chat.

"Tell me what happened last night," he prompted.

Her eyes grew sad, and she recounted the nightmare beginning with the initial attack by her assailants followed by her own bloodlust and seeking out the attackers as prey. When she mentioned Chimalma, Alton's eyebrows rose slightly.

"Has anything like that happened before?" he inquired.

"Yes, but it was a long time ago. I woke a couple of times

after nightmares with some fang marks on my pillow," she recalled. "Though it's never happened to someone sleeping next to me before. Of course, my bed partners are few and far between."

He nodded. "Our recent exploits seem to have reawakened some strong emotions in you. I recall your past has been quite violent at times. You and I have worked to try to curb such cravings. Do you remember those occasions when we've tried to channel them into safer, more focused diversions?"

She recalled the hunting experiences involving animals, as well as her occasional volunteering as a mercenary or bounty hunter for select clients just to work such desires out of her system. But it was a long time since her last diversions, and she noticed over recent years most of those cravings went dormant. However, recent activities had reawakened those longings, and she realized how strongly they pulled upon her. It was part of her nature, after all.

"I swore I'd never hurt Caleb. I've tried to protect and nurture him," she offered weakly. "Now look what I've done. He probably despises me." She recalled Caleb's distant and cool behavior from earlier that morning.

He scoffed. "Hardly. In fact, that's ridiculous. He's wary, perhaps frightened a little bit, but he still cares for you. Although it's going to take some time to work through this with him, I think. Still, it was promising that he went back to sleep next to you so recently after the attack. That should say something about him to you."

It was small consolation. She felt terrible about what happened and was still beside herself with guilt at having done that, even unconsciously, to Caleb.

Following a knock at the door, Paige entered with a curious expression. "Sorry to interrupt," she apologized.

"Caleb?" Katrina asked with concern.

Paige adopted a reassuring look. "No, he's fine. He just came in from sitting on the back porch. I just wondered when Alton's leaving so I can drive him to the airport. I'd like to keep the car for a while longer, if that's okay."

"You don't care for the economical sedan?" Alton teased.

Paige merely stuck her tongue out at the elder vampire.

However, Katrina looked sharply at Alton and asked, "Departure?"

"I returned some phone calls last night and just received a follow-up call this morning. I'm afraid that something time-critical has come up, and I'm going to be forced to return to Europe," Alton explained with some hesitation. "It seems my contact at Interpol is calling in a favor card earlier than I expected. I'm sure they didn't realize my recent information acquisition would involve me so directly."

"What's happened?" Katrina asked.

"A terrorist cell was recently infiltrated, and they need a large front of capital to facilitate further actions. Interpol has an immediate opportunity, but apparently there's no time to use conventional or official channels for the funds. Naturally, they would appreciate my financial contribution to back their immediate efforts with their promise to reimburse me later."

Katrina nodded. She had hoped that under the circumstances Alton would be able to remain in Atlanta longer.

"I spoke with Paige, and she assured me she can stay here for a time," Alton offered. "And I'll be checking in via phone and email, of course."

"I'm here for both of you, Red," Paige added supportively.

"I understand," Katrina replied before turning her attention to Paige. "And short-stuff, I can't thank you enough."

She smirked, and everyone fell silent.

"I'm sorry I can't stay. I would if I could, you know. You two are the closest thing that I've come to family since my turning," Alton quietly offered.

The women's expressions displayed some surprise at Alton's sudden revelation, and they glanced at one another. They smiled and simultaneously moved to embrace him. The group hug was heartwarming, an unusual occurrence among vampires.

After a few moments, there was a knock at the door, and Caleb's face peeked into the room with a wary expression. All three vampires separated from one another slightly.

"Is this a 'vampires only' meeting?" he asked tentatively, but with a hopeful smirk.

Katrina's tense features softened somewhat, and she crooked her finger in a beckoning motion as she invited, "Not at all. Come in."

He opened the sliding door fully and leaned against the door jamb with his arms crossed before him. "Some new development?" he asked.

"Alton's leaving," Katrina explained.

"Tonight, if I can arrange a flight," Alton added. "I have to be in Europe in the next couple of days for an important obligation. I wish I could stay, but perhaps I can visit again in the near future."

"Oh," he replied, unhappy at the news.

"But I'm staying on for a while, kiddo," Paige offered with a grin.

His face reflected a degree of relief. "For Christmas and maybe New Year's?"

Katrina sighed, suspecting suddenly that he didn't want to be left completely alone with her. A feeling of dread shot through her as she hoped it wasn't a sign of negative things to come between them.

Alton's eyes darted to Katrina, having heard her sigh, but Paige deliberately ignored it.

"Sure," Paige giggled. "I've never brought in the new year in Georgia before."

"I thought you said you didn't celebrate holidays," he recalled suspiciously.

"Ah, but I did mention parties, and New Year's involves lots of them," Paige countered slyly.

"Katrina, perhaps you could assist me with Sunset Air arrangements?" Alton interrupted.

"Sure," she replied. She moved towards the computer,

while Paige sprinted up the small steps leading to the main level of the house and pulled on Caleb's hand to draw him down the hallway with her.

Once they reached the opposite end of the house, Paige led him into the theater room and pushed the door closed slightly for privacy. He regarded her curiously as she moved closer to him.

"Katrina's really troubled by what happened last night," she whispered.

He nodded. "I realize that," he replied. "She looked horrified now that I think back on it. I just never expected that from her, that's all. I felt betrayed."

"That's understandable. But you two have to move beyond it," she replied. "You realize why I'm staying, don't you?"

Caleb shrugged. "Sure, you're worried about Katrina."

She locked her blue eyes with his and corrected him, "I'm here for you both; remember that. You're both important to me now, understand?"

He smiled appreciatively. "Thanks."

"Big sister's on duty now," she smirked while passing him to exit.

"Oh great, yet another self-professed title. What happened to the babysitter?" he teased.

She reached out and poked him in the ribs with her index finger before she exited, offering, "She'll show up as needed."

Later that afternoon, Caleb was sitting in the main living room watching television when he noticed Alton walking by with a suitcase. The tall vampire stopped in the entry to the living room and motioned to him by placing his index finger to his lips. Then he gestured for Caleb to follow him.

Caleb got up quietly, following Alton through the kitchen area and down the small hallway leading into the garage. Alton closed the door behind them and walked to the rear of the rental car with his suitcase. He activated the remote's trunk release and placed the suitcase inside before turning his full attention to Caleb with a serious expression.

"I'm departing for the airport very soon, so here's my personal email address and cell phone number," Alton offered as he handed off a business card. "Don't hesitate to contact me if you have questions or concerns, or just need to talk. Use Paige too. She cares about you both, and you already know you're safe with her if things become...darker."

Caleb's heart rate anxiously increased at the vampire's last comment. "You think things could get worse with Katrina?" he asked.

Alton soberly regarded him. "I'm hopeful that won't be the case."

Caleb considered the stately vampire. "I don't think you're being honest with me," he complained.

Alton smirked. "Oh, really? You want honesty?"

The young man looked taken aback. "Well, of course I do."

"Very well, Caleb. For the remainder of this conversation both of us will be totally honest with one another. Do you think you're up to that?"

He looked suspiciously at the tall vampire and retorted, "I'll be honest if you will."

"We'll see," Alton replied.

Caleb remained silent and folded his arms before him.

"I've mentioned to you that Katrina experienced a tumultuous past. She's moved away from higher levels of violence for years, until the recent events with Chimalma. You can be the catalyst to help her relinquish the aggression once more. Again, it all depends upon whether you're up to handling it. It would take a dedicated and determined mate to succeed at the effort," the dark-haired vampire stipulated.

"You have doubts?" Caleb countered. "So, you don't approve of Katrina's selection of me as her partner?"

"Frankly, I'm not totally convinced you're up to that role yet. But I think with some improvement, you have the potential to be a sound choice as her mate," the vampire replied smoothly. "But you shouldn't confuse being her mate with being her partner. Partnership implies a shared, equal position, and you are no equal to her, or to any vampire. Vampires are superior to humans in most ways."

"Well, that was brutally honest," he retorted curtly. "Katrina said you respected humans. Was she mistaken?"

"You said you wanted honesty. And as for humans, I do respect them in general. Believe it or not, I'm gaining respect for you as time progresses."

"Why?"

"Because you're sincere, and you amuse me," Alton replied simply. "And you seem to make Katrina happy. Her happiness is very important to me."

"Does that also make me important to you?"

Alton raised an eyebrow. "You're important to me because of your impact in Katrina's life. But you have a great deal left to prove to me before you're of greater importance. After all, I haven't actually known you for very long, and trust doesn't come easily for a vampire."

Caleb nodded. "At least I appreciate your honesty."

Alton inclined his head slightly in acknowledgement. "Now," he asked, "do you have the fortitude to confront the truth about Katrina's current condition?"

Caleb nodded agreeably, although was concerned with just how serious the conversation was preparing to turn. He didn't like the idea that Katrina's behavior might entail a "condition."

"She's experiencing a condition combining post traumatic stress disorder and something like what an addict might experience," Alton began. "You've heard of people who crave adventurous activities. They thrive on the thrill and excitement derived from their dangerous behaviors."

"Kat's an adrenaline junkie?" Caleb demanded incredulously. "Like those extreme sports fanatics?"

Alton frowned and corrected, "No, not like that. It's more like a soldier who spends the majority of their life in a war zone who adapts well to the environment and craves the danger and excitement of the hunt and the kill. A number of us -- vampires, that is -- enjoy that sort of setting. Katrina's one of those. She gradually moved away from it after having her fill of it over time, and then she wanted to explore alternate paths in her life. Unfortunately, her recent and brief exposure to those activities has brought back some of the feelings she missed from those times. Only now, she's reaping the side effects of her sudden immersion."

Caleb nodded his head, understanding the situation much better with Alton's explanation. It was a little unsettling, but he supposed it made sense.

"Caleb, all vampires are essentially predators at heart, merely in different ways. We all love our prey, so to speak. I, for one, have always considered hunting more of a parlor game played out delicately with intrigue, much like a chess match. Paige prefers a more social method of hunting, though I'm certain such a fact doesn't surprise you by now. Katrina simply prefers a more visceral, direct method."

"Am I in danger from her?" he asked tentatively.

Alton regarded him soberly. "My dear boy, we're vampires. Humans are our favorite prey. Of course you're in danger. Surely Katrina told you this?"

He considered past conversations with Katrina. "Sure, but I thought she was exaggerating somewhat. I never thought she'd actually *attack* me."

"That was unexpected, I admit. But she wasn't exaggerating. She's a potential danger to you if provoked," Alton carefully explained. "Suffice to say provoking her anger could result in unpleasant repercussions, even if it were something less than fatal."

"But I didn't provoke her, damn it!" Caleb shot back heatedly. "She scared the hell out of me."

The tall vampire remained calm, but his jaw tightened noticeably. "Well, that's just too bad for you, then. Did you honestly expect to exchange some mutual affection and just charm a violent predatory being into someone sedate and harmless? Was your sudden appearance in her life going to instantly change her, and the two of you would live happily ever after?"

Alton pressed.

His eyes reflected surprise and outrage, and he retorted, "Listen to me, Alton. I'm not afraid of commitment or hard work in a relationship, and I'm damned sure not going to give up on her. But I shouldn't have to expect to be attacked by her, either."

The corners of Alton's mouth upturned slightly, and he ventured, "I see we've struck a nerve. And are you angry with her?"

"Hell yes, I'm angry!" Caleb snapped. "In fact, I'm pissed off about it! How could she do that after she swore to protect me?"

Alton smiled sagely. "Ah yes, now we're getting at the brutal honesty."

He looked surprised, both at himself and at Alton's reaction to him.

"Do you hate her?" Alton asked.

"What?" Caleb asked, dumbfounded. "No, of course not!"

"Do you want to leave her?" the vampire asked simply.

"No," he immediately answered. "I love her."

"I see," Alton replied smoothly. "So, what are you going to do about the situation?"

Caleb's eyes played wildly before him as he searched for an answer. "I'll do what I have to do, Alton," he countered vaguely. He honestly had no idea what he needed to do regarding Katrina. It was a little outside of his experience level. *But most vampire issues are far outside of my experience.*

Alton observed Caleb's reaction, actively evaluating him. The vampire paused before continuing, "Relationships between vampires and humans are difficult at best, and you often have to wrestle with many issues to make them succeed. Frankly, most people -- most humans -- just aren't up to the task. That's because most of all, as a human, you have to be able to face your own mortality and accept the fact that someday you may just die if something goes wrong. You have to look fear in the face, Caleb, and accept it. Only then can you begin to truly embrace and accept Katrina as a vampire."

"I see," Caleb replied.

"Now, you need to determine if you're up to the task or not, and either stay or leave," Alton stipulated flatly. "I'm confident Katrina would let you live and leave, so long as you held to her rules for the rest of your days on earth."

Caleb tried to contemplate leaving Katrina and living without her. It was a painful thought, even at a cursory consideration. He glanced up to the stately vampire with narrowed eyes and saw Alton regarding him thoughtfully.

"Brutal honesty, remember?" Alton reminded with a subtle smile.

Caleb took in a deep breath and let it out slowly. "Fine, I'll work on the fear issues," he answered coolly. "Now, you're the elder vampire. What else do I need to do to help Katrina?"

Alton quietly considered him at length. "Very well. I've been thinking it's going to be a two-phase process. First, we have to move her away from the desire for violence. Later, we have to replace the violent tendencies with outlets less visceral but perhaps just as exciting."

"You already expected me to ask, didn't you?" Caleb asked suspiciously.

Alton smiled genuinely. "Well, let's just say that I was prepared in case this conversation went better than expected."

Caleb shook his head and sighed. *This guy's a regular mastermind*, he mused. "Okay, what do you recommend for phase one?" he pressed with a raised eyebrow.

Alton adopted an introspective expression. "Well, phase one involves your encouraging her with less violent activities and more displays of affection, appreciation, and intimacy. Avoid arguments or confrontations. Be understanding and agreeable. Let her know how much you need and appreciate her. Really though, these aren't uncommon techniques already successful with most women, am I not correct?"

Caleb considered that and nodded. "Sure, I can see that. I'll try."

Alton smiled supportively. "Katrina's an alpha female, so

your efforts should be appreciated. Paige might be helpful with gauging your success in phase one, but you probably already know what to do based upon your previously successful courtship with Katrina."

"Since you mentioned it," Caleb began curiously, "what is it about the fatal failures of Katrina's previous relationships? I sense this 'alpha female' business plays into it."

"Honestly, it's not really my place –" Alton began.

"Oh come on!" he retorted irritably. "I want to do this correctly, and it's not like I'm going to be able to get another male vampire's perspective anywhere else. Besides, you know her better than most since you were her mentor."

Alton shrugged. "Hm, a compelling argument."

Caleb waited patiently.

"There are alpha female humans, you know, the ones who 'wear the pants' in the relationship," Alton began. "It's somewhat similar with vampires. Alpha vampires are among the most dangerous of our kind, and as such, often command more respect and regard from other vampires. Bear in mind Katrina doesn't appreciate being challenged directly, either. That's just one of a number of alpha qualities. You may have already noticed she compels compliance in areas of your security."

Caleb nodded and raised his eyebrows. *Boy, does she.*

"Such challenging normally results in conflict, which in Katrina's past became a battle for supremacy and authority between her and her previous alpha human male companions," Alton continued. "You, on the other hand, are less confrontational and don't openly challenge her authority. This is to your advantage."

"But you seem successful with her, and you're more of an alpha," Caleb pointed out.

Alton smiled. "Yes, well, I'm a vampire like her. And I have the advantage of being her former mentor, as well as her friend. But even I as a fellow alpha have difficulties and have lost as many arguments as I've won. Then again, I'm also not her mate."

Caleb considered those revelations.

"Use your subtle nature to appeal to her, but without open-ly challenging her," Alton suggested. "I think you'll find that your gentle nature and personality will have remarkable suc-cess with her. Opposites not only attract, they often fit well together, if paired correctly."

Caleb smiled. This was the first time he considered his somewhat passive nature to be an asset. In the past, it nor-mally only resulted in his being taken advantage of. "Okay, what about phase two?"

"Let's get through phase one first," Alton suggested. "Frankly, given Katrina's past, I'm thinking phase two will in-volve less traditional pursuits. Say, perhaps, something along the lines of 'fox and hound' activities."

Caleb looked at the vampire with a dumbfounded expres-sion. "Doesn't that involve horses or something?" he asked ab-sently.

"Odds-bodkins, you Americans," Alton admonished. "Hide and seek? Something like a playful form of escape and evade. Don't worry about that now. We'll work on the details later. Suffice to say you should start exercising more. Take up run-ning or jogging and continue a regimen of upper body muscle toning."

*This is going to be harder than I thought*, Caleb ruminated. *Playtime sounds a little exhausting in phase two.*

While Alton couldn't read his thoughts, he nevertheless read the young man's body language and offered with a grin, "Don't worry. Something tells me you're going to enjoy phase two more than you think."

Caleb narrowed his eyes doubtfully. "Thanks for your hon-esty," he said. He extended his hand to shake Alton's, and the vampire returned the handshake firmly.

Alton offered, "I'm honestly encouraged after our conversa-tion, Caleb. I suspect your potential for success has improved greatly during the past few minutes. And remember your promise about trying to make Katrina happy a little each day for me."

He smiled and nodded as the tall vampire turned to return inside the house, leaving him standing in the garage alone. "Well, I did say I wanted honesty," he muttered.

Once evening arrived, it was time for Paige to accompany Alton to the airport for his return to Europe. Katrina gave her friend and former mentor a warm embrace, as well as a kiss on the cheek to send him on his way. Caleb stepped forward to shake Alton's hand, and he gave the tall vampire a penetrating look. Alton smiled slightly and winked at him in a reassuring manner.

"Thank you," Caleb offered. "It's honestly been a pleasure."

Alton regarded the young man, conceding, "Likewise. And quite honestly I can say I'm happily surprised."

He grinned as Alton slid into the driver's seat, while Katrina and Paige both shared odd glances with each another over the brief exchange between the two men. Katrina wrapped her arm around Caleb's shoulders as Paige got into the car. They both waved briefly as the car backed out of the garage.

Katrina looked down at Caleb. "You're not scared to be alone with me are you?"

He smiled briefly before looking up at her and replying in a sincere tone, "Not anymore, I'm not."

She smiled at the forwardness of his reply and kissed him briefly on the lips. With her arm still wrapped around his shoulders, she turned them towards the entrance into the house and closed the garage door on their way inside. She felt both hopeful and relieved for the first time since the previous night.

Later that night, Caleb went to bed early, and Katrina lay down beside him until he fell asleep. Then she carefully slipped from the bed and sat at her computer checking her financial accounts and other online activities neglected since the Chimalma-related distractions in their lives.

When Paige returned with the rental car, the blonde-haired vampire peeked into the sublevel room to check in on them. Katrina looked up from her computer activities and quietly made her way upstairs to Paige.

"It's too early to turn in for us vampires," Paige ventured. "How about we heat up some blood and have a chat, just like old times?"

Katrina smiled, nodded, and replied, "Sure, sounds like fun."

As the two went to the kitchen to retrieve some blood packets from the refrigerator, having moved the remainder of the supply there until the replacement refrigerator arrived for the basement, Katrina decided to broach a serious topic.

"Paige, Caleb seemed more positive this evening, and I'm feeling hopeful for how things might proceed," the red-haired vampire anticipated. "But do you think I'm a danger to him?"

Paige placed two glasses of blood into the microwave to heat and shrugged. "What do I think? I think you're both a lot better together than you are apart."

"I appreciate that," Katrina offered with a smile.

But Paige wasn't finished, and she looked her friend directly in the eyes. "I also think, since you've claimed him as your mate, it's time he knew more about your past."

Katrina nodded her understanding and sighed. Alton had made her realize how negligent she had been about that already, but it helped to have multiple perspectives.

"And one more thing," Paige said as she removed the glasses of blood from the microwave.

Katrina raised a curious eyebrow as she stared at her plain-spoken friend.

"It's time to lighten up on him," Paige insisted gently but with a serious expression. "Let him make some mistakes without feeling as though he just broke a cardinal sin. Show a little tolerance. Try a gentle hand with him for a change."

Katrina frowned as she took a glass from Paige and sipped at the blood.

"You think I've been too hard on him?" she asked. Katrina always found it difficult to accept criticism, but she realized Paige's intentions were sincere. Paige was a true, long-time friend, just as Alton was, and she didn't suspect either of them of ulterior motives.

"I think he'll be a lot less afraid to make a mistake if the repercussions aren't so severe," Paige explained. "Let some slack out on the leash. This is a great opportunity to start fresh with him."

Katrina smiled a little bit, appreciating the leash reference. She realized that she had been a little heavy-handed with Caleb since the Chimalma interruption of recent weeks. "I was more lighthearted when we met," she reflected. *It seems like a lifetime ago since I first sat in the back row of his history class watching him lecture.*

"You mean, aside from restraining yourself from killing his ex-girlfriend?" Paige teased.

Katrina rolled her eyes with a shake of her head.

"Find that same lighthearted place again," Paige urged. "Renew those feelings and relish them. He'll do anything for you, Katrina. Nurture him, and show a little patience."

She sipped at the blood in her glass and reflected on her friend's comments. "You certainly seem to have quite a way with him," she noted with amusement.

Paige smirked and conceded, "I'm playful. He likes that. It's a method that works for me. But I can be serious when necessary, and he respects that, as well."

"Your playing the role of protective big sister does seem to appeal to him," Katrina reflected.

Paige corrected her friend, "Ah, but he fell in love with the tall, mysterious, and equally protective vampire you are. I can tell he really likes that. Just be more subtle."

"Any initial suggestions?" Katrina asked.

Paige smiled with sudden realization and offered, "Sure: Christmas shopping."

The next day, Katrina and Paige slept for a couple of hours that morning, having stayed up until before dawn talking outdoors where they could appreciate the night in its fullness. Caleb tip-toed out of the sublevel room so he didn't disturb

Katrina, who took the precaution of sleeping on the couch in front of the wall-mounted television instead of risking falling asleep next to him. She seemed to be sleeping soundly when he departed the room and made his way upstairs to the kitchen to make breakfast. He courteously remained indoors so as not to alarm either of the vampires.

Once both vampires rose later that morning, they made plans for the upcoming evening. The day was spent performing simple repairs throughout the house using the various tools and supplies from the home improvement store. The new refrigerator for the basement arrived early. It was a simple effort for Paige and Katrina to carry the old refrigerator to the garage before the delivery men arrived, although the men gave the vampires a sidelong glance as they noticed the bullet holes in the door, which were sealed over with duct tape. Fortunately, the majority of blood stains were cleaned from within the refrigerator prior to the truck's arrival.

"Vandals," Paige offered from the protective shade of the garage as the sun shone brightly outside.

Caleb nearly winced at her explanation, but managed to maintain a straight face as he watched the two men load the old refrigerator into the truck.

"Pretty hostile vandals," one of the guys commented incredulously.

After the delivery service departed, Paige and Katrina easily carried the new refrigerator to the basement. Caleb marveled at the benefit of their enhanced physical strength for home improvement activities.

"I see successful business potential for a vampire moving company," he quipped with a grin, only to be given bland expressions by both women.

By late afternoon, each of them had showered and changed into casual clothes for their evening out to do some Christmas shopping. Both women were clad in designer jeans and brightly colored sweaters, while Caleb wore black denim jeans, a red oxford shirt, and his black leather jacket. Together, they looked appropriately holiday-themed.

Both vampires decided to wait until their return from the mall to consume blood, while Caleb waited to eat at the mall. They all piled into Katrina's Audi and made their way to Lenox Square. There was a complete selection of major department stores, as well as fashion boutiques. The entire mall was decorated to the hilt with Christmas décor and packed with people scrambling for gifts in the final shopping days of the season.

Caleb was amazed how easily Paige and Katrina fell into rather traditional women's shopping activities. It was hard for him to overlook the fact they were vampires, and he almost found it humorous that everyone around them seemed totally oblivious. But vampires weren't supposed to be real, and it wasn't that long ago since he hadn't suspected Katrina of being anything other than an alluring, intelligent woman of interest. Following that line of thought, he was happy they were partaking in "normal" social activities.

The young man watched with a mix of interest and amusement from the comfort of a fabric-covered chair in the shoe department as both women tried on strappy, high-heeled, designer-brand shoes at one of the mall's elegant department stores. He marveled at how they were like two college girlfriends on a shopping spree. Katrina was unable to decide between the black or bright blue, while Paige was uncertain about a bright red pair. The truth was that he appreciated how sexy any of the colors looked on their feet.

As he stared at them with a smile, both women simultaneously looked at him, as if feeling his eyes upon them. Paige grinned at him, while Katrina seemed amused by his scrutiny. The female sales clerk noted both of the women's sudden interest in Caleb and smirked at him as if she knew what was coming next.

"And what does the silent man in the chair think?" Katrina queried. "Which looks better on me, blue or black?"

He paused while glancing at Katrina's pale-skinned feet. "Both look very sexy on you, Kat," he finally replied with a grin.

She smirked and looked up at the sales clerk. "I'll take both."

The clerk nodded with a smile, obviously happy about the commission. Paige frowned and sighed and looked over at Caleb in silent question as she stood in the pair of strappy red shoes. She paraded in front of him once, turned, and walked back to stand in front of him as he stared at her pale feet.

He looked from her feet up the short height of her body until resting on her blue eyes and grinned. "Oh, yeah. Very sexy."

She smiled appreciatively and caressed the fingers of one hand playfully across his cheek. "Good boy."

"I'll take them," she announced proudly as the sales clerk raised a curious eyebrow at Caleb and glanced to Katrina, who was rolling her eyes at the display.

"He's very helpful," the sales clerk offered with a smile as she took the pairs of shoes to the counter to process the sales.

Following the shoe purchases, they made their way down the mall, window shopping. After an hour or so, the two vampires followed Caleb to the food court. They sat at a nearby table as he stood in the lengthy line for Chinese food. A large-framed college student with a flat-top haircut wearing an Atlanta Falcons sweatshirt walked up in front of him to chat with what appeared to be a friend of his, effectively cutting in line.

"Hey," Caleb announced in a stern voice. "Get in line like the rest of us."

A woman standing behind him muttered her agreement. But the young man turned to Caleb and puffed out his chest.

"Why don't you shut up and show some Christmas spirit," the man retorted.

"Why don't you show a little courtesy?" Caleb countered as he squared his shoulders, refusing to be intimidated by the guy.

Katrina stood up abruptly from her chair in clear view of the burly man and adopted a steely, lethal-looking expression. Her somewhat imposing and statuesque stance immediately captured the man's attention beyond Caleb's shoulder, and she pointed her finger at the man and motioned with her thumb for him to depart as she maintained a tight-lipped expression. The man initially appeared unimpressed until her eyes momentarily flashed bright green, and he swallowed hard as his eyes bugged out of his head. The momentary exchange wasn't lost on Paige as she sat casually observing the event.

"Never mind," the man offered curtly to Caleb as he departed to make his way towards the burger vendor next door.

"Whoa there, Red," Paige cautioned in a near whisper. "A little restraint for the local villagers, and let's keep those bright eyes of yours in check."

"Forget it. I can always claim it was a reflection from the Christmas lights," she whispered back.

Caleb glanced curiously over his shoulder at the women and noticed Katrina standing up and facing his general direction.

She immediately adopted a pleasant expression and asked, "Two Cokes for us, please?"

He grinned, vaguely suspecting what must have transpired, and replied with a nod, "Absolutely."

The oblivious woman standing behind Caleb offered, "Thanks for standing up to him. That guy sure was rude."

He looked at the woman with a humble expression, shrugged, and offered, "I guess he decided to show some Christmas spirit himself."

Caleb caught Katrina's eyes and winked before turning around to order as she smiled warmly and sat down next to Paige.

After watching him eat dinner, the women agreed to let him do some individual shopping. He was impressed that his mate was so easy-going about the topic and headed off across the mall after promising to be watchful and to call at the first sign of trouble. It was his first true taste of unguarded independence since the night he met with Chimalma at the restaurant.

Caleb purchased a bracelet for Katrina at a specialty jeweler and considered what other gifts he wanted to procure. He momentarily appreciated the crowds of people packed in the mall around him, each person taking part in the frantic final days of holiday shopping. People squeezed by each other, often with their arms full of shopping bags. Normally, the scene would be somewhat unpleasant and stressful, but as Christmas music played over the mall speaker system, Caleb merely felt happy to be there. He glanced around, wondering if Kat or Paige were stalking nearby. Once he was satisfied they weren't, he pressed through the crowds on his way to a nearby upper-level railing to consider his next destination.

He took note of a very traditional, almost angelic, rendition of "Carol of the Bells" playing over the mall speaker system. As the music began to build, he scanned the crowd on the level below and noticed a tall, brunette woman appearing to be of South American descent turn away from his view in the crowd. His heart almost stopped and his eyes bulged out as he realized the woman bore a strong resemblance to Alondra Vargas -- Chimalma! The woman wore very fashionable clothing and was about the same build as Chimalma. As the music reached a crescendo, Caleb reached for his cell phone, and the woman glanced to her side but not enough to see more of her face than her profile. The woman turned forward again and began to walk slowly in the opposite direction.

His heart raced as fear grew inside, and he selected Katrina's entry on his phone. He held his finger over the call button as he made an instant decision. He didn't want to alarm Katrina unnecessarily, and he was so tired of being afraid. He recalled his recent conversation with Alton and how he appealed to him to try to conquer his fear. Resolving he was going to do just that, his legs began moving to the nearby escalator to pursue the woman. *After all, it's a crowded mall. I should be safe enough.*

His finger still hung over the call button of his phone as he gripped his shopping bags tightly in his other hand. He moved swiftly in the direction the woman was headed while squeezing past tight throngs of people. As he tried glancing over the crowd to spot the woman again, he accidently pressed the call button.

"Caleb?" Katrina curiously asked. "Caleb? Are you there?"

He pulled the phone to his ear at about the same time he caught a quick glimpse of the dark-haired woman far ahead in the crowd, walking away from him.

"Kat?" he asked distractedly.

"Caleb? What's wrong? You sound strange," she insisted.

"Are you sure she's dead?" he asked in a quiet voice as he squeezed past two slowly strolling shoppers blocking his progress.

There was a silent pause before her urgent voice demanded, "What?"

"Chimalma. At least, I think it's her. Her hair looks almost like the night at the restaurant," he insisted quietly as he kept moving through the crowd. "I'm following her now."

"Caleb!" Katrina's voice demanded hotly. "Where are you? Stop now."

He glanced up and rattled off the names of stores as he continued walking. He frowned after losing sight of the woman again. A version of "God Rest Ye Merry Gentleman," by Loreena McKennitt, played over the mall speaker system.

"We're coming to you," she stated flatly. "Please, my love. Please stop walking," she half-pled, half-insisted.

Caleb glanced to his right and noticed the tall, dark-haired woman proceeding towards the entrance to the mall parking garage. He began moving in that direction.

"She's entering the parking garage," he muttered while squeezing past more people.

"Caleb Taylor! Don't you dare go in there!" Katrina hissed vehemently.

He was almost to the entrance doors and waited for a younger couple to enter past him before stepping into the dimly lit garage. He thought that he heard a blur of voices over the phone before the signal was lost. As he slipped his cell phone into his jacket pocket, he saw no other people and realized there was no music to be heard since exiting the mall proper.

After he took no more than a few steps into the parking garage, the glass doors burst open behind him. He whirled around with a wide-eyed expression and found himself staring directly into Katrina's shoulder. He looked up with surprise into her blazing green eyes and tried to open his mouth to speak, but she cut him off with a stern voice.

"Where?" she demanded while handing her shopping bags to Paige, who was standing at her left.

He shrugged and started to speak again, but she darted away from him and into the parking garage. Shaking his head, he looked over to Paige, who maintained a serious expression. She pushed Katrina's shopping bags at him, which he grasped with his free hand.

"We're to sit inside on a mall bench until she returns," Paige insisted as she squeezed his forearm firmly in her hand and forcefully steered him back towards the entrance into the mall.

"But if it's Chimalma --" he started to object as she ushered him before her.

"She's just confirming the target," she cut him off as they walked back inside.

Katrina tried not to use her unnatural speed in the event that mall surveillance cameras might be observing her. However, she still walked quickly through the parking garage at a rapid pace until catching a glimpse of a dark-haired woman. The woman appeared to be human, and certainly of South American decent. She continued to watch as the lady placed some shopping bags into the back of a sport utility vehicle.

The woman's cell phone rang, and as she answered it, the lady turned around to display her face more fully. Katrina was immediately able to determine that the woman was definitely human, but she marveled at how closely the person before her resembled Chimalma.

"Very close," she muttered grimly as she abruptly spun

around to return to Caleb and Paige. *An uncanny resemblance, actually.*

Paige and Caleb sat on a mall bench just inside the entry from the parking garage when they spotted Katrina stalk through the glass doors. Caleb noted that his mate's expression was milder, but still displeased. He looked up at her expectantly as she stopped before them and frowned at Paige.

"Well?" Paige anxiously demanded.

"The woman was human," Katrina muttered with a glance at Caleb. "We can't keep doing this. You know, I'm the one who triggered the detonator, and I saw the explosion engulf her. Caleb, you need to accept the fact she's dead."

Paige let out a heavy sigh and muttered with resignation, "Red's right, Caleb. We need to trust her on this and try to move on with our lives."

He was relieved, but felt an immediate sense of guilt and shame wash over him. Katrina sat down beside him on one end of the bench and looked into his eyes intently.

"But she could have been Chimalma's twin sister," she added darkly. "So I suppose I can understand why you reacted the way that you did."

His face reflected surprise, and Paige's eyes darted to Katrina's abruptly.

"Really?" she insisted. "That close a resemblance?"

Katrina silently nodded, and Paige's eyebrows rose. "What are the odds? Sorry, kiddo, I guess that was a good call after all."

"Good call, bad decision, however," Katrina admonished, although she leaned back against the bench and wrapped her arm around his shoulders supportively.

He leaned back into Katrina's shoulder and whispered, "I'm not going to run to you every time I'm afraid of something or someone."

She frowned as she pulled him closer to her and whispered irritably into his ear, "Is your male ego so fragile that you're ashamed to accept protection from me? Because you better get it through your stubborn head vampires that do that for their human mates."

He took a deep breath and let it out slowly. "I just want you to be able to respect me as something other than helpless, that's all."

Paige's eyes narrowed suspiciously as she looked sidelong at him, while Katrina's jaw tightened.

"What's that supposed to mean? I watched you challenge the guy in line at the food court. You're obviously willing to stand up for yourself when necessary. But that's apparently not good enough, so now you want to transform into someone else because you still see yourself as helpless," Katrina whispered harshly. "Did you ever stop to ask me what I wanted?"

He was somewhat struck by her retort and swiveled to the right to face her more directly. Her fingers touched his shoulder, and her hand lightly cupped the back of his neck. A momentary chill went down his spine as her hand grasped him there.

Paige's eyes widened, and she stood up and walked directly over to a nearby store display as dozens of people passed by, heading in all directions like rush hour traffic. Nobody even seemed to pay any attention to the tall, green-eyed, redheaded woman and sandy-haired, blue-eyed young man facing each other on the bench along the dimly-illuminated length of wall.

"What exactly do you want then?" Caleb asked pointedly.

Katrina paused and replied, "I want the thoughtful, kind man with the sincere disposition who I've fallen in love with already. That same man who has strength of heart and conviction, but also recognizes his own limits. What I don't want is another ego-laden risk taker with some sort of perverse death wish. I've had my fill with them in the past, and they're not a good fit for me anymore."

His eyes widened slightly, and he recalled a conversation with Alton at the estate where he'd been told about the personalities of some of her unsuccessful former partners. But he also recalled what Alton said about facing his fears in order to accept Katrina successfully as a mate. *Where is the happy medium to be found?*

He blinked, sighed, and whispered somewhat dejectedly, "I'm really trying my best, but I keep getting it wrong." He found it ironic in his momentary feeling of failure that a Vince Guaraldi Christmas tune was playing in the mall. He almost muttered, "Good grief," in classic Charlie Brown fashion, but thought better of it.

Katrina frowned and asked, "Getting what wrong?"

He shook his head. "Never mind. I'll try to use better judgment in the future."

His response confused her, and she looked somewhat bewildered. *What's gotten into him recently?*

He looked into her eyes, noting the confusion and consternation in her expression. "Can we not argue about this? Please, just kiss me and forgive me," he asked gently, hoping to try and salvage the remainder of what had been an enjoyable evening.

Katrina still felt confused, but at least he was beginning to sound a little more like himself again. However, she also recalled the conversation with Paige last evening about being more easy-going with him. She sighed while softening her grip around the base of his neck and kissed him warmly on the lips once. "You're forgiven, my love," she whispered sincerely.

When she pulled away from him, he adopted a hopeful expression. "So, where's Paige gotten off to?" he asked absently while turning back to his left.

But Paige was already sitting next to him again, and she smiled back at him with a smug expression. "All done talking?" she asked.

"For now, I think," he gratefully replied.

"Well, never mind all that," Paige insisted playfully. "Haven't you bought my Christmas gift yet, kiddo? The mall closes in another hour!"

Katrina shook her head with a smirk as he cast the sprightly, blonde-haired vampire a bland expression.

On the way back to the estate, they stopped by Caleb's apartment to pick up some additional clothes. It was the first time since the drama unfolded with Chimalma that he'd been back to his apartment. The gate guard on duty recognized Katrina's car and immediately opened the gate once Caleb waved to him from the back seat. He also noticed that they parked next to his old Honda Civic.

"Hey, my car's back," he noted brightly.

Katrina's eyes glanced at him in the rear view mirror. "Of course. I told you that night as we left the restaurant that I'd see to it."

"You can thank me later," Paige replied dryly as she exited through the passenger side of the vehicle.

Caleb grinned as Katrina exited and pushed her seat forward for his egress. The garage seemed deserted, as it was nearly eleven o'clock, and many of the apartment residents' vehicles were already parked for the evening. The three walked to the elevator, conversing casually about their shopping excursion.

As the elevator doors opened, he flashed back to the night Harry Maddox appeared wielding a pistol. But that felt like something from another time after all that happened since then, and he was impressed that he felt no fear. Some of that might have been due to the two dangerous vampires flanking him. He smiled absently and noticed both vampires staring at him curiously.

"Just thinking about how happy I am that we're here together," he replied evasively.

Both women smiled back at him, but Katrina detected there was a double meaning in his statement. Her arm snaked about his waist as the elevator made its way to the third floor. As she stood next to him, she contemplated her feelings about returning to the apartment building for the first time since the encounter with Harry Maddox. Despite the building's being Caleb's actual residence, she would have preferred that he was residing with her at the estate. While some of her feelings were due to her concerns over his safety, more of her motivation stemmed from the desire to have him near her so she could share in his life on a daily basis.

Paige's eyes darted to her friends, and she noticed Katrina's grasp on Caleb. The petite vampire absently turned her body so she was the first one standing before the elevator doors when they opened. The elevator bell dinged, and the doors slid open to reveal a peaceful hallway. Immediately following their exit from the elevator, it began its descent. The corridor was very quiet, and they only heard the sound of a television from inside one of the apartments as they walked to the end of the hall.

Caleb fumbled in his pockets for his door key and placed it into the deadbolt, but when he twisted his key to unlock it he noticed that it was already in the open position. He paused for a second as he tried to recall if he'd locked it when they last left. There was no resistance to his twist of the doorknob, and the door began to open.

"I thought we locked that," he noted curiously as he pushed the door inward.

Katrina's eyes widened as her left hand darted out in a blur to grasp his wrist, preventing him from opening the door further. She shook her head at him and used her right hand to push him towards Paige.

Paige pulled Caleb behind her and nodded once to Katrina with a stony expression. Katrina rushed into the apartment like a bullet. At that very moment, there was a *ding* followed by the sound of the elevator door's opening just down the hall.

Paige changed positions again, moving Caleb against the wall and behind her slightly as she faced the direction of the elevator. A brunette woman appearing to be in her forties and carrying a grocery bag made a peculiar facial expression at the odd scene before her. Caleb recognized her as the lady who lived with her husband two doors down from him.

"Oh, hi, Mrs. Ackers," he greeted her with a friendly smile as he moved to stand next to Paige, whose expression had softened slightly.

"Hello, Caleb," the woman noted with a pleasant smile as

she moved towards them and closer to her apartment door, though her eyes stayed warily focused on Paige.

"This is my friend Paige," he offered with a glance at the short vampire to his left. "She's a best friend of mine and Katrina's who's visiting from out of town."

Paige smiled.

Katrina appeared at Caleb's right, though only at human speed.

His peripheral vision registered Katrina's appearance. "And I don't believe that you've met Katrina yet. She's my... the love of my life." He smiled warmly at the reference, thinking the word "girlfriend" just couldn't do justice to everything that Katrina meant to him. He would have liked to have said something more substantial, like "fiancée," and he marveled that it was the first time he'd ever given thought to that level of commitment with anyone.

Katrina's hand found Caleb's and gave it a gentle squeeze.

"Pleased to meet both of you," Mrs. Ackers offered. "We've missed seeing you recently, Caleb. I hope everything's okay."

"Everything's fine," Katrina spoke up with a sincere smile. "He's just been hiding out from the world for a little while."

Mrs. Ackers smiled and nodded. "Oh, that's enviable. We'd all like some time away now and again. Well, nice to have met you both. Take care, Caleb."

"Night, Mrs. Ackers," he replied with a quick wave.

The woman opened her apartment door and slipped inside. The door closed firmly, and they heard the dead bolt slide immediately into place.

"Hiding out from the world?" Caleb asked as he looked up at Katrina.

Paige grinned, but Katrina changed the subject. "Never mind that. There's nobody inside your apartment, but it looks like your place was rummaged though pretty well."

They made their way inside, and Paige closed the door behind them. Before Caleb focused on the interior of his place, he reached out with his hands to touch both vampires on the shoulder. They both looked at him curiously.

"I'm very grateful to you both for everything lately," he offered sincerely. "I've never felt safer."

Katrina smiled warmly, while Paige considered him with a smirk.

"Finally starting to appreciate us vampires now, aren't you?" Paige asked with a penetrating expression.

He smiled and blushed a little. Then he turned to gaze upon the mess that was his apartment. Clothes were strewn over everything, his books taken from their shelves and tossed chaotically around the floor. His couch was tipped over on its back, and his kitchen stools were knocked over. The kitchen appeared fairly untouched except for a drawer and two cabinet doors left open.

His bedroom was a mess as well, with his sheets thrown off the bed, and many of his clothes from the closet and his chest of drawers were scattered around the room. The mirror above his dresser was broken, and his baseball bat was lying on the dresser top. It was difficult to determine if his place had been vandalized, or of someone had been looking for something. *But then, what do I have that somebody would want?*

"Crap," he muttered irritably. He felt like his world had been violated by the unknown intruders.

"Gawd, what a slob," Paige observed dryly.

Caleb cast a withering expression in her direction, but Katrina smirked.

"Probably done by either Chimalma or one of her hired mercenaries, because Maddox was dead before he ever stepped foot on this floor," Katrina noted absently.

Caleb sighed with resignation. "I guess I better try to get some of this cleaned up."

"We can clean this up later. Just concentrate on retrieving some clothes and things you need for now," Katrina corrected him. "And don't worry, we can run everything you bring through the laundry at my place."

The two vampires righted the furniture while Caleb picked

up some clothes and threw them onto his bed. Katrina watched him for a moment and sighed. Her expression changed to disappointment as she looked around the room.

"You don't want him to move back here, do you?" Paige asked in a discreet whisper.

Katrina pursed her lips and shook her head as she whispered, "No, I really don't."

"Yeah, I kind of figured that," Paige replied knowingly. "But he probably doesn't know that you feel that way. Maybe this is a good time to chat with him."

She smiled down at her short friend and nodded. Paige turned on the television and plopped down on the newly-righted couch as Katrina walked into Caleb's bedroom, closing the door behind her. He looked up curiously when he heard the door close and stopped sorting through his clothes.

"Caleb, I want to talk to you about something," she said while holding his hands in hers.

"Yeah?" he replied, appreciating her gentle manner.

"I realize that things have been way beyond stressful lately, and you likely feel as if you've suffered a forced relocation from your apartment," Katrina began gently. "But the truth is, despite some bumps along the way, I've really enjoyed your being at the estate with me."

He smiled. "I've kind of gotten used to being there myself."

"Do you feel comfortable there?" she asked carefully.

He considered her for only a second before answering, "You could say that." The truth was he was still getting used to life with a vampire. However, after his honest chat with Alton, he knew he was more than up to the task. And frankly, Katrina's estate felt like the Taj Mahal compared to his little apartment. The manor hosted all the amenities and grandeur he'd previously only seen on television shows about the rich and famous.

She guided him to sit next to her on the edge of his bed. Staring into his pale blue eyes, she smiled warmly at him, and he grinned back in response. "Would you consider moving in with me?" she asked simply. "On a permanent basis?"

Caleb swallowed, and his heartbeat increased slightly. It was an exciting prospect to say the least, and he really liked the idea of living with her. But he didn't want to seem like he was taking advantage of her. He realized that his net worth was likely only a pittance in comparison to hers, and he felt a momentary pang of shame for some reason. His grin faded into a more serious, introspective expression.

She noted his expression and increased heartbeat with some concern. She frowned and took both of his hands in hers again. "What's wrong?" she asked gently. "You can be honest and tell me anything, Caleb."

He paused, uncertain of how to explain his feelings. He also recalled his most recent conversation with a certain English vampire involving brutal honesty. But Katrina was more than just a vampire; she was his lover and companion. Finally, he looked into her eyes with a slightly embarrassed expression. "I really love the idea, Kat," he began. "But I don't want to feel like I'm taking advantage of you like some kind of mooch. Maybe if I could pay for utilities or something."

She smiled warmly, happy his concern was of a material nature and not a deeper emotional reservation. "Don't be silly," she chastised softly. "This will be perfect for both of us, and it's a great opportunity for you to build up your savings account. You know how you've talked about getting a part-time job to make extra money."

His mind raced back to the interview with CRE and the debacle that started the Chimalma nightmare. He shivered slightly at the recollection, causing a deeper frown to appear on Katrina's face. "Yeah, part-time work hasn't exactly worked out so well for me recently, has it?" he ventured distractedly.

She patted his hand supportively in hers and considered the issue in a more positive manner. "Well, now you won't need a part-time job, and we'll have a lot more time together," she noted aptly. "And no more commute times between seeing each other, either."

"Okay, but only if I can contribute something," he tentatively agreed.

"Oh, don't worry. She'll make you do all the housework!" Paige yelled from the other room. "Trust me, I know!"

Katrina rolled her eyes and shouted, "Thanks for your input, Paige!"

Caleb chuckled, but Paige continued speaking, evidently recollecting a conversation from her past. "'Oh, it's no problem, Paige. Just come live with me, and I'll train you and everything,'" she called from the other room. "One week later, I'm practically wearing a maid's uniform for nearly six years!"

Katrina shot off the bed and yanked open the bedroom door. "That was in lieu of an apprenticeship fee," she corrected with a sardonic grin. "And you never wore any uniform. Besides, there was free room and board, if I recall correctly. Not to mention the free combat training, financial advisement, and even a small nest egg to get you started."

"Yeah, I suppose that's true," Paige conceded with a giggle.

Katrina rolled her eyes and quickly returned to Caleb. She left the bedroom door open, all pretense of privacy lost with a vampire in the next room anyway. "So, what do you say?" she asked hopefully.

"Better say yes, or she'll be completely unbearable," Paige muttered from the other room. "Besides, I'll come in there and bite you in the neck if you say no."

He grinned and nodded. "I'd be honored to move in with you, Kat."

Katrina smiled and drew his body against hers affectionately.

"But I'm going to transfer part of my paycheck to you every month just to help pay for utilities, and I'll buy all the groceries since you really don't eat," he insisted quietly.

"That's fine," she whispered in response. She was so relieved and pulled away from him far enough to kiss him warmly on the lips. A satisfied feeling flowed through her as she contemplated the large emotional leap she'd just taken with him. It had been a very long time -- decades, in fact, since sharing living space with someone.

"You should've held out for a lump-sum nest egg settlement," Paige muttered from the other room over the sound of the television. "Or maybe a new car?"

"Oh, would you please shut up!" Katrina snapped in exasperation as she pulled her lips from Caleb's.

He fell backwards onto the bed laughing.

After a few minutes, Paige grew bored watching television while Caleb gathered more belongings in the bedroom.

"Got any spare pints of blood around here?" she called from the living room as she got up from the couch and moved to the refrigerator. "I'm hungry."

She opened the refrigerator door and immediately stared at a white dinner plate with a human heart and pair of human eyeballs staring at her from underneath some clear plastic wrap.

"Oh crap," she muttered under her breath, and then quickly shut the door. "Katrina, get in here," she whispered in a quiet, lethal-sounding voice.

Katrina heard the hard whisper from Paige. She rose from where she sat on the bed watching Caleb, while also considering the new step they would be taking in life together. She was so pleased he had agreed to move in with her, particularly considering that she had bitten him while sleeping. *Of course, I still need to work through that issue*, she considered.

"Why don't you finish gathering up some things, and I'll be in the other room?" she suggested as he smiled up at her. "And don't worry. We'll make plans to move you out of here fully before you have to return to work in January."

She walked quickly from the bedroom and into the kitchen until she was standing next to Paige with a frown and a penetrating expression. She didn't like the hard look on Paige's face, and her eyes narrowed suspiciously.

Paige silently opened the refrigerator door to let Katrina get a look for herself. Her jaw tightened angrily, and her eyes flared bright green. Paige closed the door gently. Katrina's eyes darted to the freezer, and Paige shook her head, indicating she hadn't looked yet.

Katrina opened the freezer door, and both vampires noted that among a couple of frozen dinners and a carton of ice cream was an eyeless man's head wrapped in clear plastic wrap. Katrina glared at the shorter vampire with a steely gaze, unhappiness plainly evident on her face. She recalled the gruesome photos that Chimalma had emailed to Caleb and realized they likely involved the body parts before her. *Poor bastard*, she mused.

"A Chimalma calling card, if ever I saw one," Paige whispered in a nearly inaudible tone.

Katrina nodded and closed the freezer as she stole a glance back towards the bedroom where Caleb was still picking through clothes. "She may have done it sometime after we killed Maddox," she whispered coldly. "Although we didn't exactly look in the refrigerator the last time we were here, either."

"Well, we can't call the police," Paige whispered. "But somebody's going to be missing this guy, whoever he was."

"Better to never turn up than to turn up like this. We'll dispose of everything," Katrina replied and gestured with her head towards the bedroom. "And not one word to him about this, either."

"Katrina, he's a lot heartier than you give him credit for, believe me," Paige disagreed. "He's an adult, you may have noticed."

"I'm not letting Chimalma terrorize him, not even from the grave," Katrina whispered vehemently, although she recalled her recent Chimalma-related nightmare and the horror of having attacked Caleb in her sleep. "Besides, you've seen some of his reactions recently. And what about the mall tonight? He's probably still wondering if some stray mercenary that Chimalma hired is going to pop out of a dark corner," she added after quickly moving past her previous dark thoughts.

"Him or you?" Paige countered pointedly in a whisper.

Katrina winced slightly. "Okay, I deserved that. Maybe both of us right now, I suppose. I just don't want him thinking about this, too."

"Hey," Paige offered supportively. "I'm not saying you're wrong about stray mercenaries."

"I know," Katrina acknowledged. "I'm just feeling a little protective right now with all that's happened. I won't lose him, Paige. He means too much to me now."

Paige nodded her understanding and sighed with resignation as Katrina walked across the apartment to the bedroom door and peered inside.

"Caleb, where are your trash bags?" she asked casually from the doorway.

"Oh, under the kitchen sink," he said.

"Great, thanks," she replied with a reassuring smile before rushing back to the kitchen.

Paige was already pulling the trash bags out as Katrina whispered, "Everything in the refrigerator and freezer goes, and we'll triple-bag the body parts."

"Is everything going okay out there?" Caleb called from the bedroom.

"No problems here, kiddo," Paige replied. She whispered to Katrina, "Go keep him occupied. I'll take care of this."

Katrina gave an appreciative half-smile, bent over to kiss Paige with a quick, sisterly peck on the cheek, and whispered, "Thanks, Paige. I owe you more than you could know."

Paige smiled supportively and nodded as Katrina went to occupy Caleb. "Friends may help move furniture," she muttered quietly. "But best friends help dispose of body parts."

Katrina entered the bedroom again and tried to look nonchalant as she pushed the door mostly closed behind her. She scanned the room to check on Caleb's progress. Most of the clothes were on the bed, and he was picking up fragments of a broken mirror off the floor around the dresser.

He walked past her towards the bathroom and glanced out through the crack left in the doorway. In those brief seconds, he noticed Paige putting things into trash bags, though from where exactly he wasn't certain.

He picked up the small trash can from the bathroom and started back across the room. Slowing as he neared the door, his eyes darted to the small opening between the door jamb and the door again. Once more, he was unable to tell exactly what Paige was working with, and he frowned. *What's she up to out there? The kitchen looked okay for the most part.*

His eyes slowly drifted to Katrina, and she stared back at him intently. Her expression wasn't predatory, exactly, just intensely watchful. It was as if she were studying him and waiting for some action on his part before moving. He slowed to a stop and just stared back at her with a non-challenging intensity.

*He's dying to know what Paige is doing*, she considered.

"Maybe an early Christmas gift waiting for me out there?" he ventured. *Something bad?*

But she merely stood statue-still and stared at him, although he could have sworn he saw her jaws clench slightly. Something told him to tread carefully.

He moved very slowly past her on his way back to the dresser, his eyes never leaving hers. He turned his back to her and began gingerly picking up pieces of broken mirror and dropping them into the wastebasket on the dresser countertop beside him.

"I'm learning to play nicely," he muttered quietly. *Rather, I'm learning to pick my battles carefully.*

Katrina watched him for a moment and read his body language. *He knows somehow*, she considered silently, *and he's giving me a pass on the matter.* A satisfied smile played across her lips.

He felt her arm reach around his waist from behind and enjoyed her breath against his left ear. The warmth of her body penetrated soothingly through the back of his shirt. He loved the feeling of her body against his.

"But you don't always have to play nicely," she whispered

seductively. "I really enjoy playing games with you, my love."

A shiver went up his spine, and he smiled as he resumed dropping broken pieces of glass into the wastebasket. Her right hand began helping pick up pieces of glass from around the periphery of his body as she still held onto him with her left arm.

"I'm glad to hear that," he offered quietly. "But I'm trying to learn when to play versus when not to. I don't like our occasional disagreements."

"Misunderstandings," she corrected him in a soothing whisper.

He frowned at the semantics as a quiet moment passed between them. "I love you," he whispered finally. "And I don't want to disappoint you."

Her hand grasped his right wrist as he started to pick up another piece of broken glass, and she smoothly turned him around to face her. He noticed a small smile formed at the corners of her mouth, almost as if she were pleased with something. She slowly, but firmly pressed her lips to kiss his. In return, he reached up to massage the back of her head and neck and gently ran his fingers through her long, red hair.

"I love you too," she whispered as their lips parted. "And thanks for playing nicely tonight."

There was a rapid knocking at the bedroom door, which startled him with a jolt.

"I'm going to run some things down to the dumpster," Paige announced. "Then can we please go? Hello? Starving vampire here. Villagers in imminent danger soon!"

Caleb grinned as Katrina chuckled and shook her head.

# Chapter 13

## Surprise Guest

**C**aleb never determined the nature of the concern shown by Paige and Katrina at his apartment, but over the next couple of days he felt a change in their behavior. He wasn't able to put his finger on it exactly, but they seemed more attentive to his location in and around the house. Thinking he was being paranoid, he tested the idea one afternoon by waiting until both vampires were in different areas of the house. He went into the basement where the wine and spare blood supplies were kept, shutting the door to the kitchen behind him. There he remained, quietly reading a book while perched on the edge of the workbench tabletop. After approximately twenty minutes, he heard the door at the top of the stairs tentatively open.

"Hey, kiddo?" Paige inquired.

"Yeah?" he replied nonchalantly.

She paused. "Everything okay down there?"

"Uh, sure," he said. "You need me for something?"

Another pause. "Nah, just a whim, that's all."

The door closed, leaving him sitting once more in silence. He considered the brief exchange, knowing he'd been correct. *It's not paranoia if people are actually looking for you*, he resolved.

He set his book aside and folded his arms before him while thinking about his new revelation. He'd had enough of feeling paranoid about possible threats in his life. Clearly, Katrina and Paige still harbored some concerns for his safety, even following Chimalma's death.

He had hoped that with Chimalma dead they could go back to the life that he and Katrina had been living. Instead, he still peered around corners for potential assailants. *A life lived in fear is no way to live at all.* He considered perhaps Alton was correct. Until he conquered his fear he wouldn't be able to be a better mate to Katrina. Perhaps he wouldn't be able to appreciate life truly, either.

Leaving his book on the tabletop, he walked purposefully up the stairs to the kitchen. He proceeded resolutely to the front entry area, calmly opened the coat closet, and slipped his leather jacket on. Then he unlocked the front door.

Fortunately, Katrina had ceased programmatically locking the doors, confident both she and Paige could address anyone who might attempt a forced entry. She no longer considered that someone might try to exit the house unannounced. He smiled as he opened the front door to reveal a western sky with the afternoon sunshine streaming in. A double beeping noise from the house alarm indicated the door had been opened.

*It's time for me to do what Alton told me before leaving: confront my fears firsthand.*

While chatting in the sublevel room, Katrina's and Paige's gazes abruptly met at the sound of the double beep. Katrina's eyes then shot to the security system monitor next to her to see Caleb exiting through the front door.

"Caleb!" she shouted as both vampires ran to the stairs in a blur rivaling the ability of a human eye to track.

Katrina beat Paige to the doorway and into the hallway of the main level, though Paige was close at her heels.

"Caleb!" Katrina shouted again as she ran.

They both raced towards where the sunlight was bathing the entry, heedless of the impending pain. But the front door closed in front of them, protecting them from harm.

Paige's eyes were wide as Katrina sped to the front door, slamming the flat of her hands against the solid wood and yelling, "Get back here, Caleb!"

When Katrina turned around, her eyes were blazing green

with anger.

As Caleb casually walked down the steps to the driveway, he heard a slamming sound against the front door and glanced back with a wide-eyed expression.

Katrina shouted, "Get back here, Caleb!"

He shivered, realizing that he had better continue facing the current fear, because there was already another one destined for him.

The late winter afternoon sun blazed towards the western end of the clear blue sky. He realized the sun would be setting soon, and he needed to proceed before then. When darkness fell, he had a whole new problem to confront. And while he might live through the current endeavor, he sardonically considered that he might not survive the next one.

Caleb breathed the cool air in deeply through his nose, appreciating the fresh, crisp scent of winter, and turned his face to the sunlight as he stood in the yard.

His cell phone came to life, and he glanced down to see Katrina calling him. He hesitated and considered answering it, but decided an argument over the phone while standing in the front yard wasn't how he wanted to focus his attentions.

However, he realized he was only postponing the inevitable. After setting his phone's ring option to vibrate, he walked towards the side of the house in the direction of the public park area. He'd confront his fear on a park bench.

"Caleb Taylor! Get back inside the house, right now!" Katrina admonished loudly over the small speaker near the front door.

There was a notably lengthy pause, and a much calmer version of her voice played over the speaker. "I promise I won't be upset, my love. I just want you to come back inside, please."

*Paige must have said something about her negotiation skills needing some work*, he considered.

It gave him no pleasure to put her through this, but he knew that if he didn't confront his fears he would always be dependent on others for his protection or peace of mind. Not that he didn't appreciate such protection: he merely needed to have confidence that he could stand on his own two feet. Besides, it wasn't as if there would be any danger. It had been nearly a week since Katrina's return, and no alarming events or indicators had presented themselves.

Caleb's cell phone buzzed three more times, each time leaving a voicemail indicator, as he walked through the park to the bench where Katrina had revealed her secret to him months prior. *It feels like forever since that night.*

His phone buzzed in a manner indicating he had received two new text messages, and he glanced at each message. The first one was from Paige. "She's mad. She's really mad. Come back now, kiddo."

He winced, realizing that when Paige was concerned it was a bad sign. The second text was from Katrina. "Getting dark soon. I'm coming for you." He felt a shiver from the top of his neck all the way down to his lower back.

"Oh crap," he muttered and sent a reply to Katrina's message. He typed, "Kat, love you always. C." Then he slipped his phone into his jacket pocket.

Sitting on the park bench, he stretched both his arms along the back of the bench while leaning back to appreciate the western sky as the sun began its descent. *Perhaps it'll be my last sunset, after all. It's hard to take anything for granted these days.*

New feelings replaced the anxious ones of a few minutes ago: freedom and satisfaction. He had done it: faced the fear of leaving the house unprotected and confronted the unknown. Such a small victory, though he almost wished someone would jump out of the bushes to attack him just to prove him wrong. Perhaps then, if he survived, Katrina wouldn't kill him later. *Ha! That'd be hilarious*, he mused, *kill me for leaving her protection!* The irony of the unlikely event almost made him laugh out loud.

The sun continued its descent, and he patiently awaited his fate. He was perplexed in a strange way as the late sun washed across his face in the cool breeze. *I wonder why I haven't done this sooner.* It was all very liberating to him. *Best of all, I was right. No danger is waiting to snatch my life and snuff it out. Well, at least not today, anyway.*

He chuckled and leaned back into the bench as he appreciated the remaining quiet moments and daylight.

When the sun was nearly ready to drop beyond the western horizon, he felt the chill increase with the winter breeze. He zipped up his coat up and rubbed his hands together.

He turned his head in the direction of the estate and saw a large area shielded by dense trees from the nearly completed sunset. Katrina stood like a statue in her blue jeans, black boots, and black leather jacket. Her eyes glowed bright green with what he anticipated was likely anger. Her red hair was down, and it moved fluidly around her head in the breeze like a living creature all its own. His eyes continued to take in her visage, both terrible and beautiful at the same time. She appeared both lovely and lethal, the perfect vision of a vampire: an angry vampire.

She silently regarded him, her brilliant green eyes piercing through him like lasers. He smiled, appreciating her feral beauty, and turned back towards the pink glow on the western horizon with his arms once again stretched across the back of the park bench. He lifted his face up slightly, as if presenting himself for sacrifice.

He caught a movement out of the corner of his eye and glanced over to see Paige in jeans and a red leather jacket standing in the distance just inside the forest's tree line. She regarded him curiously, and though her blue eyes weren't illuminated, her expression was one of both concern and mild disapproval.

He returned his gaze to the western sky as darkness fell on the surrounding area. His sunset was over. No sunlight remained to stave off the inevitable disagreement. But calmness fell over him, and he muttered, "Alton was right, after all. I've looked fear in the face once, and now I'm ready to face it again."

Hearing a sharp intake of breath to his left, his eyes darted to see Katrina standing not ten feet from him. He blinked only once, and she suddenly towered directly before him. He noted Paige's abrupt appearance to his right, as well. He gazed up into Katrina's eyes calmly and noted an astonished look on her face.

"Facing what fear?" she asked in a cold, level tone.

He deliberately paused and then calmly replied, "Right now, you."

She silently glared at him while Paige frowned in the background. "What?" she prompted in a steely voice. *Afraid of me?*

He smiled, looked directly into her eyes, and explained, "I'm staring fear and death in the face. Now I can truly begin to love you without fear."

Katrina was dumbfounded, while Paige's mouth gaped open slightly.

"I'm ready to die now, but I want you to know I love you and always will, no matter what," he said softly with his arms stretched across the back of the bench.

"Alton," Katrina seethed between clenched teeth. *What crap is he filling Caleb's head with now? A chat is in order*, she vowed.

The glow in her eyes dissipated slowly in the passing silent moments, and she sat down on the bench to his left. Paige closed her mouth and sat down at Caleb's right with a relieved expression. Both vampires stared at him, although Paige leaned away further in order to observe Katrina's expression.

"I love you, too," Katrina whispered with resignation. Paige casually leaned back against the bench.

Caleb used each arm to encircle Katrina and Paige around the shoulders and pulled them towards him. Both vampires conceded and shifted slightly to press against him.

"The two most important women in my world," he muttered. He turned his head to the right to kiss Paige lightly on the cheek, and then turned to Katrina to place a warm, soft kiss upon her cool lips.

She stared back with a penetrating gaze and initiated a longer kiss of her own. "Nobody's suffering retribution tonight, I suppose," she stated with a resigned sigh.

Paige grinned, turned her head to Caleb to kiss him with a peck on the cheek, and whispered, "Dodged a bullet, kiddo."

"What he dodged was an angry, deliberate fang bite," Katrina whispered.

Caleb smiled in silent satisfaction at he sat with his arms around his two favorite vampires while a nearby park lamp suddenly snapped to life, casting a glow upon them.

On the walk back to the estate, Caleb held Katrina's hand and appreciated how forgiving she had been regarding his need for a leap of faith. He gazed up at her with a cheerful smile, but she merely glared back at him and maintained a stern expression. However, as she held his hand, she lifted it to her lips and firmly kissed his skin. He gratefully accepted that, not wanting to press his luck.

At the house, Paige announced that she needed to get out for a while. Since she was a social creature, Caleb imagined that her recent sequestering at the estate was as difficult for her as it had been on him. She changed into a trendy red dress and her new strappy, red high-heeled shoes, warning everyone not to stay up for her, and departed in Alton's rental car.

"Clubbing," he ventured absently, watching out the sitting room window as the car drove away.

"You had to guess?" Katrina asked with surprise. "I'll be in the sublevel room chatting with Alton," she added darkly.

"Your lair," he amended with a smirk.

Katrina stopped, glanced over her shoulder at him with a rather unhappy expression, and grumbled, "I sometimes wish that term hadn't caught on with you."

He tried to erase a smirk as she stalked out of the room. He almost felt sorry for Alton as he considered her dark mood -- almost, that is. While the stately vampire's advice had been helpful, it had annoyed Katrina considerably in the end. His mind pondered other advice that Alton had offered and realized he would need to start a workout regimen to prepare his body for phase two. However, it was apparent he still had a lot of work left to do in phase one. He shrugged and went to the kitchen for something to eat. He had scarcely opened the refrigerator when the doorbell rang, and he went to answer it.

Katrina absently surfed the Internet while holding the cordless phone in her other hand talking to Alton. She quickly recounted Caleb's unplanned adventure that evening in a very displeased tone of voice.

"So, just what other advice have you been giving to my mate?" she demanded.

There was a pause at the other end before Alton calmly answered, "I merely provided him with some supportive advice that might aid him in his continued understanding of the vampire culture. Frankly, I feel the guidance was integral to his development as a successful mate for you."

"He's already a successful mate, Alton," she muttered irritably. "And did you tell him he needs to confront his fears more assertively?"

"Well, yes," he replied. "It's a liberating journey that will only help him develop into a well-rounded, independent person," he reassured her.

She stopped clicking her mouse in the Internet browser. "You're implying he's codependent?" she snapped.

"Well, I know that's probably somewhat appealing to you as an alpha female, but –"

"Bullshit, Alton," she interrupted. "So, you're a lay-psychologist now?"

She heard the doorbell ring and frowned at the security system screen to her left. *Kind of late for a visitor*, she mused.

Her eyes widened with horror, and she screamed, "*Caleb!*" The phone hadn't even hit the floor before she sped like a blur to the top of the stairs.

"Katrina? What's wrong?" Alton demanded after the handset dropped to the floor.

Curious, Caleb opened the front door and thought he heard Katrina yell his name. However, his attention was captured by the terrifying visage before him. A distorted vision of what used to be Alondra Vargas/Chimalma stood before him wearing all-black clothing. Her right ear was missing, and there were deep scars lining the right side of her face. The hair on the entire right side of her head was missing, save for some strands here and there, and her blistered scalp was a gaunt shade of white. Her hazel eyes blazed brightly, and she wore an evil grimace, accentuated by pronounced fangs.

"Hello, Caleb," the harsh sounding voice rasped. "Miss me?"

His eyes noted a small crossbow in her mangled-looking right hand, and it was leveled at his chest. He started to yell out, but felt his body being pushed aside as if hit by a truck. His body landed onto the carpeted floor of the adjacent sitting room, nearly a full fifteen feet from where he had just been standing.

The crossbow in Chimalma's hand fired, and the bolt caught Katrina directly in the chest with a dull thud. She gasped, but managed to remain standing as Chimalma forced her way into the entryway. The angry, disfigured vampire punched Katrina in the jaw with her free hand while firing the crossbow again, the arrow bolt catching her a few inches above the first impact point.

Pain surged through Katrina's body as she yelled, "Run, Caleb!" She grabbed Chimalma by the neck with one hand and threw her further into the house towards the kitchen.

Their two bodies became immediately entangled in a flurry of blows and clawing exchanges. Both combatants howled in bitter hatred as they smashed against furniture, fixtures, and walls.

Caleb gathered his wits long enough to realize the battle had moved further into the house. He jumped to his feet as intense fear and adrenaline surged through his mind and body. Making a run for the front door to flee, he made it as far as stepping onto the front porch before halting like a statue. "No!" he yelled in frustration.

He wasn't running for safety this time. His lover, his mate, needed help, and he wasn't about to abandon her. But his mind raced frantically as he tried to think of something he could use as a weapon. *And this time, a crowbar from the basement isn't going to cut it!* He gathered his resolve and raced back into the entry area towards the hallway and nearly ran into the wall as he tried to stop. Loud snarling noises and a series of subsequent crashing sounds came from the interior.

His mind flashed with an epiphany, and he raced down the hallway towards the study. He flipped on the light switch, and his eyes fell onto the sword in the glass case that had belonged to Katrina's husband. He lifted the casing off and cast it onto the floor. Snatching the sword from its wooden holders, he nearly dropped the heavier-than-expected weight, which shifted in his novice right hand.

Wasting no time, he raced down the hallway as fast as he could.

The two vampires continued their struggle in the formal dining room. The large table was smashed and the china cabinet reduced to rubble as they fought. Katrina's wounds were bleeding more freely as she wrestled with the centuries-old Aztec vampire. Despite her disfigurement, Chimalma seemed to have the upper hand in the battle, and Katrina felt her strength ebbing.

Katrina managed to knock the crossbow from Chimalma's grip, but the elder vampire's left hand snatched a short-bladed, curvy dagger from her waistband sheath and held it overhead as she readied to strike down at Katrina's chest. Chimalma's right hand choked Katrina's neck in a deathlike grip, while she grappled with the arm holding the dagger.

"If you're going to blow somebody up, do it right!" Chimalma spat venomously.

Caleb appeared out of the hallway holding the sword over his head with both hands, running towards Chimalma's unprotected back, hoping to strike her down. Katrina's eyes widened for only an instant, but it was enough for the disfigured vampire to notice. Chimalma's head glanced back over her shoulder, and she jerked her left hand away from Katrina's grip, throwing the curvy-bladed dagger at Caleb as he charged.

The knife flew through the air and imbedded into his upper left chest quadrant with a force that caused him to fall backwards from the impact. Intense pain cascaded through his chest and shoulder, and the sword was propelled forward across the floor from his hands as he released his grip on the hilt.

The blade skittered across the tiled floor towards Katrina, and she managed to grab the hilt as it started to slide past her. She whipped the blade upwards and plunged the tip of the sword into Alondra's heart, causing the vampire to gasp sharply. Chimalma grabbed at one of the arrow bolts stuck in Katrina's chest with her free right hand and pressed it into her further, causing Katrina to scream in pain.

But Katrina still managed to grab the hilt of the imbedded sword with her right hand and deftly snapped the end of the blade off, leaving the tip stuck in the other vampire's heart.

"Bitch!" Alondra cursed.

With one fluid sweep of Katrina's right arm, the remainder of the blade swooshed upwards and to the left, neatly separating the vampire's head from her shoulders. As Caleb looked up from the floor with horror, Alondra's head rolled across the floor, spraying a mist of blood along its path. The body slumped to the tiled floor with a squishy thud. Chimalma's head came to a stop against the far wall, an expression of shock still evident. A second later, the broken sword clattered to the floor as Katrina collapsed to her knees in exhaustion.

Despite the blade imbedded in Caleb's chest, he managed to crawl to Katrina's side as she rolled into his arms, weakly staring up at him.

"What can I do?" he urged in a panicked voice.

She felt her energy ebbing as the blood continued to seep from her two wounds, though the most critical was the arrow sticking from the area around her heart. She was exhausted from the effort of her last actions, and Katrina realized that death was finally coming for her. But instead of feeling fear, she felt an odd peace fall over her. Glancing into Caleb's shocked face, she felt genuine remorse. "Nothing, my love," she whispered. "You can do nothing."

She felt his body shaking with fear as he held her.

"You're healing?" he inquired shakily, but hopefully.

"Not fast enough," she moaned.

"No!" he demanded. "You can't die! You can't leave me!"

"Everyone dies," she whispered.

Pain surged through Caleb's chest, and he felt like he was going into shock. "Not you," he shook his head as tears welled in his eyes. "Not now!"

"I'm so sorry, my love," she whispered as a tear rolled down her cheek. She could feel the emotional pain emanating from him, which greatly surpassed the pain coursing through her own body.

"Don't do this," he pleaded as an idea dawned on him. He grasped each of the two arrows in his right hand and managed to pull them from her body. The blood flowed freely, but he used each of his hands to cover a wound mark and pressed onto each location to help stem the bleeding. Then, despite the blade still sticking from his upper chest, he forced his neck onto Katrina's mouth, demanding, "Take my blood. It'll help you heal."

She was so weak by that point, but she could feel the pulse in his soft neck against her lips. The survival instinct within her immediately wanted to bite into his throat, and her fangs protruded in her mouth. A fresh pain shot through her body, and she gasped.

"Hurry!" he urged as he pressed his neck onto her parted lips.

But she managed to turn her face from him and insisted in

ragged breaths, "No. It's not enough. Just live your life. Do it for me...for us."

He sobbed openly and gently settled her body onto the floor. Fate was so cruel to him and seemingly always had been. His loved ones were either abusive or taken from him too soon in life. He finally found the one person who made him complete, who made him feel alive for maybe the first time in his life. And he didn't want to live if she weren't there to live alongside him.

Noticing the bleeding from her body was ebbing, he ran the back of one bloody hand across Katrina's cheek as she closed her eyes. Feeling bewildered, he searched wildly in his mind for solutions. He saw the bloody, broken sword lying on the floor next to them, and an idea was born of desperation.

Ignoring the intense pain from his own nearly unbearable wound, Caleb firmly grasped the sword in both hands and pressed the edged portion of the remaining blade to his neck. Then, before he lost his nerve, he ran the blade across his throat with a painful thrust. Pain seared through his neck, and he dropped the blade with a clatter. Blood readily seeped from the hastily created gash.

"I love you," he muttered before placing his neck over her mouth.

The blood flowed onto her lips. A small spark surged through her body as she felt herself drifting into a dreamlike haze. Her eyes shot open, and something feral awakened. A rich, sweet taste was in her mouth as her lips clamped onto skin, and her arms instinctively wrapped around the figure above her like a vice.

Katrina heard a gasp from the figure, and her mind quickly returned to a conscious state. She realized with horror that Caleb was in her arms as her mouth drank furiously from him. She tried to stop, but the urge in her was too great. Her body was in command, not her rational mind. The red-haired vampire hadn't experienced thirst that strongly before, and it actually terrified her. She felt part-animal, part-higher being all at the same instant. A rush of satisfaction and longing swept through her body, yet her mind was repulsed by it. Time seemed to stop as all that existed was her insatiable thirst and his labored heartbeat and breathing.

At some point she felt stronger as her sense of conscious control also began to return. She forced her tongue onto the skin of Caleb's neck, pressing it there to prevent his continued bleeding. Terror rolled through her as she was uncertain if she had already taken too much blood from him. She sensed only a faint heartbeat from him, and his breathing was shallow.

She gathered saliva in her mouth and held it around his neck wound. Time seemed to stand still again as she impatiently waited for his wound to close. Her lips parted, and she gently licked at his wound area. She wasn't sure if she should remove the dagger from his body, fearing something might tear, and she didn't know if she had the strength to heal him.

More time passed as she lay on the floor, holding his body against hers. His breathing continued to be shallow, and she worried for his survival. She wouldn't forgive herself if somehow her hunger became the death of him. Her mind raced, wondering how he could have been so insane to do what he did. But then she also felt intense love for him, for his sacrifice. However, it would mean nothing if he died from his efforts.

*This isn't supposed to be how it ends.* She was supposed to have left him safe so he could continue his life. He deserved a normal life, one with a normal wife who could bear him children. A life where he could grow old with his partner and watch their children grow and develop. *A life without me.*

She wasn't certain what time it was, but she knew that something needed to happen for him soon. She closed her eyes, holding his body close to hers. Some strength in her body was just beginning to return, and she felt her wounds slowly repairing themselves throughout her decimated system.

*Once again, Angel Caleb came to my rescue.*

The taste of his sweet, life-rejuvenating blood still lingered in her mouth as she whispered to him, "I love you. I'll love you forever."

The rental car screeched to a halt in front of the estate, and Paige barreled through the front door with a cell phone in her hand. She tore her high-heeled shoes from her feet and cast them aside as she looked around frantically. She had driven like a demon possessed once the call from Alton arrived, and she stayed on the phone with him as he described what he'd been able to hear after Katrina dropped the phone.

"Holy crap!" she exclaimed as she made her way into the living room, viewing the carnage before her.

Her eyes took in the horrific scene in the dining room, and she rushed to where Katrina still held Caleb close to her body.

"Red," Paige urged as Katrina's weak, tired eyes looked back at her with anguish.

"He's dying," was all she managed to whisper.

"Paige! What's happening?!" Alton demanded over the cell phone.

"Katrina's injured, but recovering," Paige said hurriedly. "But Caleb's hurt badly. There's a dagger in his upper shoulder area."

"Massive blood loss," Katrina nearly shrieked.

Paige's face flashed with horror as she realized what had happened. "Katrina drank too much from him. He's dying," she muttered desperately.

"Get to the blood supply. Start an intravenous drip immediately!" Alton commanded. "Do it now!"

Paige gathered him into her arms, stripping Katrina's weak hands from around him, and ran with him to the sublevel room where she laid him gently on the king-sized bed. She raced back upstairs to the refrigerator in the kitchen and quickly sorted through the various blood types remaining on the shelves.

"Type A positive," Katrina's strangled voice called from the dining room.

Paige picked two bags of blood and frantically tried to think of where to get the other supplies she needed. "Katrina! I need tubes and needles!" she yelled frantically.

"Basement shelf...medical bag," she rasped.

Paige sped into the basement wine cellar, recalling the last time she had descended these same stairs trying to save Caleb's life. She spotted a black leather medical bag and brought it with her back upstairs. She raced back to the sublevel room where he was lying.

After checking his shallow pulse, Paige prepared the blood for him. She stuck him in the arm with a needle and attached the blood bag to the other apparatus. Grabbing a letter opener from the desk, she stabbed it into the wall above the bed with incredible force, imbedding it into the sheet rock-covered concrete wall. She hung the bag of blood from it above his head.

She glanced at the blade sticking out of his shoulder and was uncertain how to proceed. Racing back upstairs to the dining room, she found Katrina with the cell phone in her hand.

"...have to turn him," Alton finished saying.

"He won't survive it," Paige challenged. "He's too weak. And we have to deal with the dagger *now!*"

"Bring me to him," Katrina weakly insisted.

Paige carried her tall friend to the sublevel room and laid her alongside her mate. Katrina managed to prop herself up on one arm and absently dropped the cell phone onto the bed beside her. She grasped the dagger in her free hand and looked up to Paige.

"You have to close the wound," she insisted. "Just like I did after I bit him in the shoulder."

Paige's eyes became as big as saucers, and she shook her head. "I don't know if I can-"

Katrina interrupted her, "He's dying! You have to find the strength inside yourself! Now. *Do it!*"

Paige nodded furiously and motioned for her to pull the dagger out. Katrina held her breath and extracted the blade in one swift movement. As expected, Caleb's blood flowed generously from the wound.

Paige nearly leapt onto him, pressing her tongue into the gaping hole in his chest. She slurped the blood when necessary and began forcing her saliva into the wound area.

"Control, Paige," Katrina urged as she helplessly watched her friend labor at saving her mate's life.

After a time, the open wound began to mend, and Paige licked at Caleb's shoulder area until the skin was fully sealed. Her body was shaking with the effort to control her feeding urge, and she looked sidelong at Katrina with glowing blue eyes.

"Good, Paige," Katrina offered soothingly. "Get a syringe and take blood from me."

"Wait!" Alton shouted over the cell phone speaker. "Katrina's blood is too diluted with Caleb's!"

Paige paused and looked at Katrina, whose eyes showed surprise, not having considered that problem at all.

"Use mine," Paige insisted. "And screw your damned rules! He may have to follow them, but I sure as hell don't!"

Katrina was completely taken aback and simply nodded her assent as Paige grabbed a fresh syringe from the medical bag and proceeded to draw blood from her own arm.

"Saline?" Paige insisted.

"Wait!" Alton insisted. "Undiluted and directly into his wound area!"

"It might start turning him," Katrina urged in a panicked voice. "He won't survive a turning in his condition!"

"No! Unlike you, I've actually turned a human before," shouted Alton. "It won't be enough for a turning, just faster healing!"

Paige nodded and pressed the needle into the skin around the wound. She injected the entire syringe, and both vampires stared down at the sandy-haired young man with concern. "Now what?" she demanded.

"Now, we wait," Alton replied.

Tears fell from Katrina's eyes as she lay against Caleb's unconscious body, which was still breathing all too shallowly.

Paige locked down the house before the sun rose, including activating all the window shutters. Once Paige had both Caleb and Katrina settled, she took Chimalma's body and severed head out to the back yard, placing them in a shallow hole she dug to be left open to the winter sunlight. Fortunately, the winter day promised to host mostly blue skies again. The vampire returned to watch over her friends and help as needed. She also called Alton to check in and make sure she hadn't forgotten anything.

For a time, she sat at the edge of the bed with a damp washcloth, dabbing at Caleb's forehead occasionally as his body was racked with shivering that appeared to be from a fever.

Katrina slept against him as her own body continued to heal itself, and Paige looked over at her friend in support.

"I never saw this coming," she muttered darkly.

A couple of hours later, Katrina stirred. She immediately looked at Caleb and saw that his color had improved. She glanced up to the packet of blood hung above his head and noted it was nearly empty.

"How many blood units?" she asked Paige, who looked up from dabbing Caleb's forehead with a fresh washcloth.

"That's number four," Paige replied softly. "How are you?"

Katrina regarded her with sad eyes. "Stronger...and weaker." Her heart was nearly breaking with the thought that Caleb might die.

Paige nodded, understanding her double meaning. As Katrina sat up in bed, the short vampire came around to the other side of the bed and hugged her.

"Thank you, Paige. Once again, I owe you in a big way," Katrina muttered softly. "Caleb would be dead now if not for you."

Paige's voice was hard as her eyes became moist. "I'm pretty fond of the little guy, to tell you the truth."

A pang of jealousy rose in Katrina, but she urged it below the surface. She had brought Paige and Caleb together for his protection and should be happy they had bonded so well. Besides, she was confident that Caleb was her mate and lover and realized that she needed to let go of any unhealthy, possessive urges regarding him. And only a selflessly devoted mate would give his own life for hers.

Katrina smiled, hugging her friend in return. "I know you're fond of him, and I'm happy you feel that way. I think he adores you too."

Paige parted from her embrace with her. "All these years, I've become good at killing and taking blood from others, Red," she confided. "But this is the first time I've ever saved someone else's life with my own blood."

Katrina nodded supportively. "You realize that you have an implicit right to ask for something of me and of him in return," she ventured.

Paige scowled, retorting in an insulted tone, "Do you think I'm really so shallow? I'm just glad you're both still alive."

Katrina recalled the lecture she had given Caleb about vampires. She had warned him that even if they learned to appreciate his company, as a human, it was still likely to be somewhat shallow and cursory. She warned him not to be too trusting of other vampires, given their tendency for self-interest and ulterior agendas. However, even she confessed that Paige and Alton were like family to her, and she didn't necessarily place them in the same category as the other vampires she knew.

She smiled sympathetically and regarded the young vampire. "Honestly, Paige, what can Caleb mean to you after only the short time you've known him?"

Paige considered the question somewhat shyly, not wanting to meet her eyes. "At first I thought you stuck me with a really lame task of babysitting your human mate. But I've gotten to know him the past couple of weeks, and we've gone through more together than I have with any other human. You have to understand, most people go in and out of my life easily. I try not to take anyone too seriously, especially humans. They're perfect to have around for partying or sex and, of course, their blood. But when I think about Caleb, he's what having a little brother might be like, though I never actually had one as a human. It's much the same way you and I are so close, really."

Katrina smiled supportively and nodded her understanding. She realized that Caleb had a way of quickly growing on people. *Even vampires, apparently.*

Paige continued earnestly, "And hell, I walk away from people all the time. It's easy. But for some reason, I hate the thought of just walking away from him. And then seeing you again after being apart for so many years. Well, despite all the negative reasons behind my purpose for being here, it's just been so satisfying. I'd miss this feeling."

Katrina offered a sympathetic expression and admitted, "I understand. I'd forgotten just how much I missed your eclectic nature, as well as your friendship. Perhaps you should consider staying for a while."

The youthful vampire looked into Katrina's eyes speculatively and paused. "But if I make you feel uncomfortable regarding Caleb..." she began carefully. She was fully aware of how much Katrina coveted him, and she didn't want to be an impediment or interference between them. After all, Caleb was her mate.

"No," Katrina interrupted. "No, Paige. The more friends he has, the better, vampire or not. You're a good friend to him, as well as a..."

"Blood sister?" Paige ventured with a smirk.

Katrina rolled her eyes and countered, "Co-mentor?"

"Kindred?" Paige suggested with a grin.

Katrina's smile faded somewhat, and she whispered in a choked voice, "It won't really matter if he dies."

"Stop that!" Paige snapped, feeling somewhat emotional herself at the moment. "He's going to live, so quit saying that crap."

Katrina's eyes watered slightly, and she sighed. "Fine," she conceded quietly. "He's going to live. He has to."

The silence grew between them, and they looked down at Caleb's unconscious face.

"He looks so peaceful," Katrina commented softly as she

gazed onto his gentle features.

Paige nodded silently and placed a supportive hand on Katrina's shoulder as she stood beside the bed. However, she was feeling more concerned than she was willing to admit.

"Listen, I could really go for some warm blood," Katrina prompted gently. "Perhaps you could oblige?"

Paige smiled and departed the room on the welcome errand as Katrina watched her go with a thoughtful expression. She looked back down at Caleb's resting form and smiled warmly. She needed so badly for him to heal and return to her.

The evening after Chimalma's attack, Caleb stirred from his unconscious state. The injection of Paige's blood had helped to heal the area around the knife wound, and the pints of blood aided in restoring his system to a viable level. Paige was sitting at Katrina's computer in the sublevel room surfing the Internet when he woke. She quickly moved to his bedside and stared down at him.

"Katrina!" Paige called as his eyes fluttered open.

Caleb first thought he saw Katrina's face, but as his eyes regained a degree of focus, the fuzzy face morphed into Paige's, including her perky nose, bright smile, and deep blue eyes all outlined by her bobbed blonde hairstyle from a previous century. While happy to see a friendly face, he was immediately concerned that it wasn't Katrina's. He felt a swell of panic in his chest, coupled with a strong burgeoning soreness in his upper left shoulder and chest.

"Oh, please be alive, Kat," he slurred in a dry, raspy voice.

The red-haired vampire of his dreams suddenly came into view over him, and his arms flailed out and upwards to wrap themselves around her neck in a weak bear hug. But a sharp pain shot through his left shoulder and chest as he did so, and he winced noticeably. "Kat!" he exclaimed with a gasp tinged with a mixture of both sincere relief and physical pain.

Katrina's eyes were glistening with tears despite her smile as she gazed into the face of the young man who had captured her heart and soul. She maintained herself in a statue-like form above him as he struggled to use his arms to pull himself upright. "Careful, my love," she urged as her arms reached behind him to help brace his body into a sitting position.

Caleb swayed slightly, as if he weren't fully equipped to remain upright, but Katrina's arms pulled him against her body as she scooted next to him. They held each other as if the world depended upon their bodies' being pressed together into one.

"Thank God you're alive," he managed to say, despite his dry throat. He felt an elated sense of relief surge through his system as he held her in his arms. His lips found the side of her neck, and he kissed her reverently.

She smiled brightly at the feeling of his soft kiss against her skin, and she ran one hand soothingly across his face while supporting the back of his head with the other. "You saved my life yet again, Caleb," she whispered with awe. "Only this time, you gave of yourself. In the past, many humans have died as I took their blood. But no human has ever willingly sacrificed himself and rendered his blood unto me before. I'm still alive right now because of you, although it was very misguided."

He smiled, though her reference to saving her life twice made no sense. "And I would do it again in a minute for you," he assured her.

She frowned but said nothing for the moment. She didn't want him pulling a stunt like that ever again, whether for her benefit or not. But that was a topic for another time.

Paige smiled at the heartwarming scene playing out before her.

"Besides, you saved me from Chimalma," he added, soberly recalling the images of Katrina's battle with the angry, disfigured vampire.

"But not from your injuries," she whispered darkly.

A frown clouded his face as she pulled away from him so she could look into his face with a serious expression. "What do you mean?" he insisted.

"You saved me with your blood," she explained. "But you

lost too much blood yourself, and even after providing you with fresh pints of blood we had in storage, your body was dying from the wound you received."

"But —" he began with confusion. "Your blood would have saved me, just like when I was sick with the 'flu.'"

She smiled sympathetically. "Your blood was mixed with mine in such a large quantity that you diluted the strength of my vampire blood until my body could metabolize and convert it. There simply wasn't enough time for that to happen. You were dying, and there was nothing I could do to save you."

His eyes widened with comprehension, and he stammered, "But I'm alive. Then how-"

"Paige's blood saved you," Katrina interjected.

He gazed at Paige sitting on the far edge of the bed and noticed an endearing smile on her face. "Your blood? You saved me?" he asked with surprise.

Paige smirked and quipped, "Ah, what's a little blood among friends?"

But his face turned serious, and he crooked his finger at her. "Come over here," he insisted quietly.

Katrina watched intently as Paige scooted down the bed until she was perched next to him. He took the petite vampire's hand in his own and pulled on her arm to draw her closer to him.

Paige's eyes tentatively darted up to Katrina and noted the red-haired vampire's imperceptible nod of approval. She allowed her body to be drawn more closely to him and drew her arm across his waist as she leaned in towards him.

He kissed her on the cheek affectionately and whispered, "Thank you for saving my life again. That's twice in less than a week, and I'm eternally grateful."

Paige started to pull away from him, but suddenly felt Katrina's hand pressing at her back to push her further towards him. She turned her face slightly until her lips met Caleb's and kissed him once very lightly and briefly on the lips. He seemed completely surprised by that, but responded to her kiss in kind.

"You're more than welcome, kiddo," she offered, and then added in a more serious tone: "But you owe me nothing. From now on, your best interests are also my concern."

He swallowed and looked anxiously up to Katrina as she hovered above them from the other side of the bed. But instead of seeing jealousy or concern on his lover's face, he saw only a small smile of approval, and he frowned with confusion.

He felt a shift on the opposite edge of the bed, and when his eyes turned back to look at Paige, she was already gone. He heard the small panel door to the sublevel room slide shut before his eyes could even register her new location.

Looking up at Katrina with a wide-eyed expression, he asked, "What was that all about?"

"Congratulations, my love," she offered softly. "You're probably the first human to have both a vampire mate and a surrogate protector."

"What?" he asked incredulously.

The corners of her lips upturned in a partial smile. "Try to think of her as a sisterly vampire guardian-angel in your life now."

"I've never had a sibling," he whispered with wonder as Katrina smiled with refreshing approval at the idea.

The next day, Katrina exited the bathroom carrying a small basin of steaming water, a dry towel, and a washcloth and went to sit at Caleb's bedside. She placed the basin on the nightstand and looked down at him with adoring green eyes. He smiled back up at her appreciatively.

"You're too weak to shower, so I'll give you a sponge bath today," she ventured with a warm smile.

"I'm not a big fan of sponge baths," he replied darkly.

"Except when you receive them from me," she countered while removing the bed sheet to reveal his nude body before her. She gazed down at his young, lean, muscled body approvingly and offered, "You're beautiful, Caleb."

He looked away and blushed slightly as he muttered, "Men

aren't supposed to be beautiful, Kat."

"I know beauty when I see it," she admonished with a raised eyebrow and a smirk.

He said nothing and merely gazed across the room as she rinsed the washcloth in the basin and started with his feet and legs. He felt somewhat helpless and infirm lying in the bed as she bathed him, but admitted her ministrations felt much better than he expected. The washcloth was warm and soothing to his skin. But he felt a little embarrassed as he envisioned Paige walking in on him. "Where's Paige?" he asked pointedly.

Katrina smiled, sensing the reason for his inquiry. "She went out for a while this evening," she reassured him. "I don't expect her for many hours."

He seemed outwardly relieved by her response, and his body relaxed somewhat, much to her relief.

"Oh, Alton called to check on you a couple of hours ago," she offered casually as she ministered to him.

"Really? What's new with him?" he asked.

"He hopes that you're back on your feet soon," she replied. "And he left a message for you. He said, 'To be brutally honest, I'm extremely proud of that young man.'"

He smiled, recognizing the phrases used.

She raised a curious eyebrow, reflecting, "Strange, though. He normally doesn't use a term such as 'brutally honest.'"

He shrugged innocently. "Maybe some new catchphrase he's using nowadays?"

"Hm, perhaps," she replied suspiciously and frowned. A few quiet moments passed as she worked her way up his body with the washcloth.

"1823?" he asked playfully, though mainly to change the subject.

She looked at him curiously and determined the nature of his comment. *Still trying to guess my birth date*, she mused. "Nope," she replied simply.

He sighed, and she frowned with consternation as she rinsed the washcloth in the basin water. Noting her serious expression, he asked, "What's the matter?"

Katrina was suddenly struck by how brief life was for humans and how unexpectedly it could end. She also recalled a heated conversation with Alton prior to leaving on their hunt for Chimalma. He had reprimanded her for not telling Caleb more about herself. *Perhaps it's time to start having those conversations, rather than putting them off.*

"I was just thinking back to a recent conversation with Alton," she muttered vaguely. She helped him roll onto his side facing away from her so that she could wash his back.

"Oh," he replied absently. He appreciated the feeling of the sponge bath more than he had expected to.

She dried his back with the bath towel, momentarily considering how she had met Caleb when he was just a child and how he had helped retrieve blood for her. But she quickly decided that would be a topic better saved for some future date. To be honest, she still wasn't sure how to broach the subject and needed time to consider it further.

"There. Feel better?" she asked gently as he rolled onto his back again, pulling the bed sheet up to his chest.

He nodded and smiled. She bent down to him and warmly kissed him on the lips. "Thanks, Kat," he said.

She smiled back, appreciating the earnest look of innocence on his face. She loved him so much and made a spontaneous decision. "My love," she prompted as he looked up curiously. "I was born in April 1506, three years before Henry VIII became King of England, although I have no record indicating the exact day of that month," she said softly.

Caleb's mouth dropped open.

"My God, you've lived over five hundred years already," he quietly noted.

She reached out to hold his hand as she continued, "My family's name was Holcot, and I was given the birth name of Catherine. We were only of a middling level of wealth, though my father owned quite a bit of land in England. I married a wonderful, loving man by the name of Samuel Lawnder, whom you remind me a great deal of, actually. He was a farmer and a reserve soldier in the king's army, and my father bequeathed to us our initial parcel of land as part of my dowry upon marriage. The sword that I killed Chimalma with was Samuel's and his father's before him."

Caleb's eyes were wide with awe as he listened to the story unfolding before him.

"I bore two children for Samuel, a son named Hugh, and a daughter named Margery. Samuel was taken from us by the first wave of influenza ravaging the countryside. Our son and daughter both died within a year after their father, but by smallpox. I was devastated and became withdrawn and distant," she continued morosely.

He reached out with his free hand to pat her hands, which were occupied holding his other hand. "I'm so sorry," he whispered with a glassy-eyed expression.

She smiled supportively, her pain all but numbed by the passage of time and all too many tears cried centuries prior. Her voice strengthened as she stared down into his pale blue eyes and proceeded with her revelations.

"I was thirty years old and residing at my father's estate when I met a traveling nobleman who stayed with us. His name was Jean Antoine de Medici, and he was a vampire. My family had no idea and allowed him to stay as a courtesy. He held papers of introduction from regional nobles, you must understand. He stole me away in the middle of the night and took me to a large estate in the highlands. Over a period of a week I was turned, and on Saturday, November 11, 1536, I officially transformed into a vampire. It was the same year Anne Boleyn was beheaded by King Henry VIII. After the turning, my life, my world, changed forever."

Caleb was in too much shock to speak, and his heart rate increased twofold. She looked down upon him with concern, but decided that he wasn't in distress, merely astounded by her story.

"There's so much more, but we'll leave that for another

time," she whispered before bending down to kiss him.

He returned her kiss numbly, but continued to stare up at her with wonder. He couldn't believe that he had actually just heard the story she told him. "Thank you for telling me that," he whispered with sincerity and appreciation.

"I owe you so much more, my love," she replied softly and with a brief sadness in her eyes.

"But wait," he interjected as something dawned on him. "If you're from England, why don't you have an English accent like Alton?"

She smiled with amusement. "Alton embraces his English roots and deliberately chose to maintain his English accent over the years. However, I found out very quickly that the English weren't embraced positively in many parts of the world. I learned to neutralize my accent over a few hundred years. Besides, I no longer consider myself an English citizen. Now I'm a citizen of the world, and I no longer feel compelled or limited by political or national boundaries."

The explanation made sense to him and merely reinforced in his mind how wonderful the woman before him was. "You're amazing, Kat," he mumbled with awe. "Why would you want me? I'm just an ordinary human."

She smiled down at him adoringly and reached down to grasp his face in her hands. She moved her face to his until their noses were touching. "You listen to me, ordinary human," she quipped before turning serious. "You've given me the reason to want to live again. I want to share the world with you and experience everything with renewed appreciation. You've restored my interest in continued existence."

He smiled as she held his face in her soft hands. "You're a goddess," he whispered.

"Caleb," she admonished mildly as she drew her face away from his slightly.

"Well, you're at least a queen among vampires then," he amended endearingly.

She silently considered him for a moment. "Very well, my

love," she conceded with a raised eyebrow. "Then I shall be your queen, if you will have me."

He smiled adoringly. "I would have none other."

She returned his smile, kissed him passionately, and slyly asked, "As your queen, shall I also rule over you?"

"Actually, I think you already do," he replied dryly with a smirk.

"Well, yes, I suppose that's true," she considered with a smile as her eyes playfully looked to the ceiling. "But always with passion and your best interests at heart."

He nodded slowly with understanding. So many revelations had occurred in his life recently, and this was merely one of many. "I realize that now," he offered thoughtfully.

They stared into each other's eyes for another quiet moment, and then she glanced to the clock near her computer. "But now it's time for you to sleep, my love," she insisted while pulling the bed sheets up to his shoulders. "With luck, we'll have you out of bed for a couple of hours tomorrow. Then you should be able to spend most of Christmas Day feeling more like your old self."

Given everything, he had almost forgotten that Christmas was only a couple of days away. He suddenly looked forward to the event, happy to be among the living. Best of all, Katrina would be there to spend the holidays with him.

She rose, walked to the other side of the room, and turned the lights down so that the only illumination in the room was emanated from the two computer screens on the nearby hutch.

"Kat?" he beckoned softly.

She instantly appeared at his bedside.

"Don't leave. Will you stay with me?" he inquired curiously.

"Always, my love," she replied gently as she slipped the shoes from her feet, curled up next to his body, and wrapped her arms protectively around him.

*Dearest Caleb, if only you realized. I may be your queen, but I'm yours to command,* she thought lovingly as she laid with him in her arms, happily listening to the steady, strong sound of his heartbeat.

In *Sunrise at Sunset*, Katrina and Caleb battled a centuries-old foe. Scarcely three months later, are they really prepared for a London getaway?

Katrina Rawlings thought that her problems were finally behind her as her mate, Caleb Taylor, moved into her roomy estate. To her chagrin, vampires have suddenly taken a dangerous interest in the two of them. Additionally, life-changing memories that Katrina thought were safely forgotten have ominously resurfaced in her lover. On top of all that, she has to entertain unexpected house guests. How much more is a beleaguered vampire supposed to take?

An enticing invitation from her former mentor to vacation in London might be just what Katrina and Caleb need. After all, what can go wrong there, right?

**Prepare yourself for *A Bloody London Sunset*!**

**Coming soon from Rutherford Literary Group.**